THIS DISUNITED KINGDOM

Leslie / Nicholls

THIS DISUNITED KINGDOM

2020 VISION

LESLIE J. NICHOLLS

The Book Guild Ltd

First Published in 2016 by Austin Macauley
Published in Great Britain in 2018 by
The Book Guild Ltd
9 Priory Business Park
Wistow Road, Kibworth
Leicestershire, LE8 0RX
Freephone: 0800 999 2982
www.bookguild.co.uk
Email: info@bookguild.co.uk
Twitter: @bookguild

Typeset in Garamond

Printed and bound in Great Britain by CPI Group (UK) Ltd, Croydon, CR0 4YY

ISBN 978 1912575 879

British Library Cataloguing in Publication Data.
A catalogue record for this book is available from the British Library.

I dedicate this book to all those politicians, past and present, who, through corruption, self interest and incompetence, have created such a lack of interest and engagement from those they purport to represent, that they continue to survive and thrive in

THIS DISUNITED KINGDOM

PROLOGUE

MONDAY MORNING
MARCH 11TH

SOMETIME SOON LONDON

The blast ripped through Whitehall like a rusty hatchet through a rack of ribs. The torn flesh on Venetian blinds flapped lifelessly from the splintered bones of shattered window frames and fluttered through the swirling haze of smoke and dust. Slivers of glass glinted on the silent pavements below and blew unceremoniously towards the mountain of rubble where the Cenotaph once stood.

Relatives of the seventeen pedestrians obliterated by the blast would be reassured by the knowledge that they would have felt nothing. They may have seen the sudden blinding flash but would have been dead before the sound of the explosion could have penetrated their dissolved eardrums.

Those trapped inside the burning buildings were afforded no such fortune. Thirty-two of the seventy-eight office workers may have died quickly and mercifully but the remaining forty-six suffered terribly and died agonising deaths between one minute and one month after detonation. A further one hundred and seventeen innocents would remember that day for the rest of their lives, even without the charred, scarred skin and missing limbs as permanent reminders.

Looking out from his bedroom window in Downing Street, the Prime Minister hit the call button on his private video phone. Within two seconds, the solemn face of his oldest friend and closest ally appeared before him.

"You were right," the PM admitted, "Now we do it your way."

"Are the Cabinet agreed?" the other man asked.

"This is not a Cabinet decision, this is not a coalition decision, this is my decision and I am going to have to stand by it or fall because of it. The gloves are off and I am ripping up the rulebook. I need to nail these bastards!"

Three hours later, four more names had been added to the list of fatalities. None of them had been anywhere near Whitehall at the time of the explosion. Two had been sharing breakfast in their university halls, one had been found in an internet café in Kilburn and the fourth was intercepted as he turned a corner leaving his mosque in Finsbury Park. By the time their battered, bruised and burned bodies had made their way to the mortuary they would not have looked out of place amongst the blast victims. Advanced Interrogation Tactics did not always require water or electricity.

The list was likely to get even longer. One of the very few advantages of mass Eastern European immigration was the ready availability of discreet, experienced interrogation support personnel.

1

MONDAY, MARCH 11TH

It had taken five hours to assemble the Cabinet but even now, at two o' clock on Monday afternoon three Cabinet seats remained vacant. Two of their previous incumbents would never be returning to this place and while the PM had not formally asked for two minutes' silence, he did, however, need to intervene to end it.

"Malcom, Gerald and Simon were all in the same meeting and caught the immediate brunt of the blast. Simon is in a serious but stable condition. He is expected to recover but we should not expect him back around this table soon, if at all. We will determine the dates of the necessary by-elections at next week's Cabinet meeting but today is about the more immediate implications arising from the reason for their absence." The Prime Minister had managed to retain his controlled composure but those that knew him well recognised the tightness of his tone.

The Deputy Prime Minister and leader of the UKIP party cleared his throat and spoke firmly. "I disagree. This meeting was called as a direct result of the events that led to their absence and it would be an insult to their memory to defer discussions about their replacement."

1

The Prime Minister did not even look at his deputy but declared his decision would stand and that no Cabinet reshuffle or by-election discussions would be held until Parliament had been addressed and the house had been given the opportunity to mourn their memory. Neil Faraday was not normally so accommodating but, for once, having measured the mood of the room, sensitively, he sat back silently in his seat. Even in his most conciliatory mood, Faraday could not completely conceal the contemptuous expression permanently etched across his bloated face. His brown tweed jacket, mustard shirt and purple tie seemed totally incongruous in the sombre chamber, but it would take more than a mere terrorist blast to force Faraday to ditch his trademark garb. He was forty-seven years old but his overlong, greasy, greying hair, bloated, blotchy face and saddle-bagged eyes had him looking at least ten years older. Without even trying, his thin lips twisted into a self-satisfied smirk that had occasioned even his mother, reputedly, to have remarked that her first-born had an eminently slappable face.

The relationship between the Prime Minister and his Deputy was, at best, strained. On a professional level, they tolerated each other. On a personal level, they loathed each other. Graeme Mitchell had been reared as one of the new breed of Conservatives. Middle class background, state educated and an Economics and Politics graduate of Liverpool University. He had spent four years in commerce and industry as a Strategic Corporate Planner before being persuaded to stand for Parliament in his home constituency of Wirral. His Robert Redford looks, charisma, intellect and commitment to his community carried him to Westminster with a record majority and within eighteen months he was in the Cabinet as Home Secretary. Less than twelve months later, the Prime Minister of the time suffered a career ending heart attack returning from her final European Union Summit at which Britain's eventual but politically protracted and insipidly diluted exit was formally ratified. Many believe that the timing and manner of her unfortunate demise was somewhat suspicious and most definitely ominous, but nevertheless, just eight weeks later, at the relatively tender age of forty-three, Graeme Mitchell swept into Number 10 on a wave of optimism and emotion.

Despite his popularity, the next election, two years later, produced yet another hung parliament. There had been only one other coalition government since the disastrous downfall of Gordon Brown's Labour regime in the early 2000's but it now seemed that the British people had concluded that the business of governing the country was too serious a matter to be left in the hands of just one political party. Especially one which had betrayed half the population by negotiating too soft a Brexit and betrayed the the other half by negotiating any form of Brexit at all. That, or they just loved the delightful dogfights that ensued, with both coalition parties pushing populist policies to keep the electorate sweet. This time, it was the turn of the Conservatives and UKIP to rule the roost, the latter holding the balance of power with one hundred and thirty-four parliamentary seats.

Around ten years earlier, the United Kingdom Independence Party had all but disappeared from the political landscape as its former supporters had seemed to believe the Conservative Party mantra that 'Brexit means Brexit'. Only the cynical few foresaw that the dastardly machinations of the Brussels Mafia would conspire to confound those Conservative aspirations for the better part of a decade. The European Parliament were ably and willingly supported by the Liberal Democrats, Labour Party, Scottish Nationalist Party and House of Lords. Between them, they ensured that legislation passed from Parliament to Brussels to the House of Lords and pinged around like a pill on a pinball table. The deadlock was finally broken with the abolition of the upper house two years earlier.

The Labour Party had never recovered from their farcical leadership election in 2015 when their voting system inadvertently allowed Labour's opposition to elect, for them, the most unelectable candidate imaginable. Remarkably, he actually flirted with power in 2017 by seducing gullible young idealists with a vision of free further education, free health and social care for all, affordable social housing, guaranteed jobs for life at above EU average salaries and a firm pledge that everybody, everywhere, whould live happily ever after for ever and ever.

Sadly, for him, the marzipan melted on his happy house in a humungous scandal around anti-Semitism, Communism and a leaked plot to disenfranchise and imprison any child who might have aspired to inherit wealth or property from a parent. They never recovered.

The fate of the Liberal Democrats was effectively sealed when its forlorn leader lost their one and only seat to the Green Party and until the re-emergence of UKIP, the SNP and the DUP had effectively been the most influential parties of both government and opposition in Parliament as their modest presence swayed marginal votes on the most important political proposals.

The United Kingdom Independence Party was suddenly established as 'the tallest dwarf'. The flamboyant UKIP leader now positively revelled in his sworn obligation to thwart the established political party policies at every possible turn.

The Prime Minister rose and spoke clearly, assuredly and assertively. "I have invited Tom Mellor, our Homeland Security Advisor to appraise us of the current scenario, potential suspects and further threats. At this stage, nobody has claimed responsibility for the atrocity and there have been no new demands. No doubt, as I speak, there will be hordes of devious bastards huddling in corners and debating how they can make mileage out of the actions of actual perpetrators. Tom, could you please give us your summation?"

Tom Mellor had the presence and authority that his previous careers in both the military and public broadcasting had sculpted. Even at the age of sixty-two, and six foot three, he cut a handsome and distinguished figure. Highly respected and regarded both in the UK and internationally, he had been one of the few senior diplomats that had openly opposed the three Gulf Wars but had served bravely and diligently in two of them. The only visible scarring of those two tours was the permanent tanned face below his wavy grey hair.

He did not indulge in pleasantries as he knew that the majority of the Cabinet understood the contempt in which he held them. The sentiment was largely mutual but the Prime Minister's patronage afforded him a degree of courtesy, at least in Cabinet.

"You will be aware that we have at least four active insurgent organisations within our midst and each of them have demonstrated their willingness and ability to perpetrate acts of violence and terror. None have previously committed anything on the scale of this attack but members of our intelligence and security forces have been warning government for over six months that an act, or acts on this scale were likely. To the best of my knowledge, these warnings have gone unheeded, but I am sure that you will all be acutely aware of your own unfortunate, apathetic inertia in allowing these matters to escalate."

There was a degree of uncomfortable backside shuffling around the Cabinet table. Eyes lowered, gazes averted and a few notable frozen stares, but nobody spoke.

"The most active and vociferous group is, of course, IBIS; the Independent British Islamist State. They now control councils and constituencies across a large expanse on the Midlands, the North West and Yorkshire. Effectively they have created a Muslim State in the region and demand, geographically and politically to be recognised as such. We have a dysfunctional dialogue with their purported political leadership, but we strongly suspect that their more radical activists are not acting totally independently, and their actions are supported and sanctioned by their elders here and abroad. Although their demands are often shrouded in veiled threats they have never admitted to any of the atrocities that they have undoubtedly perpetrated."

The pale, thin female hand of the recently appointed Culture Minister rose hesitantly as would the arm of a shy schoolgirl in her first maths class in big school. "What, precisely, is the nature of their current demands, Mr. Mellor? Why are they not in the public domain and being debated around this table?"

Professor Mellor tried to hide his disdain but whilst his expression held up, his tone of voice betrayed him.

"We try not to provide publicity for every dissenting voice, especially those that might attract further support for whatever cretionous cause they choose to champion. However ridiculous and toxic their agenda might be, there will always be a gullible audience sympathising with their insidious views. We don't doubt that their demand to have our esteemed former Prime Minister and his Cabinet extradited to face War Crime trials would probably meet with universal sympathy but most of us would like him to serve out a sentence in Britain first. Their demand for a total ban on alcohol in the UK also has its sympathisers but they know that they can achieve this locally by simply controlling the licensing authority within the councils they control."

Tom Mellor was now in full flow. Successive governments had tried hard to suppress the extent of the IBIS agenda, but it clearly irked him that MPs and even cabinet ministers still failed to fully understand the threats that their policies posed.

"Clearly, they openly campaign for an Independent State, embracing Sharia Law but they recognise there would need to be a degree of ethnic cleansing to facilitate this. Their communities are multi-cultural, and they are still working to integrate Syrians, Libyans and African migrants but when they do so, they will undoubtedly have a compelling mandate. At the moment, there is too much resistance from the indigenous population to relocate and we fear that there will be further uprisings if both communities continue their individual separatist stances.

"We are all aware of their views on our Foreign Policy within the Middle East, but we will not, of course, withdraw from our continuing conflict with Islamist State forces. There is nothing within the IBIS current demands, or anything concrete from our

6

intelligence, to warrant or suggest an attack in this country on this scale although the threat is constantly present. Indeed, the IBIS leadership are already issuing propaganda statements and smear stories across all the fake news channels to the effect that the White Christian minorities may have committed the atrocity to undermine and demonise IBIS even further."

Up to this point in the proceedings, Neil Faraday had demonstrated his disinterest in Mellor, to the point of total disdain, by maintaining a fixed, glazed stare and inquisitive facial expression towards a perceived imperfection in the paintwork on the wall opposite. While continuing to scratch whatever seemed to be lurking upon the nail on the third finger of his left hand, he decided to join the conversation.

"Also my dear Lucy, there should be no underestimating the sinister presence of our Syrian guests who managed to penetrate our porous borders during the mass migration of 2018. The Security Services have determined that at least thirteen per cent of so called refugees entering Europe were, indeed, Islamic State fighters who could hardly believe how welcome they had been made within the communities of their sworn enemies. A further six per cent were believed to have been recruited to the European and British factions within two years of forgetting the refuge and hospitality afforded to them. We even trained them to infiltrate our establishment by creating a system of positive discrimination to provide them with jobs within our national and local government infrastructure."

Mellor paused for the continuation of Faraday's predictable diatribe and was mildly relieved when Faraday merely shrugged and nodded for Mellor to continue. The Special Advisor duly obliged.

"The Scottish Unionist Party have become much more animated of late and David Watters now claims that they have a clear majority north of the border who demand the right to be reunited with England. It is, of course, difficult to distinguish the degree of violence attributable to this noble cause from the normal levels of violence that we have come to expect from that part of the world. It is not beyond the bounds of credibility though that they could have raised the stakes, but I suspect that they would have had to call again, upon the support of Brendan Doyle's Ulster Unionists."

The Deputy Prime Minister again feigned an exaggerated yawn before requesting that the advisor skip the current affairs lecture and skip to the whodunit. Mellor was heartened by Graeme Mitchell's raised hands and the harsh glare directed at his unwanted sidekick.

"Since the Irish Republic, with the full backing of the European Union, has effectively tried to annexe the North of Ireland, Ulster has become increasingly disenfranchised. Demands to devolve and partition the North are gaining traction. It is, of course, unthinkable that the government could back down on the cowardly concessions of Major and Blair but, failing that, their bid for free relocation and housing for themselves and the Scots on the English mainland are gathering traction. The Unionist Scots and Ulstermen together form a potent threat and their patience does appear to be running out."

Everyone at the table but Faraday, resisted the temptation to remind the Prime Minister of the consequences of permitting the second referendum in Scotland that declared them an independent nation. Although a relatively junior minister at the time, Mitchell had prepared the paper proposing the plebiscite. The jibe hit him just as hard though the decision had not, of course, been his alone.

Clive Mountstevens, the sixty-three-year-old Home Secretary, broke the silence with an unusual show of loyalty to his leader. Mountstevens was a veritable mountain of a man in every sense; broad, grey, craggy and stone faced.

"The genie was out of the bottle in 2014 when the Isolationists lost by a wafer. It was inevitable that the vote would resurface as that wicked wee witch and her coven of SNP warlocks were wreaking havoc in Westminster and sucking resources north of the border.

To our eternal shame, they did so under the noses of, and with the blessing, of that maggot infested excuse for a Parliament. I am not at all surprised that a very sizeable majority now want to come back to us but they should have shouted louder at the time. Their current mass migration to Northern Ireland may be relieving the tension in Scotland but its bringing the prospect of civil war in Ireland closer by the day. In fact, it's a solution that I would personally endorse!"

Mellor strode around the table, raising his eyes to the ceiling and quietly drawing strength and confidence from the eyes that followed him, while Mountstevens looked around sheepishly for a sign of support that was noticeably and embarrassingly unforthcoming. On this occasion, Mellor seemed to welcome the Home Secretary's intervention and happily summarised the point for him.

"We can't yet rule out the joint involvement of the Scots and Ulster Unionists, but their Alliance have not, to date, conducted any hostile activity on the mainland and it would be a ground shifting departure in policy were they to do so. Likewise, the Irish Republican movement have been encouraged by Europe, this far, to campaign peacefully for unification but I'm sure we can all recall their atrocities of the 1970s."

Mellor took a hefty swig from his crystal water tumbler before continuing.

"Last, and probably least, the Liberal Democrat Party have been threatening radical direct action for months, but it is unlikely that they have the resolve and resources to pull this one off. Their focus tends to be upon civil disruption by peaceful means, but they are bound to be getting frustrated by the fact that they receive even less credibility now than they did when they were a political party. We all know of their violent opposition to the third reading of the recent bill both legalising and incentivising euthanasia but nobody within their official party would have the balls to do this. If we were talking flour bombs, or even paint bombs, maybe, but this? Never!"

The Home Secretary made no attempt to engage the speaker visually as he interrupted his flow,

"With as much respect as I can reasonably muster, Mellor, are you going to tell us anything that we couldn't read in tomorrow's *Daily Times*?"

Mellor moved squarely behind and menacingly above his seated adversary as he delivered his stinging retort:

"With a somewhat lesser degree of reciprocal respect, I must remind the Home Secretary that this is a matter of extreme Homeland Security and involves issues far too sensitive and confidential to be discussed openly around this table."

Sensing the impending downward spiral in the tone of the exchanges, the PM sought to develop the dialogue further in a more positive direction.

"There have been rumblings for some time that the Poles, Romanians, Estonians and Bulgarians were coming together to form a concerted Eastern European Action Group against the perceived racism towards them. Could they have had a hand in this?"

Mellor paused respectfully before gently refuting the suggestion.

"It's unlikely, Prime Minister. The turf war between the Eastern Europeans and the Somali community seems to be consuming all of their time and energy. They don't seem particularly interested in resolving their territorial grievances politically. Both parties seem to favour their tried and tested dialogue of knives and guns. They are too absorbed in establishing their drug and people trafficking operations to take on the wider political establishment, at this stage." Mellor added with a degree of ominous caution.

Once again, the Home Secretary pounced. In theory, he was senior to the advisor though he would never be viewed as his superior by anyone who knew either of them. He even looked inferior. Though only a year older that his subordinate, he was smaller, greyer and considerably fatter. Tom Mellor was bulletproof in every sense of the word. Since leaving active service, he carved out a successful and lucrative career as an author, broadcaster and advisor on global security and warfare. He did not need the meagre pittance that the civil service position paid him, but he relished the opportunity to deride and belittle the amateur lightweights to whom the defence of the realm was entrusted.

"I ask you again, Mr Mellor. Who, in your valued, or at least valuable opinion, is responsible?"

Neil Faraday could not resist having a peck at the advisor's exposed carcass:

"Yeah, come on, Mellor, who is your money on or are you just going to sit on that fence pulling splinters out of your arse? Jihadists, Jocks, Micks, Lily Livered Liberals or Gypsies? Just who is bombing our beloved offices right under your nose?"

Calmly, Mellor walked back to his seat and collected his papers. "I don't believe, Prime Minister, that I am paid to speculate, and I am certainly not engaged to play straight man to the buffoon sitting beside you. I am paid to gather and interpret intelligence and I have to advise you that there was not a murmur of this attack from any of our normal observation and listening channels. Whoever did this came completely under the wire and were professional and well equipped enough to maintain absolute silence, right up to the point of the explosions. No warnings, no threats, no demands and that's what really worries me. It should worry us all."

Faraday, in a rare moment of solemnity, certainly shared that worry. But then he would for, in his mind, he knew exactly who was responsible.

2

Scotland Yard Major Incident Room 3 was less a mile from Downing Street in distance but light years away in terms of urgency and energy. While the Cabinet were sitting, sedately, pondering the political implications of the blast, Detective Chief Inspector Sean Lakin and his team were frantically contacting their associates on both sides of the legal divide while scouring the screens, voice recordings and transcripts recently received from the watchers at MI7. Eleven members of the immediate team had been at their work stations for the past nine hours while one desk remained ominously empty. None of the team members could resist the temptation to glance across to Farah's desk, intermittently, but none would openly voice their fears. Lakin had tried to contact her twice but she was not at home and her video phone was dead.

He brought the room to attention.

"Listen up team! Five minutes to finish what you're working on and we start to share what we've gathered so far. I want to hear every tiny detail, every dodgy phone call, every sliver of suspicious CCTV footage and any social networking threads that might lead us back to Whitehall. Five minutes!"

As the voice levels dropped, the clicking of keyboards and shuffling of papers filled the void. One by one, the detectives turned away from their screens and faced Lakin at the head of the room, who was thoughtfully swiping and tapping the interactive eighty-inch briefing screen that was still showing the smoke and dust billowing from the Whitehall carnage. As the last chair was turning, the incident room door burst open and the thirty-seven-year-old, olive-toned face of Farah Karim seemed to light up the room. Farah's Persian beauty tended to have this effect in most situations but today, when many had feared the worst, her appearance was especially welcome, though not, apparently, to Lakin.

"Nice of you to join us, Detective Inspector," he remarked, flatly. "If you overslept and perhaps missed prayers this morning, you might have extended the courtesy of a phone call. I have been missing a senior operative at a critical time and some of your colleagues here appear to have been distracted by worrying about your untimely absence."

"I am really sorry, sir." Her words seemed to rebound from the floor with her head so low. "I have been trapped inside Victoria Coach Station. My daughter, Ava, was about to set out on a foreign school visit when they suspended all operations and closed down all communications, in or out of the station. All the screens went down, and personal devices were automatically disabled. Nobody was allowed in or out for two hours and we had no idea what was happening outside. The settings on my videophone have still not been restored."

"Well maybe you should get yourself a maid to do the school run. Or better still, a husband," Lakin retorted, to the surprise and embarrassment of the room. "Get up here and your colleagues will bring you up to speed on what has been happening in the working world."

Farah took her place next to DI Chambers, who gave her a sympathetic smile and squeezed her forearm warmly and reassuringly. An old-school gentleman, he was clearly unimpressed with his superior's outburst but knew better than to challenge him in this particular forum.

Sean Lakin strode across the raised platform at the front of the incident room. It was not so much a stage as an extended podium from which to operate the interactive digital display that recently replaced the traditional white board that had seemed to symbolise the grounded methodology of the old school copper. Lakin embraced the new technology without completely abandoning the principles of policing that he had carried with him during his twenty year career from Military Police Academy to the head of his own Specialist Investigation Unit. Still only forty one, he managed, effortlessly, to look at least five years older and frequently declared that this was the price he paid for his lengthy education at the University of Life – College Of Hard Knocks – and a spectacularly failed marriage. He often went on to comment that the divorce, however, was worth every crease and wrinkle. He was still considered to be a good looking man. Not male model material, unless a sportswear publication happened to be looking for a close cropped, chisel jawed rugby player with the obligatory wayward nose. Possibly how Matt Damon might have looked if any of his screen fights had been real. At five foot eleven and fourteen stone, he was solid and formidable.

"Okay everyone. Here's what little we know. At eight-thirty this morning, an explosion occurred in Whitehall. There are at least ninety-five known fatalities and over two hundred injured, some of whom will not make it through the day. There was no advanced warning and there have been no direct claims of responsibility. We have had the usual line of cranks declaring God's will, divine retribution, karma, etcetera and though we will, of course, follow up every line of enquiry, none of these are likely to have a thread of credibility. Phil, Pete and Chris will examining the social networking feeds for the twenty-four hours leading up to the blast when the watchers at MI7 have filtered and refined any communications and keywords from likely sources.

14

Phil Scales stood and advised that the first ten thousand transcripts were expected within the hour with a steady stream of five hundred an hour going back a further seven days. "Clearly, the three of us could not handle this without the word recognition software we have down here and though it's not too different from the programmes that MI7 use, we do tend to funnel them and home in on the more statistically significant leads rather quicker than the pen pushers."

Lakin nodded his appreciation and turned to his left and the front row of his gathering.

"Brian. Is there anything significant from the CCTV images?"

DI Chambers rose and turned to his right to address both his boss and the rest of the room.

"It seems clear that the epicentre of the blast was the Cenotaph. We have, so far, surveyed footage within a twenty yard radius of the structure over the past eighteen hours and concluded that no suspicious items were placed within the immediate vicinity. We have also slowed down the impact of the blast and there do not appear to be any incoming missiles, so our immediate forensic and ballistic investigations will focus within and below the Cenotaph itself. Just under twenty per cent of the fatalities were pedestrians in the immediate vicinity of the Cenotaph, struck down by flying and falling masonry. The remainder of the dead and injured are from the surrounding buildings from which a succession of further explosions followed the immediate blast".

"It is not yet known whether the secondary blasts were caused by further devices or by gas and oil explosions from the underground network of utilities service pipes. This will be relatively easy to determine and Rick is already working on the subterranean survey plans, including sewage and drainage passages. If it was one single explosion from below the Cenotaph, this would have been a very, very substantial device."

Chambers sat back down next to Farah, who, as a late comer to the incident room, was struggling to come to terms with the scale of the disaster. As soon as they had been released from Victoria, she had left her daughter with the rest of her school pals to resume their adventure, and headed straight for Scotland Yard. She had, of course, known that a very major incident had occurred but had never imagined anything on this scale. She had been a newcomer to London at the time of the last major attack on the city back in 2016 but still carried with her the scars of the suspicion and prejudice that her skin tone and features tended to attract back then, and to some extent, even now.

Lakin paused to absorb the implications of Chambers' assessment.

"So, Brian, are you suggesting that the device was placed strategically below the Cenotaph to trigger gas and oil explosions in the underground infrastructure. Is it not possible that the secondary explosions were a consequential by-product and that the principal target was the Cenotaph itself?"

Chambers remained seated and replied, thoughtfully.

"It's entirely possible and we will have a clearer impression when we have the utilities map of the vicinity. At one end of the spectrum of possibility, this could be a smart device, strategically positioned to take advantage of the underground infrastructure."

"Conversely then," said Lakin, "it could, conceivably, have been a smaller device designed to cause the symbolic destruction of the Cenotaph but triggering a sequence of unforeseen, disastrous consequences."

He let that thought hang there. There was little point, at this stage in the inquiry, speculating on manner or motive. Their immediate job was to gather fact and evidence. This was the specific purpose of his branch of the Special Investigations Unit. Formed in 2018, in tandem with MI7, its remit was to investigate anything, within the capital or wider afield, that suggested links to terrorism and national security. That was precisely the message that Lakin left them with as, twelve minutes later, he drew the briefing to a close.

As the team shuffled back to their individual work stations he laid a hand on Farah's shoulder, just firmly enough to stall her movement. Her colleagues in the close vicinity discreetly looked away as he advised her coldly that he wanted to see her in five minutes in the interview room. Lakin normally occupied a glass sided office in the corner of the incident room, which, although double glazed, allowed him to survey and assess the energy and mood out on the floor. The interview room, at the opposite end of the building, was totally opaque, soundproofed and secured from the inside by a keypad combination lock. There were no permanent recording devices in there as many of the conversations in this space, with both internal and external visitors, were deemed never to have happened. To the team, an invitation to the interview room was akin to the summons to the headmaster's office, back in the days when school discipline was taken seriously and seriously taken.

Farah switched on her computer, booted up, logged in and secured her screen before embarking upon the walk of shame. She entered the stark room, electing to stand rather than taking one of the leather chairs, positioned either side of the sturdy pine table. A full two minutes later, Lakin entered and firmly closed the door behind him, securing it with his personal combination code. Farah froze and felt the hairs on her arms fight against her silk sleeves. She looked to the floor and then slowly raised her head to look directly and defiantly at her superior officer.

He strode purposefully around the table and walked towards Farah until his forehead was less that one foot away from, and eighteen inches higher than, Farah's nose. His right hand closed around the crown of the back of her head and he pulled her towards him. Their lips collided, rather than met, and he kissed her fervently and passionately for at least twenty seconds. She could feel his right hand trembling against her head whilst his left arm kept her close has he slowly withdrew his face from hers and spoke slowly and falteringly.

"Have you any idea at all how worried I have been? I had convinced myself that you had been caught up in the blast on your way into work. I walked down Whitehall myself last week when I came away from your place. I traced those steps in my head. I tortured myself wondering exactly which of those fragmented body parts were yours!"

Farah looked at him through tear glazed eyes.

"I am so sorry, Sean, but believe me, there was absolutely no way of getting in touch with you. My mobile network was disabled in Victoria and the Security Services have not yet restored it. They kept us kettled there and even when I showed them my warrant card, they wouldn't let me through. I got here just as fast as I could, I promise you."

Lakin regained his professional face just long enough to assert that he would have had the head of any officer who had let her out of the area before his expression melted once again to one of pure relief.

They kissed again, this time less eagerly but no less passionately until Farah took his head in her hands, held him at arm's length and spoke directly into his lingering eyes.

"And by the way, Sean, I know that we have to keep this relationship under the radar but can we please have less of the maid, mosque and husband crap! Otherwise, you might just find yourself back in this interview room facing charges of bullying, sexism and racism; I carry a strong hand of cards you know. Just hope that I never come out as lesbian and lose a limb or I will hold the full deck!"

3

Back in Downing Street, Graeme Mitchell was still struggling to watch the distressing live feeds on his news screen as Janet, his personal assistant, ushered in John Gemmell, the chancellor, who, at fifty-three, pencil thin with rimless glasses perched upon a slender crooked nose, looked every inch the part.

Gemmell held up an apologetic hand and declared that he would understand fully if the PM wanted to defer their planning session for the upcoming Economic Update, in the light of the more pressing issues of the day.

"No, John, sit down. There is nothing at all we can do until we get something more out of either MI7 or Scotland Yard and besides, I could use some good news this afternoon."

Mitchell had every right to expect that this would indeed be good news. Despite the numerous and significant social difficulties that the country might be facing, the economy was in its strongest position since the heady days of the Thatcher regime. The pound had rarely been stronger against the euro. Back in 2018, when Greece ditched the currency and defaulted on its European debt, the pound was worth one point two euros.

19

Now, one would have to pay one point six euros for one of the much coveted English pounds. Albeit reluctantly, there were still many individuals and businesses within the membership of the European State that were desperate to do so. English exports to Europe had, of course, become significantly more expensive, but since the eventual British withdrawal from Europe around the turn of the decade, the Americas, South East Asia and China had become their most significant trade partners. Scotland were still in the European Union so it was still possible to sneak some tariff free French wines and German cars across Hadrian's Wall but this was considered to be a most unpatriotic as well as highly illegal practice.

The first few years out of Europe were hard as the British in general and the English in particular had to find new markets for their exports. They were forced to do so while rebuilding their own agricultural and manufacturing base to produce all those goods that for the previous forty years had travelled over or under the sea, further lining the pockets of the corrupt Europeans who controlled the shipping lanes and transportation systems, as well as the goods they carried. The immediate removal of restrictive laws and trade practices made the restoration of the rural and industrial infrastructure much faster and less painful than anyone could have imagined, aided, crucially, by substantial investment from their new allies in China. Over sixty per cent of English electricity was now generated by Chinese-owned nuclear reactors and thirty per cent of new social housing was funded by the Yen.

Unemployment was decimated and the government of the day congratulated itself on the decision not to have repatriated the wave of Eastern European migrants that had fled the abject poverty within their own flawed and failed political flirtations with the Super state. Such was the demand for labour in the fields, factories and offices that unemployment and welfare benefits were virtually withdrawn as anyone who wanted to work could do so and those who didn't were made to.

The combination of inward investment, substantial increase in tax revenues and dramatic reduction in welfare benefits generated unprecedented growth in the English economy to the extent that it rapidly became one of the most buoyant in the Western world and the envy of their erstwhile European partners. Not all of the former British Isles shared this meteoric economic recovery. Britain's departure from Europe coincided with the second Scottish devolution vote which, this time, opened the vote to both English and Scots. The criteria for the declaration of independence demanded that either fifty one per cent of the Scottish electorate voted for separation or a minimum of thirty per cent of the combined population. Both criterion were comfortably exceeded and the Scots heralded their independence in a blaze of tartan clad, malt fuelled exuberance.

Fittingly, the Welsh had followed like sheep in demanding their own referendum though nobody in the world, let alone in Wales, could quite understand where they thought they could generate sufficient revenue to stand alone. Many suspected that, with most of the political debate and rhetoric conducted in Welsh, the population had misinterpreted the meaning of independence, believing that the extent of their freedom simply extended to spending tax revenues, rather than actually raising them. Common sense prevailed and they remained within the now Disunited Kingdom.

Scotland was welcomed, open armed, into the European Union immediately. They were wooed by a more accessible market for their oil and some misguided perception of economic and national security. This suited the English as, without the necessity to create artificial borders, the differentiated currencies and national identity cards ensured that the two adjacent economies and cultures co-existed, albeit with vastly differing degrees of fortune.

The economic implosion of Scotland was heralded two years following independence with the almost complete collapse of the North Sea Oil Industry. Decline in global manufacturing had led to dramatic downturns in consumption. This was exacerbated by the Confederation of Muslim States or, as it was then known, ISIS, gaining control of a large proportion of the Middle East's oil fields and flooding the market with cheap oil to fuel their armament costs and, simultaneously destabilising Western economies. The rapid development of fracking technology spread quickly from North West England throughout the country to the point at which the country became not just self-sufficient, but a significant fuel exporter.

Not surprisingly, a growing number of disaffected Scots quickly reviewed and bemoaned their decision to elect independence. Within months of the oil collapse, an estimated seventy per cent of the population were claiming that they had voted against devolution and the demands for repatriation grew. Westminster held firm and while politicians just about resisted the temptation to gloat, they ensured that the tame media did their bidding. The dire economic plight north of the border led, inevitably, to social and civil unrest. Scottish Nationalist Party members and its voters became regular victims of violent verbal and physical attacks.

Across the water in Northern Ireland, which was still officially a part of the United Kingdom, the Unionist, protestant community were becoming increasingly isolated. The so called Peace Agreement, brokered by highly discredited British Government negotiators, had effectively handed power to the Republican South and they gradually took control of land, jobs and housing, assisted by huge European Union grants. The absence of a hard border between the two states was of greater concern to the EU than to Ireland or the United Kingdom, who seemed relaxed about the virtual annexation of their territory. The Westminster Government seemed to shrug their shoulders claiming that democracy must run its course but it seemed inevitable that, rather than a united Ireland, the island was on course to revert back to the state of the quasi civil war of the 1970s onward.

Ulstermen and women demanded protection from the English motherland, threatening and perpetrating acts of terror when it was not forthcoming.

A growing number of Scots had sympathised with the cause of Northern Ireland and, sensing safety in numbers in a unified cause, they joined forces with the Ulster Unionist movement and formed the Unionist Alliance. Two sets of unsettled outsiders with no sense of belonging and no voice.

Economic Nirvana, it seemed, did come with certain adverse social consequences and there was little doubt that Europe was doing its best to fan the embers in Ireland to create a damaging and distracting blaze.

Gemmell swiped his personal computing device and the screen came to life on the Prime Minister's wall. The economic charts remained positive. Gross National Product had grown for the sixtieth month in succession, imports at an all-time low, and employment numbers at an all-time high. The downside to this phenomenon was a worryingly high rate of inflation fuelling personal financial uncertainty and social unrest.

"As you know, Graeme, we have been allowing the economy to overheat for too long with the manufacturing economy in the private sector underwriting the increasing cost of the public sector. We are out of balance. Nobody wants to work in our schools and hospitals. Nobody wants to collect rubbish and nobody wants to police the streets any more. Some families are now earning enough from one member working in the private sector that their partners are choosing to stay home. I can't believe that the Minister for Work and Pensions with his strategy team didn't see this coming. We have to flatten this out. If we simply raise wages in the public sector we fuel inflation even further and outprice our goods in the export markets. If we don't raise wages, the services suffer and we have to import more immigrant labour to prop up the numbers. Before we know it, we have created the European State on our own doorstep that the public rejected."

Mitchell knew that this was a highly simplified version of the truth and probably spun to reflect some of his Chancellor's less savoury political views. Nevertheless, political commentators at home and abroad had foreseen and foretold of the cancer of economic indulgence. A nation eating itself away, virtually gorging upon itself.

"You are right, John. Something needs to be done both politically and socially to restore equilibrium but you know the mood of this Parliament. This government, this Cabinet, this regime and the majority of the establishment are still celebrating Brexit and remain drunk on its fumes. We somehow need to engage with them, without bringing this fragile prosperity crashing down around our heads. At the moment though, we happen to have an even more pressing national crisis to resolve."

Gemmell looked at Mitchell hesitantly before reluctantly posing his question.

"Don't you think that the two issues might just be related?"

Gemmell had remained steadfastly silent at the earlier Cabinet meeting but it was not his style to express his views and opinions in open forum. He much preferred the relative comfort of a one to one with his leader.

"What? Some sort of socio-economic insurgence? A people's uprising? Organised and perpetrated by who? Disaffected social workers? Disgruntled teachers? Police? Nurses for God's sake?"

"Of course not, Graeme, but never underestimate the resolve of the Liberal Movement. Their political agenda has been completely undermined since they crashed and burned at the end of the Con/Dem coalition in 2015. They were, you might say, *ConDem'd* to obscurity. They are dead but they won't lie down."

The Prime Minister suppressed his instinct to simply bat this thought away.

"Do you have any evidence at all to substantiate this suggestion? Is there any intelligence from the watchers to even support the vaguest notion of treason?"

"Well, clearly not. Otherwise Mellor would have suggested it this morning," Gemmell replied.

"Not necessarily, John, you heard what Mellor said. He doesn't peddle speculation or opinion. He only deals in facts."

"Well the fact is, Graeme, that we have just suffered the most aggressive terrorist attack in a generation at a time when this country should be basking in economic glory, not burying our dead. You heard Mellor today. He and the watchers have been warning us to be on our guard for some time. While you have been focussing on international diplomacy and I have been balancing the books, the Home and Foreign Offices seem to have grown as green and flabby as their toady permanent secretaries. Today is a wakeup call. A particularly unpleasant one but then nobody likes to be shaken out of a peaceful slumber and beautiful dream."

As if to underline the sentiment, Mitchell's personal videophone trilled loudly, shaking both men out of their deep pensive state. Gemmell withdrew diplomatically and Graeme, gingerly, opened the screen to see his old friend's rather self-satisfied grin.

"I have a name for you," he declared. "Game on!"

4

It was four o' clock in the afternoon in Istanbul as one very weary traveller collapsed onto his single bed in a modest three star hotel in the centre of the city. His thirty-minute journey from the airport had been uneventful and without the encumbrance of hold luggage he had disembarked the aircraft and cleared immigration just over an hour ago. Throughout the vast yet still crammed arrivals hall and in the main airport concourse he had noticed sizeable gatherings huddled around the overhead television screens, watching smoke and flames arise from above some of the world's most famous landmarks. Smart angled cinematography had actually made the blast impact seem much more widespread than it actually was and a casual observer might be forgiven for believing that Big Ben was about to fall. The traveller knew, full well, the extent of the damage and was more than pleased with his handiwork.

His flight had taken off from Heathrow just minutes before the Whitehall blast and just over an hour before the authorities had closed all the international exit terminals from England and Wales. He always knew that he would be cutting it fine, particularly with the notorious early morning air traffic control delays at Heathrow

26

but he was not unduly worried. His passport was in order, there was nothing incriminating within his regulation sized cabin baggage, and he was, of course, an upstanding citizen who knew his way around airports due to his frequent and extensive business travel. This was, for him, just another day out of the office.

He allowed himself two minutes on his back to gather his composure before turning on his personal communications device and viewing the long list of missed messages. All from the same number. Although he was confident that the calls would have been untraceable he was still angry that the caller had made so many attempts to contact him so soon after the event. Though his device was smart enough to remain totally discreet, the caller obviously wasn't. He presumed that he was expected to ring back but this was a man who rarely did what was expected and even more rarely submit to the whim and will of others. He poured himself a large Highland Park, savoured the first sip and swallowed the remainder and lay back to reflect upon his morning's work.

Back in London, the caller was becoming increasingly frantic in his attempts to reach the silent cell phone. He also knew that both their devices were well out of reach of any communications monitoring or even advanced Intelligence Service scrutiny and he was therefore becoming more irate with every ignored message.

"I don't care where you are, who you are with or what you are doing. Ring me back you bastard and tell me what the fuck you think you are playing at!"

He knew, of course, that his anger was futile. The man had been paid, and was now invisible. He would remain so for as long as he wanted to. In fact, the London caller never actually wanted to see him again in his life as he suspected that doing so might bring it to an abrupt and untimely end. He did however want – no – need an explanation as to why his instructions had been so wildly misinterpreted, or, even worse, completely undermined. His services had come with the highest commendations and his professionalism, right up to the point of execution had been exemplary. So what then, was his new agenda?

The anxious caller surveyed the montage screen on his wall mounted plasma screen. Of the forty eight images he could have selected, one of them was a weather bulletin, the other forty seven depicted scenes of devastation, carnage, weeping wounded, bewildered bystanders and outraged politicians. He expanded them in turn. Starting with the blast scene and moving gradually to the grim faces of the leaders of the Western and Eastern worlds. United in their disbelief, they resolved to track down and punish the perpetrators. Even Jürgen Schulke, the German president of the European Super state expressed his concern. The world was awash with an outpouring of grief, sympathy and, most of all, blatant and unashamed hypocrisy.

He closed the screen and keyed the contact again. This time the device sprang to life and a vacant expression stared at him silently.

"What the fuck are you playing at?" hissed London.

"Firstly," replied the contractor in a slow, calm, deliberate tone, "I have done as you desired, I have detonated a device in your designated location. Secondly, as a measure of goodwill, I am giving you one of your famous supermarket special offers: you purchase one, you receive one free! You might, therefore, be safer staying home tonight; or better still, away from the capital altogether. And thirdly, if you ever key this number again, my London connections will destroy you just as quickly and as absolutely as I destroyed your pathetic warmongering monument." The contactor clicked to close the call, coldly and clinically.

Minutes earlier, in an office not far away from the recipient of that call, the Prime Minister had just opened his own videophone to see the reassuring face of his old friend again. There were no niceties; there did not need to be as they had always known when one wanted to talk and the other wanted to listen.

"I have a name for you. Game on."

"Go on," urged Mitchell.

"Adnan Abadi. Syrian National. Twenty six years old, arrived here four years ago on a refugee ticket. Lives alone near Bloomsbury and reading politics at the London School of Economics."

"What do you have on him?" asked the PM.

"Very little," the other man admitted, "other than he wasn't where he should have been this morning and that absence undoubtedly saved his life."

"And do you know where he is now?"

"Well if you're quick," his friend grinned, "your people should find him in custody suite 3 in Holborn police station. Don't tell them I sent you."

***

Twelve minutes and a cascade of four phone calls later, DCS Sean Lakin was receiving his orders from the commissioner of the Metropolitan Police.

"We need to keep this pretty low key and under the radar, but we need one of your specialists to interview a suspect that we currently have in custody over at Holborn nick."

"Okay, sir," nodded Lakin. "What's he in for? I assume it is a he?"

"Yes," confirmed the commissioner. "It's a he. A Syrian national named Abadi. As far as Holborn are concerned, it's an assault and probable GBH but we are much more interested in the events that led up to his arrest. We need to know his every move from six o' clock this morning. Though not necessarily every movement."

The commissioner smirked at his crude and rather inappropriate attempt at humour before continuing.

"The source of the tip-off is all a bit vague, I'm afraid, but it sounds like it could be either official intelligence or a senior copper's snitch, but there is definite interest at the highest level."

"Would you like me to go across personally?" offered Lakin.

"No, that might set hares running. Let's keep it discreet. Holborn have already been advised that your people are on their way to quiz him about another line of enquiry that you're pursuing and that he might be able to help you with."

"Right, sir, I shall have someone there right away."

It was precisely five-fifteen in the evening when Detective Inspector Farah Karim arrived at Holborn custody suite 3.

5

Adnan Abadi's day had begun, as usual, at six-thirty in the morning but that was destined to be the day's only passing semblance to normality. By the time he had arrived at his college, he was physically and emotionally ragged. The aftermath of a terror attack delivers a unique experience of participation to anyone seeing, hearing or, especially, feeling the event. Adnan had felt as involved as it was possible to be and walk away unscathed. His upbringing in Syria should have given him a thorough preparation for every facet of life under terrorism but it had been so long since he had experienced it that he had almost forgotten the guilty rush of infused adrenalin as he surveyed what had been done, what he had seen and what he had heard.

He had been just eight years old when he saw his mother, father and only brother blown to pieces by a missile outside his school. In his excitement to join the family on their way to their weekend retreat, he had left his sports kit in the classroom and had run back to retrieve it. A weekend in the hills would not have been possible without his new Nike trainers. As he returned from the classroom and ran through the front doors, the searing heat of the blast threw

31

him backwards as four cars, their occupants and sixty three pedestrians were obliterated and scattered across a hundred yard radius. Adnan was less than a hundred and fifty yards from the road and wondered, to this day, whether any of the warm, wet, glistening, red and grey body fragments that hit him were from his own loved ones.

He never discovered whether the missile used in the attack was British, American, Russian or Saudi Arabian. At the time, it hardly mattered. His country was being ripped apart by a pride of feral lions, feasting upon a starving wildebeest. That was how it was, living in the newly liberated Syria.

Eighteen years, two months, three weeks and five days later, the Whitehall bomb exploded. It would have been his parents thirty-fifth wedding anniversary, not that they would have celebrated such things. They had simply devoted their love, time, energy and finances to giving their son and his brother the life they could only have dreamed of. How sad and ironic that it was their devotion to education that had eventually blown them apart.

It was almost ten o' clock when the tall, lean, black haired, brown eyed, handsome latecomer joined the study group and ten sets of eyes focussed upon him with varying degrees of surprise, relief and bewilderment. Professor Hollamby was first to break the awkward silence in his reserved and rather dramatic tone. He was not nicknamed Dumbledore for nothing.

"Adnan. Thank God you're all right, my boy!"

The members of the group all knew that Adnan had been selected to represent the group in an exclusive audience with the Minister for International Affairs that morning. His purpose was to discuss how Britain's thirty billion pound aid budget was to be deployed in helping to secure the future development, peace and sustainable harmony of countries whose populations had sworn their hatred of their white, Western Christian benefactors. Despite being the logical choice, his selection had created unbelievable tension and jealousy within this ruthlessly ambitious group of future global business leaders and diplomats.

"I didn't get to see him." Adnan mumbled. "I don't suppose I ever will now."

Nicholas Roberts had been declared critically injured in the secondary blast and was not expected to survive his horrendous injuries. He had, as he was accustomed to do, been sipping his Earl Grey as he looked out of his first floor window onto the briskly populated but beautifully civilised pedestrian parade below him on Whitehall. The blast from within his office had thrown him through the window and onto the pavement below.

There were eight people in this particular study group. All post graduates, five chasing graduate diploma status and three pursuing masters degrees. International politics was a popular course at the LSE but these eight select students were the absolute cream of their college and destined for global greatness. None of *them*, Professor Hollamby frequently mused, would be on the merry-go-round of knowledge recycling in sterile, professional academia. Not that this made them very nice people. Brilliant minds often sheltered tortured souls and their intense study created a layer of autism that all but destroyed any modest pretence to the strangulated interpersonal skills they may have feigned in their early months with the group.

They also lived in an age in which international politics embraced open discussion on religious, tribal, cultural, political, dynastical, doctrinal and secular issues. Not long ago, in the early second millennium, such conversations would have caused outrage, brought almost certain legal sanctions and closed the educational facility. Today, one did not need to be a shaven-headed, knuckle dragging, Neanderthal, National Socialist to express controversial right-wing views. The United Kingdom Independence Party shared government and its leader sat beside, though wider on the right of, the Prime Minister. Faraday's son, however, a podgy and equally unpopular parody of his daddy, sat, at this very moment, just to the left of Adnan Abadi. Under any other circumstances, the two would never have been seated so closely together. They barely managed to share the same room without spitting fine sprays of thinly veiled venom but today, there just happened to be only one spare chair within the circle beside Quentin Faraday and Abadi felt the need to collapse into it.

Never one to miss an exciting, contemporary, educational exchange, Professor Hollamby, almost gleefully, pronounced that the events of that morning would no doubt create too much distraction for the students to absorb the riveting lecture he had prepared, so he had suggested an open discussion on the cause and effects of terrorism and its legitimate use as a political lever. He basically wanted to 'put it out there' and have his multicultural students scrap like rats in a sack.

The dynamics of the debate had initially taken the form of two moderate contributors, Jos der Linden from the Netherlands and Jean Francois Martin of Paris pleading dramatically to the remainder of the group for suggestions as to how and why violence of any form could have a legitimate place in any aspect of modern society. It would not be long before two of the other group members conspired to provide an insight.

Inevitably, the discussion focussed upon a former British leader, now languishing, comfortably, no doubt, in private quarters in an austere facility on the Isle of Wight, writing the next instalment of his personal and political memoirs that would see him move to a much warmer island in the Caribbean upon his release in nine months' time. There was speculation within the group, with some degree of foundation, that one of the possible motives for today's attack was the steadfast refusal of the Westminster Parliament to hand him over to the Iraqi Government to face a war crimes trial upon his release.

History had been written, rewritten and rottenly written on the legitimacy of the three Gulf Wars. Nobody, not even Quentin Faraday could argue that the intervention of the West had not only taken one hundred times the number of lives that the deposed and deceased despotic leaders had disposed of, but had paved the way for a succession of even more murderous regimes.

The flash point occurred when Abadi spoke passionately of the disgraceful treachery of the British Government in actively encouraging the Syrian population to take up arms against their unpopular and undemocratic leader, only to stand back when, under the eyes of the West, an even more unpopular and undemocratic regime took up the challenge. Abadi would never know whether the missile that wiped out his family was dispatched by the Syrian Government, the rebel insurgents or well-meaning Westerners but it hardly mattered. The effect would have been equally devastating, whatever the source.

Abadi argued rationally, calmly but passionately, that Britain had a responsibility back then to intervene and provide relief effort and a peacekeeping force to restore some form of civilisation to the wretched innocents of his sad nation.

Faraday countered, dismissively, by asking:

"Which of us, in this circle, would dare to intervene if we saw two rabid Rottweilers fighting over a piece of rotting meat in a rat infested alley? The West did the world a favour by setting these two factions against themselves and ridding the planet of a couple of hundred thousand new terrorists. And don't give me the innocent women and children crap! The women and brats are more likely to have bombs strapped to them than their cowardly husbands and fathers. We rid the world of vermin. Who amongst us would risk infecting ourselves...?"

Before he could continue, the chair crashed around his head and shoulders and Abadi grabbed him by the throat and dragged him to the floor, pounding him with fists and feet until Faraday's face was reduced to a shiny, red-pepper-fleshed pulp. There was little doubt in the minds of the group members that had they not dragged Abadi off, Faraday would have been reduced to that piece of Rottweiler meat that Faraday had so graphically, but fatefully, described.

This was not a good day to call the emergency services. Police and ambulance crews right across London were stretching every sinew, either attending the Whitehall scene or strategically positioned at other potential target sites. The first aid facility at LSE was comprehensive. Faraday was receiving attention within three minutes and when the ambulance crew eventually arrived, around twenty minutes later, they found him conscious, barely, with an oxygen mask covering his swollen and bloody face.

Adnan Abadi remained impassively at the scene. He had turned away from his bloodied victim and sat quietly, with his elbows on his knees, chin resting on his grazed fists, as if in meditation, waiting for the police to arrive. Hollamby had called the university security team but the two burly, bull necked guards surveyed the scene and stood, nervously, supposedly securing the exit, rather than approaching the crazy man in the middle of the room.

A full eight minutes later, the guards stepped aside as four uniformed policemen entered the room, the first two with Taser guns drawn, and slowly approached Abadi who rose, obligingly and offered his outstretched wrists. The younger of the two officers read Abadi his rights, confirmed his understanding, and led him away. This would be a major snatch for the team; arresting the lunatic who had beaten the Deputy Prime Minister's son half to death. Although the truth would emerge down at the station, there would be wild tales of superhuman strength, struggle and heroics in four different pubs that weekend.

Professor Hollamby, still dazed by the events of the last half hour, shepherded his remaining students back to the blood spattered circle in the centre of the room and developed the theme of whether violence could ever be justified in retaliation to racism. Thankfully, it was a short debate.

6

Detective Chief Inspector Sean Lakin had called just three members of his Special Investigations Unit team together following his phone call with the commissioner. The remaining nine were aware that Chambers, Karim and Churchill had received the tap on the shoulder and barely raised their heads from their screens as the three special investigators followed Lakin into the interview room. Each member of the team trusted Lakin implicitly. They knew that he viewed every one of them as a precious resource, each with a particular skill, a special purpose and specific role to play within every investigation. They just correctly assumed that the three selected for this particular briefing would be following a new line of enquiry that needed to be investigated in parallel to the monumental tasks being performed at the nine occupied workstations. Lakin did not believe in briefing for briefing's sake. New information could be a time consuming distraction to existing lines of enquiry and most of the team still harboured hopes of actually getting home that evening.

Lakin closed the door and simply told the three that he had received a rather vague, but compelling piece of intelligence from an unnamed but reliable source, a good few levels beyond his own pay grade.

"The suspect's name is Adnan Abadi, a Syrian postgraduate student at the LSE. There is nothing, as yet to directly link him with the Whitehall blast but he is currently in custody at Holborn nick facing charges of aggravated assault and actual bodily harm."

Chambers was the first to speak:

"So why is an assault of interest to us, Guv?"

Lakin looked at each of the three in turn as he delivered his answer.

"Well, setting aside the fact that he has just beaten the living shit out of Neil Faraday's first-born, the Foreign Office registrar noted that he had an appointment with the Minister for International Affairs director this morning and failed to turn up."

Detective Sergeant Roger Churchill took up the dialogue.

"I suspect that a good number of people failed to turn up for Whitehall appointments today. The area is still sealed off and for all the registrar knows, Abadi could be rehearsing his questions from under a pile of rubble."

Lakin nodded as he replied.

"Abadi's appointment was a late arrangement as a favour to the Foreign Secretary. The planned meeting was for 9 a.m. and non-cleared visitors to Whitehall are all advised to arrive up to one hour ahead of time to undergo security clearance. He should have checked in around the time of the blast. He would have been directly in harm's way had he met the appointment."

"Lucky lad," smirked Chambers.

"Maybe so, maybe not," Lakin replied. "Farah, I need you to get over there this afternoon and take over from the local squad. As far as they are aware, they are investigating a violent assault on a high profile, possible political victim. That alone is sufficient justification for this team, you, to be involved. We need it to stay that way for the moment. Conduct the interview alone, with our own discreet recording device."

"What about his lawyer?" asked Farah. "He is going to pick up immediately on my line of questioning?"

"So far, he has declined the offer of representation. He hasn't even asked for his phone call. If he does reconsider his position when your interest becomes clear, we have lined up a solicitor with grade-A clearance. We clearly have a limited time to hold him so it's vital that we get to work as quickly as possible and work on the hoof.

"Brian, I need you to get hold of Abadi's citizen file and feed Farah with anything that might help to focus her line of questioning.

Roger, link up with the watchers and find out everything you can about Abadi's life in Syria before he gained his refugee status and citizenship. Three years seems a pretty short time to get his full ticket and you might be able to turn up whether there was anything unusual in the process. Again, keep Farah in the loop. Okay guys, get to it."

As the three of them turned to leave he placed a hand on Farah's shoulder to delay her exit. As much as she had desired a reprise of the morning interaction, she knew that it would not be forthcoming. They were now both in fully functioning business mode.

"Do you need any help down at Holborn, Farah? I would prefer you interview him alone but I am hoping that you will be receiving a steady stream of information from Brian and Richard. Will you be able to process and stay focussed?"

Farah was a very highly skilled interrogator. Part of her training had followed the principles applied to news broadcasters. Delivering news stories and interviewing headliners while receiving information and instructions, through invisible headphones, from a team of researchers and producers.

"I will be fine," she assured him. "The enhanced audio visual functions on Digispex now allow us to switch off the sound and transfer the voice message into live and recorded text. I can switch in and out of either mode through my lens or tablet screen."

"Okay," said Sean. "It could be a late one. Have you got someone to look after Ava or do you want me to sort out a sitter? I might even be able to get there myself later?"

"No, its fine, thanks Sean. Ava is with her school group in a hotel for the night. They are hoping to take Le Shuttle tomorrow or, failing that, they will be coached to Dover for the ferry. We have completed the obligatory hugging."

With that, she squeezed Sean's hand and smiled warmly. "So there's no excuse for not coming round for a post interrogation interrogation!"

Farah strode back to her work station and closed down her screen. She was confident that by the time she had reached Holborn, her tablet would contain a thorough briefing of the events surrounding Abadi's arrest and a transcript of the Holborn interview. She would allow herself thirty minutes to assimilate this information and prepare her own line of questioning.

She understood, and completely accepted that the principal reason for being posted to this interview was her own background. London was the most multi-cultural capital city in the world. Over fifty per cent of the population had not been born in the city, and nearly sixty five per cent of those had not been born in the country. The early waves of immigration had been from the old British Empire. In the nineteen sixties and seventies Britain opened its borders to Indians, Pakistanis, Africans and West Indians, all of whom provided much needed resource in many essential, labour-intensive sectors.

A steady stream of immigrants continued as a result of Britain's European Membership until the government finally conceded that they had totally lost control of their borders and the island was sinking and suffocating under the burden of overpopulation. And then there were the political refugees. Millions of Middle Eastern men, women and children sought sanctuary in Europe as the bombs crashed down around them. Germany, Austria and France were most heavily targeted but Britain was deemed by most to be the Promised Land. Migrants from Syria, Iraq, Iran, Afghanistan and Egypt all justifiably felt that they had a right to settle here as, invariably, it had been Britain and its bullying big brother America that had destroyed their homelands.

Farah had been one such refugee. She had been fortunate to escape Iran with her parents, husband and baby daughter just over thirteen years ago. Her father, an Iranian civil servant, had been helpful to the British Embassy in Teheran on a number of occasions; so many, in fact, that their move to Britain had been rather more hurried than any of the family had anticipated. Six years later both her parents had died of natural causes, her father of a massive heart attack and her mother of pancreatic cancer. One of the few cancers that had not yet been defeated by health service advances.

Her husband had returned to Iran within two years of arriving in Britain. In truth, she had not been at all sorry. She quickly realised that the subjugation that she had tolerated in Iran was neither the norm nor acceptable in democratic Britain and it also became apparent that her husband had probably been more interested in her father than herself, though with no sexual interest in either. The Iranian Intelligence Services had no respect for family. Farah's daughter, Ava, had been the one good product of their short marriage and mother and daughter doted upon each other, especially now, with no living relatives.

In Iran, Farah had been a brilliant student and talented linguist. The British Embassy in Tehran had no hesitation in recommending her to the British Intelligence Services, but the demands on her time would have been far too onerous and potentially dangerous to her life with Ava. She eventually opted for a career with the Special Investigations Unit within Scotland Yard where again, she had turned down numerous opportunities of promotional transfer to preserve and maintain her promises and commitments to Ava.

Given her earlier experience in Victoria, Farah elected not to take the tube but walk the mile or so to Holborn. She would use the time to assimilate her thoughts and plan her approach. The walk also helped her to appreciate the state of confusion, apprehension and, yes, terror on the faces of those who had ventured back out onto the streets. As she stepped from the pavement to cross the Strand, Farah froze as her whole being responded to the sudden, deafening crash behind her. She recovered momentarily, shielded her head in her hands and turned, sharply, towards the commotion. A pallet load of canned food had fallen from a hand truck as it mounted the kerb on its way to the Aldi store.

Such was the heightened emotion of the event that a similarly shocked passer-by picked up a tin that had rolled towards him and hurled it directly at the driver. Had Farah not been so focussed on her mission at Holborn, she might have intervened to prevent the brawl that followed. As it were, she continued along the unusually quiet thoroughfares until, fifteen minutes later, she approached the rather apprehensive desk sergeant at Holborn. There were still certain people who were intimidated, rather than enchanted, by her exotic features.

The station superintendent had been alerted to expect Ms Karim and to afford her all cooperation and courtesy. He led her to his own office and she took the seat graciously offered. If Superintendent Holden had felt at all affronted at the intervention of Scotland Yard he did not show it. He strongly suspected that the identity of the assault victim had led to the commissioner's phone call and the decision to move the inquiry to the special investigation team.

"Would you like to speak with the arresting officer and incident investigator?" he asked. "In this instance, they are actually the same person. All hands to the pump today."

"That would be most helpful, thank you," replied Farah. She knew that to have declined the offer would have been construed as either arrogant or discourteous, though she would certainly not allow anything declared in those earlier exchanges to influence or prejudice her own line of questioning.

PC Coyne joined them. He was in his late-twenties, around two metres tall and more generously proportioned than his doctor or wife would have desired. He opened both his electronic notebook and witness interview, the latter also recorded electronically and verified by the thumbprints of both participants to the interview. Coyne had been relieved though somewhat surprised by how compliant, almost docile, the prisoner had been throughout the arrest and charging process. He had not requested the presence of a lawyer and had nobody he needed to call. He admitted the assault but claimed only a vague recollection of the events that immediately preceded it. He claimed that he thought that Quentin Faraday was about to assault him and used the chair to defend himself. He had remained calm and composed throughout the interview and was now resting in a holding cell.

Farah thanked the pair and asked if she might have a few minutes alone to review her own notes and review the interview video on Coyne's tablet before seeing the suspect herself in the secure interview room. By this time, she had downloaded a good deal of background detail from DI Chambers and within fifteen minutes she was led down to the small, windowless room where Adnan Abadi awaited.

7

Neil Faraday burst through the door of the Home Secretary's ante-room and looked down upon the shocked Mountstevens through blood red eyes. His fists were clenched and he did not so much speak as growl, intimidatingly.

"I want that bastard caught, I want him charged, I want him remanded and I want him in the shittiest cell on the most dangerous landing of toughest block in the hardest prison in the land!"

"Good afternoon, Neil," Mountstevens looked up from his pile of papers. "Nasty business with Quentin. How is he by the way?"

"Thankfully, he has regained consciousness. He has a broken jaw, three missing teeth, a fractured skull and two broken ribs. He also has internal bleeding and the doctors say that it's too early to rule out brain damage. Yes, Clive, it's a nasty business and the nasty bastard that did this nasty business is going to suffer for the rest of his nasty, miserable life."

"Look, Neil, I can fully understand your position but I can't discuss this with you now. I was expecting someone just as you

44

came through the door and it would be unfair to keep him waiting. What I can tell you is that we have a suspect in custody and he is being questioned by the Yard's most senior team."

"Well bloody well make sure he stays behind bars for the rest of his stinking, rotten, miserable existence. Or better still, give me a baseball bat and ten minutes with him."

As Faraday turned to leave, the door opened into his outstretched hand, stubbing and painfully bending back his fingers. If he had been enraged when he entered the room, he was positively incandescent as he left and bumped into, quite literally, the Home Secretary's next visitor. At one metre seventy, Naveed Choudhry was half a head smaller than Faraday but their eyes were drawn together by invisible laser lines of mutual hatred.

"What the fuck is he doing here, Home Secretary?" demanded Faraday.

Choudhry answered for him. "Like you, Mr Faraday, I am the leader of a democratically constituted political party. I polled more votes than you at the last election and had it not been for the blatant gerrymandering of the proportional representation system, my party would have secured more parliamentary seats than yours. I have an appointment with the Home Secretary and assume that you do not, so please run along and let two serious politicians discuss the serious matters of the day."

The image of his bruised and battered son flashed to the front of Faraday's mind as his fists clenched and veins in his neck protruded. Just in time, he recovered just enough control and composure to heave a disgusted sigh, walk around the self-satisfied Choudhry and exit briskly down the ceramic glazed corridor.

"Please sit down, Naveed," invited Mountstevens. "It's not my place to apologise for Faraday but his son his in a serious condition in hospital."

"Battered to within an inch of his life," noted Choudhry. "Rumour has it, by a Muslim. A rumour of course, generated and circulated by Faraday."

"Well between you and me, Naveed that seems to be the case and the argument that led to the confrontation was certainly politically, if not racially motivated."

Choudhry accepted the statement dispassionately and calmly replied. "Well that might be so, Home Secretary," signalling a switch from pleasantry to formality, "but this morning's tragic events have created enough inter racial tension in our communities, without that oaf fuelling the fire."

Naveed Choudhry was the leader of the British Muslim Party which now held forty three parliamentary seats. The BMP were considered to be the moderate and rational face of Muslim politics in Britain, their MPs respected for their ability to represent legitimate constituency issues without constant reference to the rhetoric of race. His nephew, Rahim, however, was not held in such diplomatic esteem. At thirty-five, seventeen years younger than his uncle, Rahim was the self-appointed, undemocratically elected chairman of the IBIS: the Independent British Islamist State. They were, of course, neither independent, nor a state and publicly at least, were a major embarrassment to Naveed Choudhry who was a well-respected politician at home and within the extended Commonwealth.

Naveed continued. "As far as I am aware, there is absolutely no evidence that this morning's atrocity was in any way linked to IBIS or any other group associated with the British Muslim community, but already, the thugs are on the streets and gathering outside the mosques. I need your assurance, Home Secretary, in that police presence and security will be heightened in sensitive areas. IBIS have not claimed responsibility and have issued a statement distancing themselves from it."

"I read the statement," nodded Mountstevens. "I particularly noted their regret at the loss of at least eight Muslim lives. Not surprisingly, no such sentiment for the Christians, Hindus, Jews and Sikhs killed in the blast. But then, sensitivity and inclusiveness never were strong suits of IBIS. Also, we both know that there are cells

46

of ISIS in this country and no doubt, finding sympathy and refuge within the so called Islam Territories of Northern England."

"Such speculation is unjustified and unhelpful, Home Secretary. You will also recall that I, personally, helped to unravel the ISIS plot three years ago that has seen a number of its high profile leadership enjoying hospitality at His Majesty's Pleasure. For all we know, the bomb may have been planted by the Scots, the Irish or the Eastern Europeans and all I am asking is that you issue a statement denouncing the immediate association with Islam and demanding that there is no ill placed retribution against our communities."

Clive Mountstevens liked Choudhry. Naveed was the eldest of two sons born in Blackburn, Lancashire to a Pakistani immigrant father who had worked from the day he entered the country to the day he died, in one of those cotton mills which used to punctuate the landscape across the North West of England. Naveed chose not to follow his father into the textile industry and identified that there was a severe shortage of ethnic teachers in the education system. He gained a scholarship to grammar school and a university bursary in Lancaster and was fast-tracked into a teaching role in Blackburn. He developed an interest in local politics, served as a councillor and within three years headed the Lancashire County Council education authority. It was no surprise when, at the age of thirty-seven, he became Britain's first Muslim member of parliament with the Labour Party.

His younger, brother, Akram, did follow his father into the mills, where he worked tirelessly for thirty years before dying of lung and chest infection for which his son Rahim, held the mill, the health authority, the trade union, the Labour Party and the monarchy responsible. Rahim sought solace at the mosque, fastidiously studied the Koran and volunteered as an advisor to the rapidly expanding immigrant community claiming as much in benefits for his clients and himself as he could legitimately, and illegitimately, prise from the state he despised. Like his uncle, he developed an appetite for politics but did not call it this at the time.

In Rahim's mind, he was rallying the Muslim community against local prejudice and discrimination. He was forming and leading groups of naïve friends and relatives to stand up to the gangs of white youths that constantly taunted them. He was cajoling the community into maintaining and upholding the disciplines and traditions of their race and discouraging the liberal integration that threatened to infiltrate and weaken their culture and religion. He joined the Labour Party, took an active interest in local politics and at the tender age of twenty he became a councillor for the Audley Range ward of Blackburn Borough Council. He continued as an active and outspoken Labour councillor right up to the point at which Tony Blair's Labour Government waged war on Iraq when he resigned and stood as an independent candidate. It was only twelve years later when he formed the party demanding the formation and establishment of an Independent British Islamist State, that he considered himself a proper politician.

Naveed Choudhry continued his appeal. "The British Muslim Party has no sympathy with ISIS and has no association with IBIS. All we seek to do is provide representation for our constituents to live peacefully and practice their traditions and culture in accordance with our religion. We protect the right to educate our children in Islamic schools and to shelter them from what we consider to be some of the excesses of Western liberal attitudes to sexuality. We offer no threat and I hope you will agree that since our formation, we have done everything possible to promote the cause that is possible to be both British and Muslim."

Mountstevens gently nodded his acknowledgement of the points his fellow parliamentarian had made. "Naveed, everyone in this house recognises and appreciates the efforts that you, your MPs and many of their constituents are making to bring greater harmony amongst our communities. There are however, still too many people in this country who cannot, or will not, differentiate between Al Qaeda, the Taliban, ISIS, IBIS and the BMP. To them, you are all Muslim fanatics, driven by a declared and open obsession to convert the world to Islam, by whatever means required. I know it's unfair but it just puts an even greater imposition upon you to condemn the terrorist factions."

"And we will do so," Naveed promised. "If and when it is proven that Islam was involved in this atrocity. The State Broadcasting Corporation and Sky News have already invited me onto their screens to denounce acts of terror and I told them what I will tell you now. For me to do so would be tantamount to an admission that Islamic factions were involved. Have the SNP, the United Alliance, the Irish Republican Party or the Liberal Party been asked for a similar denunciation? No! Of course they haven't. You, Clive, you and your government need to take control of this situation, calm the nation and find the culprits."

On that point, Choudhry rose, shook the Home Secretary's outstretched hand and set off towards his own, much smaller workplace down the Westminster corridor.

Back in his office, Choudhry locked the door, sat behind his desk and withdrew his personal communication device. One of the privileges of a party leader is a private, soundproofed, allegedly bug free office. Even so, he chose not to engage the remote, hands free video function and placed the device to his ear and mouth as he keyed the speed dial. His nephew answered almost immediately.

"I have been trying to contact you all day," complained Rahim.

"And I have been trying to avoid you all day," countered Choudhry. "Word might not have reached you in your medieval state of Lancashire, but there has been an outrageous atrocity perpetrated here in London."

"Really?" replied his nephew. "I have been so busy watching newsfeeds on the devastation of Western carpet bombing in Baghdad, Cairo and Tripoli that I have not had too much time to catch up with your minor English incident."

"I presume you will be denying any involvement?" asked Choudhry

"I have yet to decide," mused Rahim. "I am pretty sure that none of our official factions were responsible but it seems too good an opportunity not to claim some responsibility, if nobody else wants it."

"And what about ISIS, ISIL, IS, Daesh or whatever the warmongers are calling themselves this week?"

"As you well know, Uncle, I have no jurisdiction over ISIS nor them over us. We simply share a few common beliefs. I really cannot think why ISIS would want to do anything to harm the British people. Why, without their government's wonderfully generous actions in removing their fiercest enemies, ISIS could never have been established. While Saddam Hussein, Gaddafi and Assad were in power, nobody would have dared rise up against them. ISIS will be eternally grateful to Britain and the US for removing those heroic despotic dictators and clearing the way for a fundamentalist Islam Middle East."

"So it was not you or your followers?"

"Uncle," pleaded Rahim. "Why would we need to do this? Our babies are our bombs. In less than fifty years there will be more Muslims in Britain than Christians and then we will see the true power of democracy. We are amassing untold wealth. While the British people waste their money on alcohol, drugs, tobacco, excess food and foreign holidays to burn their skins, we are preserving our wealth to buy properties and businesses. Not only will we dominate the population, we will dominate the economy and you, of course, can be prime minister, if you live that long."

"Don't give me that, Rahim. Patience is the policy of my party. Your demands seek only to antagonise and alienate. You may well be able to walk all over the English but the Eastern Europeans are nowhere near as accommodating. They too, have worked hard to infiltrate this island and they will not give up their territory easily."

"And when the time comes, Uncle, I am sure we will be able to rely upon our like-minded comrades in ISIL to lend us whatever support we need to cleanse this grubby little island of its dirty natives, infidel intruders and the decadent society they have built together."

"Rahim," sighed his uncle, not waiting for the answer before closing down the call. "From whom did you inherit so much hate?"

8

The regime at Holborn was not at all comfortable with permitting Farah to interview Adnan Abadi alone, in a secure, enclosed and isolated interview room. Such precautions were not usually employed when interviewing an assault suspect but then, neither was the presence of an officer from the Special Investigations Unit Team, or SUITS as it was frequently, though inappropriately, labelled. The fact that the victim had been the son of the Deputy Prime Minister was the official explanation given though some in the station were already putting two and two together and making one hundred and twenty-six. The current number of Whitehall fatalities.

Farah was accompanied into the secure area where the interview room was at the end of a corridor of sixteen cells. Although they were supposedly self-cleaning, the stench of sweat, urine, excrement and vomit always tended to linger longer than the transit guests. Farah resisted the temptation to spray Chanel No 17 under her nose as this would, undoubtedly, project the wrong image to both prisoner and guards.

"There is a panic button on your side of the interview table and two officers will be positioned right outside the cell. We will also keep the suspect cuffed to the table." reassured the Duty Sergeant. Farah thanked him and entered to cell quietly and confidently. "Good evening, Mr Abadi," she said.

Abadi did not return the greeting but simply looked her up and down in a somewhat suspicious but nonetheless admiring manner. Farah removed her computer tablet from her bag and activated the video and audio recording devices. She then donned the oversized, but still fashionable spectacles that gave her both normal vision from the upper element of the varifocal lens and a set of autocue notes within the lower. The tiny earphones on the arms of the glasses provided a live feed to anyone wishing to comment on the interview exchanges relayed back via her tablet. In this instance, that someone was Detective Superintendent Sean Lakin.

"Mr Abadi. I am Special Investigator Farah Karim." She deliberately concealed her rank, as experience told her that seniority in a woman could be intimidating to certain cultures. "You have been arrested in connection with the assault upon Quentin Faraday. I have studied the transcript of your earlier interview with Detective Sergeant Galligan and there are some inconsistencies and supplementary questions that I need to put to you."

DS Galligan's interview and subsequent transcript had been comprehensive. The suspect had been totally open about his background in Syria, claiming that he no longer had any affiliation or affinity with the region and no living relatives. He was creating a new life in Britain, his ambition was to become a political journalist and he focussed all his time and energies towards that goal. He had no girlfriend nor, for that matter, any male friends. The closest he came to social contact was within the confines of his course and his weekly kickboxing class. He was physically fit, he worked out regularly and running was his preferred form of relaxation. He admitted to a history of mental illness for which he took moderate medication in the form of a mild antidepressant to control the occasional mood swings brought about by the trauma of his youth.

Abadi looked directly at her with his head tilted nonchalantly to his right as he spoke. "Are you the token female Arab in the team, trotted out every now and then to establish empathy with fellow sand monkeys?"

"No, Mr Abadi." she replied, equally unfazed. "I am a senior investigator from Scotland Yard trotted out regularly to interview vicious criminals of all ethnicities and religions and I just happened to be first back from lunch today when the department pisspot was emptied and your name was dredged from the bottom of it, so shall we proceed?"

Abadi smiled and nodded.

"Mr Abadi, or can I call you Adnan?"

"I think, Farah, that since you are probably here to ensure that I am incarcerated in some stinking prison for a significant part of my life, you should drop any pretence towards familiarity and afford me the customary formality. Mr. Abadi will be fine."

"Is that where you believe you will be going, Mr Abadi? To prison?" Farah prompted.

"Well not if there is any natural justice in this country but I suspect that the words of a Syrian refugee will sit less sympathetically with a jury than the son of the Deputy Prime Minister."

"You assaulted the son of the Deputy Prime Minister, Mr Abadi, in what appeared to be an unprovoked attack. He is in a serious but stable condition in hospital but a few hours ago you could potentially have been facing a murder charge."

"I acted in self-defence," muttered Abadi, unconvincingly.

"Eight witnesses saw it differently, Mr Abadi," challenged Farah. "They claim that you reacted violently to something Mr Faraday said during a heated debate."

"This is not my recollection, Farah. I considered myself to be under attack. I have already discussed this in great detail with a male officer earlier today. What is your interest in the matter? Do you not trust the young man?" If Abadi was deliberately trying to draw the Queen of Spades, he was playing a very cool hand of cards.

54

"The assault," continued Farah, "occurred during a morning in which London appears to have suffered a terrorist attack in Whitehall, the heart of British Government. You viciously attacked the son of the Deputy Prime Minister. Now it is perfectly possible that the two events are completely unrelated but my department is required to investigate all possibilities."

"So now I am a suspected terrorist?" pleaded Abadi incredulously. "A mass bomber?"

"Is that an admission, Mr Abadi?" queried Farah, softly.

"No it is not, Ms Karim." Abadi kept his composure. "You, more than most, ought to be aware that not all Muslims are bombers."

"Are you a Muslim, Mr Abadi? I hadn't realised."

This initial parrying was nothing more than an attempt by Farah to establish some form of rapport with her suspect and to get him accustomed to speaking to her. At this point, she wasn't particularly concerned by what he said and was encouraged by the fact that he seemed willing to engage. The exchanges were being broadcast live via Farah's laptop to where Sean Lakin and Brian Chambers were watching and listening closely. In turn, bullet points were appearing upon her screen and Digispex but verbal messages from Scotland Yard were kept to an absolute minimum as Farah found these more distracting than the removable screen script.

"Mr Abadi," Farah began to get down to business. "You arrived at your college this morning just before nine-thirty. Would you mind telling us where you had been prior to that time?"

"I left my flat at around seven-thirty, I walked to Russell Square and took the tube to Westminster where I had an appointment at the Office of International Development. While I was underground, the bomb exploded and the tube network was suspended and exits closed. I got out around nine and walked along the embankment, up to the Strand and across to the LSE."

"Who told you it was a bomb?" Farah enquired, calmly. "There is some speculation that it may have been a major gas and oil explosion."

55

"I guess I saw it on the screens or heard it on the news. I can't remember."

"But if you walked directly from Westminster to the college and were then escorted directly from there to here, where would you have watched the news? Were there screens in your study room, or your cell? Was there a radio in the cage of the police van?" Farah's Digispex had already told her that there weren't and at least Abadi didn't try to bluff it out.

"It was probably an assumption on my part. That seemed to be the topic of debate in the study group and you yourself have just told me that I am a suspected terrorist."

Farah returned to the morning journey. "Mr Abadi, are you familiar with the acronym FRT?"

"Would that stand for Farah's Relentless Tenacity?" Abadi smirked, "Feeling Rather Tired? Or Farah's Rather Tiresome, perhaps?"

"Facial Recognition Technology is the advancement of Close Circuit Television technology. A facial image, captured on CCTV, is broken down into individual pixels and reconstituted into a file that is as unique to an individual as a fingerprint. This is why the wearing of balaclavas and burkas was banned on the public transport system in 2016. Your image was indeed captured entering Russell Square tube station at seven forty this morning. You took the Piccadilly Line and emerged from Leicester Square eleven minutes later. You re-entered Leicester Square at nine forty-one, took the southbound Northern Line and exited Charing Cross at nine forty-seven. You made no attempt to go anywhere near Westminster or Whitehall this morning, Mr Abadi. Why was that?"

Few investigators had Farah's skill of assimilating screen data into lucid narrative as effortlessly as she appeared to do. This confident and assured delivery seemed to rattle Abadi for the first time since their eyes met around forty minutes ago.

Abadi sat back in his chair. His right arm stretched across to his left armpit and his left hand covered his face and chin. His downturned head would have given a full house to any amateur psychologist playing Body Language Bingo.

Eventually, perhaps twenty seconds later, he lifted his head and spoke. "I had no intention of meeting Nicholas Roberts that morning."

"You passed up a plum interview with the Minister for International Affairs? An aspiring political journalist, offered a gig that your classmates would have crawled on their knees over broken glass to have made, and you stood him up? Do you realise how incredible that sounds, Mr Abadi?"

"Exactly!" Abadi asserted. "I was carefully selected for the interview, as you were today, purely because of my background and ethnicity. I was expected to be so grateful to meet the great man, so thankful for the scraps of foreign aid thrown at my homeland, so envious that Britain could afford these pathetic, patronising pay-offs that I simply refused to play the game. I was making my own political statement to the minister, and my professor, that the process for allocating Foreign Aid is almost as corrupt as the regimes for which it is destined."

Farah listened intently to his explanation as she was carefully trained not to be led by her predetermined instinct. "So how would such a gesture have made any impact upon the political landscape?"

"I was expecting a confrontation back at the LSE and hoped that the ensuing publicity of a mere student snubbing a minister would make the headlines."

"So why," Farah played along, "did you not declare this when you returned to the study group and to me when I asked you about this morning's movements?"

"Because," Abadi pleaded, "the events of this morning overtook me, the gesture would have seemed totally futile and my absence might have, and indeed did, attract suspicion."

They stared at each other for what seemed like minutes, but was probably less than fifteen seconds. Interrogators were trained to embrace silence and the *Negotiation for Dummies* textbook will tell you that whoever breaks the silence first, loses. Farah was about to ignore that rule as the message materialised in front of her eyes. Before she had the opportunity to speak, Abadi opened up to her.

"The fight with Faraday was part of that strategy but it went too far. I was enraged, outraged by his vile diatribe. I rose to challenge him and I am sure that he made the first move. I retaliated and that's all I can recall."

"Would you like to tell me about the numerous searches for ISIS on your computer and the email traffic between yourself and their high council in Afghanistan?"

Abadi looked genuinely shocked. "How did you access my computer? Have you searched my flat? That's illegal!" he demanded.

"We had just cause to search your premises, but as it happens, we don't need to access your device to monitor your conversations, Mr Abadi," Farah countered. "The intelligence services are capable of intercepting traffic without touching your devices. You have been a person of interest for some time now."

"I am to be a political journalist," he countered. "I need to research all dimensions of the political spectrum. I am proud of my ability to have established a dialogue with them but this does not mean that I support them."

"But when we did access your device, we found a number of encrypted files, detailing the components and construction of explosive devices. Is this part of your academic studies too?"

Abadi slumped backwards, deflated and declared, "I think perhaps I now need to take up your colleague's kind offer of a lawyer. Interview over. Goodbye, Ms Karim, Farah."

It was nine-thirty on that February evening when Farah finally signed out of Holborn police station and stepped out into the cold, frosting street. The sky was mostly clear but an eerie mist lingered a mile or so south where the Whitehall Arc lights illuminated fragments that still fluttered and flew from the site of the explosion.

It could, Farah thought, have been the souls of the dead, fulfilling their summons to the heavens.

Farah flicked open her mobile device and clicked on the video message icon. She smiled, involuntarily, as the beaming face of her fourteen-year-old daughter shone out at her. She was clearly excited but also noticeably nervous from her earlier experience at Victoria. Ava had completed a slow one hundred and eighty degree sweep with her videophone to reveal a large white vessel, brightly illuminated by a bank of floodlights. "Hi Mama, we have given up on the tunnel but the school have managed to get us on the seven o' clock ferry from Dover. If you're free before we sail, call me coz I don't think we get a signal in the sea, or the channel or the ocean or wherever we are going. Anyway, take care, don't worry, speak soon and I love you, Mama."

This was especially poignant for Farah as it was the first time that Ava had ever been away from home alone, which was why she had been so insistent on seeing her off that morning. She closed the device and looked around at the unusually quiet streets. It would have taken around thirty minutes had she walked back to her smart terraced house in the edge of the highly desirable Shoreditch area, but it had been a long day so she headed for the Holborn tube, took the central line to Bank and the Northern Line to Old Street, from which it was a three minute walk to her street.

As she rounded the corner and approached her house, she was too busy fishing for her keys at the bottom of her business bag to notice the quiet, electric vehicle pull up across the street and the bulky, black jacketed male haul himself out of it. It was only when Farah had unlocked her door that she felt his presence, his breath on her cheek and arm around her neck. Startled, scared and relieved in less than one second she grabbed Lakin's arm and greeted him with a torrent of abuse, a push and a long passionate embrace. Lakin emerged from her arms and grinned:

"When I saw the interview end earlier than anticipated, I thought you might appreciate a debriefing."

"Don't you want to talk about the interview first?"

Farah received her answer as they went inside, straight upstairs and stripped frantically. It had been a ridiculous day for both of them and neither had the will to battle their emotions. Their bodies fused in a frenzy of frustration, anxiety and raw desire until, twenty minutes later as they reached the crescendo of their passion, the earth, quite literally, moved for them as they heard and experienced the second explosion of the day.

9

The following morning's meeting between Mitchell, Faraday and Mountstevens had already been planned prior to the previous evening's bombing of Cleopatra's Needle. The London needle was situated in the City of Westminster, on the Victoria Embankment near the Golden Jubilee Bridges. It was close to the Embankment underground station and was presented to the United Kingdom in 1819 by the ruler of Egypt and Sudan Muhammad Ali, in commemoration of the victories of Lord Nelson at the Battle of the Nile and Sir Ralph Abercrombie at the Battle of Alexandria in 1801. The significance was not lost on Neil Faraday.

"If this is not the clearest possible message that the Muslims are, once more, bringing terror to our streets, then I don't know what more you need them to do!" he howled. "Do they have to paint the dome of St Paul's green and gold and stick microphones on it to wake you two up to reality?"

The Home Secretary offered both hands in a calming gesture. "Neil, I completely understand your frustration but I spoke with Mellor and MI7 this morning. Both advised that there is absolutely no evidence of Islamic links to either blast. We don't even know, at this stage, if the two are connected. Mercifully, there was not a single casualty in last night's blast. In fact, Google Earth imagery shows it coming down like one of Fred Dibnah's steeples with all the debris falling towards the Thames. It's as though the perpetrators waited for the area to be clear and angled the blast to cause as few casualties as possible. This hardly replicates yesterday's Whitehall attack. The first one was designed to kill while the second was carefully planned not to."

"Unless," the Prime Minister added, "one of them went badly wrong?"

The other two looked puzzled as Mitchell continued.

"We are now certain that the bomb at the Cenotaph was laid below the structure itself, within or under the foundations. There is an easily accessible system of sewage and drainage tunnels down there and they run parallel to, and only feet below, the new oil and gas pipes laid in 2019 to connect with the East Kent fracking fields. It's only supposition at this stage, I am told, is that it's perfectly feasible that the property damage and civilian casualties were collateral damage caused by secondary energy explosions."

"And where, if I might enquire, did this vital information come from and why, as Home Secretary, did it not come through me first?"

The PM stood and placed an arm upon his colleague's shoulder. "Look, Clive, this is totally unofficial and unsubstantiated but my brother in law is a senior executive at Quadrania Energy and they are in something of a flap, wondering if their infrastructure might have been a contributory factor. I assured him that your people will be working overtime to get a forensic investigation completed but such an unsolicited, personal approach to me, at least lends some credibility to the possibility."

"If that were to be the case," pondered Faraday, "it's just possible that the two explosions were just designed to be the symbolic destruction of iconic sites, commemorating military achievements.

If you ask me that points the finger even more squarely at Islamic State."

"Let's not get too carried away with supposition until we get something more concrete from either MI7, Mellor or Home Office Forensics." Mitchell intervened. "Let's work, at this point, from the known to the unknown. Clive, what do you have so far?"

The Home Secretary fired up his tablet and the images projected onto the wall beside them.

"These are images from the Whitehall scene taken from stored satellite images, immediately before, during and after the blast. You can see that the Cenotaph explodes upwards and although there is a spread of stone onto the pavements, the majority of it falls back down within a forty yard radius. We can see from the 'before' images, that this would directly account for the deaths of just six pedestrians who happened to be crossing close by. As you can see, there seems to be a delay between the Cenotaph going up and the bricks, glass, debris and flames exploding outwards onto Whitehall. This is where the majority of fatalities were incurred. As you say, Prime Minister, we expect to have an interim but conclusive forensic report by the end of the day."

The group observed similar footage of the evening blast on the embankment. The evening darkness was an obstacle to clarity but the sudden burst of light illuminating the red granite hurtling into the Thames rivalled the spectacle from Sydney Harbour Bridge on New Year's Eve.

The Home Secretary went on. "There have been no claims of responsibility or serious gloating and goading. I spoke with Naveed Choudhry yesterday who conveyed his distress and sympathy on behalf of the British Muslim Party." Mountstevens glanced at Faraday, who had, of course, gate-crashed the meeting.

"Well that's big of him," sniped Faraday, "but why wouldn't he? We are all British aren't we?"

"Well yes, Neil, but there have been no such messages from the Scottish or Irish separatist parties."

"And none," resumed Faraday, "from the Independent British Islamist State!"

"No," admitted the Home Secretary, "there have not, but Choudhry has spoken with his nephew who categorically denies any involvement."

Faraday launched right back at him. "Even if I were to trust that slimy, treacherous snake of a nephew, there is a subtle, but very significant difference between having any involvement with it and having knowledge of it. We all know that that IBIS is just a UK cover for the global Islamic State movement and they have supported terrorism here and overseas for three decades. Rahim Chatha is a fundamentalist activist who will not rest until he has established Sharia Law within the Northern Territories. And do you think they will stop at Birmingham, Lancashire and Yorkshire? Will they hell! They are already buying up property and forcing people out of the belt through Northamptonshire, Hertfordshire and Surrey. They will soon have the country in a pincer movement and I am convinced that all the IS terrorists in Belmarsh have been trafficked through his party."

"No," countered the Prime Minister. "You may suspect it, Neil, but you can't prove it. Just as you couldn't prove that European Union Activists were responsible for sinking those North Sea fishing boats last year! These are very sensitive and delicate political times. We have enough issues to face at home and in the Middle East without pissing off Europe as well!"

This really seemed to light Faraday's touch paper as his cheeks reddened and his mouth went off like a Roman candle. "I am Deputy Prime Minister of this country and leader of the second biggest political party. I was duly appointed and my party was elected to defend the rights of English people against any and all of the silent enemies here, in Europe and further afield who managed to achieve with two pieces of paper, what our predecessors fought off with two World Wars. I enjoy a curry and a kebab as much as the next man. I value being able to buy a packet of fags at the corner shop twenty-four hours a day and I even drink the odd glass of German lager, but I will not lie down and see us trampled over again, by either Europe or the Arab world! Your predecessors created this shit! You can't solve Eastern problems with Western values. When you replace a dictatorship with a democracy, you are just paving the way for a new dictatorship. Arabs don't do democracy. Arabs don't talk, they throw stones. When the stones stop hurting they shoot and when the shooting stops, they bomb! That's just how it is; birds fly, dogs bark, Muslims murder!"

Perhaps realising that he had just crossed the border between Syria and hysteria, Faraday sat quietly and allowed the Prime Minister to fill the embarrassed silence.

"Clive, tell us about the suspect you have in custody."

"Well, it's clearly too early to call it but your tip-off seemed to have some substance. Even if he hadn't attacked Neil's son, there are too many questions about him that remain unanswered. We know relatively little about his family allegiances in Syria. He has taken a very active involvement in Middle Eastern politics since his arrival here. He is a loner with no known friends or acquaintances but neither does he appear to be especially devout. We certainly have enough to detain him and it is my recommendation that we get him out of Holborn as soon as possible and get him remanded to Belmarsh. Clearly, it's not my decision but we do have some fairly friendly magistrates in Holborn."

"I would like ten minutes with him before you move him," Faraday growled.

Neither man doubted that he was sincere in that wish, but at his age and in his physical condition, both knew that such an encounter would not have ended well for him.

"He will certainly feel at home at Belmarsh," continued Faraday, now on something of a roll. "His Islamic State buddies will be hanging out the banners for him. They will be cracking out the sweet green tea tonight all right!"

Belmarsh Prison was built on part of the east site of the

former Royal Arsenal in Woolwich, and became operational on 2 April 1991. It was conveniently adjacent and adjoined to Woolwich Crown Court, which meant the prison could be used for high-profile cases, often those concerning national security. Between 2001 and 2002, Belmarsh Prison was used to detain a number of people indefinitely without charge or trial under the provisions of Part 4 of the Anti-terrorism, Crime and Security Act. It soon became known as 'Britain's Guantanamo Bay'. The law lords later ruled that such imprisonment was discriminatory and against the Human Rights Act but it was still primarily used for the detention of prisoners for terrorist related offences. In September 2006, the number of such prisoners was fifty-one. Now, that number had risen to over four hundred and fifty.

"Have we anyone currently undercover at the moment in the Ulster Democratic Unionist Party and The Scottish Unionists?" asked the PM

"If he tells you that," laughed Faraday, "They wouldn't be under cover anymore would they?"

Mountstevens ignored the oaf's childish intervention and directly addressed Mitchell. "Both organisations are on the radar, Prime Minister. We have received intelligence that some form of civil unrest is expected but we believe that they are more likely to hit Edinburgh before they take us on. The Unionist Alliance seem to understand the stupidity of wrecking a country they want to re-join. Whether we have anyone infiltrating the organisations is not a matter for me but we do have sensible and supportive political representation in the form of Brendan Doyle in Belfast and David Watters within the Unionists in Edinburgh."

"Are any other names coming out of MI7?" enquired the PM.

"Well not names, exactly," Mountstevens replied, rather hesitantly. "Facial recognition technology flagged up a face at Heathrow yesterday that seems to have attracted interest from both the Border Agency and MI6. We share FRT technology and data with our allies in the US and the Non Confederated European

Countries and one particular face has been flagged by the American, Swiss and Greek authorities. There is nothing that anyone can pin on him other than the fact that he seems to be unfortunate enough to be in certain cities when bad things happen."

"So why the lack of a name?" asked Faraday.

"It's not the lack of a name," said Mountstevens, through ten clasped fingers in front of his mouth. "It's too many of them. The face seems to belong to five different individuals living in Libya, Egypt, Malta, Spain and Turkey."

10

HMP Belmarsh could never be described as exuding a relaxed atmosphere but the activities of the past two days had created a heightened sense of tension and mistrust. While most other prisons in England had been expanded since the 2019 Justice Bill, the operational capacity of Belmarsh had remained at nine hundred and ten since its last refurbishment in 2008. This was not due to a lack of potential occupants but a deliberate policy of keeping the number of dangerous, maximum security prisoners below one thousand. At the best of times, the place was a potential powder keg. Today was not the best of times; today the powder keg was on a long, though as yet, unlit fuse. Almost all Belmarsh inmates were high-risk offenders; murderers, rapists, kidnappers, serial killers and terrorists. Almost a quarter of inmates were convicted or suspected of crimes against the national security of the country. The establishment was a showcase of ethnic, cultural, religious and political diversity with its occupants all sharing one thing in common: they were very, very dangerous and unpredictable people.

Governor David Thornton had been at his desk since seven-thirty that morning. Normally he would leave his home, just six miles away, in an exclusive but well populated area of Woolwich, and either run or cycle to work. He would shower his impressive two metre frame before changing into his trademark plain grey suit, white shirt and maroon tie. The tie used to be red until the prison psychologist advised him that this was just too provocative a colour for these surroundings. Between themselves, his officers referred to him as Sir Stephen, referencing his rowing prowess and an uncanny resemblance to his hero: Redgrave. This morning, he could not indulge himself in the luxury of the great outdoors and parked his three-year-old Audi A10 in his reserved space between the first and second security fences.

Too early to call upon his faithful Naomi, he made himself his first cup of coffee of the day and sat upright at his desk to monitor his newsfeed. Images of both of yesterday's blasts were prolific upon the mosaic screen, interspersed with accompanying messages from related government departments. When his red videophone rang, he was startled and relieved that he had arrived so early but even then he wondered whether he might have missed an earlier call. When he opened the screen he was puzzled to note that the screen view had been suppressed and the voice was clearly not that of the Home Secretary for whom this line of communication was normally reserved.

"Governor Thornton," the voice projected. "You don't know me but you will have recognised that I have access to the highest level of communication. As we speak, I am keying the agreed security passcode into the screen to validate my authority."

"Yes, sir, I can see and recognise the code. Please continue." Thornton did not even think about questioning why this individual had access to the code. It was absolutely known and understood in approximately fifteen positions of high authority that anyone using this line of communication must be treated with the utmost respect and gravity.

"Thank you, David. Please don't read anything untoward in the absence of the Home Secretary in this conversation. He is alive and well but Platinum Command Ten D, has agreed that he should not be compromised by this conversation. Please confirm that you understand me."

Thornton instantly recognised the third and final security clearance and knew that this interaction was sanctioned by the Prime Minister himself. "Yes sir, I completely understand."

"Good. Later today, or tomorrow at the very latest, you will be receiving a remand prisoner who will be held on assault charges. You will recognise him as the perpetrator of the attack upon Quentin Faraday and so far as the staff and inmates are concerned, this is his reason for being remanded. I am discussing this with you and you alone as I need you to inform me directly and immediately of any unusual incident or activity while under your care. He should be afforded normal rights of association and only isolated in a life threatening scenario. I cannot emphasise highly enough the importance of contacting me, personally, any time, night or day, should anything unusual occur and, as I don't expect you to be on duty twenty-four-seven, you will need to brief your most loyal and trusted member of staff to keep you informed."

The caller did not need to ask Thornton whether he understood as David confirmed this willingly.

"I fully understand, sir, and will select two highly trusted duty officers to keep me appraised at all times."

"Thank you, Mr Thornton, and I am sure you will understand me when I say that I very much hope that we do not have occasion to speak again," and with that, he closed the connection.

Despite its maximum security status, or perhaps, because of it, Belmarsh tried to observe a typically balanced prison routine with equal focus on safety and association. Sixty per cent of cells were designed for multiple occupancy and the single cells were not necessarily for solitary confinement but more suited to some of the prison's less sociable clients. On most days, the corridors and communal areas would seem little different to a hospital or college with guys milling around, some moving purposefully, some just leaning against the walls and doors chatting but everyone, inmates and officers, understood the underlying menace of the place and its ability to implode without notice. There were numerous classes and activities available but rehabilitation was not a key focus as most convicted inhabitants knew that it was unlikely that they would return to society young enough to either make an active contribution or pose a credible threat. Inside, however, there was little to lose other than sparse privileges and so fear of further offending was always front of mind. The gymnasium and exercise yards enjoyed high occupancy levels as muscle, energy and testosterone were just as viable a currency in Belmarsh as phone credits and narcotics.

For all the governor's attempts to normalise the facility, he ensured that the regime was rigid and robust. Officers were no longer issued with batons since an incident four years ago when two officers were overpowered and their batons used against them and six other prisoners, leading to three fatalities. Most officers now carried Tasers that were coded to their own grip pattern and could not be used by any other party. Others carried longer range tranquilliser guns, again, personalised to them, and them alone unless reprogrammed. Sanctions were restricted by human rights but punishments were applied for an array of offences ranging from loss of communication privileges, loss of association time, solitary confinement, suspension therapy and mind manipulation, which could also be used sparingly as a reward.

Of the latter two, suspension therapy was the least prevalent and most serious. Persistent violent offenders would be held in individual prison pods and tranquillised to the point of being semi-comatose. They were fed, and drained, intravenously and could be held in this state for up to four months. Prisoners who had endured this treatment testified that they were aware of their predicament for the whole period and recognised no distinction between sleeping and waking hours. They were awake, aware but completely incapacitated. There were few reoffenders in this category.

Mind manipulation was an extension of virtual reality technology. Mainly used as a punishment, prisoners would be strapped into a chair, not dissimilar to those that used to be deployed by twenty-first-century dentists. They would be injected with a drug to render them susceptible to the images about to be transmitted to them and then subjected to up to twenty minutes of virtual reality intrusion. To the participant, however, there was nothing virtual about the experience as they suffered the terror and horrors to which they had subjected their victims, without the physical impact. Most common scenarios included acts of terrorism, bombings, executions, and beatings, abuse of family members, simulated amputations and drowning.

At the other end of the spectrum, less frequently deployed in such institutions, there were untold joys to those who were deserving of, or could afford the leisure based versions of the treatment.

Amidst the innovative technologies and new procedures, many parts of prison life were as they had always been and one of the most important privileges for the inmates were personal visits from friends and family. Close contact was rarely granted and most meetings were conducted through mesh or toughened glass, depending of the level of risk deemed to be associated with the visit. Glass minimised the passage of illegal objects and substances whereas mesh simply challenged the ingenuity of the participants.

A couple of hours after David Thornton's intriguing call, one such visit was just concluding. Khalid Farooq had met his visitors from behind glass for the six years since he had entered Belmarsh as an energetic thirty-four-year-old and had resigned himself to the fact that the best he might hope for would be to touch his wife and four children between the mesh sometime before he died in there. On this occasion it had been his wife, Ayesha, and eldest son, Ahmad, on the other side of the glass. As Prison Officer Scott Douglas led Farooq away and back through the security labyrinth he delicately tried to improve the prisoner's mood.

"That boy of yours is growing unto a handsome lad. How old is he now?"

"Fifteen, Mr Douglas. Similar to your own boy I believe."

Douglas was not at all surprised that his charge knew such details. "Fifteen next week, as it happens. He's got his eyes on one of those Nike sport suits your boy was wearing but I'm afraid that's a bit out of my league. By the way, I hear that there's a new arrival on his way here that you will probably want to be having a word with. His name is Abadi."

"Thank you, Mr Douglas. I am sure that your boy will have a very happy birthday."

Scott Douglas had been considered to be one of the new breed of Belmarsh custodians when he had arrived just under two years ago. He was optimistic, inquisitive and showed a genuine interest in the issues and motivations of his charges, irrespective of their background or crimes against society. He was a very youthful thirty-seven years old and this thick black hair and smooth tanned complexion had already marked him down as an object of fantasy for a number of those prisoners who were unable to satisfy their desires with their cellmates. It now seemed that the system had got its dull decaying teeth into Douglas and he too, was drifting into the crevices of corruption that differentiated block from block and wing from wing in structure alone.

They continued through the next two security gates without exchanging another word. They both understood each other and Douglas only ever spoke to Farooq out of the watching gaze of the many CCTV cameras on the wing. Khalid Farooq was a big man in every conceivable sense of the word. He stood one metre eight and carried one hundred kilos of hard, solid body mass. His physical stature, however, was of secondary importance to his reputation and resources. Despite his incarceration six years ago for his part in the foiled May Day plots to bomb Manchester's Trafford Centre and London's Brent Cross Shopping Complex, simultaneously, he was, to many, still the most feared man in

Britain. The carnage was narrowly averted as an undercover operative had managed to warn the emergency services just four hours before the bombs had been due to explode. Seven thousand shoppers had been evacuated to a safe distance before seventeen devices were disabled and a further three car bombs detonated at a safe distance from the public. The identity of the agent was never discovered but he and twenty-three more of Farooq's former squad were found dead, tortured and horribly mutilated over the course of the following fifteen months. It was widely accepted, but never proven, that Farooq continued to run Islamic State affairs in the UK from his prison cell in Belmarsh.

Officer Douglas escorted Farooq all the way back to his cell. It was a multiple, designed to hold four prisoners but was only occupied by three. His companions were Kamran Hassani and Usman Masood. Hassani had been imprisoned with him as a co-conspirator in the Trafford Centre plot. Masood was convicted, two years later, of beheading a regional newspaper editor in Bradford who reported and blew open a paedophile ring operated by seven Pakistani males from a mosque in Bradford. What Masood lacked in intellect he more than made up for in blind stupidity and a desire to hurt people. Both men were now Farooq's most trusted lieutenants, with very different briefs. Officially, they were disowned and denounced by the leadership of the Independent British Islamist State. Unofficially, they were both feared and revered by it.

Contrary to common perceptions, even the most influential and resourceful inmates at Belmarsh resided in fairly spartan conditions. The popular impression of cells, laden like Aladdin's den or Del Boy's parlour were simply myths and fables. Governor Thornton ensured that even though he could not prevent the hierarchy existing, he could prevent the visible and physical manifestation of it. It was one of the few powers that he was able to exert over the evil but scrupulously careful Islamist leader.

It was not long after Farooq returned to his cell that the huge outer perimeter gates of the prison compound slid sideways to allow the entry of the white prison transit van and the two flanking electric police motorcycles. Ten minutes later, Adnan Abadi was being processed.

11

Unusually that morning, Farah failed to beat the seven o' clock alarm. She was under no pressure to do so having worked late last night at Holborn. Had Ava been at home, the pounding beat of her techno classical music chip, the thundering water against the Perspex shower wall and the high pitched whirring of the microwave hair drier would have stirred her a good two hours earlier but today, Farah was tired. Lakin had left her shortly after they had been startled by the Embankment blast two miles away. Such was the intensity of the explosion they both heard it and felt it, despite its most unfortunate timing. Sean advised that he would be tracking down the source of the unknown blast and, if allowed access to the area, would go directly there before heading into Scotland Yard. His earlier years of Special Forces training had conditioned him to sustain long periods of activity without the need for sleep. Farah knew that it would have been futile and naïve to have offered to accompany him. Nobody at the Yard knew of, or remotely suspected their relationship which had started just under eighteen months ago when they had both attended a terrorist recognition conference in Harrogate. Their passionate embrace in the lift, after a late night drink in the bar, came as no surprise to either of them. It just seemed the natural fusion of the latent chemical elements that they had developed over the previous six months. Ava, inheriting her mother's gift of perception, suspected and approved of their relationship. She had also inherited her mother's gift of discretion and knew not to speak of it.

"Ava!" Farah sprang to life and reached for her videophone. She knew that even this early, Ava would be in the middle of her beauty regime but would still have disturbed her had she thought her daughter might have been in the deepest of slumbers. She desperately needed to see her face and hear her voice. The screen expanded and slowly came to life, as though waking and stretching from a long night's rest. The complex digital tones signified connection to a foreign network and within seven seconds, Ava's beautiful smile, only partially hidden by long, wet black tresses, was beaming out at her.

"Darling, how are you? Is everything okay? Are you having a good time? Was your crossing all right?

"Fine, yes, yes and yes Mama and I love you too! We arrived in Paris at around four this morning. Security guards at Calais, I think it was, were horrible. They kept us waiting for ages and searched our coach and all our bags before we could leave the port. Miss Atkins told us they were just singling out the Brits to teach us a lesson for leaving the EU!"

"Possibly, darling, but it might also have had something to do with the suspected terror attacks yesterday. Did you hear about the Embankment blast last night?"

"We did Mama. We were watching coverage on the ferry newsfeeds and on the coach. I tried to call you from the boat but communications were blocked at sea and the reports told us that there were no casualties so we were all relieved. We are absolutely knackered but we insisted that Miss Atkins went ahead with this morning's city tour."

"I bet you did," Farah grinned. "I also bet that you will sleep through the street tour commentary and wake up when you reach the Eiffel Tower! Anyway, I get the message, you're busy and you have a face that needs painting."

"So perceptive, Mummy! Let's speak later. I love you! Mmmmmmmm mmmmmwwah!" and Ava was gone.

Farah smiled, kissed the screen and held it to her cheek until the first tear ran over it.

Considering her troubled early childhood, Ava had coped and adapted wonderfully to Western life. She had been in Britain since the age of one and barely remembered her father who had walked out on them when she was just two and a half. She could remember no ferocious arguments between her parents, there were none; but neither could she recall nor understand the cold, mental cruelty to which her mother been subjected by a man living in a Western culture with strict Eastern values. Towards the end of the marriage, though, strictly speaking, it was still not over, she suspected that her husband had simply been using her to monitor her father, who was a high ranking diplomat in Iran's Foreign Office. Years later, her suspicions were confirmed, beyond reasonable doubt.

Farah showered, donned her Lycra and packed her business clothes in her backpack, demolished three slices of pineapple, a grain bar and a strong black coffee before hitting the street and gearing up to the three mile, thirty-five minute run to Scotland Yard. The roads were unusually busy so early on this Tuesday morning as no doubt, there would be road closures and diversions closer to the city and the river. Farah thought it strange, yet somehow reassuring, that the response of Londoners to two blasts within twelve hours, was to take to the streets even earlier to get to work, rather than hide themselves away at home. Although acutely aware of the normal hazards of running through London, Farah possessed the remarkable ability of focussing on every step of her journey while assimilating the geographical, political and social landscape through which she traversed.

London had become accustomed to the fact that acts of terror were just one of the premiums to be paid for living in one of the most influential, affluent, inspirational and multi-cultural capitals in the world. Tourism was a significant source of revenue and income although the profile of visitors had changed radically over the past twenty years. Britain's complete withdrawal from the European Union led to an instant reduction in European tourists, partly due to the political backlash to the country's perceived arrogance and partly due to the high rate of the pound sterling against the euro. Today's visitor would have to fork out twelve point three euros to get their hands on one of those beautifully crafted pints of English ale.

Conversely, tourism from China, South Korea, Russia, India and Brazil was booming as these growth economies and close trading partners sought to explore where their wealth was invested. North America was still an important political and trade ally but its citizens were notoriously insular and particularly risk averse where terrorism might be a remote threat. Relations between Britain and the USA became rather strained in 2017 when perhaps the craziest man in the world became the most powerful man in the world.

England in general, and London in particular, had been more than a remote threat for the last twenty five years. Although the Good Friday Agreement of 1998 effectively brought to an end the threat of IRA bombings it was a commonly held view that the next wave of terror might come from disaffected Ulster Unionists who saw this not as an agreement but an appeasement.

The agreement acknowledged that the majority of the people of Northern Ireland wished to remain a part of the United Kingdom but that a substantial section of the people of Northern Ireland, and the majority of the people of the island of Ireland, wished to bring about a united Ireland. The agreement reached was that Northern Ireland would remain part of the United Kingdom until a majority of the people of Northern Ireland and of the Republic of Ireland wished otherwise. Should that happen, then the British and Irish Governments are under 'a binding obligation' to implement that choice. The sole political voice of dissent was the Democratic Unionist Party.

Feeling equally disenfranchised, the 'no' voters of the two referenda for Scottish independence considered the DUP to be a natural ally. Most of the Scots who had voted to stay within the United Kingdom had been middle class, middle aged, well educated, politically moderate professionals or business owners. They had correctly foreseen the economic, political and social chaos that an independent Scotland would descend into. Predictably, as their oil revenues abated, their health and welfare costs soared out of control, their exports failed to materialise, tourism ground to a halt, unemployment soared, civil unrest exploded and kilted troops took to the streets, the ranks of the middle-class dissenters were swelled by younger, angrier, more desperate protesters determined to get their hands on what they perceived to be their share of the United Kingdom's prosperity. In 2021, the Unionist Alliance was unofficially formed.

They demanded injections of cash from the UK, in the form of foreign aid and investment into Scottish Unionist and Ulster communities together with the right to be repatriated to homes in England and Wales. They reinforced their demands with protests marches on the streets of Edinburgh, Glasgow and Belfast though these had little impact of course upon their English neighbours. It was widely suspected therefore that it would only be a matter of time before their voices landed more loudly, closer to home.

To date, however, the Unionist Alliance threat had remained, largely, latent but since 2005, the United Kingdom had been subjected to regular and frequent acts of terror in the name of Islam. These began with attacks on the London public transport system and spread throughout the nation with riots, bombs, beatings and beheadings by those professing to despise the Western culture while taking full advantage of the freedom it provided to express and manifest such hatred.

The recent roots of conflict pointed towards the illegal invasions of Iraq, Afghanistan, Libya and Syria, though most political and military observers would identify Britain's part in the creation of the state of Israel as the root of all evil. Religious fanatics harked back to the medieval crusades while the more pragmatic would simply blame the millions of disaffected Muslim youths who had embraced the doctrine that it was their sworn duty to convert the world to Islam.

Add to this cauldron, pitched street battles between the Romanians and the Poles, the Poles and the Hungarians, the Hungarians and the Romanians and the Poles, Romanians and Hungarians. Farah often found herself conscious of the fact that few dared to venture onto the streets alone, let alone a tall, strikingly beautiful Asian woman clad in clinging black and yellow Lycra. She ran through the streets like a beautiful, sleek cheetah and arrived at Scotland Yard just before noon, relieved again, at not having needed to bare her considerable teeth. Relieved at reaching her immediate destination but frustrated by her inability to determine the direction that her investigation should be taking.

12

The weary traveller in Istanbul was now very much alert and watching various newsfeeds and political commentaries on the large wall mounted monitor of his Istanbul hotel bedroom. His videophone had beeped twelve times in the past three hours to signal that he had received a series of missed calls. The calls had, in fact, been made to a device that was now at the bottom of the Bosporus and via an account that had already been removed from all communication company records. The traveller had installed complex, untraceable software to alert him when anybody tried to contact him on the now defunct device. He enjoyed another spoonful of room service fresh fruit salad, poured himself another strong, thick black coffee and hit the key to contact his impatient caller. The connection was opened within two rings and the traveller began to speak

"Mr Black," he opened, fully knowing that this name was a ridiculous and totally futile attempt at hiding his true identity, "I believe that I advised you during our last conversation that it was to be precisely that: our last one. On this occasion, I shall put this down to early onset dementia, but if you ever try to contact me again, you WILL die."

"I am entitled to some answers," Mr Black demanded. "Why the carnage in Whitehall? Why the bomb on the Embankment? I am assuming of course, that was down to you?"

"Your assumption is correct." replied the traveller, pausing to sip on the gloriously rich coffee. "I believe you British call it multitasking or, perhaps, optimising productivity. When I was a boy in Nicosia, my father ran a small courier business. One man and a windowed van, he was frequently hired for journeys to the airport or shipping terminal. Whenever he could, he would try to arrange a return fare, be that people or parcels. He called it back loading. So while I was in London, Mr Black, I followed my father's lead and did some rather lucrative back loading. It seems that you are not the only person in the world that does not admire your architecture and infrastructure. Now please listen to me very carefully. I have afforded you the privilege of this communication as a past valued customer but if you ever try to contact me again, I promise you, your future will replicate your adopted name. Goodbye, Mr Black."

The traveller finished his coffee and lay back on his bed; not to sleep but to study his maps. His next journey could not be made by air. His luggage allowance would have been woefully insufficient and the screening devices would have erupted like a nightclub laser light show. No, this journey was to be no planes, just trains and automobiles. But first he had a couple of calls to make.

To his clients, he was known simply as 'Colin'. It had never even occurred to him to create a more exotic identity like Jackal, Panther or Scorpion. He had just needed to avoid using his own name of Mehmet Osman and adopted the name of his childhood football hero Colin Kazim-Richards who had scored a wonder goal for Galatasaray against their fiercest rivals and former club Fenerbahçe. Kazim-Richards was considered to be something of a soccer mercenary in Turkey, having played for all three major clubs, including Beşiktaş, as well as undertaking a number of assignments in England and Scotland. Mehmet could not resist the irony of it all: An unscrupulous Turkish Cypriot, for sale to the highest bidder and never happier than when dragging down defences in England!

Mehmet always considered himself to be a Cypriot first and a Turk second. On the 16th of August 1960, the island of Cyprus became an independent state, the Republic of Cyprus, with power sharing between the Greek and Turkish communities. Archbishop Makarios III was elected as president by the Greek Cypriots and Dr. Fazıl Küçük was elected as vice-president by the Turkish Cypriots. However, in December 1963, in the events known as 'Bloody Christmas' when Makarios III attempted to modify the constitution, Greek Cypriots initiated a military campaign against the Turkish Cypriots and began to attack Turkish villages.

By early 1964, the Turkish Cypriots started to withdraw into armed enclaves where the Greek Cypriots blockaded them, resulting in some 25,000 Turkish Cypriots becoming refugees, or internally 'displaced persons'. This resulted in the UN peacekeeping force being stationed on the island as well as an external migration trend of thousands more Turkish Cypriots to the United Kingdom, Turkey, North America and Australia.

With the rise to power of the Greek military junta in 1974, a group of right-wing Greek extremists, who supported the union of Cyprus with Greece, staged a coup. Turkey responded robustly with an all-out invasion of Cyprus. Greece's junta collapsed and the Turkish invasion effectively resulted in the division of Cyprus. The Turkish intervention resulted in the occupation of some thirty-seven per cent of the island in the north. Mehmet's family remained in Nicosia, within sight of the United Nations' Green Line and although he grew up alongside Greek Cypriots, his father never failed to remind him of the treachery of both the Greeks and the British.

Growing up, as he had, amongst the multinational United Nations Peacekeeping forces he developed a fascination for the military and was proud and delighted to be called to Ankara at the age of seventeen, to serve his national service. He took to army life as though he had been born into it. No training was too tough, no task was too hard, no discipline was too rigid, no order too outrageous. He was proud, at the age of nineteen, to become a career soldier as opposed to the three hundred thousand or so conscripts who made up over eighty per cent of the nation's armed forces. He was first deployed in the Turkish Land Army and quickly singled out for his physical prowess, technical awareness, ingenuity and single minded determination. He was transferred to the 1st Commando in Talas where he attained promotion to the rank of 'Uzman Cavus', broadly equivalent to Sergeant in the British Army. His final deployment was an attachment to NATO as one the 'Rapidly Deployable Turkish Corps'.

This culminated in a tour of Syria as part of the totally futile attempt to unravel the disastrous Western intervention that had facilitated the twelve-year insurgency during which Syria fought a civil war; a war against Islamic State and ultimately, a war against the civilised world. Mehmet served with distinction and was one of the fortunate few to return home in one piece. He would, however, be scarred for life by the sight, sound and scent of burning babies, hacked limbs, gouged eyes and acid-infused bodies that had suffered in the name of freedom and democracy.

He was honourably discharged and returned to his family home in Nicosia. On his homeward journey he reflected upon the fact that even as an articulate, educated and intelligent man, he had absolutely no idea who he had been fighting for, who he was supposed to be killing and what he was meant to be achieving.

While he had been overseas, an equally monumental struggle had been occurring in his homeland and he was totally and utterly shattered to discover that his beloved parents and only sister had died in an explosion during the recent, economically fuelled, Greek uprisings in Cyprus.

It was then that he became 'Colin'. Homeless, stateless and shameless. No accountability other than to himself.

Now, at the age of thirty-eight, he was almost as fit as in his prime, certainly as smart, even more technically aware and a hundred times more dangerous. He was also very wealthy and very, very, handsome. His NATO nickname had been Rock, after the American actor Hudson. He was proud of the physical similarity but disgusted by his doppelganger's sexuality.

His connections with NATO and deployment in Syria had provided him with a network of contacts across the military and political spectrum. Like Istanbul, he considered himself to be the bridge between Eastern and Western culture and those seeking his services knew that politics, religion, right or wrong had no bearing on his choice of assignments. He would do what he wanted to do, when he wanted to do it, where and for whom he chose. Neither was money the determining factor. He had killed a man for a single lira and maimed another for a million. He had charged less for destroying a hotel in Athens than a café in Jerusalem.

The Cenotaph had not come cheap and it was a delightful bonus to be able to 'back load' the job with the Embankment. The loss of life at the Cenotaph did concern him though. He hated the thought that Mr Black thought him unprofessional enough to either disobey his instruction or, even worse, make a mistake.

For his next assignment, it was necessary to travel back across Europe overland. The logistics were complex but at least half of the groundwork, as it were, had been completed during his last mission. Multi-tasking and back loading. He now needed to transport a considerable quantity of explosives, or at least the constituents to construct them, over one thousand seven hundred miles. Some of the items were already on their way. Some were already there, waiting for him. Others he needed to source and transport within the next five days. His client had been most specific about the location and timing of this job and it was to be one of the most spectacular and devastating that he had ever undertaken.

13

As Farah had suspected, Sean had stayed at his office all night as was obvious from his shaven face and clean white shirt. He tended to make more of an effort in his grooming regime at the Scotland Yard shower room than he ever did at home. He was tired but there was nothing to suggest this in the energy and enthusiasm he exuded as he strode around the floor placing hands on shoulders and patting the backs of his equally enthusiastic team.

"Five minutes, team! Gather your stuff and let's see where the last twenty-four hours have taken us."

It seemed strange to Farah that only one day ago, she had been about to wave Ava 'Bon Voyage' at Victoria when their plans came crashing down around them. Now, she felt very relieved that Ava was out of the country, safely away from the chaos and allowing Farah to concentrate all her attention towards the investigation.

The team moved, like a column of industrious ants, towards the top of the room where they sat, perched or stood around their leader, rather than in front of him. Lakin felt good in the knowledge that he always, quite literally, had his team around him.

"Okay, here's what we have." Lakin flicked the switch on

his remote handset and the screen behind him flashed to life, projecting six simultaneous images of the Cenotaph, Whitehall and the Needle, or what was left of them. Together with photographs of Quentin Faraday, Adnan Abadi and Tom Mellor. "Brian, would you take us through the forensic reports on the two blasts?"

Detective Inspector Chambers took the handset from Lakin and expanded the Cenotaph and Needle images.

"Initial Forensic reports strongly indicate that the primary devices used in both explosions were caused by a similar Cyclotol compound with, almost certainly, the same remote electronic detonation devices. These devices appear to be highly sophisticated, long range ultra sound delivery systems capable of penetrating the thickest of security walls and deep subterranean bunkers. They were first developed in Russia but have been used extensively in recent Middle Eastern campaigns."

Brian Chambers was almost puffing his chest out in pride as he revealed these technical and strategic details but would have been totally out of his depth if he'd received a question as he had only been briefed on the topic ten minutes earlier by the Home Office forensics expert. Most of the team realised this and none, therefore, saw any mileage in giving him a hard time.

"It appears that both sites were accessed via subterranean sewage and utility service tunnels although it is unlikely that the perpetrator would have simply sneaked down a manhole from the street. The amount of explosive compound deployed and the sophisticated detonation system would probably have taken days, rather than hours, to lay."

Lakin was the first to interrupt the flow. "Brian, there was some doubt yesterday as to whether he Whitehall offices and residential buildings were the result of collateral damage caused by explosions of gas and oil lines, triggered by the initial blast. What's the view on that?"

"Highly unlikely, boss," declared Chambers confidently. "The primary explosion was definitely below the Cenotaph but we believe that there was a deliberate explosive train in place with carefully laid pyrotechnic boosters to the secondary and tertiary sites. Not only were they deliberate, they were specifically sited to cause the maximum impact in the most densely occupied and strategically important buildings."

Having exhausted his notes, he quickly sat down in a manner suggesting that further questioning would be unwelcome.

DI Rosie Hunter immediately stood and took the attention away from Chambers. Rosie was a highly experienced officer in her early forties and spent most of her time liaising with the intelligence services in a delicate two way dialogue that supported both parties without compromising either.

"The strategic positioning of the secondary and tertiary devices are leading MI7 to believe that the perpetrators had access to detailed information and floor plans of the impacted Whitehall departments and perhaps even architects plans of the infrastructure, foundations and underground utilities supply routes. No, Sean, this was no accident." Rosie was one of the few members of the team respected sufficiently to address him so informally.

Lakin remained seated and brought to life the image of Adnan Abadi. "We received the name of Adnan Abadi from a high level Home Office source. Possibly Tom Mellor himself," said Lakin, as he flicked the switch to position Mellor's mature distinguished image alongside that of the young and rather shifty looking Abadi. "Believe me, if Mellor was the source, it's a lead worth following. Roger, what have you been able to turn up on his background?"

"Very little, I'm afraid, guv." DS Churchill rather sheepishly admitted. He recalled Abadi's tragic family loss when the boy was just eight years old. "He came from a reasonably influential middle-class family in Damascus. His father had been a successful oil trader and his mother was an English teacher and freelance translator, undertaking contracts for the American and British consulates.

After the death of the family he was taken in by a Red Cross facility to help deal with his physical and mental scars. He was there for over six months and when he was nine, he was transferred to an international orphanage that catered primarily for the displaced children of Syrian and allied service personnel. It was, by all, accounts, a highly regarded institution and he was there by grace of his close relationship with the head of care at the Red Cross hospital, and a substantial portion of his father's estate which was still being picked over by carrion sniffing lawyers and moderated by his charitable hosts.

"He followed a pretty normal education, or as normal as it could be in what was still pretty much a civil war zone, but his file had him marked down as a loner, socially awkward and with occasional violent tendencies. It was impossible to divorce himself from the religious and political turmoil of the state and it was reported that he grew up with no allegiance to any particular group and was perfectly happy to strike out against anyone unfortunate enough to disagree with him. There was enough in his trust fund to see him through college in Syria but he was forced to leave the country after a confrontation with one of the senior religious scholars of the college that would have resolved itself with a bullet in the back of his head had he not managed to get out of the country.

"It seems that he managed to withdraw all the available cash from his inheritance, significantly depleted by his crooked trustees, and with a generous donation to the Red Cross they helped him to attain entry to the UK with refugee status. Despite his social deficiencies, his academic brilliance and political awareness secured a place at the London School of Economics where he has been studying for the last four years."

"That's quite a lot for a declaration that started very little, Roger." Laughed Lakin and the room seemed to agree by offering up chuckles that over-rewarded the joke but released some of Churchill's tension.

"Thanks," said Churchill, "but there are far too many gaps there for me to feel confident in my appraisal."

"Farah." Lakin pointed. "You met the man yesterday, what do you think?"

Farah related the circumstances surrounding Abadi's arrested, illustrated and punctuated by the before and after images of Quentin Faraday; the before looking like a cherubic photo from an American Ivy League yearbook, the after, resembling an African Witch Doctor's rattle.

Farah rose and clicked the notes page on her tablet.

"He is undoubtedly articulate and extremely intelligent. Socially awkward is something of an understatement. This man would make Hannibal Lector look like Ronald MacDonald. He is cold, calculating and clearly, very violent."

"Would you say he was radicalised?" asked Lakin

"Not in the accepted sense," replied Farah. "He is, undoubtedly powered by a political anger but this does not seem to be the customary Muslim/Christian thing. I don't see him as a brainwashed Jihadist and he seems to be balanced in his criticism and animosity towards both factions. It's as though his childhood experiences have turned him against all forms of formalised conflict but he is ready, at the drop of a hat, to unleash his own form of retribution to anyone daring to offend him."

Chambers interceded. "Is there anything to link him to either blast?"

"Well," continued Farah, "he was in custody at the time of the second but given the types of sophisticated detonation technology you outlined earlier, that certainly does not rule him out of the equation. As for Whitehall, had he upheld an appointment in the Ministry of Overseas Development that he was scheduled to attend, the white overalls would probably be scraping him off the ceiling as we speak. For me, he did not offer a credible excuse at all for not being where he should have been and I had no hesitation in recommending that he be remanded for the assault and pending further investigation on the terror charge."

"Well it seems that the CPS and judiciary agree with you, as he is currently being transferred to Belmarsh," advised Lakin.

Rosie Hunter rose again. "If it was Abadi, it is most unlikely, indeed, bordering upon impossible that he could have done this alone. According to the Border Agency he hasn't been out of the UK since he arrived here four years ago and smart as he might be, he couldn't have created these devices out of a few Fairy liquid bottles in his Marylebone bedsit."

"Where are MI7 looking?" asked Lakin.

"The obvious contender is ISIS. They have had no major successful attack in the UK since the shopping centre atrocities of 2015 and they are still smarting that we have their former top banana, pardon the expression, and his two goons in prison here."

"They may be in prison here," interrupted Roger Churchill, "but that doesn't seem to stop them from directing operations from their cells. Okay, they haven't had a 'Biggy', but we can all identify a number of explosions and assassinations that seem to have their greasy stains all over them."

"Either them," added Chambers, "or their playful little faithful puppies in IBIS."

"Rosie, do MI7 have anything to link IBIS to this?"

"Of course there's nothing concrete," Rosie conceded, "but Rahim Chatha, the IBIS leader was on the news last night and came as close as he could legally do to endorsing the attacks without claiming responsibility for them. In his broadcast he questioned how long the Muslim majorities in the areas of the Midlands, Lancashire, Yorkshire and North London can be prevented from following their lifestyle and law while being exposed and subjected to the abhorrent behaviours and rituals of a so called Christian society. His words, not mine!"

Peter Morris, the team's senior media researcher chipped in. "That statement prompted a predictable response on social media sites with Natter almost melting down with the barrage of Nationalist Party posts calling for civil action on the streets of the Muslim controlled councils. The calls have been supported and endorsed by the Unionist Alliance who have openly said for the first time that they are bringing their campaign to mainland England to recover their rights to citizenship from what they call the silent invaders."

Lakin turned to Rosie again. "Do MI7 have a view on the Unionist Alliance?"

"They certainly do." Rosie confirmed. "They have been monitoring communications between the parties for some time and they also have two of their representatives on their payroll. Openly, the Alliance are looking for political dialogue to demand a protected homeland in Ulster or a pledge to resettle them in England. That is their official stance, but Doyle and Watters advise that there are more militant factions who are becoming tired of talking and want more direct action from their leadership. They claim that they still have access to a vintage arms stash from the Troubles but, more worryingly, there are European allies who would be happy to support them with finance and resources to destabilise the government."

"Could they be working with IBIS?" asked Farah.

"Absolutely not!" affirmed Rosie. "The Unionist Alliance want to drive IBIS out of their northern territories and reclaim those counties for themselves. They are becoming desperate."

"Right," Lakin clapped his hands to bring the room to order. "We have Abadi in custody and the intelligence services will no doubt take over that inquiry. Brian and Roger, I need you to continue to investigate the scenes to establish how and when the devices were planted and where the materials were sourced. Rosie, keep close to MI7 and remind them that we are happy to support them in looking at IBIS and the Unionist Alliance. We are called the Special Investigations Unit for a reason. Let's live up to it!

"The rest of us: back to the streets, the screens and the files. Peter keep watching Natter, Twitterama and the rest of that sad, crazy, virtual world that freaks inhabit. If only the idiots knew how easy they made life for us they would never go near those network sites again. Back to work. And talking of freaks, I have an appointment with the commissioner."

14

Adnan Abadi was experiencing the full gamut of emotions as he made the short journey in the confined cell of the prison van from Holborn to Belmarsh. Fear, anger, humiliation, frustration, stupidity, incredulity cycled, but it all kept coming full circle round to fear. He had never been inside a prison before, but in Syria, he had been brought up to understand that they were brutal, merciless and masochistic institutions where inmates were incarcerated at the will of, and often for the entertainment of the state and its local law lords. All too often, he had seen some of the more liberally minded teachers and academics in his orphanage, schools and college dragged from their desks, battered with batons and stunned by cattle prods. Some returned months or years later; or rather the grey empty shells of their former existence did. Hunched, limping carcasses with drawn distorted faces from which peered nervous, twitching suspicious eyes. The fortunate ones simply disappeared.

As a politics student, he understood that the British judicial and penal system was supposed to be rather more civilised but as with most organisations, there were formal and informal systems to circumnavigate. In the prison service, the formal system was

95

highly organised, highly structured, overstretched, undisciplined and hugely inefficient. The informal structure was transparently hierarchical, ruthlessly disciplined and brutally efficient. The mighty minority ruled and the malleable majority complied, submitted, or died. Adnan Abadi had spent a lifetime trying to make himself invisible but suspected that this was to be his greatest challenge.

His processing procedure was remarkably genial. He was addressed as Mr Abadi and treated with courtesy and respect throughout the hour long ordeal. Signed in, strip searched, medically examined, interviewed, briefed, and advised on the dos and don'ts and the etiquette of life behind bars. As a remand prisoner, he had the option of retaining his own clothes but even without the advice of the reception staff, he recognised that this was hardly consistent with his desire to blend in rather than stand out. There might have been some puzzlement on the part of the administrators as to why a prisoner remanded on assault and bodily harm charges would warrant a stay at Chateau Belmarsh, but they quickly put this down to the identity of his victim.

It would have been unusual for a new prisoner to be afforded an audience with the governor, so David Thornton just happened to schedule one of his prison walks to coincide with the processing of today's intake. He passed closely enough to exchange pleasantries with his staff and to take and develop a life-sized portrait of his intriguing new charge at the front of his inquisitive mind. Thornton simply nodded in the direction of Adnan Abadi as he began the long walk through four securely gated chambers before arriving on B Wing, where he was escorted briskly by Prison Officer Scott Douglas, to his single occupancy cell at the furthest end of the landing. At this time of day, the inmates were still locked in their cells, but they recognised that two sets of footsteps clanking, out of step and irregularly down the open steel mesh flooring, signalled the arrival of a new playmate. Bizarrely, as though he were a landlord welcoming a new tenant to a penthouse apartment, the officer took Abadi's hand in both of his and shook it firmly.

Abadi looked down at his hand, at Douglas' face in puzzlement and entered his cell.

As the cell door groaned to a close behind him and the harsh clunk of the bolt punctuated his confinement, Adnan slumped to a seating position on the thinly padded, rigid bed with his head in his hands. He had not consciously made the decision to either laugh or cry but the latter gradually transformed into the former as he tried to make some sense of the bizarre series of events that had led him here.

He thought back to that first mysterious telephone call that he was required to take in the college principal's office in the relatively safe suburb of Haria, fourteen miles from Damascus. The man sounded kind, sincere and honest. He seemed to understand Adnan's sense of inadequacy and promised to provide him with a purpose. That first phone call led to others, and a series of electronic messages before Adnan finally mustered sufficient trust to accept the proposal. Though they had never met in person, Adnan came to respect his mentor as a surrogate father figure but was smart enough to know that the emotional bond was unlikely to be formed nor reciprocated. It was, however, his opportunity to leave the traumatic memories of war torn Syria behind him and pursue his dream of a European education and career in political journalism.

He was barely twenty-one at the time and although he was an exceptionally intelligent young man, his educational journey in Syria had been constrained by his circumstances, resources and the limitations of a fragmented education system in an even more segmented country. Regularly, over the next twelve months, he had been summoned to attend meetings, interrogations, evaluations, interviews, role plays, physical activities and outdoor camps to prepare his mind and body for his next level of education at the world famous London School of Economics. It would have been too risky for his sponsoring organisation to have facilitated his official entry to the institution and so refugee status was facilitated by an Egyptian member of the United Nations peacekeeping committee in Syria, who was also able to call upon an ally in Britain to arrange the entrance examination, which was passed with a result so high that it came dangerously close to embarrassing both parties.

He had now been studying in London for just under four years leading a frugal, but comfortable life. He was so totally immersed in his studies and research that many of his cohorts suspected borderline autism. It was known that he had no family and never spoke of friends, so it was a source of intrigue when his videophone trilled and he invariably left whatever he was doing to move to a place of sanctuary before engaging in conversations that ranged from ten seconds to ten minutes. Every time he returned, there was no noticeable change in demeanour. It was as though he had been engaged in one of those infuriating market research cold calls that used to plague phone owners in the early part of the century, before they were banned under human rights legislation.

He reflected upon that last phone call, just one hour after Whitehall exploded. Adnan turned sideways, stretched out and closed his eyes. He somehow knew that he needed to clear his head of all such thoughts if he was to survive this place.

At precisely twelve noon, there was a loud whirring sound and a succession of simultaneous sliding locks leading to a cacophony of sound that seemed to herald the collective waking of the wing. Those who wished to, and were allowed to, were able to wander outside of their cells, mill around the gangway, hang over the netted balconies or congregate in the hall below to play table football. Pool had long since been banned after to many incidents of cues being used as clubs and spears or balls stuffed into socks as a makeshift mace. The inmates had an hour's association time before lunch, two hours in the exercise yard, classes, supper and seven o' clock lock-down.

Adnan stayed in his cell as he was not yet ready to acknowledge the new world he now occupied.

His isolation was remarkably short-lived. The door slowly opened inwards to reveal two large smiling Asian faces atop fittingly large bodies. Their grey tracksuits might have been sprayed on to their bodies with touches of black applied to accentuate the sculpted muscle tones. They clearly visited the prison gym regularly but probably passed on the yoga and Pilates classes. As a politics student, rather than a hackneyed con, Abadi recognised the visitors as Usman Masood and Kamran Hassani; vicious terrorists, probable ISIS lieutenants and definite followers and henchmen of the most hated and feared man in the prison, if not the land, Khalid Farooq.

Masood spoke first. "Just wanted to pay respects to our new hero on the block, man. Everybody on da wing will be wantin' to touch da knuckle of da man dat done dat racist faggot Faraday's kid. Just a shame you couldn't of gotten to da old man as well, innit?"

Abadi was sure that Masood could speak perfectly good English if he chose but this contemporary dialect was popular in prisons amongst Asians and blacks who seemingly revered and imitated a comic folk hero named Ali G.

Adnan was visibly shaken by the intrusion but felt that to ignore the visitors would not conform to required B Wing etiquette. "I was advised not to speak about the crime for which I have been remanded. I was told that nobody would know what I was in for. Has there been something on the television or news tablets?" he enquired meekly.

It was Hassani's turn to speak now and clearly considered himself to be more of an intellectual than his partner. "Radio Belmarsh is much more informative than the standard news channels, friend. Faster, more detailed and available exclusively to private subscribers only."

"An we 'ear dat you is not just 'ere for smashin' up dat faggot kid eetha. Ma man Kamran 'ere is callin you da new Guy Fawkes already!"

Adnan Abadi froze. He had heard that the prison grapevine was even more virulent than Facebook but he was genuinely shocked

99

to learn that he was known as the accused assailant of Quentin Faraday and totally astounded by his apparent implication in the London bombings.

"I, I don't know what you mean," he stuttered. "I've been charged with an assault but nothing else and I was told that none of the details of my case had been released to the press."

"Don't be so modest," Hassani grinned as he approached the cowering Adnan. "Everyone on the wing would big you up for bashing the ponce and if you were to be the man with the fireworks there would be quite a few brothers in here who would kiss your cheeks for that one too."

"There would be uvvers dat would slit ya cheeks and all for dat job, of course, but don't worry man. We is da only subscribers to Radio Belmarsh and us likes to keep noo news to ourselves for a while. Information is power, like, innit?" Masood moved his hands like a puppeteer as the words fought their way from his distorted mouth. It was considered strange for someone so patently illiterate to be allowed so close to the Scholar but it was assumed that his strength, brutality and absolute loyalty were sufficient compensation. The officers frequently joked that what Masood lacked in brains, he more than made up for in stupidity.

Hassani placed his huge hand under Abadi's right armpit and gently, but firmly encouraged him to his feet. "You're honoured, Adnan. Your first morning here and Mr Farooq, the Scholar has invited you to morning coffee. It's easier to get to see the governor than it is to get to see the Scholar so we'd better not keep him waiting had we?"

Adnan knew that he had heard the expression 'resistance is futile' somewhere but though he could not recollect the source, he absolutely knew that it was most appropriate here and now. He tucked his chin into his chest, thrust his hands deep into his pockets and walked slowly between his two escorts, along the inmate-lined corridor as if walking down the aisle of a crematorium to the waiting priest and the final curtain call.

15

Mirroring the mood of the mourning, the capital city shifted with the angry drifting clouds over those two March mornings and developed with a solemn gathering intensity. Stunned silence had switched to shock and panic with the realisation that this was a cynical attack upon a culture as much as upon a nation. As the fatality and casualty count multiplied, so did the number of nations afflicted. The brunt was borne by British nationals filing their way into their hitherto, mundane Monday march into civil service but the numbers were swelled by British immigrant Asians and Eastern Europeans earning honest pounds, fastidiously cleaning the premises that now lay stark remnants of the magnificent architecture that this most noble avenue once represented.

As with the clouds, shock shifted to disbelief, disbelief to outrage and as the afternoon skies darkened, the voices of anger shrieked revenge and retribution. The retribution was random as hands waved and fingers prodded violently towards those where previous pernicious prejudice pointed. Focus upon Islam was immediate for therein lay recent history. Random examples of Eastern European inequities quickly emerged to further darken the murky skies over Greater London. Further afield, those fearing the Unionist Alliance backlash reminiscent of the IRA troubles had little trouble themselves in conjuring the link towards the abandoned former faithful in Edinburgh and Ulster. Within hours, the nation had turned upon itself.

Those most distant from personal tragedy were most vociferous. Hourly updates on tablet news pages escalated the outrage. Broadcast journalists from around the globe swooped to secure the most dramatic scenes of swirling debris and carrion, employing their most practised expressions of solemn grief to accompany their fatuous reports of racist rhetoric founded upon pure journalistic speculation.

Meanwhile, those most immediately affected spared no thought toward the political implications of the abhorrent events and simply suffered the silent dignity of knowing that their lives and those of their loved ones had changed irrevocably. Across the nation and across the globe, millions feared for the modest mathematical chance that a friend or relative might have been in the wrong place at the right time. A host of inevitable, almost predictable, insensitive self-dramatists told tales of non-existent near misses, oblivious to the hostility fermenting within those that had suffered actual losses.

Over the past two days, the Prime Minister and his Deputy had been too heavily engaged in media bulletins and international communications to have been actively involved in the investigation process. That task, quite rightly, had lain with the Home Secretary and his Head of Homeland Security.

The government press officer, Propaganda Anderson, as he was uncharitably known, had assigned specific communication tasks to both men, more in keeping with hierarchy than either personal preference or suitability. Mitchell was immediately despatched to Buckingham Palace to brief King William on the atrocity and the likely scenarios. He was also required to support the Foreign Secretary in briefing NATO and the ambassadors of all the countries whose citizens had been killed or injured in the blast. Faraday, meanwhile, was given the rather less diplomatically challenging task of speaking publicly to television, radio, internet news and printed press. His tone was rather less sensitive and significantly less objective than that of his leader and without specifically naming either group, he made it perfectly clear that he believed that blood and rubble stained the hands of Islamic State and its UK satellite, IBIS. Thinly veiled references to other cultures 'abroad and within our midst' saw Naveed Choudhry, the official British Muslim Party leader, almost apoplectic in his denouncement of such irresponsible broadcasting by a Cabinet Minister on subsequent programmes. No comment was offered by Choudhry's nephew, Rahim Chatha, leader of IBIS. Rahim would not even share his uncle's surname, let alone his political platform.

The Home Secretary had convened a series of short but intense meetings with Tom Mellor to demand action from Homeland Security and its three intelligence services. Mellor explained that MI5 were actively engaging their agents and resources in UK based organisations recognised to be a potential security threat to the country. It was a tricky task as their sleepers were required to react quickly but without jeopardising their cover and longer term operations. Likewise, MI6 were tracking the international threats, of which there were many, but reported no apparent foreign state involvement. MI7, the newest of the agencies, was specifically engaged in high technology intelligence gathering from communications sources that not too long ago were deemed illegal and even now, not publicly acknowledged. In truth, MI7 could, given greater resource, monitor the phone calls, texts, emails and social network accounts of every person in the country. Accessing the information was one thing; disseminating it, filtering it, isolating, assessing, interpreting and investigating were different tasks altogether, hence the very close association and working relationship with Sean Lakin's Special Investigations Unit.

At a more practical level, Mellor advised that the military forensic team had ascertained the explosions at both the Cenotaph and Needle had been created by underground devices, probably laid up to ten days earlier and detonated either remotely, in real time, or certainly in the case of the Needle, with a remote timing device. The explosives deployed in all the devices, one on the Embankment and four in Whitehall had been secreted in, or above, sewage tunnels or utility pipelines. Discussions were already underway with the water authorities and utilities providers to ascertain whether any work had recently been undertaken in either location. Simultaneously, in a belt and braces manoeuvre, they were checking with London Transport and Westminster Council to determine whether licences had been granted, as required, to access the subterranean workplace in London Underground or sewage service tunnels. The results of these enquiries would be passed immediately to the Commissioner of the Metropolitan Police for follow-up investigation.

The mood across the mainland had become increasingly tense. Two days had elapsed since that first eruption and a steady flow of steaming bile and toxic suspicion was oozing from the two terror created craters. Further tremors were feared, anticipated and imagined as the initial shock in London led to a more widespread understanding that the fault lines were likely to spread quickly, over the surface and underground. Recriminations were random and rife, bordering upon riot proportions.

The absence of any message of disassociation or sympathy from IBIS was callously and creatively conjured by Rahim Chatha to antagonise his detractors and encourage supporters in equal measure. Rahim had never admitted that IBIS was anything other than a political entity, dedicated to the establishment of a true Islamic State within Britain. When openly challenged, since the party's inception six years earlier, about the regular though infrequent disturbances, beatings, arson attacks and occasional murders in the white indigenous settlements amongst IBIS strongholds, he would merely shrug and point to the increasing levels of frustrations amongst an Islamic majority that was rarely recognised and increasingly marginalised. There were few attempts to engage Chatha at a political level and Tom Mellor was cautious about escalating tensions by identifying IBIS as a suspect in the explosions. He did, however, feel that there needed to be a conversation to gauge the man's true feelings towards the campaign of terror. He explained his plan to the Home Secretary.

"There have been some worrying disturbances in Blackburn, Bradford, Leeds and Birmingham where factions from the English Defence League have clashed with IBIS gangs. Chatha will secretly be delighted by these developments as it will give him the opportunity to claim that the Islamic community is, yet again, under threat from state sponsored racism. I suggest that we should be proactive and send some formal representation to discuss security with him."

The Home Secretary removed his glasses and pondered the suggestion. "Are you suggesting a direct dialogue with MI5?"

"No, Home Secretary, I believe that the IBIS hatred of our intelligence services is so entrenched that contact from any of the MI branches would be inflammatory and counterproductive. I am suggesting a lower-key approach from the Special Investigations Unit on the premise of discussing the recent disturbances and issues surrounding the future security of those communities."

"Doesn't that cut directly across the three local police authorities in those areas?" Mountstevens challenged.

"Not at all. We would brief them first but as this is clearly an issue that crosses policing boundaries and could even, potentially, involve Unionist Alliance members in Scotland and Ireland, we are perfectly justified in involving the national SIU. We are engaging him on the premise of discussing their own security, while seeking to ascertain whether there might be any reasons for the EDF to instigate these specific disturbances."

"All right," Mountstevens nodded. "But keep it low level. This can't escalate into another accusation of racist victimisation. Moving on, is there anything of significance coming from overseas?" The Home Secretary was referring to MI6 but felt that not referring to it by name was somehow protecting the integrity of the organisation.

Mellor sighed, and formed facial expressions and hand movements indicating that he struggled to know where to start in answering, but eventually he did.

"We recognise that we are on a war footing with Islamic State in Syria, Iraq, Afghanistan and Egypt. The view from MI6 is that if IS had wanted to conduct a mainland strike on Britain, they would have the capability of doing so in a more intense and prolonged initiative. Although their resources are strengthening, they are still fighting on too many fronts and are not yet capable of an all-out offensive unless, or perhaps rather until, Saudi Arabia is officially in their camp.

"That said, they report a pattern of digital traffic triangulating between Istanbul, London and Riyadh immediately before and immediately following the Whitehall and Embankment bombings. Timing and coded content strongly suggest that there is a connection between the communications and the events. Agents in Istanbul are in place and actively monitoring signals but we have not yet isolated any suspects."

The Home Secretary was in no mood to accept any of Mellor's report as constructive progress, though he would, of course, present it that way when he met with the PM later that day. "So, we have no concrete leads from forensics, an Arab in custody on an assault charge, potential riots in the North, denials or silence from the main protagonists and a bit of phone tapping across Europe. Is that about it?"

"That's hardly an accurate representation of my account, Home Secretary, but perhaps when you get someone to read my written report to you later today, you might grasp some of the finer points of detail. Will that be all? I have important people to speak to." Without waiting for an answer, Tom Mellor left the room.

As Mountstevens watched him walk, he reluctantly reminded himself that he respected the man's knowledge, experience and professionalism almost as much as he despised his success and popularity. The Home Secretary was old school, the oldest in fact. The only son of an immeasurably wealthy landowner, Eton schooled, Oxford educated, woefully dim but well enough connected to have become a career politician and had survived in and out of various cabinets for the past thirty years. He landed this post because he was the only candidate upon whom both Mitchell and Faraday could agree, though he was distinctly down their respective lists. He considered himself to be an honourable man. There was, after all, honour in well-intended conspiracy and deception was there not?

He was snapped from his self-congratulatory state of warmth by a cold shudder when his red private line buzzed and he switched on the set to see and hear the Commissioner of the Metropolitan Police, Nigel Pollard. Pollard, as ever, was courteous and efficient though inwardly uncomfortable at the prospect of having to conduct a rather complex conversation with his boss.

"Home Secretary," Pollard began, without preamble or pleasantries. "We have had the initial responses from London Transport and Westminster Council regarding licence applications for underground infrastructure access. There have been forty=two licences granted within the last six weeks to eight service providers ranging from sewage drainage, rodent clearance, pipe maintenance, foundation strengthening and electrical cabling. Only two of those licences were granted to operate in both the Whitehall and Embankment locations and both were for routine utility services pipeline maintenance on behalf of South East Utilities. Work in both sites was subcontracted to a Dagenham based Polish excavation team, an electrical engineering contractor in Ealing and a specialist subterranean welding operation from Scotland. They specialise in North Sea oil installations and are one of the few capable of handling such a technical task. MI7 are checking out their businesses as we speak and running the rule over the personnel deployed on these jobs. We should have fuller details by close of play."

"Thank you, Nigel." Mountstevens replied. "Have you also enquired as to whether any of these three business have recently been engaged at any other sensitive sites within the capital?"

"No sir, we have not, though that is, of course a very pertinent observation. In fact, I shall have them checked out on a wider national scale."

"Yes of course, Nigel, I was about to suggest that also. Let me know what turns up. While you are on, I have asked Mellor to have someone have a quiet word with Rahim Chatha of IBIS. Low key, under the radar stuff. Probably something your Special Investigations Unit could handle." Mountstevens terminated the call and congratulated himself on finally contributing something remotely positive to the investigation.

It was just over two hours later when the commissioner briefed DCI Lakin, and Sean, in turn, phoned Farah to ask whether she had ever been to Blackburn, Lancashire. When she confessed that she had not yet enjoyed this particular pleasure, Sean advised her that her geographical and political boundaries were about to become broadened. He also suggested that this was such a sensitive project that he would prefer to discuss this with her away from the office. Her place? "Eight o'clock?" he smiled.

16

The murky sea of inhumanity parted as Adnan Abadi, piloted by Hassani and with Masood in their wake, navigated their way down the rippled walkway that connected the opposite shores of the wing. Other inmates conspicuously diverted their eyes as a precaution against both Masood's unpredictable rage and the possibility of being called as a witness to what this audience might yield. Purposefully, they strode past prisoners and prison officers. Hassini even exchanged pleasantries with Officer Scott Douglas advising him that the new boy had asked to meet the Scholar so as to understand better 'how things worked around here'. Douglas had merely grinned, surprised that the meeting had taken so long to organise.

As they reached the open cell at the end of the corridor, Masood touched Abadi's shoulder to stop him while Hassani took up position slightly in front of, but almost wedged alongside the Scholar before summoning the other two inside. Abadi immediately noticed that the cell was much larger and lighter than his own. Probably five metres by four, a double bunk along the left-hand wall and a single bed, diagonally opposite in the right hand corner.

109

At the end of the single bed was a wall mounted desk and shelf structure. In front of this was a seating unit that cleverly concealed the toilet, next to the four misty, barely transparent blocks that formed the source of natural light that was supplemented by an inaccessible ceiling mounted bulb.

Khalid Farooq had positioned himself immediately below the lamp and in front of the window so that the light reflected away from his ankle length, pure white gallabiyah and white satin kufi to project an almost ethereal presence around this tall, heavy-bearded entity. He was only permitted to wear this ceremonial garb in his cell following a protracted human rights debate two years earlier. He surveyed Abadi for what seemed a minute but was probably only a third of that; his piercing eyes burned through Abadi's quivering body. Finally, the Scholar spoke.

"We hear of chaotic times in the capital. I am sure that if you had wanted to beat the idiot offspring of our mutual enemy half to death, you could have achieved this with some degree of privacy, rather than under the glare of your whole fraternity."

Abadi remained silent for a couple of seconds before realising that he was expected to justify his action.

"You are remarkably well informed, Mr Farooq, but I must assure you that the episode was not premeditated. While I certainly do not regret the outcome of the altercation, I suspect that I shall be forced to regret the consequences of my actions."

The Scholar remained impassive as he replied, "I can understand why you would consider your incarceration regrettable but sometimes we must all face consequences for acts we perform for the greater good. Sadly, the beating of an odious son of an equally odious bigot will hardly register in the annals of our mighty international struggle. I am told, however, that there might be a more significant reason for visiting us."

"With all due respect, Mr Farooq, I am visiting you because I was brought here and cannot understand why the presence of one such as I in this place should be of any interest to your good self."

Abadi kept his head bowed as he spoke but his eyes constantly monitored movement around him.

The Scholar moved menacingly forward. "Tell me what you know of the other events of the past two days, and before you answer, think carefully because I am not asking for detail that is freely available in a standard news bulletin."

Abadi was surprised that Farooq had arrived at this point so soon and did, as counselled, think very, very carefully about his answer.

"I know that every British brick destroyed is a step closer to a purer landscape in this vile country. I know that every British Christian killed is a step closer towards the will of the one true God and I know that every drop of blood spilled provides the ink with which to write the names of our fathers and forefathers who will be avenged by Jihad. I know that I am destined to play my part in our ultimate victory but that beating an oafish student has no part in this plan."

"But bombing London does?" quizzed the Scholar.

Adnan Abadi now knew that his subsequent answers could well determine whether he would leave this prison, or even this cell, alive.

"If, as you have graciously indicated, I would be applauded for bringing down one infidel in the form of Faraday, how might I have been rewarded for bringing down two hundred of them together with two of their ridiculous monuments to imperialism?"

"Would you deserve to be rewarded for these deeds?" the Scholar's tone and demeanour was becoming more menacing as he approached to within two arm's length of the student.

Abadi instinctively moved backwards but only a matter of six inches, before his right shoulder connected with Masood's left one. "If one man were to be able to perform such a deed alone, what greater glory could such a man achieve given the opportunity to lead a greater organisation on the side of the Prophet?"

At this, the Scholar scoffed and his face twisted. "Such a man could achieve nothing if he were locked in here for the rest of his life or even a period of years for a mindless pointless assault. Such a man would have proved himself to be stupid and undisciplined."

"But if such a man were to be assured that there was a way out of here to join the forces of international Jihad, would such a man not have proved his value and be deserving of even greater power and glory?" Abadi afforded himself a more confident expression but this was immediately stricken from his face by the back of Farooq's huge hand.

"No, you fool, it would not!" Farooq grabbed Abadi's face in his right hand and dragged the man towards him. "Such a man would have proven himself to be a liability to our eternal cause. Such a man may have jeopardised the lives of others who are working together for collective triumph, not individual glory!"

The Scholar's fingernails were digging into Abadi's cheeks like the jaws of a cobra around a mongoose. Abadi's eyes were bulging with fear as the Scholar released his grip and threw him back into the waiting body of Masood, in disgust.

"Such a man will have alerted the security forces in Britain and abroad, causing our true brotherhood to abandon a glorious campaign that would have taken down more than two meaningless monuments and a handful of ridiculous civil servants!"

The Scholar's eyes were wide with fury as he continued slowly and deliberately, "Such a man will have brought shame and danger to innocent communities here in the British Muslim territories and more bombs upon our brothers at home. Such a man will be as useless to me as blunted knife, so I ask you again, what do you know of the events of the last few days?"

"I didn't do it," pleaded the retreating Abadi. "All I did was attack a fellow student who mocked the cause of our brothers in Syria. The assault was not connected to the bombings."

"So, one minute ago you are a martyr and now you are simply a mindless moron?" scoffed the Scholar. "But what if I were to tell you that any man who would have the courage and initiative and guile to perpetrate such acts of terror, striking at the very heart of the British establishment and at the seat of government, would surely gain a seat by my side? What if I were to tell you that such a man were destined for greatness and a legend within our brotherhood? Would you now be such a man?"

Hassani now stepped forward, sensing that it was only now safe to join the interrogation. "But then, Scholar, if this man before you were such a man, he would have proved himself to have been a coward and a liar in denying his actions so therefore not such a man after all."

"Yes indeed, my friend, that is a sound observation," nodded the Scholar as he turned again to Abadi.

"So what are you, Abadi? Are you a courageous and committed Jihadist who strikes terror at the heart of our enemy and demoralises them in the eyes of our followers and the Muslim world? Are you a stupid meddler who interferes in matters of which you know nothing and risks the lives of our brothers? Or are you just a fool with a bad temper? Tell me who you are. Tell me what you are."

Abadi cowered as he answered, anticipating a blow that never came. "I am a fool with a bad temper."

The Scholar positioned himself so close into his prey's face that Abadi could see hairs from his flaring nostrils and smell the breakfast egg on his breath. "Then why is a bad tempered fool brought to the highest security prison in the country? Where were you questioned? Who interrogated you?"

Abadi began to feel slightly less intimidated but knew that events could quickly turn on one wrong answer or one wrong question. He breathed deeply and answered slowly. "I was arrested at my college and charged with assault at Holborn Police Station. Later I was interviewed by some woman from Scotland Yard who wanted to know why I was not near Whitehall that morning when I should have been. So it seems that I am here because I am a fool with a bad temper who was not in the wrong place at the wrong time. If I had turned up for a meeting in Whitehall I would probably now be dead."

"And now because you *didn't* turn up at Whitehall you might still be dead. I find coincidences very difficult to accept. They would not send you here without a very good reason and I am going to discover what that reason is. Be assured that before you leave us today, I will know whether it was you behind this folly and if not, why you are really here."

Then the first blow came. Then more followed by a strangely disciplined, almost choreographed sequence of moves that suddenly became less artistic and more frenzied, culminating with the appearance of the toothbrush holding a thin razor blade where bristles had once been. This was not designed for oral hygiene unless the removal of a tongue fell within that particular category.

Less than one minute later, Adnan Abadi emerged from the cell, first staggering, then crawling and finally slithering towards his cell, smeared and trailing blood like a snail on a pavement. There was no commotion and little emotion from those who witnessed his exit from the Scholar's cell. This was not an especially rare occurrence and it was not in the interests of prison harmony to draw attention to any activities relating to this part of the wing. It was only when Prison Officer Scott Douglas saw the bloody, slimy entity from the platform above that he immediately hit the large red button on the landing to signal lock-down. Most of the prisoners were relieved to have the reason to retreat from the scene and those that would have preferred to stay and watch were aware that armed guards would be on the wing within seconds to ensure that it was enforced.

Scott Douglas was one of the younger and less experienced of the team that charged onto the wing but he wasted no time in taking control of the situation, instructing Officers Woods and Gordon to monitor lock-down while Glenister and Morris were advised to get to Farooq's cell to hold the occupants under surveillance, if only through the safety of the rectangular spy hole through the cell, which was not yet closed.

Douglas dragged the lifeless body along the corridor, stopping occasionally to apply CPR. His hands were slipping from the victim's blood smeared chest. He was shouting words of encouragement and at one point he thought he heard a vague response but felt it more important that he get Abadi back to his cell and secure him inside. Two minutes later, as he was explicitly instructed, he immediately phoned the governor who answered on the second signal.

"Governor Thornton, sir," choked Douglas. "Adnan Abadi is dead."

17

Apart from the obvious disruption to London transport, Ava's school trip to Paris had been perfect timing. Farah and Sean had been struggling to create space for each other and were constantly dodging the missiles that came their way from all directions. There were no extra marital considerations; Sean was divorced and Farah a widow. There were no religious or cultural taboos to be avoided. Both were pragmatic enough to recognise that organised religion was simply a cynical form of control and in their minds, nobody naive enough to admit to such beliefs should be allowed to hold positions of authority. Farah had no family to condemn her and Sean knew that his parents and older sister would instantly take her to their hearts when, eventually, he introduced her to them. Ava knew and admired Sean as her mother's boss and close friend. Farah would not tell her of their true relationship as it would just pass the burden of secrecy on to someone who would barely understand why it had to be so, and, unlike Farah, would receive no compensation for her commitment.

Their relationship had to be secret for professional reasons. Sean had promoted her almost three years ago and a good six months before the start of their relationship but pride, professionalism and protocol hung over them like a horse hair veil; heavy, dull, uncomfortable and slightly smelly. Such a relationship would be frowned upon in most police forces, would be positively discouraged within Scotland Yard and absolutely intolerable in the sensitive world of the Special Investigations Unit. Both Sean and Farah believed that the feeling they had for each other was probably love, but neither seemed sure enough to sacrifice the careers that they both pursued with a passion they were certain of.

He arrived at her place the previous evening at eight o'clock precisely. Farah suspected that he had probably timed his tube journey and hung about the station to ensure that he arrived bang on time. Though he had a key, he would not let himself in. It somehow seemed like a level of commitment that neither deserved. He knocked, she opened, they hugged, they kissed passionately and they hugged again; this time just holding each other and looking into each other's eyes as though desperately trying to grab a glimpse of the thoughts and images that lay behind.

They made conversation together. They made dinner together, they made love together and then they made plans together. Sean shared the relevant details of his conversation with the commissioner. They planned how the trip to Blackburn should be made, how the meeting had been arranged, how the interview was to be approached and the insight she should be looking for. Lakin's last words to Farah were: "Whatever you do, watch out for Chatha. He's as smooth as snake shit, twice as slippery and ten times as toxic. MI7 call him the Teflon Cleric; everybody knows that IBIS is a front for the radicalisation and recruitment of IS Jihadists and the provision of safe haven for their exiled returning heroes. They have just never been able to make anything stick. Be careful, Farah, he is the embodiment of evil."

They made love again and planned how they would spend another wonderful evening together when she returned tomorrow evening, no shop talk allowed. They knew that this was a promise that neither was likely to keep.

At nine-thirty the following morning, Farah was seated in the standard class quiet coach, rear carriage bulkhead, facing travel, window seat, shared table, power point and high speed connectivity on the Virgin HS3 service to Manchester. She had considered the Euston to Preston West Coast route with the shorter transfer to Blackburn but with the Manchester journey now only taking one and a quarter hours, the slightly longer connection from Manchester was the more sensible option.

The HS3 rail link was created by a long scalpel incision through the torso of middle England. The gash exposed the diseased sternum of the region but made no pretence towards remedial action. Arrow straight, it dissected communities, surgically removed golf courses and veered only to avoid the occasional church, mosque and country residence of three Members of Parliament.

She considered herself fortunate that the seat to her right was vacant and when the train pulled out of Euston, the large gentleman on the other side of the table moved to his left so that both had half a table each and as much leg room as they required. More importantly, Farah could study the files on her tablet in the knowledge that nobody would be looking over her shoulder or glancing sideways at her highly confidential briefing document. There was much to read about Rahim Chatha. She read how his love for his father and distress at his death shaped his hatred for the capitalist establishment. She read of his passion for local politics, his alignment to the Labour movement, and his acrimonious split from the party over Tony Blair's foreign policy towards the Middle East in the nineteen nineties.

Leaving Labour did nothing to dampen his political fire and indeed, his ambition soon turned to obsession when the elders of his Blackburn community urged him to form a party to specifically support and promote the interests of Muslims, not just in Blackburn, but within all the major UK conurbations with Muslim majorities. He was a conscientious and committed scholar, a charismatic communicator and an evangelistic leader. The growth of the United Kingdom Independence Party from 2005 onwards was exactly the catalyst he needed to tear Muslim councillors away from their traditional Labour roots and stand under independent Muslim banners. As the number of councillors multiplied and more councils migrated to Muslim control it was almost an inevitability that the divergent independent councils were encouraged to come together under the auspices of IBIS, in pursuit of an Independent British Islamist State. At its outset IBIS was considered to be as disreputable as its sworn right wing enemy, the English Defence League and while the latter was driven to obscurity by Britain's moderate multicultural majority, IBIS continued to spread their influence throughout the North West, Yorkshire and the Midlands.

Rahim Chatha travelled extensively to the Middle East war zones of Afghanistan, Iran, Iraq, Libya, Syria and Egypt, promoting religious, political and charitable crusades and, in return, he frequently held court in Blackburn and London, welcoming a succession of highly dubious heads of Middle East movements. He polarised opinion within the UK Muslim community and held numerous heated public debates with his uncle, the legitimate head of the government recognised British Muslim Party. To most moderate observers, Rahim Chatha was considered to be the most dangerous British politician since Enoch Powell.

Sean Lakin had phoned Chatha personally the previous day, to advise him that as the leader of IBIS, albeit not a political party yet recognised in Westminster, the Special Investigations Unit had a responsibility to ensure that the civil unrest and threats of violence against their group had not gone unheeded. He was sending one of his senior investigators to try to ascertain why such acts were being conducted and who might be behind them. Lakin had tickled every single nerve end of Chatha's ego and arrogance, so the meeting was readily agreed and arranged. He had not mentioned that his representative would be a woman as this would, undoubtedly, have resulted in a much less harmonious exchange.

By the time she had absorbed the twenty thousand word dossier, the train had pulled into Manchester Piccadilly station and the train manager had to gently announce to Farah, in person, that the train had indeed reached its destination. So immersed in her studies was she that the three loudspeaker announcements had gone completely unnoticed. As had the rather large man who had been paying her a rather unhealthy interest over the past hour or so.

As Farah alighted the train and crossed the concourse towards her connecting service, she sensed a rather different climate in Manchester to that in London. It was early March and she had worn her customary black suit and long grey overcoat but quickly began to wish that she had forsaken her beige silk blouse for a woollen jumper. It was not just the temperature that struck her as being very different. Farah had not travelled extensively throughout the UK and although she was totally accustomed to the modern multi-cultural London which she now called home, she was taken aback by the prevalence of more traditional Islamic garb and the relative absence of Western fashion.

The thirty-five minute journey to Blackburn was uneventful, but Farah was fascinated by the contrasting landscapes of the countryside the train traversed. Through the densely populated suburbs of Salford and Bolton the carriages seemed to emerge upon a different planet where the purple vegetation of rolling barren moorland stretched out to the magnificent contours of the Pennines; the natural division between Lancashire and Yorkshire. Would that the world were still so simple with geographical features rather than religious doctrine dividing populations

As agreed, approximately fifteen minutes from Blackburn, Farah phoned her office to relay her current position. This was immediately relayed to the Lancashire Constabulary who had agreed to have a driver waiting for her at Blackburn station. She used the last ten minutes of her journey to load data onto her

Digispex and to rehearse in her mind, the agreed rationale for her visit and the delicate, diversionary route she would attempt to follow from protector to inquisitor.

The train squealed to a reluctant stop at Blackburn station and before she had stepped from the carriage she had noticed the young uniformed officer standing alongside the carriage in front of hers. It might have been the clicking of her heels on the old concrete platform that caused him to turn but it was clear that he had been given a detailed description of his charge. He was neither surprised nor disappointed by her approaching appearance. He smiled warmly as he stretched out his hand. "Inspector Karim. Welcome to Blackburn. I am PC Ernie Pemberton."

"Thank you, Constable," Farah returned his welcome, and his smile. "I hope you haven't been freezing here for too long."

"Freezing, Ma'am? This is like a summer's day in Blackburn. Let me help you with your overnight bag."

"No, its fine thanks. It's only equipment and files. I am travelling back down this afternoon."

Pemberton seemed surprised that she had travelled so far for such a short visit. "Oh, right then, we'd better get on our way."

It was a short walk down a sloping subway that led out to the front of the station and a wide expanse known locally as the Boulevard. Years ago, this had been the central hub of the city where the stark but striking cathedral, that gave the town its elevated status, overlooked a vast bus station. Blackburn had been a significant town in the heart of the Industrial Revolution. It was home to the country's largest concentration of weaving mills which in turn generated engineering businesses, which of course required breweries to lubricate the workforce. It was the concentration of labour that attracted the early immigrant community in the late nineteen-sixties and now the Asian community accounted for around eighty per cent of the two hundred thousand population. The mills had been closed years ago and the demand for beer had trickled to a drought. Commerce and industry in the town now revolved around retail outlets and taxis to transport the population to and from them. The vast majority of the workforce were council employees.

The drive from the station to the town hall had hardly warranted the provision of a vehicle but Lancashire Constabulary and Sean Lakin had insisted upon it. The town hall was erected in the nineteen-seventies and, at the time, was considered to be a seriously radical example of modern architecture. A tall, pale, grey structure rising from the very centre of the city with magnificent views to the surrounding hills and the Ribble Valley beyond. As leader of Blackburn Council, Rahim Chatha had the whole of the top floor for his personal team but there was something almost sinister to be confronted by his beaming face on a huge portrait hung behind the reception desk. Pemberton had parked in the designated spot right outside the front door and escorted Farah to the desk where, when he announced that Detective Inspector Karim had an appointment with Mr Chatha, the male receptionist performed an exaggerated double take before inviting her to sign in and take a seat. Pemberton offered to wait but she thanked him for his kindness and courtesy and asked whether he, personally, would be on duty for the return journey. He smiled as he hoped that he would.

She had arrived ten minutes early for her two o' clock appointment and was not at all surprised to find herself waiting until two twelve before she was invited to take the lift to the seventeenth floor. She entered the lift alone and was met by another ageing male assistant whose long grey beard almost obscured his stained red tie. Farah was not normally of a nervous disposition but the combination of Sean's parting words and this strangely hostile arena had her nerve ends tingling as the assistant generously declared, "Mr Chatha will see you now."

18

"Governor Thornton, sir," choked Douglas. "Adnan Abadi is dead."

"Say that again," demanded the governor. David Thornton was not given to dramatic phrasing but he simply did not believe what he had just heard. A new prisoner, one that apparently warranted the interest and intervention of an unknown government grandee seemingly hovering somewhere between Downing Street and Thames House, had died less than two hours after arriving into his care.

"He was killed, sir, but not before he took out three of our highest profile convicted Islamic State terrorists. Khalid Farooq, Kamran Hassani and Usman Masood are all dead in their own cell. One fractured skull, one apparent broken neck and one ripped throat."

"Lock those two cells immediately. Close down the wing and let nobody near any of the bodies. I will be down in five minutes." It took Thornton less than fifteen seconds to locate the call back button for the mysterious caller that had briefed him earlier. He instinctively knew that his own personal investigation before

123

making the call would have been contrary to the caller's instruction. The device was answered within seconds with a curt, "What's happened?"

"Adnan Abadi is dead, sir, but it seemed that he died killing three high profile terrorist prisoners on his wing. It's impossible to say at this stage who was the aggressor but we have four dead victims."

"Listen carefully, Mr. Thornton. I will be sending Home Office personnel to remove all four bodies immediately and bring them to our highest security pathology and forensic facility. Give the team any help they require in bagging the corpses but get them out of there without delay and make sure that the only humans to see my team are officers. Impose a total lock-down and instruct your officers to discuss these events with nobody. And I mean nobody! No doubt we shall have a further conversation in due course to determine how your regime could have allowed this to happen but, in the meantime, be under no doubt that this is a matter of the absolute, utmost highest level of security."

Abadi had already been secured in his cell by the time Thornton arrived on the wing. He did not enter. The sight from the viewing screen told him everything he needed to know. The lifeless, stationery corpse, twisted into the most unnatural position of agony and apparently oozing blood from every limb was a truly sickening sight. Thornton quickly withdrew and took the short walk along the landing amid the fevered shouting, cheering, jeering and banging that came from the cells of the others who sensed or smelled blood and death.

This time, Thornton nodded towards the cell and instructed Douglas to open it. He managed to move it just far enough to allow the governor to squeeze through without stepping on the corpse immediately behind it or smearing himself with the gooey red and grey matter that was gelling on the edge of the cell door at just around his head height.

It was only a matter of minutes earlier that Usman Masood's head had collided with the edge of the cold steel door with such force, that a five inch long, three inch wide cavity was created from the crown of his pointed shaved cranium, behind his ear, to the point at which the base of his skull connected with his neck. As Farooq had approached to instigate the beating, Abadi had swiftly swivelled and crashed the point of his right elbow into Masood's tight temple. Before the big man could drop to the floor, Abadi grabbed his stunned head with both hands and smashed it against the steel corner before pushing the body towards the advancing Cleric. For safe measure, he stamped on the fallen man's neck, crushing his wind pipe.

Hassani was now directly behind Farooq and there was insufficient space between the bunk and single bed for the two to advance in parallel. As Farooq's progress was halted by Masood's bloodied mass, Adnan Abadi leapt forward, stabbed both thumbs into the Cleric's eyes and with the palms of his strong hands covering the screaming man's ears he pushed his head sharply backwards into Hassani's face. As Hassani fell backwards over the toilet and into the table, Abadi changed his grip on Farooq's head and, in one seamless action that involved the Cleric's chin and right shoulder, his head snapped backwards as his neck was broken.

Hassani had recovered composure sufficiently to stagger to his feet, only to fall over the body of his master as it was pushed towards him. As he stumbled forward, Abadi's right hand emerged from the pocket of his track suit bottoms with a crude but deadly knife, crafted from a toothbrush and the sliver of blade from a prison issue disposable razor. The handle of the brush, which had been filed to a fine point, was thrust into Hassani's right eye and as Abadi withdrew it, he turned his hand deftly and slashed the screaming man's throat from right to left. The blade was narrow and though it cut the skin, it had not severed any critical veins or arteries. The adrenalin seemed to pump through Hassani's right eye as he launched a counter attack on Abadi. Although the toothbrush was still in Abadi's hand, it was encased in Hassani's two fisted grip and for the next half minute, both men endured punctures and slashes as they played out the ultimate game of wrist wrestling. The gash in Hassani's neck was widening and when Abadi finally managed to manoeuvre his knee under his opponents bleeding chin, it took only one fierce jerk to tear the man's neck apart and rip out the strained strands of pipework that lay behind.

As Adnan Abadi slowly and painfully lifted himself clear of the two bodies below him he was unsure how much of the blood that smeared his tracksuit had leaked from his own punctures and cuts rather than the liberal coating from the two dead adversaries from whom he was desperately disentangling. He stumbled backwards over his third victim, applying a shiny red coat of blood to his back as he turned himself over and crawled to the door. He used the cell door's external handle to drag himself to his feet but managed to stagger less than four yards before crashing back to the floor of the landing where blood from his wounds dripped through the open steel gantry onto the concrete below.

By this time, quite a crowd had emerged around the cell but none had dared to approach to investigate the commotion. Prison Officers Douglas, Glenister and Morris were running along the corridor ordering the prisoners back into their cells as the lockdown alarm was sounded.

Scott Douglas instinctively took control of the situation, directing Glenister and Morris towards the Islamist's cell as he supported the crawling Abadi back to his. Once the prisoners had been securely locked back into their cells he called for two of the armed guards to put down their rifles and help them to get Abadi back to his cell. So blood-soaked was he that the trio struggled to hold onto him and as they hurried him through the cell door, Douglas dragged the thin mattress from his bed, threw it on the cell floor and lay the barely conscious prisoner upon it. Abadi's glossy black hair was now streaked with thick stripes of clotted blood which transferred a perfectly shaped red circle into the porous grey mattress. The two guards were immensely impressed by the care and attention applied by the young officer as he clearly tried to apply a number of resuscitation techniques before Abadi pulled his head towards him and forced out his three last words, "It wasn't them…"

The nearest Home Office Pathology and Forensics facility was situated just eight miles from Belmarsh, at the Royal London Hospital at Whitechapel. Two ambulances, with outriders had been despatched to Belmarsh within seconds of Governor Thornton's phone call and he was given explicit instructions to have staff at all gates grant immediate access as soon as they saw the distinctive vehicles and uniforms approach. The instructions further specified that Abadi's body was to be removed in the first vehicle.

The journey from Whitechapel to Belmarsh would normally take around twenty-five minutes but the presence of police outriders was able to trim a full ten minutes off that time. Thornton was at the front gate to personally supervise the access and rapid progress of the two ambulance teams through the seven different gates and security points between the outside world and Abadi's cell wall. Prison Officer Scott Douglas had been standing guard, nervously, outside the cell and was already inserting the key when he heard the stampede of feet on the outer gantry and sliding gates at the entrance to the wing. Two paramedics pushed past Douglas, one checking for the pulse that would not be found while the other was quickly laying out the black body bag. Governor Thornton fastidiously observed the process but at no stage sought to intervene. He was normally the most calm and rational of men but was becoming increasingly overwhelmed by the bizarre events of the past few hours that could, conceivably, spell the end of his hitherto stellar career in the prison service.

Seconds later, the other team marched past towards the cell at the opposite end of the landing and the teams almost collided as the first two paramedics wheeled Abadi back through the labyrinth of gates, gullies and gangways, out across the deserted yard, through the inner and outer perimeter fences and into the waiting ambulance. The crew loaded the trolley into the grooved reception frame that formed either a mobile hospital bed or a makeshift mortuary. The driver signed the requisite release document while the second attendant climbed into the back with the body. In less than a minute, the ambulance, escorted by one of the outriders, was on its way back towards Whitechapel. The entire operation, from the first phone call from the governor to the ambulance leaving the prison, had taken just under thirty minutes.

It took the second crew significantly longer to certify death, chalk out the floor, photograph the scene and remove the twisted, bloodied bodies of Farooq, Hassani and Masood. The mood of frustration on the wing was turning to frenzy as the bored but excitable inmates sensed that something sensational was happening, as if they could smell the blood right under their noses. Governor Thornton knew that it would be impossible to keep a lid on this as too many prisoners would have seen what had taken place before lock-down. These three particular individuals were feared, revered and hated in equal measure within the Belmarsh community so the danger of further disturbances was clear, present and almost inevitable.

Right at this moment, David Thornton was almost hoping that the mystery Minister, as he had come to think of him, would suspend him and relieve him of the inevitable aftermath on the wing.

At one-thirty that afternoon, the first of the two ambulances returned to the Royal London Hospital and cleared the security barriers at the far side of the building before being halted before the sliding door that protected the ramp down to the segregated Home Office Pathology and Forensic Laboratory. Having carefully driven down the ramp, the sliding steel door was sealed closed and the ambulance reversed up to the open doors at the end of the laboratory corridor. Only corpses destined for special Home Office investigation entered or left by this portal. The pathologist, one of three at the unit with high security clearance was waiting at the door with a tall, distinguished looking man in a navy blue striped suit.

They both stood aside as the ambulance doors opened and three bulky body bags were offloaded onto gurneys and wheeled down the corridor.

The other ambulance arrived just as the third body had been removed and the first vehicle moved away from the loading bay. The vehicle door was opened efficiently, the trolley released from its holding rails and the driver and his assistant were ushered down the corridor, through an automatic double door into a brightly lit, sparklingly clean chamber with white tiles around three walls and a bank of large, stainless steel drawers on the fourth. The pathologist piloted the trolley towards the end compartment of six on the second tier from the floor which allowed the body bag to be slid, rather than lifted into the open drawer. The paramedic pair exchanged a few solemn words with the pathologist as the blue suited observer unzipped the body bag from the head down, to reveal the shaven headed, bearded, bruised face of a young Asian man who had long since ceased to care where, or how, his broken, battered body had been brought to rest.

"I think I can safely sign the death certificate," said the pathologist, "but the body will need to be formally identified."

The blue suited official stepped forward. "It appears that the deceased has no living relatives but the guard to whom he was assigned in Belmarsh is on his way to conduct the formal identification. I think that the sooner we can get this man identified and cremated, the better we might all sleep."

19

Farah took a deep breath, tightened her jaw, contracted her muscles and strode confidently into the vast, imposing council chamber. Chatha expressed no outward animosity towards the woman in front of him but remained seated with his hands firmly placed on the large boardroom table in front of him. Even if he had been inclined to proffer a handshake, the expanse of the table simply served to emphasise the distance between them, both geographically and culturally. Chatha, seated, seemed taller than the one point six metres his file declared and he certainly looked closer to fifty years than forty. The copious quantity of grease on his straight, side parted hair served to disguise both the grey at his temples and control the unruly strands that would otherwise have fallen over his cold brown eyes. His long, thin, wispy, black beard was bordered with grey and Farah would not have been surprised to see him stroking the straggly growth to a point.

"I do apologise for the delay, Inspector, but just as you arrived I was required to take a call from my wife, who has just received some terribly distressing news about one of her cousins."

Farah nodded compliantly and resisted the temptation to delve into the cause of the distress, as Chatha had, to her mind, clearly invited.

"Please don't worry, Mr Chatha. In my profession, I tend to cherish and value any opportunity presented to catch up on the endless stream of administration that pours down these devices." Farah held up her videophone as if to reassure herself and demonstrate to him, that she was only one button away from support, should support be required.

"Yes indeed," affirmed Chatha, solemnly. "I am sure that you will have many messages to monitor, especially in such turbulent times. So how can I help you, Inspector?"

"Well," began Farah, somewhat surprised that there had not even been the offer of a glass of water, let alone a cup of tea before they got down to business. Perhaps the phone call from his wife was genuine and he really did need to conclude the meeting quickly. "I believe that my Chief Superintendent advised you that we hope that we might try to help each other in this particular instance. We are all aware that the London bombings have heightened animosity towards the Muslim community, and the last thing that the police and security services need is an outbreak of racially fuelled disturbances that will divert resources from the most important task of tracking down the perpetrators."

"We appreciate your concern, Inspector, but I am sure that the local constabularies, supported by our own community reservists, will be able to contain the isolated pockets of discontent."

"Of course, Mr Chatha, the Serious Investigations Unit has total confidence in our local colleagues but our interest is at a national level and we simply seek to ensure that the incidents that have occurred within each of your councils are recorded, coordinated and investigated thoroughly. Our most immediate interest is in establishing whether there is a tangible link between the disturbances in Blackburn, Bradford and Birmingham."

"Well of course there is a link, Inspector. All of these acts were perpetrated by mindless, bigoted, racist thugs who have been encouraged to use the bombings as an excuse to declare open season upon our Muslim brothers."

Farah leaned forward, tilted her head slightly to her right before enquiring, softly but confidently, "Who do you believe might be encouraging such behaviour, Councillor, and why would anyone wish to do so?"

"Come now, Inspector. You know as well as I do that when any act of terrorism is conducted on these islands, the finger of suspicion is immediately pointed towards my people. We have little doubt and, in some cases, solid evidence to substantiate the fact the many of these acts are sponsored by EDL and UKIP activists, simply to stir up further hatred towards us."

Farah hoped that her visible hostility towards Chatha's use of the phrase 'towards my people' had not been too apparent to him. "And it is precisely such evidence that brings me here today, Councillor." Farah smiled, inwardly delighted by the councillor's invitation to validate her visit. "Which particular incidents are you referring to, and what evidence do you have to substantiate your assertion, sir?"

Chatha gave no indication that he had recognised taking the bait so subtly cast by Farah.

"The beheading, two years ago, of the young English soldier in Glasgow was not the action of a Muslim, it was a revenge murder by one of the many SNP supporters who believe themselves to have been cast aside by your government. The bus bomb in Liverpool last year was not an act of Jihad but one of the first assaults from the Irish Unionists on your mainland. In both instances, the authorities and the media turned the spotlight towards my people and your government deliberately downplayed the involvement of the Unionist Alliance. We have obtained clear evidence to substantiate our claims but your media still used these events to further fuel hatred towards us."

Farah noted the repeated and open use of the phraseology of 'your government', 'your media' and while she knew that both accusations were, in fact, valid, she pushed against the open door. "So if you had clear evidence of this disgraceful transgression, did you pass the evidence to the police or security services?"

"No, Inspector, we did not. Firstly, nobody would have believed us. Secondly, we would have been pressured into declaring how we received such evidence and thirdly, we knew, absolutely, that the authorities had exactly the same evidence but chose to have suspicion face towards us than to openly admit that conflict was opening up on another front."

While Farah knew and understood that this might well have been the case, she might also have added that it also served Chatha's purposes to have more hostility cast towards them.

"Mr Chatha. In this particular instance, the police, security services, politicians and media have gone to great lengths to emphasise that there is no evidence to link the London bombings to any Islamic organisation and yet the civil disturbances sprang up almost immediately, in four diverse areas, within minutes of each other. Do you have any views on how and why such attacks might have been coordinated?"

"I refer you to my earlier answer, Inspector. Racist thugs, social media and a political campaign to discredit and isolate our communities."

"Then we must work together to eliminate these criminal elements from our society but we need your help in doing so. Have there been any other possible catalysts for yesterday's attacks, other than the bombings?"

"I am not sure what you are driving at, Inspector. What other motive might a racist thug need?"

"I am just wondering, Councillor, whether or not your party had been holding any more underground rallies, any more secret Sharia courts or entertaining any high profile overseas visitors to address your followers?"

For the first time during the interview, Chatha let down his guard and unleashed his contempt.

"Had any such event taken place, I am sure that your people would already have known about it and I strongly resent your attempt to turn my communities from innocent victims of violence to political perpetrators."

Farah kept an even temperament and responded calmly, "I can assure you, Councillor that this was not my intention and I sincerely apologise for any perceived offence I might have inadvertently caused. I am simply seeking to establish whether or not there are any other potential lines of enquiry that we might pursue on your behalf."

"And if there were, Inspector, why would this be on our behalf. Surely you have the interests of our whole nation at heart here?"

"Yes of course, Councillor," admitted Farah, and consciously kicked herself on the shin for such a careless remark.

The interview continued for a further forty minutes or so. Farah skilfully turned the focus back towards high profile members within the Muslim community who might consider themselves to be particular targets with a view to providing added protection. The offer was promptly dismissed by Chatha, who immediately recognised this for what it actually was: a semi-legitimate attempt to have the security forces monitor known activists within IBIS.

Farah tried to draw Chatha on his relationship with his uncle and the legitimate British Muslim Party. He would not be drawn. She tried to explore his own political ambitions and why his party had not sought to contest Westminster seats. He simply replied that it would be hypocrisy to sit in a chamber that he did not recognise and support a state that he wished to dismantle.

The two sparred, Farah jabbing, Chatha blocking with Farah winning easily on points. She took no particular relief in this pyrrhic victory as she recognised that his reluctance to fight back was more to do with contempt than confidence. He simply refused to belittle himself by engaging with this young girl.

Before concluding the interview, Farah saw the need to retrieve the situation, if only superficially.

"We completely respect your rights, Councillor, as a registered political party, to hold political meetings and express views that the mainstream, majority population might find challenging. We also recognise that you will, from time to time, invite, or at least attract visitors from some of the more extreme factions of your faith and we have a duty to ensure their safety while in our country. At the same time, I know that you will appreciate that we are aware that you might also, inadvertently of course, be opening your communities to foreign visitors whose presence may not be benign and we also have a duty to ensure that your communities and the wider population are protected from their presence also. Let me assure you, Councillor that the Special Investigations Unit will be working closely with the local forces to minimise social disturbances and we would welcome your support in passing on any information that will enable us to do so."

Chatha rose to signify the end of the meeting and, in the absence of a handshake, he bowed his head slightly and thanked Farah for her kind offer, which he and his fellow councillors would consider carefully. As soon as Farah left, Chatha immediately resumed his earlier encrypted digital conversation.

Farah took the elevator back down to the reception area and sat quietly for a full two minutes, reflecting upon the hour long exchange. Although she had never actually felt threatened in the council chamber she had undoubtedly sensed a sinister presence and did not need to remind herself that she was no more than one hundred feet and two degrees of separation from evil.

She looked outside into the bright but crisp midday sunshine and considered taking the short walk back to the railway station. She quickly reconsidered, understanding that to do so might be seen as ingratitude to the local force and, more importantly, a glaring dereliction of security protocol. She keyed in the code for Blackburn Police Station and less than five minutes later, Constable Pemberton had completed the short journey. He smiled as he collected Farah from reception and escorted her through the front door of the town hall and on to the promenade of the shopping precinct below. As they made the short walk to the squad car she noticed that there were hardly any people walking alone. There were small groups of black clad women with prams, huddles of young men talking excitedly at shop corners and elderly men, shuffling two by two in front of their women. Farah now felt even more relieved that Pemberton was at her side.

"Well," he asked, "how did you find our esteemed and charismatic council leader?"

"Charm personified," smiled Farah as she slid into the front seat beside him. The distance between the town hall and the railway station was less than a mile but the complex traffic system around Blackburn transposed this into a ten minute journey. There was a small set down area in front of the station and, on their arrival, a battered blue minicab occupied the last space at the rear, while two rather large burqa clad figures struggled to extricate a pushchair and suitcase from the back seat. Sensing Farah's frustration but not wishing to flaunt the law by parking illegally, Pemberton left the electric motor ticking over in neutral while he went over to help the struggling carers. He might have noticed that something was wrong had he seen that there was no child waiting to occupy the push chair. As he wrapped both his arms around the contraption, the larger of the two ladies stepped back towards the police car, where Farah was busy keying data into her device.

In one seemingly simultaneous motion, the figure pulled open the passenger door and a thick hairy arm thrust out from beneath the burqa, pinning Farah in behind her seat belt while the other hand held acrid smelling cloth over her nose and mouth. As she struggled, vainly, to shake her assailant off, she saw the other figure behind Pemberton raise a heavy bar and smash the policeman on the back of the head. Farah was dragged from the police car into the back of the cab, wedged between the two black swirling forms. The old, wizened Asian taxi driver drove away quickly leaving a bleeding policeman sprawled across an empty suitcase and redundant pushchair. The whole episode took less than fifty seconds.

20

Prison Officer Scott Douglas reported, as instructed by his governor, to the reception area of the pathology department of the Royal London Hospital with the prospect of identifying Abadi's corpse beginning to drain his elation at his brief time away from the grim, foreboding atmosphere of impending doom at Belmarsh. He signed in and sat in the cold, stark waiting room until a young female attendant in pale-blue cotton scrubs collected him with one of those nondescript expressions that neither feigned grief nor disrespected the dignity of the visitor. After a brief, silent walk down two long corridors, Douglas was met by the Blue Pinstriped Suit and the White Coat. White Coat dismissed Blue Scrubs. "Thank you Kate. I will buzz you when Mr Douglas is ready to leave."

"Yes, Professor Houston." She dutifully replied.

Houston introduced himself and announced Blue Suit simply as "an observer from the Home Office". Douglas nodded knowingly towards the observer.

"Mr. Douglas," continued the pathologist, "I understand that you are the only person immediately available to identify the body of Adnan Abadi. Thank you for agreeing to do so. I understand

138

that there is some urgency in having him processed and cremated. Probably a religious thing."

"Possibly, sir," agreed Douglas. "I wouldn't know about any of that but Mr Abadi was under my jurisdiction for a brief time and I was by his side at his death so I would indeed be able to identify him."

"Excellent, how fortunate!" Houston rubbed his hands, totally failing to recognise the impropriety of his exclamation. "Come this way please."

If the reception area had felt cold and stark, the pathology laboratory to which he was then led reminded him of one of those ice hotels that he had once seen in a Reykjavik tourist video. While the temperature was undoubtedly controlled, it felt particularly cold though this was perhaps the illusion of the brilliant electric light, perfectly diffused across the pure white tiles on the floor and walls. They strode across to the bank of cabinets on the far wall and Professor Houston paused for a moment, with his hand gently resting upon the handle. "Are you okay with this, Mr Douglas?"

"I guess so. I don't suppose he can look too much worse than he did back in his cell and I expect you have cleaned him up a bit and, perhaps sprayed him with something?"

"Quite." Houston pulled out the drawer, paused again and folded back the grey sheet from the corpse's face.

Douglas looked down and slowly moved his cupped hands over his nose, as if either in prayer or anticipation of a non-existent odour. His first glance at the bruised, battered and totally unfamiliar face of the young, bearded, shaven-headed Asian conjured a vision of a small open top sports saloon car spinning off the road into a wall or a body falling from a multi storey car park. He suspected he would never know and didn't really care what twist of fate or circumstance had carried this anonymous unfortunate here as he solemnly nodded, "Yes. That is Adnan Abadi. Do you need me to sign anything?"

"No that won't be necessary thank you. I can take care of the paperwork and get the body released to the undertakers. There seem to be enough witnesses to negate the need for a postmortem in this case. Thank you, Mr Douglas, you have been most helpful. I will have my assistant show you out." Houston moved over to his stainless steel desk and pressed the small buzzer which, alongside a small phone and a large folder, were the only items on it.

Less than a minute later, Kate returned, smiled and motioned Douglas to walk with her. Blue Suit muttered something to the pathologist and followed them to the reception area where Scott Douglas signed out, walked into the car parked and breathed in a lungful of lovely polluted London oxygen. He sensed the Blue Suit alongside him as he walked across to the governor's Audi which he had borrowed for the short journey.

"Well done, Scotty. So far so good."

"Thank you, sir. It's a bit strange identifying dead bodies when one is more accustomed to causing them." Douglas grinned. "Will you really get away without the formal postmortem and inquest?"

"In this day and age Scotty, mention the words *public interest* and *national security* and politicians can get away with most things."

"Well I shall leave that to you, sir. I had better get going. As you can imagine, I have a bit to do before I get back to the prison. If you could give me an hour or so before contacting the governor and telling him I have done the deed and I'm on my way back, that should give me plenty of time to tidy things up back at my place."

"Roger that, Scott! I will call you this evening to discuss phase two."

***

My Place to Scott Douglas, was a small secluded cottage on the edge of Birchmere Park, a quiet beauty spot and nature reserve less than three miles from the prison. The modest but ridiculously priced gardener's cottage had been rented for him during his brief career at Belmarsh but even if he had felt the inclination to invite fellow workers back there, they would have wondered at how a poorly paid screw could afford such a lovely property. He had a back story, just in case, of course. His old aunt, a retired and respected historian was in a care home and the property was subject to an equity release scheme to fund her residency until her inevitable expiry. Scott was simply a live in caretaker with a bag packed and ready to go when required.

He parked the governor's car across the end of the walled driveway so that anyone approaching the cottage from the front would be required to do so via the neat, lush gravelled drive and thus within sight and sound of both living room, hallway and master bedroom. He keyed a message into his handset, pressed send and inserted the first of the two robust Chubb keys into the heavy oak door. The text message ensured that he was not met by a bullet between the eyes as Adnan Abadi stood in front of him, just beyond the door but out of sight from the path. "Welcome back, buddy! How did I look?"

"A damn sight younger and a whole lot better looking than you do now! How are you feeling? You look like shit!"

"And I feel like it. How much of that crap did you pump into me back in the cell?"

"Just enough to keep you dead to the naked eye but I would have had to have given you the full dose if the governor had insisted that the prison quack come down to see you. Thankfully he was so spooked by the suits that he did everything just as he was told."

Adnan Abadi had, indeed, taken a pretty heavy beating in Farooq's cell but nothing more than he had endured before, either during his brutally intensive training, or occasionally in the field. His mind was programmed to endure pain and his body conditioned to absorb the most robust physical intervention. He was perfectly conscious as he left the cell and though Scott Douglas did not doubt his partner's thespian ability, the deftly administered phial of a carefully blended ketamine barbiturate solution guaranteed the authenticity of Abadi's fading consciousness as he bundled him back to his cell.

Adnan trusted Scott implicitly but could not resist his next question. "So what would have happened if the governor and prison doctor had insisted upon examining me before the release?"

"Plan B, Adnan. There's always a plan B… and in this case, a plan C! Plan B; I would have injected you with the second ketamine phial that would have slowed your blood pressure and respiration down to a trace. If the doctor had spotted that you were still with us, we would have bundled you into the ambulance, but sadly, you would have passed away on the journey… around ten seconds after our tame paramedic administered the Epinephrine shot to bring you round: Plan C!"

"And by the unlikely, but nonetheless disconcerting scenario that the adrenaline did not kick in quickly enough, was there a plan D?"

"Of course there was my friend. You get burned, the boss loses an agent but thankfully, the smart, good looking one is still on the case! And with that in mind, I need to get back to Belmarsh and hand in my resignation. The horror of the murders and the trauma of identifying your corpse is far too much for a sensitive soul like me to survive."

"Who was he? My doppelganger?"

"A twenty three year old RTA victim. Spun off the road at speed apparently, with dope in his system. Should have been cremated yesterday but let's just say we kept him on a low light until you got here! They burned a couple piglets. Shame really. If the congregation had cleared off sooner they could have had a free barbeque at the wake!"

"Sensitive as ever, Scotty. You're all heart. Before you go, you need to feed it up the line that I am absolutely certain that Farooq and his goons had no idea who carried out the bombings, and if ISIS or IBIS had been involved, it would not have happened without their knowledge or blessing. In fact, they were seriously pissed off by the thought that I had done it and were ready to do me damage, or even take me out because of it. They hinted that the bombings might well have thrown a spanner into the workings of an even bigger plot that might be about to unfold."

"We suspected as much," agreed Scott, "but we still kill three birds with one stone if you pardon the clumsy pun. First, we prove, pretty conclusively that this wasn't an IBIS backed action. Second, we get rid of three of the most dangerous Islamists in Belmarsh and we know for sure that they have been the brains and brawn behind the eight murders in there that I was sent in to investigate. And third, their deaths will undoubtedly flush out their sponsors and contacts on the other side of the wall. Whether they are related to these particular London bombs is almost irrelevant. We all know that IBIS have been behind most of the terror attacks in Britain since 2015, and this might just be the lever to prise the lid off."

"It already seems that IBIS areas are coming under attack from far right groups who *want* them to be responsible and that gives the authorities a legitimate excuse to get within their communities on the pretext of protecting them. If they now, as we suspect, seek retribution for the Belmarsh Three, by blowing their peaceful-party pretence, we are better placed than ever to get under their skin. Anyway, I suggest you shake off the remains of your barbiturate-induced nap and get your report prepared. Our lord and master suggested that he might be in touch later. Meanwhile, I have a resignation letter to tender."

Scott Douglas was upbeat and singing along to the old county music tracks booming out from his governor's personal music system in the Audi. He had been in that prison too long and was finding it increasingly difficult to wash the smell of sweat, urine, fish, cabbage, and human detritus away as he walked from the gates at the end of each shift. He had also come close to blowing his cover on more than one occasion but the information that he had passed to MI7 had undoubtedly saved many lives. He also had to admit to himself that that he quite enjoyed the challenge of smuggling in the phones, alcohol, tobacco and weed (never anything harder) and the small fortune that he had amassed in doing so was a healthy supplement to his MI7 salary. They didn't even deduct his prison officer's salary so it had been quite a lucrative eighteen months but all good things come to an end he chuckled.

He was just about to park the Audi in the governor's space when his second and most secure device buzzed in his pocket. As he pressed the button and his *real boss* appeared on the screen, his euphoria suddenly drained.

"Scotty, that resignation letter you have in your pocket. Just keep it in there for another few days. I might just have a couple more shifts for you to see out."

21

As a geographic and metaphoric merging of East and West, Istanbul is the only city in the world spanning two continents. The magnificent Bosporus flows through the heart of the city; Europe lies to the west, Asia to the east.

For almost two thousand years, this amazing metropolis had been the pillar of some of the world's great empires, serving as capital city for the Romans, the Byzantines and Ottomans. Each left their unique signature upon this remarkable landscape. A new identity was now emerging.

Inside the sprawling city, the secular and the sacred mingle; minarets with nightclubs and dusty prayer rugs with boutique bars. The idea of Istanbul as collision between East and West revealed itself immediately, with monumental churches, elaborate mosques and Roman ruins.

The seemingly endless list of iconic attractions drew millions of tourists to swell this vast city of over seventeen million inhabitants, wondering at the new sights that await around every corner but also thrilled by the dangers that might lurk in the alleyways.

Preposterous and prosperous in equal proportion, Istanbul had numerous neighbourhoods, designer stores, a Grand Bazaar the size of two football pitches, and a thriving art and culture scene. The Museum of Modern Art, conveniently located beside the pier where ships docked, was a popular attraction for those joining and disembarking cruise ships.

In summer, the height of the season, one could find as many as four liners a day docking there. Today, there was only one. The Oceanic Line, *Princess of the Waves* was busily loading food, drink, supplies and passengers ahead of its 5 p.m. sailing for her eight day itinerary taking in Crete, Sicily, Sardinia, Corsica, Marseille and disembarking in Barcelona.

The couple exiting the museum and strolling hand in hand towards the ship had already checked in two hours earlier, unpacked, taken lunch in the deck ten Sea Spray Buffet before disembarking again to take in a few final local sights before their big adventure. He looked relaxed and confident as they approached the security station. She was less so. This was not so much a fear of sailing as her discomfort in walking out in public for only the fourth time in her adult life in the decadent Western tourist garb of jeans, T-shirt and sweater. At least, she consoled herself, her legs were covered.

The Philippines security guard scanned their sea passes and smiled as he offered his customary greeting. Passengers frequently wondered whether the use of the Christian name with a title was a form of impertinent friendship or simply a lack of understanding of how Western Christian and surnames worked. "Welcome back aboard, Mrs Christina, welcome back aboard, Mr Richard."

22

Lakin had accompanied Farah to Euston that morning before heading into the Yard. They had sat opposite each other on the Northern Line tube and walked briskly together up the escalators and onto the concourse of the mainline station before they doubled back down the few steps to the underground car park. They moved into a dark, secluded corner and it was only there that he held her hands, drew her close to him, moved his arms to the sides of her head and kissed her intensely. This was not a kiss of passion, or lust but an embrace of sheer, unmitigated love. He just wanted to hold her, to caress her, to love her and to protect her. He felt ashamed at having to do so in the dark. He felt even more ashamed when, at last, they unlocked their embrace and Farah headed back to the concourse while Lakin walked across the car park and joined the taxi queue.

The traffic that morning had been particularly heavy with more commuters than usual travelling overground to avoid the perceived dangers of the tube system. They were probably in greater danger from falling masonry in the streets than in the tube but he understood the misleading sense of freedom that the sight of sunlight provided. It was during that journey that he reflected on his lack of freedom to openly embrace the woman he truly loved. The previous night had been the first time that they had actually slept together and woken together. It was, for him, the most wonderful feeling he had ever experienced. To wake, quietly, and feel her smooth, warm shoulder against his chin. He had gently raised himself to look down upon her serene form as she lay, breathing softly beneath his gaze. He had marvelled at her beauty for a full three minutes before succumbing to the need to hold her, to mould into her, to adore her, to worship her.

It was during that taxi ride he realised that more than anything, he wanted to experience that feeling again. He wanted to experience that feeling every day, for the rest of his life and he would do whatever was needed to make it happen. It would entail a transfer for one of them; possibly even a change in career from the SIU to another branch of the police or intelligence services. It would be more likely that Farah would make this move but Sean determined at that moment, that, if necessary, it was a modest sacrifice that he was prepared to make to be with the woman that he knew, beyond any possible doubt, that he wanted to spend the rest of his life with. He checked the time of her return train from Manchester and booked a table, thirty minutes after its scheduled arrival at their favourite Lebanese restaurant on the Edgware Road. It was only then that he considered the possibility that Farah might not actually want the same thing.

It was just after ten-thirty when he arrived in his office and after a detailed briefing update from inspectors Brian Chambers and Rosie Hunter he was ready for his twelve o' clock meeting with the commissioner. Their initial discussions were centred on Adnan Abadi's background and the profile drawn by Roger Churchill had certainly placed him firmly in the frame as a significant person of extreme interest.

The conversation progressed to the maintenance work undertaken at the two sites by the Polish excavation contractors, the electrical engineering business based in Ealing and the Scottish specialist welders.

"We have made solid progress in contacting the three companies involved in the two maintenance sites. Altogether, there were nineteen workers involved in the two operations, fourteen of whom were present at both sites, two exclusively at Whitehall and three at the Embankment. We have the names of all the individuals involved and we have commenced the process of tracking them down and interviewing them locally. All three businesses have been highly cooperative and we only have three workers that we haven't yet located. Two of them are with the Polish excavation squad, where each of them worked at one site in isolation and a Colin Richards who was subcontracted to work at both sites by Caledonian Specialist Alloys, a welding business based in Aberdeen.

"The Polish guys are on a job in France and Richards is a freelance subcontractor to Caledonian who seems to move around a lot. He is a highly qualified specialist, said to be one of the best in his line of work and constantly in demand internationally. He is thought to be back in his base in Italy and our current priority is to track all three of them down for interview."

Lakin paused and waited for the commissioner to absorb the update. It didn't take long. Commissioner Pollard, despite being only two years from retirement, was as sharp as a pin. You don't get to that level in the Metropolitan Police and, more importantly, stay there, without possessing quad-core microchip analytical skills and the judgement of job.

"Abadi fell into our hands too easily. He may be involved somehow but its Richards, the specialist engineer that interests me the most. The Scots connection, his specialist skill, the roaming brief, his apparent departure from the UK... find him, quickly!"

Lakin nodded in agreement. "Yes, sir, we will clearly keep investigations ongoing on all fronts but Richards, Abadi and the Poles will be our immediate priorities, in that order. If any, or all of these were involved, the next and perhaps most important question, is who is the paymaster. This is not the work of a lone fanatic."

"IBIS have to be the most obvious contender," pondered Pollard, "but I wonder if that's too obvious? I am not sure how these atrocities would further their domestic, political ambitions but their known affiliation to Islamic State is the more feasible connection. The Western Allied forces have been giving them something of a pounding in Syria and it would be understandable, indeed predictable, for them to try to strike back on our doorstep."

He seemed to hover over the word, *predictable*, as though to suggest a lack of diligence somewhere within the chain of command. Lakin thought better of pursuing this train of thought and simply advised that he had one of his most senior investigators interviewing Rahim Chatha, in the spirit of complete mutual cooperation, as they spoke. Lakin noted the deep frown appear on Pollard's brow and was relieved to have been spared the challenge of his response by the red flashing alert on the commissioner's personal desk screen. He discreetly turned away to allow his superior to access the message. As Lakin saw Pollard's expression change quickly from stunned amazement to horror, he motioned to leave.

"No! Sit down, Sean, you need to see this!"

The commissioner pressed the button to activate his wall mounted screen which was immediately animated by the grim face of Tom Mellor staring out at them.

"An almighty shit bomb has just descended upon Belmarsh!" If Mellor's language seemed inappropriate, his tone and demeanour was certainly on script. He grimly and slowly continued. "Adnan Abadi is dead. He died at around noon today, less than two hours after arriving at Belmarsh. It seems that he had a welcoming committee of Islamic State and IBIS activists, who tortured and beat him to death."

The commissioner was first to respond. "Abadi is clearly a loss to the investigation but the perpetrators are presumably an equally valuable line of inquiry?"

"They would have been," replied Mellor, "if the three of them were not lying alongside Abadi in the morgue."

Now Lakin felt obliged to join the conversation. "Somebody got to the killers after they assassinated Abadi?" His mind was spinning at the possibility.

"No, gentlemen. It appears that our innocuous politics student brutally killed three of the hardest and most feared Islamic radicals before succumbing to his own injuries."

The commissioner was incandescent. "How the hell was this allowed to happen? Why wasn't Abadi in isolation? Why wasn't he under protection, for God's sake?"

Mellor was calmer in his response. "You will recall, commissioner, that, officially, Abadi had been remanded to Belmarsh on assault charges. There was no mention on the custody sheet of the suspected terrorism link. The prison regime acted appropriately throughout."

Lakin regretted his response almost as soon as it left his lips. "Allowing four high profile inmates to tear each other to pieces is appropriate? Sorry, Mr Mellor, this is beyond ridiculous! There must be something seriously wrong at Belmarsh for this to happen. This was not a random assault. Somebody knew that Abadi was a terror suspect and until we find the source of that leak we must assume that our investigation has been blown apart!"

"I agree with you, Chief Superintendent, and that is why this is now your number one priority."

The three continued to discuss the identities of the dead ISIS and IBIS activists. There was an inconvenient truth within the Home Office that Belmarsh, the country's most secure prison, was also probably the source of most of the country's many attacks on infrastructure and individuals over the past ten years. Digital communications devices were, of course, banned in Belmarsh but civil rights dictated that prisoners must have rights to association and access to external visitation and contact. Committed fanatics with nothing else to do could devote their lives, behind bars, to plotting, planning and directing campaigns as well as recruiting the foot soldiers to carry them out. They, quite literally, had time to kill.

Mellor was now warming to both Pollard and Lakin; so much that he felt comfortable in widening the context of the conversation.

"There are now two additional security issues to be addressed. First, when the word gets around Belmarsh that Farooq, Hassani and Masood are dead, there will be allegations of racist assassinations and inevitable threats of retribution. There will also be a power struggle within Belmarsh to establish a new Islamic hierarchy and a similarly hostile response from the non-Muslim prison community."

Pollard was reluctant to reply as his remit did not extend to within the prison service but he felt that his input was being commissioned.

"That will undoubtedly be the case, Mr Mellor, but I hope that the Home Secretary will authorise the implementation of emergency measures in the prison. I am no expert and I understand little of the logistics but I don't believe that a prolonged lock-down would be in the interests of long-term security. I would suggest that you call in all available prison officers, extend the shift rosters and, selectively, block by block, wing by wing, give the prisoners greater rather than less freedom to associate."

"You mean fewer prisoners out of their cells at any one time, but more frequently?" clarified Lakin.

"Absolutely." affirmed Pollard. "Selective association, segregated meal times, enhanced food and entertainment… and a closer relationship with the guards. The prisoners should not be made to suffer for events that were not of their making. This would also limit the opportunity for open power lobbying and conflict within and across the two principal convict communities."

"Sound advice," nodded Mellor, "and please call me Tom, by the way, as I seem to be the only civilian around here. I will ensure that we relay this conversation to the governor. Our most immediate concern, however, is that the tensions that might be apparent within Belmarsh will obviously be replicated across the wider community. We can lock Belmarsh down. We can't lock the rest of the country down."

"That's not strictly true, Tom," Lakin interjected. "While I am not suggesting you do so at this stage, you do have the power under the 2019 Homeland Security Act to impose regional curfews."

"And just imagine how that would be interpreted and portrayed by IBIS," Mellor scoffed. "I am sure we can all read the headlines now. *Peaceful Muslims Persecuted... Islamic Round Up... Return of the Ghettoes...* A PR nightmare for the government and a propaganda coup for IBIS. They could not have engineered a better outcome themselves."

Just as Lakin was about to agree, his own phone buzzed in his pocket. He knew that the call would be of the highest importance as he had blocked all but three callers from his device for the duration of the meeting. When he saw the anguished face of Brian Chambers before him he accepted the call without even excusing himself.

"Boss," Chambers almost choked. "Blackburn Constabulary have called. Farah Karim has been abducted."

23

Farah was awakened by a series of harsh slaps to the side of her face. Some of the impact had been dampened by the heavy cotton of the black hijab that covered most of her head and much of her face. A strong jet of water from a portable jet wash sprayed directly into her eyes, nose and mouth ensured that her senses quickly became focussed on the terrifying sight in front of her.

She was shrouded in a black burqa and bound to a heavy wooden chair. Her hands were laid flat upon the table in front of her and secured by two metal semi-circular clasps, fixed to the surface. Farah noted the reddish brown stains ingrained into the table and even before she saw the long heavy hunting knife at its far edge; she immediately recognised them as blood.

These, and two other chairs at the other side of the table were the only items of furniture in the cold, dark damp cellar in which she was encased. There were no windows, one door, slightly ajar at the top of eight concrete steps. She quickly deduced from the old pipes on the walls and barrels on the floor that this was an old pub cellar. There were hundreds of old pubs in the Blackburn area where alcohol consumption had largely been driven underground.

154

Two tripods pointed towards her from the opposite corners of the table. One supported a small video camera, the other a bright arc light. Standing alongside each tripod, as though in some bizarre ritual parade, were tall figures dressed in dark blue boiler suits and black woollen balaclavas concealing all but their cruel, dark eyes. This was a scene that she recalled all too well from numerous terrorist abductions she'd had the misfortune to investigate. Few had ended well.

The man opposite and to the right of her spoke. "We have your videophone and we need to know the passcode. We also need to know the contact details for your head of department which we are sure will be in the memory."

The second man waited for ten seconds for a reply before directing the jet wash one metre from her face and unleashing a torrent of cold, stinging needles towards her mouth and nose. What felt to Farah like thirty seconds, was actually less than ten but she had choked repeatedly from the blast and her eyes seemed to have been forced to the back of her forehead.

"The sooner you tell us, the sooner we make contact and the sooner you leave here. We have your warrant card so we could easily get what we need to know online, but it will be much quicker and easier for you if you tell us." The first man had spoken calmly in a slightly accented voice and a sinister, unnerving tone.

Farah knew this to be the case and was only surprised that they had not yet been able to bypass the crude phone security and access her system themselves. "My access code is 436986 and my line manager is Detective Chief Inspector Lakin," she spluttered. "He is in the contact list as DCI LAKIN."

As the first man nodded towards the video tripod his accomplice carefully moved it away and replaced it with one of the chairs. The first abductor settled into the chair and scrolled through Farah's now unblocked videophone. Although it was department issue, the make and model was widely available so the kidnapper was able to find Lakin's details easily.

The second man, who had yet to speak, had now positioned himself at Farah's right hand shoulder after switching the spotlight directly into her face. They all seemed slightly surprised at how quickly the connection was made when Lakin's face appeared and Farah heard his amplified digital voice on loudspeaker. "Inspector Karim, are you hurt?"

Her abductor remained perfectly calm as he turned the screen towards Farah and projected her image to Lakin. "As you can see, she is alive and will remain so just as long as you meet our demands. Three of our brothers have come to harm in one of your institutions and we now fear for the well-being of others. When I give you their names, you will persuade your superiors to have them released and in forty-eight hours from now, on Friday at 5 p.m., they will be delivered to a venue in the north of England and exchanged for your whore of an inspector. Forty-eight hours is enough time to have a release order signed by the Home Office and if more time were requested, it would indicate to us that their release would never be approved. At that point we will commence the return of your inspector to you in stages such as this…"

The silent accomplice swiftly drew a pair of secateurs from his boiler suit pocket, grabbed Farah's left hand, lifting it harshly from the table and snipped off the top of the little finger, just above the knuckle. The caller allowed Farah to scream, then sob for twenty seconds or more before indicating to his accomplice to gag her. She then writhed in agony amidst the muffled obscenities mouthed beneath her muzzle. He then spoke slowly and chillingly into Lakin's stunned face. "I will contact you again in exactly one hour with my demands. Have someone with you who can authorise the release." The phone screen went blank.

Lakin had stood in the corner of the commissioner's office during this brief exchange so that Pollard and Mellor could witness the video call but the terrorists could not see them. Stunned, bewildered and visibly upset, Lakin turned towards the commissioner with a look that needed no spoken word. Pollard looked back at him firmly and declared:

"We don't do deals with terrorists."

Lakin regained enough of his composure to suppress his instinct to plead and somehow, calmly replied. "But neither do we sacrifice senior police officers, sir. Somehow, this all links back to the bombings and our best hope of getting to the bomber could now be through Inspector Karim. If we appear to go along with them, we may have a chance of cracking this. If we reject the proposal out of hand, a police officer dies and the trail goes cold."

"Firstly, Sean, there is absolutely no evidence that this has anything to do with the London bombings. Your officer was in Blackburn on a fishing trip when three Islamists were murdered in one of our prisons. One of them had family connections in Blackburn." The commissioner held up his hand to prevent Lakin's intervention. "Secondly, how and why could the prison murders be linked to the bombings when Abadi was only remanded on assault charges? And thirdly, there have been eight abductions and eight beheadings in Britain in the past seven years, and we have yet to catch the evil bastards responsible for any of them."

"So this is our chance, sir," Sean pleaded. "I totally agree that we should not be seen to do deals with terrorists but if both sides agree to keep this under the radar as a condition of trade, we give ourselves the chance of getting to them before, during or even after any possible exchange. Those bastards don't know the meaning of the word honour. I suggest we convince them that we are ready to do the deal and grab them. Render them if required, but even if they aren't behind the bombings, we will learn a lot about other events... past, present and future. In the meantime, by all means, have the Blackburn police chase down the local connection to the dead guy."

Tom Mellor was still online and watching this exchange through the screen on his office wall. Pollard and Lakin seemed oblivious to his presence and both turned to the screen in surprise when he interjected.

"He might be right you know, Nigel. There is no rule that says we have to play by the rules and perhaps it's time that we raised the stakes a little by stepping down to their plate, if you'll excuse the scrambled metaphors. Let's at least hear what their demands are before we rule the possibility out of hand."

The commissioner pondered the possibility before conceding,

"Mr Mellor, Tom… this matter is just as far out of my jurisdiction as is Belmarsh but I am now involved and I have to express an opinion. This is not how we do things in this country but perhaps it is time to adopt a different approach. For what it's worth, however, I would add one absolute caveat. If the video of Inspector Karim in their hands is released to the public, there can be no question of a prisoner exchange, even a bogus one. We would have to meet the challenge head on and face the consequences."

Lakin jumped in before Mellor had the chance to reply. "But we both know that those consequences would be *head off*, sir! They would not think twice about hacking her head off and pissing into her neck! I agree that we force them to keep the negotiation quiet but in this case, we do whatever we need to do and justify our actions later. The Geneva Convention does not apply to the war on terror, sir," he added respectfully.

The commissioner turned to Mellor. "Karim is Lakin's officer, Lakin is one of mine but ultimately, Tom, this has to be a call between the Home Office and Number 10. May I respectfully suggest that you test the water in Whitehall while Sean and I wait for the call?"

"I will be back to you within the half hour," said Mellor confidently and the screen went grey.

There followed a very awkward and uneasy silence between the two senior police officers. The commissioner understood that Lakin would do everything in his power to ensure the safety of his inspector and Lakin knew that the commissioner could not be seen to sanction any suggestion of a deal with terrorists, even a bogus one. Britain had been torn apart by terrorism for over a century at the hands of Irish terrorists on both sides of the religious and political divide, and Tony Blair's capitulation in the Good Friday agreement was supposed to have been the end of it. There had been a period of relative peace, in Britain, if not abroad, until the London bombings of 2005, committed by British Muslims in protest against the country's invasion of Iraq. Since then, there had been regular, sporadic outbursts of terrorism, abductions and beheadings in the name of Jihad and in support of the virtually continuous war against Islamic State since its emergence in 2012, in the wake of the Western induced Arab Dawn. The new political landscape had now brought its own new challenges.

Commissioner Pollard broke the silence. "You have to prepare yourself Sean. The Home Secretary will not allow this. Your best hope is to work with the local team in Blackburn and rely on traditional police work."

"With respect, sir, you said it yourself. Eight previous abductions with refusals to engage ended with eight brutal executions. We wouldn't be looking for a needle in a haystack, we would be looking for the eye of the needle in the whole farmyard. The population will clam up. IBIS will make an disingenuous appeal for her safe return while drafting their demands on the other side of the page. They have elevated the abuse of our tolerance to an art form. Our failure to retaliate is not seen as civilised moderation, it is seen as stupid, illogical weakness. We cannot continue to combat Eastern savagery with Western idealism. We need to hit back and…"

It was probably good timing for Lakin that the screen alert stopped him from saying something he would inevitably regret, as both men spun round to the image of Mellor beaming down upon them. He spoke solemnly but boldly.

"I have just concluded a conference call with the Home Secretary, Foreign Secretary, Defence Minister and Prime Minister. Clive Mountstevens is vehemently opposed to any negotiation, as is the Defence Minister. Robert Brockington would support a covert, unofficial intervention so Graeme had the casting vote. He is equally uncomfortable but recognises that the time might have come to try a different approach. He will privately support a covert operation but if it goes wrong and we are publicly embarrassed there will have to be a scapegoat. I think you can guess who that might have to be Sean?"

Lakin juggled the contrasting emotions that fought for the tip of his tongue and he simply replied, "It wouldn't be the first time my balls have been on the chopping board, but if we are going to do this, I am going to need your help M. Mellor."

The commissioner nodded towards Lakin, then to the screen, shrugged and left the room as though to indicate that he had just witnessed a conversation that had not happened.

24

Farah was grimacing and possibly sobbing inside but determined not to let her emotions suggest weakness in the eyes of the inhuman savages that seemed to delight in her torture and torment. The initial pain from her finger was agonising but she was not expecting the second, even more excruciating trauma as the smaller of the two captors pressed an old hair straightening device against her finger stub, perhaps as a crude attempt to cauterise the wound, but more probably as a method of taking Farah's pain to a whole new level. She sat, gently rocking in her seat, unable even to massage her half finger with her shackled left hand. She knew that she was in shock; she knew that her adrenaline was helping to control the pain but wondered how much worse it was due to become and what further agonies they planned to inflict upon her.

Though she completely understood her perilous predicament Farah told herself that resignation, submission or self-pity were not options. She had to remain focussed and she had to remain positive, if only to divert attention from her throbbing wound. She focussed on the positives: she was alive, they had snipped her little finger rather than a full one or worse. They had kept their balaclavas on to mask their faces even after the conference call; they would not try to protect their identities if they were planning to kill her. Ava was in France so she will not be aware of her mother's absence and therefore neither need worry... yet. Sean is aware of the situation and she was confident that he would do everything within his power, authorised or unauthorised to get her away from these savages and she knew how persuasive he could be. She was in a bad place, she concluded but she had rescued people from worse ones.

Next she turned her thoughts to her captors. They looked sinister in their dark blue boiler suits and balaclavas. She could not allow herself to be intimidated by their dress so she reverted to her psychology lectures and focussed on how power, and the perception of power, could be shifted by positive thought. She could not continue to view them as superior. They could not be allowed to retain their all-powerful personae. She had to bring them down; to belittle them, to undermine them, to disrespect them. Farah repositioned their boiler suits as ridiculous romper suits and their balaclavas as children's wrestling masks. She thought of their faces beneath the masks and saw Laurel and Hardy; two bumbling hapless lackeys incapable of original thought. She christened the bigger one Laurel and the smaller one Hardy and already they had become marginally less fearsome. She then imagined them alone in a room, unarmed, with Sean Lakin, and they now appeared positively vulnerable. She almost pitied them.

Hardy had pressed a cotton wool swab over her finger stub and secured it with a crudely wrapped bandage. He also positioned a small bottle of mineral water in front of her with a straw protruding from it to allow her to sip and lubricate her mouth and throat. No words were exchanged. No apologies, no thanks.

Her captors seemed worryingly calm. They showed no signs of agitation, no panic and no impatience. They communicated to each other calmly and quietly in a language that Farah would not have been able to decipher even if they had spoken loudly enough to be heard. They sat together in the corner of the room, facing her and she occasionally caught a reflective glimmer as their eyes turned towards her. She thought about engaging them in conversation but quickly decided that at this stage, some three hours into her ordeal, there would be no benefit in doing so and she could be inviting further brutality. She waited, wondering where she was and tried to recall the moments before, during and after the chloroform cloth drained her consciousness. She knew that she was asleep during the journey but tried to remember whether she had dreamed and whether her sleeping images had been subconscious insights, images or sounds. She remembered nothing but the slaps and the spray that awoke her.

The conversation in the corner became slightly more animated and it seemed clear that they were preparing for the next phase of her ordeal as Laurel nodded to Hardy and motioned towards a black rucksack from which he drew a long, black hunting knife with a black handle and a twelve inch long, gleaming serrated edge. He held the knife by his side as he positioned himself alongside and to the left of Farah. Laurel switched on the arc light and positioned it towards Farah's face. Unable to shield her eyes from its piercing beam she clamped them shut and turned her neck as far as she could to her right, unaware of the inviting expanse of flesh that she had exposed to Hardy and his gleaming blade.

Laurel spoke in perfect English, with more than a hint of the dialect that one might associate with the former Lancastrian mill town.

"We are going to make a brief film to send to your superiors to encourage them to speak favourably with us. You will hear me threaten you and you need to know that if our demands are not met, my threats become promises and my promises become reality. Speak only when I tell you to and say only that you have suffered no further harm but you fear that further amputations will be commensurate with any procrastination on the part of your colleagues."

He set the digital recorder in motion and positioned himself at Farah's right shoulder. He spoke clearly and calmly into the screen with none of the fanatical hyperbole that used to accompany the archetypal textbook Jihadist ransom demands of the early 2010s.

"By the time you receive this link, exactly one hour will have passed since you last saw your whore. By now, you should be in the presence of someone of authority with the will to save your agent's life. If your government chooses not to do so, the people of Britain will be given an open invitation to a public beheading. You will need a period of time to comply with my demands and so there is a forty-eight hour stay of execution, during which we will communicate regularly, promptly and clearly. For every incident of procrastination or duplicity on your part, this woman will lose another part of her body. If our demands are not met within forty-eight hours, her head will be removed. She will now confirm to you that she has suffered no further harm." He touched Farah's shoulder to prompt her statement.

"I have not been harmed further but I know that I will be, as they have indicated, if their demands are not heeded." She chose her words carefully using heeded rather than met. It may have been an insignificant semantic gesture but to Farah it was her own show of defiance. Laurel and Hardy suddenly didn't seem quite harmless again but she fought back against those thoughts.

The kidnapper spoke again. "There are a large number of our brothers in your Belmarsh Detention Centre and they are clearly unsafe in your hands. We seek to rescue four of them before they are murdered and in return, you will receive your agent, alive." Her captor was also playing with words, knowing that *agent* would be far more provocative than *officer*. "These are the names of the prisoners you will release: Mehmet Hussain, Ibrahim Bengasi, Mohammed Sayed and Abdallah Afzal. They will be back with us by the weekend. You have exactly one hour to discuss my demands with your leader. You will then activate the link at the end of this message and we will video conference. I will then give you details of the exchange procedure. If contact has not been made by 7.30 p.m., we will remove one finger every five minutes. When her fingers are gone we start on the toes."

He strode slowly to the recorder and switched it off. He expertly downloaded the recording on to a USB device and transferred this to a secure laptop. Using a scrambled and untraceable GPRS network he sent the message and internet link to Sean Lakin's mobile device. He then sat back and waited. Beneath his balaclava he was grinning widely, looking forward to whatever the outcome was to be.

25

Tom Mellor had taken the short trip from his makeshift Whitehall office to Scotland Yard and was locked in a very private and very serious discussion with Sean Lakin in conference room B. The conference room was situated in the heart of the building and brightly lit to compensate for the absence of natural light. It was soundproof and automatically swept every three minutes for hostile listening signals from the high penetration, ultra sound, and alien satellites known to be aimed at such sensitive facilities. Within this room, all communications were totally secure and although images and sounds were transmitted electronically, they passed through a series of gateways and filters that prohibited the communication to be downloaded and saved onto the recipient's device. If an external source tried to capture the sounds or images, they would simply record white noise.

As soon as Lakin's phone vibrated on the boardroom-style table, he grasped it and hurriedly viewed the message. He keyed a code into his device, a corresponding code into the conference room control deck and the wall sprang to life. Lakin stood quietly, clenching his fists, gritting his teeth and swallowing back the bile as he watched an officer he greatly admired and a beautiful woman he loved, degraded and abused by two cold, clinical and cynical thugs. The message was short, brutally blunt and not even the sound of Farah's proud voice could permeate the cloak of despair that enshrouded Sean Lakin. There was no possibility of the authorities sanctioning this. Not even the maverick with whom he now shared the room. Mellor sensed his mood and quickly broke the silence. "Right. We'd better get moving if we're going to get her back by the weekend."

"Can we really do this?" questioned Lakin, almost in disbelief.

"The Prime Minister and Home Secretary have entrusted me with this matter. The Prime Minister, I presume, because he wants me to succeed; the Home Secretary because, no doubt, he wants me to fail spectacularly and get me off his back for good. I have no intention of obliging the bloated toad so readily."

"Exactly what authority and resource do you have, Tom?"

"Listen to me carefully, Sean. I was put into this role because the challenges we face domestically and internationally are unlike any that we have ever faced in our history. Conventional intelligence, diplomacy, strategy and policing, with respect, are useless against forces that have no regard for human life; especially their own; and we are even facing enemies who, possibly only months ago, were our own loyal British citizens. I'm not 007. I don't have a licence to kill but I am trusted and empowered to push the boundaries. Not everybody thinks the way that I do. Your own boss disagrees with me but I hope you are not going to let that stand in our way?"

"The commissioner is not a policeman, he's a politician and, *with respect*, I am not in the habit of letting politicians stand in my way. I will do anything... and I mean anything, to get my officer back."

"That's what I thought you might say, Sean. Let's be clear though. We are both putting our careers, and probably your balls, on the block here. You will need to trust me and my circle of like-minded ministerial and military colleagues implicitly."

"That goes without saying, Tom, but I still have a team to lead and they will be right behind me."

"If we can use them, I am sure they will be, but for the time being, I suggest you hand current day-to-day issues over to your number two. You are likely to be pretty occupied for the next couple of days. This is how I am expecting it to pan out..."

Mellor and Lakin spent the next fifteen minutes hypothesising, plotting, double guessing, speculating and rehearsing for one of the most crucial conversations that either man would ever engage in. They began by bringing in one of the division's most trusted technology geeks, though they suspected that tracking the kidnapper's internet location would be a hopeless and futile task. They were not wrong but vowed to try again during the planned live interface that was about to begin. They had agreed that Lakin was to be the only face that the kidnappers saw and that he would assume complete authority over the negotiation unless tactically, he decided that the need to defer to higher authority might be a valid ploy. This was to be a card they must use sparsely as they agreed that this would immediately diminish his credibility and jeopardise the process. He hit the keys, activated the ether and opened the connection. The screen opened into a dark room with Farah still tied to the chair flanked by her two abductors. The taller one spoke first: "You are punctual, Superintendent Lakin, this is a good sign."

Lakin did not seem perturbed that his rank and identity was known. Both were accessible to anyone with access to a laptop and an inclination to understand Metropolitan Police procedure.

"You have me at a disadvantage," replied Lakin. "You know my name. If we are to be communicating as closely as I believe we will be, I need to know what to call you."

"I have a number of very significant advantages over you, Superintendent, and identity is the least significant of them. If it helps you, you may address me as Tariq and my colleague as Haq. Quite appropriate don't you think? Please do not use this new found familiarity to try to indulge in pleasantries. We each should have only one purpose in this conversation."

Lakin could feel the goose pimples on his flesh rise and harden at the tone of Tariq's voice and the arrogance of his vocabulary. If anything, his utter contempt for this individual actually helped him to remain calm and focussed.

"I am empowered to negotiate the exchange of my officer for our prisoners and I am happy to proceed as soon as possible." He stated.

"Firstly, Superintendent," retorted Tariq, "This is not a negotiation. I am not stating demands, I am issuing instructions. Secondly, your happiness, or otherwise, is immaterial to me. We will proceed at my pace. Do you understand me?"

"Yes, I understand you Tariq, and while I have no desire to negotiate with you, I do have some conditions of my own that will need to be observed."

Tariq turned to Haq and nodded to him once. Haq removed the secateurs from his pocket and prised Farah's right hand from the table. Farah's scream was possibly the most horrific sound that Lakin had ever heard and the terror blazed from her eyes as the blades hovered over her hand.

"You clearly did not understand me, Superintendent. We must try harder to help you."

"Wait! I am not trying to antagonise you and I am totally committed to making this exchange happen but, unlike you, I am answerable to a higher authority." Lakin played to his adversary's sense of superiority.

"I am answerable to Allah; you will be answerable to this woman."

"If another hair on that woman's body is harmed, I will not be permitted to continue with the exchange. That is the first of the conditions that my government has imposed upon me." reasoned Lakin.

"The first? You dare insult me by suggesting that there are more?" Tariq's cool demeanour was suddenly turning and Lakin

169

needed to interpret whether this was rage or concern that he was detecting.

Lakin tried to calm the situation by responding in a quiet, measured tone. "Nothing more than you would expect, Tariq. First, the police inspector suffers no further physical harm. Secondly, her capture and the planned prisoner exchange is kept absolutely confidential. No reporting, no leaked videos and no triumphal parading of the returned prisoners or your hostage."

Tariq seemed to be surprised at the relative modesty of the demands. "You are not a foolish man, Superintendent, so you must realise that I am holding all of the cards in this game and even if I agree to your conditions, we can broadcast anything we like once our prisoners are returned to us."

"You are holding a police officer, Tariq, but as you know, the British Government can be remarkably dispassionate in its care of service personnel. As you have already pointed out, a number of your comrades are currently incarcerated in our prisons and while I am sure that the authorities are doing everything they can to ensure their safety, racial tension is high and resources are stretched. If the kidnapping or murder of a police officer were brought to the attention of prison officers, who knows how they might react?"

"I warn you, Superintendent, do not threaten me!" Tariq's voice was now wavering, but was it fear or fury Lakin wondered.

"This is not a threat, Tariq. I want to make this exchange without any further harm to inmates or friends and relatives in your own community and I am sure that you would not wish to be held responsible for any new uprisings... before, or after we have concluded our business. Tell me where and when you want this to happen and I will get into action immediately. I will, however need to see regular evidence that no more harm comes to our officer."

"Your conditions are acceptable to me." Tariq was doing his best to retain face though he now knew that the cards he was holding were not quite as strong as Lakin's hand. He and his colleagues had never really understood why their enemies had always been so protective of those prisoners that had been so stupid, careless or unfortunate to have fallen into infidel hands. Perhaps the authorities were now wising up to the new rules of war. In Tariq's book, the first rule of war is that there are no rules and if his opposite number was now thinking the same way, he might just need to give more consideration to the fate of his captured fellow Jihadists. Still, he thought, this would not be the first time that single queen had beaten a pair of aces. "You will have the prisoners released and have a helicopter, with at least eight seats, available to deliver them to a location in the north-west of England within forty-eight hours. You will hear from me again at two o' clock tomorrow when you will assure me that my instructions are being followed."

"I shall look forward to speaking with you, and to my officer." Lakin added.

The screen went black. Lakin sat down, held his head in his hands and breathed out deeply. He was surprised to feel the cold sticky sweat transferring from face to fingers. Superintendent Sean Lakin was a tough, smart and experienced policeman but he had never been deployed as a hostage negotiator and had never been called upon to save the life of a woman he loved.

Tom Mellor stepped from the shadows.

"You did well, Sean. You did very well indeed. Just the right balance of deference and defiance. Their type do not respect compliance. They detest weakness. They will not take you for granted."

"Can we deliver, Tom? Can we spring the prisoners? Can we get the helicopter? Can we make the trade?"

"Do you mean, *can* we, Sean, or are you really asking *should* we?"

"Both, I guess." Sean was clearly struggling with that question and found himself wondering how he would respond if the hostage had been a Blackburn police constable.

"Desperate times demand desperate measures, Sean. There is no rule book in play here and if there is, we will rewrite it. How do you fancy being a co-author?"

"Right now Tom, I think I would rather be a writer than a copper but I will do anything to get that woman back safely."

"Right then. You need to get back to your team and take care of the other lines of investigation. Make absolutely sure that nobody says a word about your officer's abduction. We have already put a gag on Blackburn. I will handle the prison authorities and the transportation. There are one or two of my old service colleagues who would be very happy to take the controls of that chopper and my old regiment would be delighted to lend me a sniper. I will call you tomorrow to pull all this together."

They shook hands and Mellor walked briskly from the conference room. Lakin could not help reflecting on how much Mellor seemed to be relishing his responsibilities and just hoped that this was not just a game to him and an opportunity to revisit unfinished adventures and unattained glory.

26

Richard Collins was one of Mehmet Osman's least used identities but the United States passport always seemed to impress European border staff. His English-American accent was strong enough not to attract suspicion. His ability to lighten his Mediterranean good looks with a simple melanin reduction agent, his hair with some liberal grey streaking, his eyes with blue tinted contacts and his cheeks with some uncomfortable but surprisingly pleasant face putty, would have fooled all but the most sensitive facial recognition technology. As it happened, he need not have worried because cruise line immigration staff were amongst the least robust of any major international transport mode and he and his lovely wife Christina had been ushered on board in record time the previous afternoon, only to endure the obligatory but ridiculously orchestrated safety drill just one hour later. Safety drills used to be something of a rite of passage for virgin cruisers, thrilled by the sense of peril but equally certain that there was no danger of such a vessel going down. That all changed in 2012 when the *Costa Concordia* was sunk off the shore of Italy by an arrogant oaf of a captain, showboating to his relatives on the nearby coastline and desperately trying to

173

impress his teenage girlfriend and member of the ship's dance company.

Since then, safety drills have been undertaken more rigorously, but most attendees still showed the same degree of interest and enthusiasm that they probably showed on the aeroplane that flew them there as the waitresses went through the motions of explaining how they should behave in the event of a crash that they all knew would kill them. Seasoned cruisers would lie on their sunbeds until the very last beep of the seven tone alarm before nonchalantly and grudgingly trudging to their muster points, making it perfectly obvious that they did not need to be there as they were more familiar with the lifeboat drill that the fifteen-year-old Indonesian stewards to whom their safety had been entrusted. There were relatively few casualties on the *Concordia* but maritime experts reflected upon the fact that had the event happened further out at sea, the casualty count would, undoubtedly, have been higher. Others frequently speculated on the fact that cruise liners, with upward of six thousand passengers and crew on board, might make a compelling and attractive target for a terrorist attack. Richard and Christina had also considered the possibility.

Mehmet tended to rotate his identities so frequently that he found it helpful to use combinations of previously used given names and surnames; Colin Richards, Richard Collins and recently, in Italy, Ricardo Colino. Today, he blended comfortably with his fellow cruisers as he sat out on deck, eyes glued to his tablet although unlike them, he was not *reading* a thriller, he was plotting one. He had studied every one of the ports of call and was carefully considering his numerous options for disembarkation and onward travel. It seemed such a shame that he and his allocated bride would not be able to enjoy the full, twelve night voyage that his fellow passengers had paid handsomely for. Not only was cruising the most luxurious and relaxing form of travel, it was also the safest. Mehmet made a mental note to take another one someday under less demanding circumstances. For now though, he lay in the sun, sipping his double espresso while drawing gently on, and savouring the mild vanilla aroma of his filtered Café Crème cigar. Life was good.

His wife for the week had signed up for the galley tour to discover how a brigade of chefs laboured twenty hours a day to provide far more food than even the greediest sloths on this floating calorie factory could consume. Her fellow curiosity seekers gasped in awe at the sight of the four thousand lobsters thawing on stainless steel preparation tables and were thrilled by the thought of the hundred thousand eggs to be consumed on the cruise, lying end to end and stretching the perimeter of every deck of the ship. Christina feigned interest but, in reality, was totally engrossed in the conversation she had struck up with the ship's provisions master, but then he was a very close friend of her cousin in her other life in Libya and this meeting had been meticulously planned for months.

As provisions master, Abdul-Aziz had pretty much total control of the procurement, logistics and storage of all food and beverages, and their containers, loaded and unloaded at the various ports along the voyage. This was a position of responsibility and on shore, would have commanded a much higher salary than the four thousand US dollars per month paid by the cruise line. With such unique access to products moving on and off the ship, without the intense scrutiny of customs and gangway security, his potential for supplementary earnings was frequently exploited and Abdul was much in demand. He politely and discreetly assured his client that everything was in order and her very specific instructions and requirements would be completed in full within the next three days. Until then, he advised, she should just lie back, relax and enjoy the cruise.

This was a completely alien concept to the young woman. Where she came from, ships were for the transportation of food, oil, weapons and ammunition. The sight of men and women aged from eighteen to eighty offering their almost naked bodies to the sun was an abomination. The food they consumed was abhorrent, the alcohol was evil and the sight of men and women, cavorting to music together in public would have been unbelievable had she not witnessed this with her own eyes. She could not lie back, she would not relax and enjoyment was the last thing she expected of this voyage.

27

Clive Mountstevens and Neil Faraday were rather surprised that the Prime Minister had kept the welfare services budget review in the diary but Mitchell was resolute in advising them that he had made the commitment to Jo Greenfield, his Work and Welfare Minister so it would be bad form to allow terrorists to dictate the parliamentary timetable. The debate was less than a week away and this inner sanctum of four needed to be fully aligned on the more controversial elements of the proposed policy. Pleasantries were exchanged and the two Conservatives and UKIP, Greenfield, were genuinely pleased and relieved to hear that Faraday's son was recovering well in hospital with no signs of permanent damage. Mountstevens was perhaps ill advised in asking whether Faraday had any part in Adnan Abadi's untimely departure from prison but Faraday simply declared his mixed feelings of delight that the taxpayers would be spared a costly trial but disappointment that he had not personally been there to witness or participate in the process.

Ms Greenfield was a relatively new Cabinet member although at the relatively tender age of thirty-three, nobody was surprised to see her around the cabinet table. An accomplished barrister, specialising in European employment law, her experience, outspoken stance on the folly of EU regulations and her tall, elegant stature crowned by perfectly coiffured, strawberry blond tresses marked her out as a favourite in both government and the media. Her single status was more a reflection of her daunting demeanour than her obvious glamour, upon which no one would ever dare to comment; openly at least.

She sought to include three radical proposals within the welfare bill and was aware that her first battle would be to gain approval within this room before meeting the anticipated hostility of the house. This would be the third presentation of her plans and she hoped that the enforced dilution of the reforms would now gain approval to be presented to the wider Cabinet, especially as more pressing matters might be distracting her peer group. Her first proposal was the obligatory placement of dependent single mothers within parenting complexes. For far too long, she had argued, irresponsible young women, or increasingly frequently, irresponsible young girls, had deliberately become pregnant to avoid the more rigid demands of the workfare programme, and to secure housing and financial benefits. More so, the quality of accommodation and level of benefits rose proportionally with the number of offspring generated, thereby fuelling an unsustainable rise in population. This sector of the population was consuming the great majority of the social housing that the government had fought so hard to secure over the past ten years. Baby farming had now become a top three issue for the electorate, overtaking the concerns on European immigration which had slowed to a trickle since Britain's departure from the union.

Greenfield's bill, she contended, was straight forward, fair and effective. Any single female parent with no sustainable means of support would be given three options: They would have three months to produce a legally binding declaration that a partner, relative or friend would finance the upkeep of the child and provide adequate proof that the provider had the means to do so.

Failure to do so would default to one of the remaining two options. Firstly, the child would be removed and offered into fast track adoption to the long list of childless couples throughout the England and Wales. The streamlined process would see the child rehoused within six weeks to pre-approved parents, with no rights of declaration to the original parent. The second option would be the placement of the parent and child, or children within a purpose-built hostel community in which similarly placed single parent families would be required to live together and work together to raise their children. They would receive no financial benefits but would be entitled to weekly food rations. Utilities and essential services would be paid by the authorities and the individual mothers might be able to earn treats for performing services beyond their required roster duties. The hostels would be supervised by parenting specialists who would oversee childcare and ensure discipline within the facility.

The hostels themselves would be built or converted by unemployed males, with an emphasis on enforced labour resource directed towards the named absentee fathers. Redundant mills or factories and other brownfield sites would provide the basic structures. The cost of building and maintaining these centres would be recovered within two years by the cessation of housing, child maintenance and unemployment benefits. Ms. Greenfield had deliberately presented this proposal first as she considered it to be the least contentious of her radical reforms. Her assessment and confidence were well founded.

The only resistance came from Faraday who still favoured his own proposal of chemically induced reversible sterilisation for all fourteen year old girls, who could then apply for the process to be reversed from twenty years onwards with the granting of a carefully vetted parenting licence. Reluctantly, he accepted that the religious and administrative issues surrounding this measure would delay its potential implementation for years. More importantly, he had been advised, privately, that King William and Queen Catherine would vehemently oppose this measure so he gave a grudging nod to the hostels.

The second measure related to unemployment benefits. Although unemployment levels had reduced dramatically since the exit from the EU and the reduced levels of immigration, there were still issues to address. There was still a reluctance on the part of many so called indigenous British people to take jobs in the service industries and public sector that hitherto, had attracted immigrant workers. A bill had been in force for three years now, enabling the withdrawal of benefits from anyone unwilling to accept such work, or deliberately getting themselves dismissed. There were, however, still quite a large number of unemployed men and women who could not be placed in such roles and Ms Greenfield was now proposing that working families could apply to have a state supported unemployed person allocated to them to help with childcare, care for elderly relatives, gardening, decorating and car washing. The service would be free of charge but the recipient family would be responsible for supervising the quality of work undertaken and submitting weekly reports to trigger benefit payments. A number of challenges were raised to test the credibility of the bill but none were considered to be insurmountable and in any case, the Labour and Liberal Alliance opposition would be easily out voted.

The third proposal was, undoubtedly, the most sensitive and politically explosive. There were understood to be over three million disenfranchised Scots who had voted to remain within the United Kingdom in the 2018 referendum. Unfortunately for them, the English were also given a vote and the havoc that had been wreaked upon them by the mischievous Scottish National Party abusing their power in Westminster had caused most voters south of the border to vote, effectively, for Scotland's expulsion from the Union. Interestingly, the Scottish vote suggested that there were just under two million pro-unionists at the time of the vote but their numbers had now swelled by fifty per cent. Add to these, around one million Ulster citizens, anxious to leave the North of Ireland since its controversial unification by the majority Catholic Republic there were at least four million former British passports holders now demanding the right to be allowed entry to England. While this was not specifically a matter for the Work and Welfare Minister she was clearly concerned about the potential damage that legal or illegal immigration would have on the English and Welsh economy. She therefore sought to propose the establishment of a Celtic state within Wales with phased migration, subsidised by the Irish and Scottish Republics who would transfer the value of housing and unemployment benefits within their nations to fund the regeneration of North and South Wales. This was to be a forty-year plan for housebuilding and a commercial and industrial infrastructure to support the enlarged community.

The principle was compelling but the practicalities less so. Both Ireland and Scotland were financially fragile, and would both require a second bailout from the European community to help fund the migration. Both states might welcome the benefit of transferring their disgruntled and disenchanted former countrymen over the border and across the sea but EU support would, no doubt be conditional upon Ireland and Scotland relaxing their tighter immigration controls to allow EU migrants to fill the houses and jobs vacated in their lands.

While everyone around the table could see the long-term merits in such a proposal, Prime Minister Mitchell was quite adamant that to put this white paper to parliament at such a sensitive time might be an invitation for even greater turmoil and terrorist activity. Jo Greenfield feigned disappointment but secretly congratulated herself that two out of three wasn't bad and when she was Prime Minister, not too long from now, this proposal would definitely resurface.

Before closing the meeting, the Prime Minister asked the Home Secretary to update the room on the progress of the terrorist enquiries and uprisings within Belmarsh and IBIS communities. Ms Greenfield took it as a huge compliment that she was permitted to stay for this briefing though somewhat surprised that the Prime Minister seemed to be linking the three topics. They were, however, all within the jurisdiction of the Home Secretary so they might, in fact, be three separate briefings. It was quickly apparent that this did not seem to be the case.

Addressing the bombings first, Mountstevens advised that links had been identified with both blast sites in so much as three contracting companies had been deployed in both areas working on underground infrastructure projects from where the bombs were thought to have been sited. All the workers from each of the companies had been identified and interviewed with the exception of one. A Colin Richards, described as a freelance specialist metallurgist, who, despite a seemingly British name, was said to have spoken with quite exotically accented English. His security clearances required photographic identification and MI7 have run his image through all of the facial recognition software at border control. They got a hit on a gentleman called Faisal Alborz boarding a flight for Istanbul at around eight-thirty on Monday morning. All the intelligence agencies were now instructed to treat this as their highest priority.

Mountstevens moved on quickly to discuss the events at Belmarsh and did not risk his credibility by suggesting that the death of a suspect in the bombing at the hands of three high profile ISIS associates, might be a simple coincidence. The terrorist attacks had triggered right wing English parties to create disruption in IBIS strongholds. The death of the three ISIS convicts was thought to have prompted the sinister kidnapping of an inspector from Scotland Yard's Special Investigations Unit, after interviewing the leader of the Independent British Islamic State party. The Home Secretary advised that his Special Security Advisor, Tom Mellor, was personally coordinating the operation to secure the return of the hostage.

The police service and army reservists were on red alert. The possibility of further terrorist atrocities and riots in Muslim communities could not be discounted, even though there was still no evidence that Islamic forces were responsible. He qualified this statement by referencing the previous discussion regarding Scottish and Irish unionists and the possible involvement of a worker contracted to an Aberdeen engineering company.

Jo Greenfield was highly excited by the revelations from within this inner sanctum, though she did chuckle inwardly that they did make her discussion on gymslip mums seem rather tame by comparison.

28

Farah had not slept. Her hand throbbed, her back and neck ached from almost twenty-four hours bound to a bare metal chair in a cold damp dark cellar. She tried to remind herself that she was a strong, courageous, intelligent and resourceful police officer. She recalled the horrific experiences that she had witnessed as a young girl and resolved that she would not give these two amateur thugs in dungarees the satisfaction of seeing her beg for mercy. She knew that such weakness would simply multiply the degree of contempt in which she was held. She had been handled very roughly as they dragged her, blindfolded, into the cellar. They had kicked and punched her as they shrouded her in the moist, heavy black garb that she presumed the smaller of them had been wearing at the time of the abduction. They made it clear that her status as a female police officer was doubly offensive to them. She was not just a whore but a whore of the state and responsible for the oppression that their brothers were suffering here and abroad. She had steeled herself for interrogation but, thankfully, it hadn't happened... yet. She was party to the video conversation with Sean and was both hopeful and worried that he would be planning something independently as she was certain that the authorities would never give in to the demands of terrorists, especially within their own shores. She was gradually resigning herself to death and began to imagine how it would feel to have her throat ripped apart by a hunting knife. Would she choke on her own blood? Would she agonisingly bleed out? Would the slash sever her nervous system and close her down quickly and painlessly? She almost wished she had watched those hideous beheadings on websites so that she might have some idea what to expect and then she concluded that it was better not to know and to imagine the least horrific outcome. Her overriding thoughts were for Ava. She was immensely thankful that her daughter would be having the time of her life in France, blissfully unaware that she was unlikely to see her mother and only living relative again. She consoled herself with the fact that she believed that Sean would look after Ava as his own; if, that is, he wasn't killed in the process of trying to secure her release.

She was not stupid. She did not live in the optimistic false hope of a special services rescue operation. Somehow, she had to get her captors to unshackle her hands from the table. She could not just sit here totally defenceless. She thought of the numerous still photographs she had seen of beheading victims kneeling passively before their executors, waiting for the blade to strike. She vowed that she would not be so compliant. If she were able, she would go down fighting. They would not release her hands out of kindness, so she needed to find a compelling reason to motivate them to do so.

She had lost track of time and was beginning to fear that the next deadline might have passed and the dungaree twins would be back at any time to hack off more digits… or worse. She may have put on a very brave face externally but the large, loose black shroud hid a shivering, bruised, goose pimpled body and a terrified soul. Farah was shaken from her dark thoughts as the bolt on the cellar door was slid back and footsteps descended the stairs. She was encouraged to see only the smaller one, Laurel, emerge and rather than secateurs, he carried a bottle of water and a filled pitta bread parcel. It was as though she had subliminally connected with him as he placed the food and drink on the table and unshackled her damaged hand. She pleaded with him to release her other to allow her to massage it. Her captor lost all semblance of kindness as he spat. "Rub it between your legs, whore!"

Hunger protest was not an option. The gesture would have been wasted on them and she desperately needed water to smooth the rough dry nerve ends that she imagined were protruding from the lining of her throat after the involuntary screaming of the previous evening. She was also dehydrated to the point of deliria. Farah didn't think she would be able to eat as her whole body was consumed by fear. She convinced herself, however, that if she was to stand any chance of fighting her way out of this cellar she would need to build up her badly depleted reserves of energy.

Hardy, the one who called himself Tariq, came down the stairs and switched on the spotlight. She expected that this might be the prequel to another video amputation but he seemed satisfied that the blinding light in her face was terror enough for the moment.

"It seems that you are more valuable than we imagined," mused Tariq. "Your commander has agreed to our demands. Perhaps we asked for too little in return?"

Farah was surprised and relieved by the statement but more so by the fact that the boiler suits were still wearing their balaclavas. She was smart enough to understand that this could have been nothing more than a ploy to buy the services more time to engineer a rescue attempt but she had to hang on to every positive and milk it for all she was worth. "Thank you," she sobbed, almost sincerely, "could you now please release my hand so I eat properly and care for my injury?"

"Why not?" shrugged Tariq. "The feet remain secured. We are civilised me and you are not going anywhere." He nodded to his junior who reluctantly obliged.

***

Mellor and Lakin were working very discreetly and effectively together. The younger man was handling the hostage situation at the front line, organising the logistics and liaising with the captors, while the wily old warrior was oiling the wheels and securing the equipment and personnel to undertake the exchange. They had agreed that the number of people involved in this exercise would be kept to the absolute minimum if they were going to secure Farah's release and keep the integrity of the government intact. So far, Mellor had contacted the four people that he needed to satisfy his obligations and unsurprisingly all, eventually, agreed to his requests; some more willingly than others.

Sean had delegated day-to-day responsibility to Brian Chambers and Rosie Hunter. Rosie was secretly delighted with this, although she felt slightly guilty that her chance at the top job had come at the risk of Farah's freedom, or even her life. Brian Chambers was rather less relaxed and took personal umbrage in the fact that he was not joining Sean on the rescue mission; in fact Sean had not even discussed the details of the task but at least he had confirmed that it was happening. Chambers would be far more useful keeping a handle on things back at the Yard, especially since Rosie was already on her way to Scotland via Blackburn. The Virgin West Coast service stopped at Preston where a secure delegation would be waiting for DI Hunter. Lakin had made it absolutely clear to them that it was vital that news of Farah's capture did not leak beyond those four walls.

At precisely 2.00 p.m., Lakin's videophone pulsed. He activated the screen and was met by a pair of cold eyes peering out from a slit in the balaclava as Tariq spoke into the remote microphone.

"Confirm to me that everything is on schedule, Superintendent." The directness of the statement and stern tone of voice had been carefully chosen to intimidate.

Lakin was in no mood to be pushed around and did not dare to show any personal feelings for Farah. "How can I confirm that everything is on schedule when I have not yet been given a schedule to observe? I can confirm that we have a mandate to comply with your demands and so the sooner you tell me how you want this to happen, the sooner I can get down to detail. First though, I need to see and speak with my officer."

Tariq turned the phone towards Farah and in the dim light of the cellar, Sean could see Farah's face, still partly concealed by the primitive headwear bound upon her. She held her hand up to the camera. Nothing as trite as a wave but an indication that she was alive and that her hands were now free.

"Let me speak with her," demanded Lakin

"No." replied the captor. "She may speak to you but if you try to issue any coded instructions to her you will simply bring more suffering upon her. Her body may be in our hands but her well-being is, for now, in yours." Tariq walked to the table and passed the phone to Farah. "You speak, he listens." There was no particular reason for this condition other than the exertion of control. He remembered all the details of his training.

Farah realised just how long it had been since she had last spoken and was not sure whether the stutter she had developed was from lack of normal motor skills or her morbid fear.

"I am all right, sir. Cold, hungry and sore, but no further harm has come to me."

She wished she could have told him more but was conscious that she must act as his lieutenant and not his lover. In truth, she was neither cold nor hungry but felt that her captors would not wish her to sound too comfortable. She too had been well trained.

Tariq snatched the phone back. "And none will, just so long as your boss here delivers against his promises."

"And I have told you that we want the officer back but you need to understand that the release of your friends is a complex and sensitive issue. We need as much detail as possible now to enable us to comply with your wishes." Lakin almost choked on his subservient words but he, too, knew the role he needed to play. Reverence now, revenge later.

"Our four bothers will be released tomorrow at 2.30 p.m. They will be transported to the north-west of England in a commercial helicopter with eight seats, including the pilot. Two places will be taken by yourself and, I will allow you one armed guard. The seat beside the pilot will be vacant. You, personally, will film the loading of the prisoners into the helicopter and transmit the video message to me in real time. I need to see you climb into the helicopter with them and you will continue filming during take-off. Your phone will be fully charged and you will hand it to Mehmet Hussain. He will continue to transmit for the duration of the journey. Do not try to claim that this will interfere with the controls. It will not."

Lakin simply nodded. "Alright so far." The armed guard concession threw him slightly as this would have been one of his demands. He would now have to think of another to balance the negotiation.

Tariq continued as if he were a call centre advisor offering technical advice to reboot a computer. "You will fly directly to Barton Aerodrome, eight miles north-west of Manchester where you will set down and refuel the aircraft. There you will be met by our own co-pilot. He will sit beside your pilot and issue the instructions for the short, final part of the journey. When you land, your guard may stay with the prisoners and two pilots. You will walk to where we will be waiting with your officer. Haq will have a gun to her head as I presume your guard will have his gun on the hostages inside the helicopter. I will cross to the aircraft and when I have confirmed that all is in order your guard will leave the helicopter and exchange places with Haq."

Lakin was running the scenario through his mind. "That

doesn't work Tariq. If Haq has a gun on me and my officer, what is to stop him shooting us both while my guard is walking back towards us?"

"I will be unarmed, Superintendent. If Haq were to shoot you and your officer, I would expect that your guard would be capable of killing me and his hostages. This is not a schoolyard game, Superintendent. These are not foxes and hens we are exchanging. We both have much to gain and much to lose."

Lakin had expected no less but had two further conditions: "My pilot crosses with my guard and we have access to whatever form of transport you used to arrive at the exchange point."

"That goes without saying, Superintendent."

"I would prefer that you said it anyway, Tariq." said Lakin, "I have always been a little anal about small details like that."

"So be it, Superintendent. Your pilot crosses with your guard. I will contact you at two-thirty tomorrow and you will be ready for take-off."

Lakin tried to hold the other man on the line a little longer. "I would prefer it if we could schedule another call to ensure that we have been able to get everything in place at our end."

"I am sure you would, Superintendent, but I have every confidence in you. Two-thirty tomorrow."

29

Governor David Thornton's world had been turned upside down over the past forty-eight hours. He had been regarded as one of the most successful and progressive leaders in the prison service, universally admired amongst his colleagues and clearly destined for a fast-track career progression in the civil service. Now it was all imploding and though his rational thoughts guided him to the conclusion that none of these events were attributable to him personally, he had been in the service long enough to know that mud sticks to a governor just as stubbornly as the stink of urine and vomit sticks to the walls of a cell. And his day was just about to get worse.

Even the ever faithful Naomi had seemed rather more distant today as she advised him that he was to expect a call from the Home Secretary himself at three o' clock. It was as though she, too, could smell the slightly unsavoury odour of failure emanating from his office and was already preparing herself to welcome his successor. It was very rare, if at all, that the Home Secretary would speak personally to a governor; the head of the prison service would have been the customary conduit. Thornton suspected that

191

the call would not be to commiserate on his recent run of bad luck. He was, however, surprised and confused by Mountstevens' tone when he took the call.

"It's a terrible business, Thornton. Of all the departments and services that fall within my remit there can be no doubt that you chaps get the shittiest end of a very shitty stick. To spend your whole lives sweeping human detritus from cell to cell, trying to prevent all manner of savages from ripping each other apart while having to pretend that you are expected to rehabilitate the pond life you get within your walls must be soul destroying."

"It can be quite challenging, Home Secretary, but we have to believe that we are serving some purpose here. Even if it's only to keep the rest of you safe while we do our best to control the worst of the worst that find their way into here."

"Quite so, Thornton, quite so, and that's why I am calling you today. It's complicated and I am not at liberty to share everything I know with you but the listeners at MI7 have picked up on a definite plot to create even more mayhem at Belmarsh. You will know better than I do, David, that you are sitting on a powder keg there and it is only the dedication and courage of you and your officers that has prevented this kind of bloodbath from happening more frequently. There is an extreme faction of the English Defence League who have connections, probably members, inside your institution and they have specifically targeted four of your inmates for execution within the next twenty-four hours. The exchanges suggest that even if there is a complete lock-down, there is still a way of getting at them, which might suggest some kind of collaboration with your guards. We will help you to get to the bottom of that in due course but the immediate priority is to get those four men out of there. We are told that there would be widespread civil unrest amongst the Muslim community if anything happens to another four of their folk heroes so soon after the last trio of terrorists was terminated. What do you know about Mehmet Hussain, Ibrahim Bengasi, Mohammed Sayed and Abdallah Afzal?"

"I obviously know why they are here, Home Secretary, but there has been nothing to suggest that they have been continuing their regime of terror on this side of the wall. Indeed, there was a suggestion that they might even be a steadying influence following the deaths of their erstwhile compatriots."

"Which is precisely why we suspect they have been targeted, David. There are some very sinister forces at work out there and we strongly believe that all this can be traced back to the Whitehall and Embankment bombs. If we can get them off your hands before anything happens to them, we might just be able to get something from them."

"I see," said Thornton, quickly seeing where this was leading. "So you want to get to them on the premise of saving them from the bad guys and telling them that the bad guys are their guys?"

"Something like that, David. As I said, it's complicated, but we need to get them out of there quickly. You need to prepare them for transfer to HMP Manchester tomorrow. They are to be moved at two hours' notice and we will be sending in a helicopter tomorrow at two o' clock to get them out of here."

"A helicopter? Surely you are not planning to land it inside the prison? That would cause a riot!"

"No, we want you to have the prisoners cuffed, hands and feet at the front gates by one forty-five and told that they are being transferred out of there for their own protection. The roads are too dangerous. In fact, we can't be sure whether the hit was planned to happen in here or whether they were double guessing us and planning to hijack the van."

"Or could they be triple guessing you and planning to bring down a chopper?" Thornton questioned, now warming to the intrigue.

"We can't really be sure of anything other than the need to get them out of there before their death reflects badly on Belmarsh… and you."

That comment stalled any further possibility of challenge from Thornton and he readily acquiesced to Mountstevens' supplementary suggestion. "It was also suggested that they are escorted by the officer that tried to save Abadi. They are more likely to trust him. Douglas, was it?"

"Yes, sir, Scott Douglas. I am sure he will be up for the task."

"Good man. Have him there with the prisoners at the gate tomorrow. He will be in good hands. One of our top SIU superintendents is supervising the transfer and we have drafted in a retired Special Services pilot to fly the helicopter. Your man, and your prisoners, will be in safe hands."

Mountstevens closed the connection and turned to Tom Mellor. He would have preferred to have rinsed his tongue with bleach and scraped it with a wire brush before continuing the conversation. The Home Secretary was a consummate politician but such lies did not trip easily from even his tongue. "I have squared it with the head of the prison service and, as you heard, Thornton is onside. You need to know though that I don't like setting either of them up like this."

"Listen, Clive," Mellor assured him. "This won't rebound on the prison service. It's high time the intelligence boys took one for the team."

Mellor had no such qualms in preparing Scott Douglas for his surprise meeting with the governor. The original plan had been to have him resign due to trauma and stress but Mellor recognised that this prisoner exchange was likely to be anything but straight forward and although Sean Lakin seemed an able copper, the skill, courage and resourcefulness of Scott Douglas made him rather more optimistic that this might just end well after all.

Scott Douglas had been brought to Mellor's attention five years ago when he was thirty-two. A bright grammar school boy from Stafford, he had ignored his parents' wishes to go to university and follow them into medicine. Instead, he had left school at the age of eighteen with A-levels in geography, history and IT. If his parents were disappointed by him snubbing a medical calling, they were positively distraught when he showed them his acceptance letter for the Royal Marines Commando induction programme. At five feet eight, straight black hair and a rounded, almost chubby face, he always looked more of a holiday camp entertainer than a trained killer and this innocuous, deceptive appearance had got him into, and out of, many scrapes during his formative years in the marines. He saw action right across the Middle East but served with particular distinction against the official IS forces in Syria and Libya.

Almost inevitably, after three years in the marines and having attained the rank of sergeant he was invited to Hereford to try out with the regiment there. He was readily accepted and his intense mental and physical training took him to another level. Although he still relished the physical confrontation, he became more intrigued by the challenge of more covert operations and his team executed four successful search and rescue missions in Iraq, saving British, French, American and Japanese hostages from certain brutal beheadings. A captain at only twenty-five, he had already been identified as someone that the intelligence services might want to look at later in life but as conventional warfare was gradually being replaced by airstrikes, drone attacks, long range bombardments and chemical warfare, Scott Douglas was persuaded to make the transition to MI6 rather sooner than even Mellor might have hoped.

Although Adnan Abadi had been recruited by, and still worked for the CIA, he had been seconded to the British intelligence services just over two years ago in a cross fertilisation exchange programme designed to support the theory that the 'relationship' was still 'special'.

The special relationship had, in fact, been ripped apart in 2016 by the publication in England of the 'Chilcott Report', a supposedly independent report investigating the events leading up to the British invasions of Iraq and Afghanistan. Publication of the report had been dragged out for almost a decade to allow former Prime Minister Blair sufficient time to cover his tracks, stash his cash and negotiate safe transit to whatever safe haven he should now have been basking in. Although this was a report into the British Parliament's actions, the United States would never forgive Britain for exposing the turgid and sycophantic conversations between Bush and Blair that totally discredited both leaders, and their nations.

While Britain and the United States still had a number of common interests and common enemies, successive US presidents had publicly stood shoulder to shoulder and slapped the backs of British Prime Ministers while privately tickling their tummies and patting their heads. Relations between the two nations took a notable nosedive in 2017 when one Donald Trump was elected president. In the run up to the election, when the then Prime Minister of the UK was asked to express her view on the two candidates she caused something of a diplomatic stir by declaring her immense relief that only one of them could be elected. Although Hilary Clinton had remained the bookmakers' favourite throughout the campaign, it finally emerged that the American public would prefer a self-confessed septuagenarian misogynist with orange skin and a large golden shredded-wheat formation on his head to a woman tainted with suspicions of financial impropriety and failing to protect her troops abroad. The rest of the world wondered at a political system that could allow two such inappropriate candidates to contest the position of leader of the Western world. Most English politicians now asserted that the two nations shared little more than approximate skin tones, l broadly transferrable language and a love of hamburgers.

In the true spirit of Anglo-American relations, Abadi was briefed to report back even more about the British intelligence services than the IBIS groups he was supposed to be monitoring. Despite this, he and Douglas worked well together. They had formed a strong partnership during three previous operations but both recognised exactly which side the other was on.

Abadi was still recovering from the physical, mental and medical effects of the last few days but had been alerted that he would likely be transferring out of the UK within the next few days under a new identity. He had been given two days to learn to be Adam Albano, the British born son of a Maltese hotel magnate and his English lawyer wife. Both, tragically, now deceased in the most tragic yachting accident that the CIA had never witnessed. The real Adam had gone down with them. The CIA often sailed in murky waters.

***

Sean Lakin had just finished a conference call with John Haworth the Chief Constable of Blackburn and DI Rosie Turner who had just left the Lancashire town and was now in a budget hotel room in Aberdeen. She was eagerly pursuing the compelling link with the Scottish connection in the maintenance work at the blast sites.

Both Rosie and the Blackburn police had interviewed Rahim Chatha who protested that he was unsure what had upset him most; the abduction of a recent guest to his town or the suggestion that he or his political party might be responsible. Rosie reported that Chatha's indignation oozed out of his arrogant snake skin pores like venomous sweat and sympathised with the Chief Constable who was required to maintain a working relationship with the most senior, but most corrupt politician in the north of England.

Nobody knew anything about the abduction. Nobody had seen it, nobody had heard it and nobody had reported it. The only visible evidence was a rather large lump on the back of PC Pemberton's head and an abandoned taxi. Conversations with Chatha's staff, the receptionist and the taxi company led nowhere. The official taxi had not even been despatched at the time the abduction took place. The town hall receptionist had suddenly been taken ill but none of his immediate family could shed light upon his chosen place of convalescence. His extended family were scattered around the country, and the globe. The local police were now involved in a 'Missing Person Investigation' but secretly commented that it would have been easier to locate Terry Waite in Beirut than Farah Karim in Blackburn.

Sean Lakin had always known that the responsibility for getting Detective Inspector Karim back to Scotland Yard and, more importantly, back to his home, would rest largely with him.

30

"What the fuck do you think you are playing at, Mitchell?"
Faraday's face was now almost as distorted as his son's as he
launched into his tirade on the Prime Minister, having almost
kicked over the highly polished Cabinet office drinks cabinet. "I am
the Deputy Prime Minister for fuck's sake, not the fucking butler.
You can't agree to a fucking hostage exchange with IBIS bastards
without fucking consulting me!"

The thought of Faraday being anyone's butler amused Mitchell
but wisely, he only smiled inwardly.

"Calm down, Neil. You are, as you say, The Deputy Prime
Minister, not a dockyard union official and I am, remember, the
Prime Minister. I am empowered to make the final decision on all
matters of national security."

"But to swap a fucking lady copper for the top brass of ISIS
UK? We don't do deals with terrorists remember? Have you been
shagging her or what?!"

Mitchell had known that there would have been a negative
reaction from Faraday, which was why he elected to tell him after
the plan was in motion rather than delay the decision-making
phase. Even he, however, was stunned by this outburst.

199

"Firstly, this is not a hostage exchange, it's a critical stage in the bombing investigation and an attempt to avoid any more terror attacks on this scale. Secondly, you know that we don't do deals with terrorists. Thirdly, judge me on the outcome, not the action… and fourthly, if you ever insult that brave police officer or myself in that manner again, I will knock your thick bloated head off those dandruff showered shoulders of yours."

Faraday was not letting this one go. He never missed an opportunity to strike out at his nemesis and the fact that this occasion actually happened to seem justified was something of a bonus.

"Hundreds of people have lost their lives this week. Hundreds more are injured. Thousands of our citizens are mourning for their dead and wounded and your response is to release four convicted terrorists from prison. Is that the deal? Let them go and they will promise not to detonate any more bombs? What kind of leadership is that?"

Mitchell was fighting to stay calm. Faraday was renowned for having listened rather less than his classmates in school and rarely showed any signs of tact and diplomacy, but this was one of those displays that social media was invented for.

"A police officer is being held to ransom, not the country. The intelligence services are investigating links between the bombs, the suspected bomber who battered your son, three dead goons who murdered him, the underground ISIS hierarchy at Belmarsh, the political connection with IBIS and a potential rogue faction in Blackburn. We appoint advisors to advise us and pay the police and military to act upon that advice. You, on the other hand, are paid to make British people believe that they are still living in a democracy, because only a failed democratic constitution like ours could accommodate and tolerate an incompetent, bigoted fool like you. Now piss off and play with your Lego. I will tell you when you need to know something… if I think it might be within your limited capacity to comprehend."

Mitchell briskly walked out leaving Faraday stunned and with the blank expression of a defecating Labrador.

***

Sean Lakin was warming to Mellor's style and approach but he tempered his affinity with his healthy distrust of politicians; especially those that had arrived into power via a circuitous route of military service and the broadcast media. Mellor had arranged a meeting in a private dining room of the Guinea, his favourite pub in Mayfair. When Lakin arrived, he found Mellor sharing a generous buffet with a younger man who was introduced to him as Scott Douglas. Mellor explained, albeit ambiguously, that Douglas was a member of the security service and his recent undercover assignment in Belmarsh made him the perfect escort for the prisoner exchange. He invited both men to help themselves to the bar and the buffet as they waited for the third and final member of their team to arrive. Lakin afforded himself the luxury of a pint of Heineken and had never, until now, appreciated the skill involved in serving the golden foaming liquid. He certainly would not have paid full price if this particular fobbing specimen had been passed to him by a barman. Scott Douglas grabbed a mineral water while Mellor flexed his right arm around a cask hand pull and pumped himself a pint of London Pride.

The three of them stopped talking as they heard footsteps ascend the wooden stairs and the door creaked open. Mellor's face beamed as a tall, wiry, grey haired man of around sixty strode into the room.

"Phil, it's great to see you. Thanks for coming at such short notice."

"No bother, Tom," the tall man grinned, "I do everything at short notice these days. Long-term planning never seemed sensible under your command and I'm surprised to have made sixty-two. If I'd known there was a chance of me getting there I would have taken better care of myself!"

They hugged warmly and shook hands for rather longer than both had probably intended. "Let me introduce the team now that we are all here," Mellor declared grandly and proceeded to tell Phil Thorley as little and just as much as he needed to know about his two new colleagues. Phil Thorley was well accustomed to such ambiguity and fully understood, from experience, that it was unwise to get too close to men that might die alongside you, or watch you die. He last served directly under General Tom Mellor in Iraq in 2003 when he was a young thirty-something Captain in 3 Regiment, Army Air Corps.

The regiment's role in the UK was to provide aviation support to 24 Airmobile Brigade, now 16 Air Assault Brigade bringing together the agility and reach of airborne forces with the potency of the attack helicopter. 3 Regt AAC was part of the coalition forces that took part in Operation Telic (Iraq) during 2003 when Captain Thorley was one of the most junior officers to fly the Apache attack helicopter. During the course of the campaign he had flown countless missions rescuing almost as many comrades as the enemies he killed but none were more grateful than the big man in front of him now. Phil Thorley had risked his life when landing his Apache in the middle of a fierce firefight at a makeshift base on the outskirts of Basra. He saved Mellor and three senior members of the United Nations Corps from certain death at the hands of Iraqi rebels. He should have received a medal. Instead he received a reprimand for endangering the army's most expensive piece of kit. He left the army soon after but kept in regular contact with Tom Mellor who introduced him to a security organisation that paid ten times as much as the Queen paid him for a quarter of the hours. The work was legitimate but there was no pretense that this was for Queen and country; this was for wife and daughter. His last mission was in Syria in 2014, where he was part of a team commissioned by Mellor to destroy a chemical weapons facility that the British forces were not allowed to go near. They succeeded, but only just and anyone that doubted the presence of chemical weapons in the conflict was invited to visit Phil Thorley in his private hospital bed in Amersham where he spent eight weeks recovering from the gas and bacteria that had permeated his protective clothing and set to work on his skin and organs. From then on, Mellor was rather more selective in the jobs he lined up and this, in fact, was the first operation for over two years, though they still maintained regular contact.

Introductions over, Mellor advised the team that he had chartered a Eurocopter EC155 from Battersea Heliport and recommended that they get down there after lunch to review the seating arrangements and take a trial flight to familiarise themselves with the sounds and sensations that might impair their judgement during this dangerous day out. Each member of the team had definitive responsibility. Lakin would liaise with the captors and handle any last minute negotiations that might arise. Scott Douglas was responsible for the secure transportation of the four prisoners and the safe return of Inspector Karim. He would be armed with a Home Office standard issue Glock 29, as would Sean and Phil but in addition, Douglas would carry a Heckler and Koch G3 which would double as a sniping rifle to ensure that the team and their hostage were protected before, during and after the transfer.

Phil Thorley, of course, would have total control over transportation and navigation. His first two take-off and landing points were known to him: Belmarsh Prison and Barton Aerodrome, but he would not be told the prisoner exchange venue until they had refueled at Barton. Mellor emphasised, very slowly, very clearly, that each man had their own critical role to perform but in any pressure situation, there needed to be a leader and that leader was to be Phil Thorley. His rationale was simple; the most crucial decisions were likely to involve the helicopter and Phil was the only person who could fly it. Secondly, although he was considerably older than the other two, he was considerably more experienced in this type of operation and likely to be the most objective. Thirdly, Mellor reminded them, it was his balls that would be on the block first and he preferred to place them in the hands of his old friend.

Lakin and Douglas nodded their agreement and they studiously plotted the critical path of the following day's mission. They were conscious, of course, that their plan would need to be flexible enough to accommodate any unexpected demands that they fully expected the kidnappers to impose and they agreed each other's degree of discretion before Thorley would be required to make the final call. They timed the pick-up, the transfer from the prison gates to the helicopter; how they would bundle the handcuffed prisoners in and where they would sit. The four would sit together, in a row, now cuffed by wrists and ankles, on the leather bench seat at the back of the helicopter, facing the front. Sean and Scott would sit directly opposite them with their backs to Phil, and the vacant jump seat next to him. They estimated that the flying time to Manchester would be around ninety minutes, depending upon wind conditions and they would consume around half a tank of fuel. The refueling stop would take around twenty minutes and they then estimated a further twenty to thirty minutes flight time to the handover venue. With any luck, Sean thought, he should have Farah back by his side by four-thirty.

They discussed the transfer logistics, as best they could, without knowing the terrain. They could, however, determine and agree a formula that would ensure that the exchange exposed both parties to similar levels of risk with Scott Douglas, his Heckler and Koch G3 and Kevlar suit acting as referee.

When they landed, the prisoners and the auxiliary pilot picked up at Barton, would remain in their seats in the tender care of Thorley and his Glock. Sean and Scott would move towards the transfer site where Farah should be waiting with her guards, while Scott would take up a position from which he could, if required, take out the captors and the helicopter. Farah's captors would then move to the helicopter and Phil would join Sean, still being covered by Scott. Simple; what could possibly go wrong?

31

Rosie Hunter was tempted to ring her boss with the outcome of her meeting with Caledonian Specialist Alloys Ltd, a specialist marine exploration business based in Aberdeen. Although she was furiously ambitious she was also fiercely loyal and decided not do anything that might distract her superintendent from the highly complex and sensitive task that consumed him. Her meeting had gone well. James McPherson, managing director and an archetypal red haired, ruddy faced fifty-something dour Scot was keen to point out that he was not one of the lame-brained lunatics that favoured independence and was only too glad to help the English police. His loyalty was, Rosie noted, perhaps influenced by the many contracts his firm undertook for English utility companies and councils. Nonetheless, he was genuinely forthcoming in the matter of Colin Richards.

"Not only is he one of the finest technicians I have ever encountered, he is the only man I know that can work equally effectively below ground and in the darkest, most confined spaces imaginable. Gregor here, calls him the Mole!"

His partner chuckled and added, "The Multi-Tasking Mole: he is a welder, an electrician, a mechanic, an engineer and if we'd stuck

205

a brush up his arse he probably would have swept the Channel Tunnel for us while he was down there!" Gregor Hansen was McPherson's cousin, business partner and operations director.

"The Tunnel?" Rosie repeated. "He worked for you in the Channel Tunnel?"

"Aye, Miss," Gregor continued, "two weeks before the London jobs. We had him contracted for twenty days, excluding weekends. He was twelve days in the English side checking and replacing cables and sensors for the service tunnels that the maintenance teams use. Nothing critical or related to the running of the service but we have had the routine maintenance contract for the last three years and the Mole is perfect for the job. He can fix anything, anywhere."

"Which is why he is in such great demand," added McPherson. "And so bloody expensive!"

"Presumably you keep a file on Mr Richards, even though he is not a direct employee. May I see it?

"Of course you may, Inspector. We keep meticulous records on all our contractors. We have to, given the security procedures we need to observe for most of our undertakings." McPherson rose smartly and took four steps to the regulation stainless steel filing cabinet to the left hand side of his desk. Rosie did not doubt that everything on all their employees and contractors was computerised but McPherson was from the generation that would insist on having everything printed and placed in this buff folder.

Rosie leafed through the folder. There were the usual personnel forms, scantily completed with minimal detail. No permanent address, no next of kin, just a mailing address to a PO Box in Italy, an email address and a mobile phone number. Although Rosie realised that these could all by now have been closed down, they were undoubtedly valuable but her eyes widened when she arrived at a small cellophane bag containing a collection of cards.

"What are these?" Rosie asked, as casually as she could maintain.

"Security passes." declared Gregor proudly. "Issued and returned before and after every job."

Bingo! Thought Rosie, praying to herself that the master craftsman was not meticulous enough to wipe down the cards before he handed them back.

"Look," said McPherson, in that warm, sincere and reassuring tone that only a mature Scot could manufacture, "if this is about illegal immigration or tax avoidance, I can assure you that he never spends more than a month at a time in the UK and I am pretty sure that we are the only British, sorry, Scottish… or UK company he works for. We keep him as our little treasure. Our secret weapon."

"No, it's nothing as serious as that," Rosie lied. "Just a missing person inquiry we are following up from our colleagues in Europe. Could I borrow this file please? I promise we will courier it back to you when we have scanned everything."

"Of course, you can. I would be surprised if anyone in Italy would declare him missing though. He never seems to stay there long enough."

Rosie thanked the two partners for their generous cooperation and made her way out of the building to her waiting hire car. If she could get back to the airport within thirty minutes, she noted, she might be able to check in for the six o' clock flight and avoid a four hour wait at possibly the worst airport in Europe, where every seat in every lounge seemed to be occupied by a seventeen stone oil worker with a container of alcohol glued to his right hand. Rosie had promised to phone Brian Chambers immediately after her meeting but, with the need to make the early flight, she opted to call him from the airport. She hit the start button, but before she could select 'drive', she was startled and frozen to the wheel by the sudden bang on her window.

***

Brian Chambers had also been busy discussing Colin Richards with his counterparts at MI7. This particular intelligence agency was created in 2015 to support the work of MI5 and MI6 and was borne out of the old General Communications Headquarters in Cheltenham. Its creation was in response to the growing need to monitor telephonic, internet and social media communications in the wake of the rise of ISIS indoctrination and recruitment within the United Kingdom. Previous government regimes had failed to authorise such a body, oversensitive to the backlash of phone hacking accusations and perceived threats to civil liberties but the Conservative Government of 2015 initiated its development, though to most citizens, quite deliberately, it was perceived merely as a renaming of the GCHQ facility. In reality, the new MI7 functionality rendered former GCHQ capability the comparative equivalent of holding a very dense glass to a particularly thick wall. Tom Mellor had been the principal advocate of the agency and when challenged by the then Defence Minister on the potential outcry, should the nation ever come to understand the full penetration of the unit's monitoring capability he simply responded: "Fuck 'em! If they have something to hide its all the more reason to watch them." And so MI7 was created to secure, protect, reassure and spy on UK citizens and as far overseas as its many satellites could penetrate. Within the corridors of power, its agents were known simply as 'the listeners' and 'the watchers'. They communicated liberally with their sister agencies and cooperated fully with the police, particularly the Special Investigations Unit with whom they were indirectly linked.

Chambers had spent the best part of two hours driving across to Cheltenham as, ironically, neither he nor his counterparts at MI7 were keen on conducting such meetings other than face-to-face. They also tried to avoid meeting at their London analysis centre. They clearly understood that if such technology were available to Little England then the real world powers were more than capable of 'out listening' them.

Using the employee information from the Westminster Licensing Agency, the identities determined by border control from passport and facial recognition technology and the fact that their prime suspect had travelled from Heathrow to Istanbul on the day of the first bomb, they started their search. They concentrated initially on calls from the UK to Turkish landlines and mobiles from the time of the first explosion that had failed to connect during the time in which the Heathrow flight was in the air. They then focussed on calls from the same numbers to the same Turkish devices that connected within four hours of the Heathrow flight landing. There were over seventeen thousand such calls, the majority from South East England. They narrowed the search to calls from and to central London locations in the expectation that the bomber might be appraised of the extent of his mission's success. It was also acknowledged that there would be a huge number of calls out of central London to worried relatives, advising that the callers were alive and well. Word search technology hunting phrases including the words, bomb, blast, terrorist, destruction, etc. was not especially helpful as these terms would be used widely after such an event.

They filtered the results by searching calls to known devices associated with the assumed names of the suspect and triangulated on communications from devices in the UK, Turkey and other global locations that had taken place during both the aftermath of the first and second bombs. On both occasions, using GPRS data, they established a pattern of calls of similar length and frequency, from Whitehall in London, Paris and Riyadh to the same device in Istanbul and calls returned to the Paris and Riyadh devices. Simultaneously, the listeners were monitoring email traffic between the same locations and focussing on sites where telephonic and computing devices had communicated to recipients within the same two hundred metre radius. The results were not deemed to be conclusive but corresponding phone devices and IP addresses in Whitehall, Paris, Istanbul and Riyadh were deemed worthy of further investigation. It was not possible to isolate telephone numbers from the listeners' technology as all decent devices now incorporated basic security, but each communication contained its own unique tone and frequency, almost like sonic DNA. It, did, however, require further technical investigation and feet on the ground to turn frequencies and tones into flesh and blood. Brian Chambers was despatched to concentrate on Whitehall. Sister Agencies would be working further afield.

**

The bang on the window instinctively caused Rosie to slam her foot onto the accelerator but with the automatic gearbox in neutral, all she achieved was the plaintive squeal of an anguished engine. The large, looming figure jumped back, but then slapped a brown bag against the windscreen. Rosie swung her face to her right and saw a startled Gregor Hansen mouthing obscenities and motioning her to wind down the window, as though unaware that they were now operated by switches. "It occurred to me, Miss Hunter, that if you were looking for fingerprints on his security passes you might want to pick some of that DNA off his overalls. Are you sure you wouldn't like to tell a curious old man what this is really all about?"

When Rosie had arrived at the airport and finally called Chambers, they spent the first thirty seconds talking over each other like a pair of love-struck teenagers on their first call after arriving home from a holiday romance. There would never be any emotional entanglement to get in the way of their professional relationship as Brian was a boringly contented, confirmed bachelor and Rosie was currently engaged in a relationship that was anything but boring. Chambers recalled his earlier meeting and still in absolute awe and fear of the capability that he had witnessed, he suggested that he meet Rosie on her return flight to the city airport and discuss their collective breakthroughs over an expensive Metropolitan Police funded dinner in Canary Wharf. With this information in their hands, they had no doubt in concluding that they were worth it.

32

Governor Thornton barely managed to disguise his naivety and his fury by expressing surprise that the four transfer prisoners were sitting in their cells with their belongings already assembled as he informed them that they were to be transferred out of Belmarsh for their own safety. They grinned at the governor and sat, excitedly, like four schoolboys about to embark on their first school trip to the zoo. Despite Thornton's best efforts to control the use of communication technology, it was clear that they had known, almost as soon as he had, that they were to be shipped out. Of all the possible scenarios that ran through his head, the one that he missed was that they knew better than he did why they were being moved. He told them that they were to leave the prison at ten o' clock, under the supervision of Prison Officer Scott Douglas and Detective Superintendent Sean Lakin. He chose not to disclose the mode of transport in case they displayed either a dislike of flying or being manacled together like slaves on a chain gang.

Lakin and Douglas were in the governor's office studying the files on the four terrorists. Mehmet Hussain, and Ibrahim Bengasi,

211

were both serving life sentences for planning and perpetrating bombings in Britain and Gibraltar. The British plot had been foiled, saving the lives of hundreds, if not thousands, of Tottenham Hotspurs supporters when MI7 intercepted the plan to detonate suicide vests in the stands of White Hart Lane. The Gibraltar bombing did happen; killing three suicide bombers, Somali citizens who had arrived in Spain via illegal boat traffickers and twenty-seven tourists in the Military Museum high in the caves of the landmark rock. Hussein and Bengasi were both students at Leeds University and were one of the listeners' early successes in monitoring and extracting detailed evidence from emails and more sophisticated web communications. They had both been in Belmarsh for the past six years and were revered and reviled in equal measure by the various factions within the prison.

Mohammed Sayed and Abdallah Afzal had both been extradited to Britain from Egypt for their part in the bombing of the British Embassy in Cairo in the years following the so called peaceful revolution, then referred to as the Arab Spring. The extradition process lasted almost three years as legal wrangles ensued as to whether they should be tried in Egypt, upon whose soil the crime was committed or in Britain, whose Embassy they had breached and whose eleven citizens they had murdered. The prospect of losing a billion or so pounds in foreign aid eventually swayed the decision to send them to Britain where, they too, were now serving life sentences with no possibility of release.

During his time with the Metropolitan Police, Sean had been presented with opportunities to transfer into the intelligence services and reading these files, he began to wish that he had considered those offers more carefully. The police service tends to frown upon prisoners being killed or maimed during arrest whereas the intelligence services seem to adopt a more pragmatic approach. Scum such as these might well have disappeared and eventually expired following months of sophisticated but robust interrogation and right at this moment, reading these files, Sean would have relished the role with the wet towel, electrodes or even a simple baseball bat. He also found himself contemplating the fate of the two balaclava-clad cowards holding Farah but concluded that her safe release was paramount and nothing else mattered… for now.

***

RAF Northolt is a small airfield near Uxbridge on the north-west side of London. Its RAF function is principally administrative and was therefore happy to share its runway and logistics facility with private charters and commercial freight movements. It was here that Phil Thorley was making the final checks, in and around the Eurocopter. Although he was not completely familiar with this particular aircraft, his practice session yesterday had shown him everything he needed to know in terms of functionality so he was now concentrating on issues of security. The four seats in which the prisoners would be seated were in one row at the rear of the cabin, facing forwards towards the two seats which would be occupied by Douglas and Lakin. There were no suitable anchor points to which the prisoners could be shackled, other than the standard seatbelts. Lakin and Thorley had therefore agreed that they would simply use two lightweight aluminium struts, through which to thread the handcuffs and ankle braces to link and limit the movements of the four men as they would not be able to unfasten their seatbelts with their hands cuffed behind their backs. Finally, Thorley loaded the case containing three handguns and the rifle that had now been waved through by RAF security and he was cleared for take-off.

Governor Thornton had ordered the fenced and gated car park at the front of the prison to be cleared to allow the helicopter to land. It did so at nine forty-five, with the power of the rotors rippling the rainwater on the wet tarmac as though to create a dry platform for boarding. Thorley had angled the landing to ensure that he could see his passengers approach on their journey from the prison.

Inside, the governor had signed the transfer documents and formally handed the prisoners into the custody of Superintendent Lakin, as it was on the advice of the SIU that the prisoners were being relocated. The four prisoners were handcuffed behind their backs and a length of chain passed through the four sets of cuffs to link the men together. Their ankles were also secured by manacles and a length of chain, eighteen inches long, to allow them to shuffle the short distance from the prison gate to the waiting aircraft. Lakin issued a final briefing:

"You are going to walk together, in single file, to the helicopter. When we get there, one by one, you will be removed from the chain link, your wrists will remain cuffed but your ankles will be released to allow you to climb into the craft where you will take your seat in bare feet. This part of the transfer will be supervised by our pilot and he would like to assure you that your safety and comfort is the least of his concerns. If you act suspiciously or disobey his direct instructions he will shoot you in the knee. He will apply first aid to ensure that you don't bleed to death but he doesn't carry pain killers in his kit bag."

Lakin paused as the prisoners looked at each other for strength in numbers but courage appeared to be in short supply as they remained silent and looked distinctly uncomfortable. They figured, quite reasonably and astutely, that this big man did not like them very much.

"Once in the helicopter, Officer Douglas here will secure your ankles again to keep you safely in your seats. Please resist the temptation to kick him as he does so because if I see any of your feet moving more than six inches backwards or forwards as he performs this task, I will crush the toes of the offending foot with this pair of pliers from the emergency tool kit. Please observe those small details, sit back and enjoy the flight."

The human freight was loaded without incident and secured to their seats by the cuffs and lengths of metal linking them together and keeping them rigid. Lakin and Douglas sat opposite, handguns out of sight but to hand if absolutely required. Phil Thorley undertook the final checks, secured air traffic clearance and lifted the machine sharply from the ground while simultaneously turning through one hundred and eight degrees for the flight north. The prisoners seemed to be relieved but, as instructed, none spoke.

Lakin was expecting a call from the kidnappers but not quite so soon. It was as though someone had told them that the craft was in the air, which was perfectly possible from one of the Belmarsh cells. Although the telephone technology allowed the call to happen, the noise from the rotors above made it difficult to converse. Lakin confirmed that they were airborne and expected to be landing at Barton for refuelling in just over an hour unless the wind resisted the two hundred and fifty knot progress of their transport. Tariq advised where to refuel and warned that his own pilot would be there to supervise operations, supported by a backup team of snipers with high powered rifles.

Thorley seemed in constant contact with the ground. All helicopters flying in the London city control zones are subject to an air traffic control clearance and particular visibility criteria. In the main, pilots navigate by visual reference to ground features with only limited radar assistance and are required to fly along designated helicopter routes. These routes have been selected to provide maximum safety by avoiding flying over built up areas as much as possible. Lakin would not admit it but his face seemed to betray the fact this was very far from his preferred mode of transport.

The three good guys were under no illusion that they had just embarked upon possibly the most dangerous mission of their careers. Farah's captors clearly wanted these four prisoners back safely so there was little threat to the men in the air but they had considered and discussed the possibility of being attacked and overpowered during the refueling operation at Barton airfield and had agreed contingency protocol to prevent this from happening.

Only Thorley would leave the cockpit to supervise refueling while Sean and Scott would be training handguns on their four guests. This was part one of the potential Mexican standoff. The second stage, at the handover point, would prove to be a greater logistical and security challenge.

Although the flight path initially took them away from the city, Sean could not help but look back past the heads of the four prisoners and wonder whether or not these individuals had been directly or indirectly involved in the bombings just days earlier. Sure, they were incarcerated at the time, but everybody knew that it is possible to run major crime organisations from a prison cell and it was clear from the fact that they were now sitting in front of him that they were important cogs in the ISIS war machine. His thoughts then strayed towards Farah, as it was just as likely that they were involved in her kidnap or, at the very least, they were the main beneficiaries of it. Worst of all, he felt sick to the pit of his stomach that here he was, a senior police superintendent, complicit in their release. Although he almost convinced himself that his actions were a necessary step in the potential tracking of the London bombers he knew that the likelihood of this materialising was remote and that his sole motivation was the release and return of his girlfriend. He asked himself how he would have felt if Farah had been the wife of a politician or businessman and he did not like the answer he received. He did vow, however, that the exchange of prisoners would not be the end of this matter although he had little confidence in the flimsy follow-up operation they had agreed with Tom Mellor. He realised that he was staring directly through these four figures of hate and his expression was leaving them in no doubt whatsoever of his true intentions. They could only hope that their brothers in the north had prepared the handover carefully enough to ensure that their backs would never be exposed to the sniper rifle that sat beside Phil Thorley in the left hand front seat.

If Thorley had any emotions at all towards this operation, he managed to mask them completely. He had not spoken a word to his companions and had only exchanged the most cursory of conversation with the ground authorities. His expression was beyond neutral; distant, distracted, calm, but nonetheless, focused. Sean remembered Mellor's explicit instruction that Thorley would have the final say in all operational matters and for the first time in three days he questioned Mellor's judgement. Thorley was, no doubt, loyal, reliable, experienced and as tough as they possibly come but he just did not seem engaged in the operation. Just a taxi driver ambling along above the high roads.

Scott Douglas harboured no such concerns. He knew Thorley by reputation and the reputation dictated that this was a man who would do anything, absolutely anything, to get the job done.

33

Adnan Abadi was also on the move. Or rather, Adam Albano was. In an amazing transformation from 'dead man walking' to 'new-born working' Adam was now leaving a meeting at the London division of MI7, having spent the morning with Paul Cruse the Deputy Director, Rosie Hunter and Brian Chambers. As soon as Rosie Hunter had reported back from her meeting in Aberdeen the humongous computing power of MI7 had sprung into action analysing trillions of bytes of data attributable to the various identities of one Colin Richardson. His fingerprint profile had already been circulated to the service's cooperating agencies and this, overlaying the facial recognition technology and voice frequency profiling had allowed them to isolate and triangulate a series of telephone communications and data exchanges between Istanbul, Paris, Britain and Riyadh. It would have been infinitely more helpful if the voice profiling had actually recorded words but in the absence of recorded conversations, the unique voice patterns had plotted a sequence of calls, from two days prior to the bombings to three days afterwards. The conversations before the first bomb had been principally between South London and Riyadh with a couple of calls isolated to a Whitehall GPRS point. The subsequent calls were mainly between Istanbul and Paris. Adam Albano was now boarding the 10.07 Eurostar service to Paris, armed only with a set of GPRS coordinates triangulated around Montmarte.

Rosie Hunter was to focus on the London and Whitehall signals while MI7 requested the help of the sister agency MI6 to follow the trail to Istanbul. They all knew that these leads were at best tenuous but many inquires had previously blossomed from even tinier seeds. The intelligence agencies had a specific personality profile for their investigating officers; patience, meticulous attention to detail, positive attitude, resilience and the ability to see a clue in a vanishing cloud were all prerequisite. Strictly speaking, Rosie was not part of the service but she was certainly displaying the credentials.

The communications between Saudi Arabia and Istanbul were fairly predictable. Istanbul, gateway to Asia was also a crucial waypoint to Syria and the heart of ISIS. Riyadh, Saudi Arabia openly expressed revulsion towards the paramilitary activity of Islamic State while blindly pumping millions of oil dollars into the arms and tanks of its fanatical membership.

The London call patterns were intriguing, strongly suggesting that if Richardson was the bomber, he continued to communicate with a colleague he left behind, in or close to, of all places, Westminster.

There were, of course, long standing links with ISIS throughout France who, being the first European country to outlaw the public wearing of religious face covering paraphernalia, had suffered the wrath of Allah and his blind fanatics for over twenty years. The tensions within France had further escalated since the withdrawal of Britain from the European Union as hundreds of thousands of illegal immigrants who used to pass through France, en route to an easy life in Britain, were now forced to remain on the soft-cheese side of the Channel. This in turn had created a massive surge in membership for the Front National, founded in 1972 by Jeanne

Marie Le Pen who was succeeded by his daughter Marine. It seemed that the party's hatred of all things Islam was now only surpassed by its venomous hatred of the new, independent United Kingdom.

So with four majestic haystacks hiding one tiny needle, the United Kingdom switched on its mighty magnet and drew in, disseminated and analysed every single byte of transmitted data that might lead them to Colin and whoever he was in league with.

***

As two thousand fellow passengers filed down the gangways to join tour coaches, taxis and local buses, Richard Collins and his delightful new bride for the week, Christina, sipped coffee on the balcony of their cabin watching their fellow cruisers flock, sheep-like, to explore the tourist highlights of Sicily. Richard, as Ricardo Colino had been here just under two years ago on a trip that made him two hundred thousand Euros richer and a rather famous Mafiosi family two much loved members lighter. Since boarding in Istanbul, they had docked in Crete, where Richard had spent most of the morning in an internet café on the beautiful harbour side of Chania trading laborious logistical details of the mission he would be embarking upon on Sunday morning, when the ship was scheduled to dock in Marseilles.

Tomorrow, Saturday, they would be pulling alongside in Naples where the ship's provisions master, Abdul Aziz, would be taking on board another massive haul of food, drink and cleaning materials. Three of those small containers, alongside three that were loaded in Crete, would not pass Abdul's strict quality control procedures and would be offloaded again in Marseilles.

Colin and Christina waited another hour or so before walking down the gangplank, declining the obligatory photograph with the Sicily Lifebelt on the quay, and strolled independently, away from the port towards the beautiful old town of Palermo. They followed a group of Indonesian waiters, laughing pushing and slapping each other heartily as they sought out the nearest Starbucks or McDonald's where they would congregate outside, taking full advantage of the free Wi-Fi to contact their loved ones, far away, to tell them how bored, lonely and miserable they were feeling. A hundred metres ahead of them, they spotted Aziz who was heading towards the large coffee house in the spacious market square where they had arranged to meet to discuss remuneration and the unscheduled disembarkation process at Marseilles.

34

Phil Thorley had been given the coordinates for the Barton Airfield and told by Lakin that they would receive details of their subsequent destination from the second pilot who would join them after refuelling. They were approaching Manchester from the south having broadly followed the route of the M6 motorway before veering west towards Bolton. Barton is little more than a small field nestled close to the sprawling retail Mecca of the Trafford Centre which is infinitely more popular with families on cheap days out than with discerning and dedicated retail therapists.

As the helicopter descended, Lakin's phone trilled and Tariq gave him precise instructions of where to land and how to refuel. They were to put down in a wide open section of the airfield, marked out by two white vans and a yellow fuel truck. The pilot was to switch off the engines, refuel under the supervision of Tariq's comrade who would guide the helicopter to the exchange point. Lakin, Douglas and the prisoners were to remain in the helicopter. Sean relayed the instructions to Thorley who simply nodded his acknowledgement and took the aircraft down.

Immediately on landing, Douglas uncoupled his seat belt as Thorley passed him the rifle. He barely had room to shoulder the weapon and there was less than one hundred degrees of forward peripheral vision but this also served as a degree of protection for Lakin and himself. Thorley climbed out of the cockpit and stood beside the man he assumed to be the second pilot (the one of the three men wearing a baseball cap rather than a balaclava and not holding a pistol). If there was any expectation of code of respect between fellow pilots, it was not apparent here as the two men barely acknowledged each other, let alone communicated.

The refuelling was completed by one of the two armed guards and when the fuel level had been verified, one of the armed balaclavas withdrew, walking backwards with his gun trained on Thorley, while the other drove the fuel truck clear. Thorley walked towards the left hand side of the cockpit but the balaclava passed baseball cap a gun and motioned Thorley back to the pilot seat. "You drive," he said. "Our man covers you and takes over after the transfer."

It was as if Tariq had sensed or anticipated Lakin's concern as his phone rang again. Tariq's voice was as cold as ever but Lakin now thought he could sense a nervous tone as he snapped the instruction.

"Your man brings the aircraft to us. My man makes sure he behaves. You will now switch off your phone and hand it to your escort who will give you the new coordinates. We will meet in less than twenty minutes. Your pilot also hands over the gun that you, no doubt, gave him."

Lakin had expected this. The bad guy in the cockpit could not hold the gun and fly the helicopter. Nor were they ever likely to allow Lakin or Douglas to transmit the details of their destination by phone. The kidnappers would have known that the helicopter's route would be constantly monitored but must have felt confident that they could complete the exchange quickly, securely and with a guaranteed getaway. Lakin and Douglas were now becoming increasingly agitated while Thorley just sat and waited for instructions.

The coordinates were keyed into the navigation equipment and they took off for their rendezvous: Darwen Tower.

The octagonal Jubilee Tower, as it was officially titled, overlooked the town of Darwen in Lancashire and was completed in 1898 to commemorate Queen Victoria's Diamond Jubilee. It was also said to celebrate the victory of the local people for the right to access the moor. It was opened to the public on 24 September 1898. At 85 feet (25.9 m) in height, walkers could climb to the top via the internal staircase to admire the views of North Yorkshire, Morecambe Bay, Blackpool Tower, Cumbria, the Isle of Man, North Wales, Derbyshire, elsewhere in Lancashire, and surrounding moorland. Today, there were only three people at the summit of the tower and they were looking to the east only.

Access to the hill on which the tower was erected was limited to one public highway and would only allow motors to drive to within one mile of the summit. Two tracks allowed walkers access to the hill but today, each gate was supervised by a burly man in a yellow council vest advising that the hill was out of bounds as the area was due to be sprayed with chemicals that would eradicate a fungus threatening the delicate heathers and hardy gorses that decorated and protected the tower itself.

Farah stood at the top of the tower, encased in a clear Perspex dome. Her hands were securely fastened behind her back and they had now removed the burkha that she had worn for the past three days and stood in the business suit that she had carefully chosen for the meeting with Chatha. She felt grubby, bedraggled, disheveled and humiliated. She stupidly told herself that even if Sean would ever forgive her for getting herself captured and forcing him to compromise his principles, he would wonder what he ever saw in her as she stood here like a crumpled *Big Issue* seller. She then reminded herself that while Sean might have declared that the exchange would take place, she doubted that he had received the authority to do so. She had little doubt that a plan had been formulated to confront rather than comply with her kidnappers, but standing as she was, on this isolated, cold, misty moor amidst two armed men, with at least four others dotted around the hill, she could not envisage a positive outcome. Her thoughts turned again to Ava. At least she had been spared the anguish of the kidnapping. She will have had a wonderful holiday and Sean, if he survived, would look after her.

On any other day but today, they probably would have heard the helicopter before they saw it but the swirling mist fought with the howling wind to confound both senses. Sight just defeated sound as the looming craft broke through the mist and approached the tower at a height of no more than two hundred meters. As if from nowhere, two figures emerged from the gorse below in hi vis yellow overalls, waving bright flashlights. Phil Thorley spotted them immediately and wondered how many others might be secreted away in the undergrowth. The two spotters removed their yellow suits, arranged and pegged them in a cross on the ground and withdrew as mysteriously as they had appeared.

Farah's gaze was fixed upon the approaching object as it hovered and now throbbed over the hill sending gorse, reeds, moor grass and two pairs of yellow overalls in a centrifugal whirl. She was dragged out of her dark thoughts and pushed towards the damp stone steps that led to the base of the monument. As she stepped out onto the steps surrounding the octagonal base, the cold wind from the moor seemed to merge into the warmer draught from the helicopter rotors, rippling her cheeks and blurring her vision. She felt the barrels of the two pistols in her back, unsure whether they were there as a direct warning to her, or a concealed threat to her rescuer. She resigned herself that it was likely to be both and that she and her Heathcliff were doomed to perish upon this wild and windy moor.

Thorley brought the craft down expertly through the swirling wind and landed smoothly and evenly. He had not intended to switch off the rotors until instructed to do so and, predictably, the instruction came at gunpoint. The passenger's gun was an irrelevance as Lakin also had one trained upon the back of his head and nobody was really sure who had the most to lose. Sean's phone rang and the silent co-pilot handed the device back to its owner. Tariq was barely audible through the wind but the two had rehearsed the exchange protocol thoroughly so the call was little more than the prompt to proceed. Scott Douglas remained in the rear with his hand gun on the Jihadists and the rifle barrel at the baseball cap. Sean Lakin alighted, shocked by the force of the wind and the starkness of the landscape from which the tower stood, two hundred meters away like a moon rocket ready to launch.

He could clearly make out Farah, flanked by her two boiler suited and balaclava-clad captors. As agreed, one of them walked towards the helicopter, pistol in hand, and matched Sean step for step as he walked from the helicopter. After around one hundred paces, they were alongside each other, around fifteen meters apart, and equidistant between the tower and the aircraft. At this point, exactly as planned, Scott Douglas emerged from the aircraft, handgun in pocket, rifle in hand and waved his signal for the next phase of the transfer to commence.

The first captor moved away from Sean and walked towards the helicopter. Simultaneously, the second captor, Tariq, Sean presumed, began his walk towards the ground vacated by Haq. This was Sean's cue to walk, at last, towards the object of his mission, and, increasingly, he realised, his very being. He was conscious that at this point, the baseball-capped accomplice in the cockpit now had the four prisoners and Phil Thorley under his control, but Scott Douglas held the rifle and could take out any of the their opponents with ease. The balance of power was still pretty even, so long as there were not more conspirators hidden in the distant hedges. Sean was becoming more confident with each step. He passed by Tariq with barely a glance, knowing that Scott had him covered.

Farah could hardly believe that this was happening and was beginning to convince herself that she might see her daughter again after all, but she knew at first hand, her right one in fact, just how ruthless and uncompromising these people were. She thought of moving back into the shelter of the tower but needed to see how this was going to unfold, even though she was helpless to affect proceedings. Sean was now close enough for her to see his face. His grim expression a measure of both his concern that the operation was not yet over and perhaps his shame that soon it would be. As he approached Farah and took her in his arms, as any commander would support a rescued subordinate, two shots rang out, piercing through the howling wind and causing moorland birds to take their flight of frenzy in all directions.

Sean dragged Farah into the safety of the tower and looked back from behind a huge supporting pillar towards the aircraft. Tariq was down on one knee, Scott was lying motionless on the ground as the helicopter rotors sprang into life. Haq had climbed into the cockpit, behind his baseball capped comrade and pointed the gun directly at Thorley. "Either get this machine off the ground within ten seconds or you will have a bullet in your head and my colleague takes the controls. Your choice."

"What about your buddy back there in the grass?" Thorley asked.

"He made a bad choice," Haq replied. "Now fly or die!"

Tariq rose slowly and turned towards the tower with his gun in front of him. He moved slowly towards where Sean was secreted pondering his choices: "blow the bastard's head off or torture his songs out of him?" The choice became academic as Tariq stumbled to his knees again and fell face forward into a gorse bush. His last act on his way to paradise was to lift the gun in his blood soaked hand towards his temple and pull the trigger.

Scott sprang up from his prone position and dashed towards the cover of the tower, not knowing whether there would be sniper fire from the moorland ground cover. He stumbled onto the steps just as the helicopter was hovering above its takeoff point and soared upwards at an alarming rate, its engines screaming. As it climbed, its rotors whined against the absurdity of such a bulbous object attempting to defy the laws of gravity and aerodynamics. Thirty seconds later, the law won. The helicopter could not sustain such an ascent and at just under two hundred meters the screaming stopped, the rotors ceased fighting and the capsule plummeted into the ground with a deafening explosion that temporarily silenced the howling wind.

35

Despite being over 50 miles from the nearest shore based communications mast, Mehmet Osman had secured an excellent signal strength on his handheld device as he knew exactly when its satellite was overhead to afford him five minutes of valuable, and completely confidential conversation... for the sender at least. He was pretty sure that by now, the listeners at MI7 would have latched on to one of his identities, most probably Colin Richardson and would have collated and mapped the network of devices with which he had connected over the ten days. Up until now, it would only have been possible to triangulate his contacts to within a two hundred yard radius of their location and no content would be visible or audible. He now decided that his friendships should be shared with a wider social network as he manipulated the numerous security codes and filters on the adjacent computer in his cabin.

He caught his own mischievous grin in the stateroom mirror as he waited for his client to pick up the call. "Ah, Mr Black. I am so glad to have caught you to apologise for my rather unpleasant demeanour when we last spoke. I felt it appropriate that I call you to apologise and to thank you for your kind payment which has now been securely deposited in my Cayman Islands account. Perhaps you could come and see me out there so we can share a drink and reflect upon what we both achieved together."

"I think you must have a wrong number and I am putting down the…"

"Don't do it, Mr Black. I would consider that to be very rude and I do not tolerate rudeness, even from my most loyal clients, let alone a new boy like you."

"Are you mad?" came the response. "We agreed that we would never speak again and I would much rather stick with that arrangement."

"I am sure you would, Mr Black, but having reflected upon our arrangement, I now feel that the unbudgeted body count at Westminster must be worth a bonus though I am still happy for you to have the Cenotaph for free. To be honest, a like-minded sympathiser of yours across the Channel footed the bill for that one."

"There were not meant to be any bodies at all so there will be no bonus, even if I could afford one, which I bloody well can't!"

"I can understand your position and even sympathise with your complaint. Customer satisfaction is very important in my business, Mr Black, so perhaps I should offer you a refund? Would you like the funds transferred into your Coutts account in London or Lloyds in Geneva. I have both numbers from your earlier kind transfers."

"What the fuck are you playing at?" Black spluttered. "I don't want your money and I don't want anything more to do with you!"

"Well I am truly sorry to hear that, Mr Black. It has always been helpful to have friends in high places but I must respect your decision. Have a nice life, Mr Black."

The connection ended with 'Mr Black' looking down at the handset that had landed on the desk in front of him as it slipped from his ice cold, sweaty hand. He retrieved it, relieved that his position afforded him the immunity from phone taps, to which ordinary Members of Parliament were not privy.

Osman calculated that he had at least seven minutes remaining to make the next call though the signal would hold slightly longer as he knew the recipient to be at home in Paris. The brief conversation had followed a similar pattern. The recipient had been equally horrified by the call, particularly as the party had gone to extraordinary lengths to conceal the identity of the client. Conversations and cash transfers had been diverted through two continents and four countries, but the assassin had pinpointed the client and was now speaking on the home device.

"How can you politicians be so ungrateful?" mused Osman. "I give you exceptional service, above and beyond your expectations and even offer you a refund, but still you seem to revile me. I very much hope that your partners in Saudi do not learn of your disrespect towards me. Although their royal family has untold wealth, I am sure they would be horrified to learn that you, a mere go between, has offended both them, and me, by rejecting my kind offer. I bid you adieu, et bon chance, Madame."

The bemused Parisienne clutched the phone to her forehead and the repeated tapping created a wide canyon through the deeply layered foundation cream on her smoothly sculpted skin.

These conversations were not conducted out of mischief or malevolence. Osman did not play games, nor was he politically motivated. His sole motivations were success and survival. That meant never underestimating his clients, however stupid, naïve and unprofessional they might seem. The very fact that they had secured his services spelled danger. Osman was not an assassin that could be hired down the pub for a fistful of fivers. He was a professional mercenary, renowned and reviled in equal measure and only accessible to those with the highest network connections. He also had one crucial and distinct advantage over his clients; he knew exactly who and where they were. His message to them was clear. He could destroy them with one flick of a switch.

He was confident that his own device was being monitored but its content and location would be untraceable, despite the best efforts of the UK and US intelligence services. By throwing them a few scraps in the form of his two clients, he knew that the focus would, temporarily, be diverted to them but without enough data to actually locate them. Even if, by chance, they were tracked down, none of his clients ever knew his identity or whereabouts. His identity was known only to one other person in the world and access to his unique services was limited, almost exclusively, to the international political community. This was one of the many benefits of having such a close friend embedded within the offices of the United Nations, with the ability to point him towards potential clients with problems that only he might be able to resolve. His last act in active military service had been to save the life of his superior who was now a modestly paid military advisor with the UN Security Council. Together, they had formed a hugely successful and lucrative partnership by facilitating some of the most high profile and daring attacks on property and persons on both sides of the invisible moral equator.

It was entirely possible that physiological and psychological experiences of Osman's years of front line service had somehow diminished his capacity to differentiate between good and evil though it was not unknown for him to kill for money and donate the proceeds to build an orphanage. If questioned, he would probably declare that boredom and cynicism were his prime motivations.

Osman switched off his phone, keyed a few digital commands into his computer and strode out onto his stateroom balcony. He looked up to the clear blue sky as if straining to hear the world's security forces scrambling to scrape together the contents of the digital feast that he had just thrown overboard.

36

Sean shielded Farah's face from the heat as the helicopter exploded only yards from the point from which it had risen so slowly and dropped, vertically, so quickly. By now, Scott Douglas had joined them at the base of the tower and they all retreated behind the huge concrete pillars as the flames roared upwards and outwards, fuelled by a tank filled less than thirty minutes ago. There could have been no survivors.

"Jesus Christ!" howled Sean. "What an almighty cock up! How the fuck did it all turn to rat shit so quickly?"

"The only thing that went wrong," replied Scott, calmly and coolly, "was the first guard topping himself. My shots were meant to both wound him and destroy his weapon but I didn't bank on him having a backup handgun to blast himself off to paradise."

Sean and Farah looked at each other, totally confused, before staring back at Douglas who, by now, was videoing the scene on his handheld communications device.

Sean was the first to speak, though his mind did not seem to be in total control of the words that were forming in his mouth.

"Seven men are burning to death over there. Four prisoners

233

entrusted to our care, two, God knows who the fuck they were, and we probably never will, and one of our own. A good man, a service veteran, an innocent civilian and you can't see what went wrong? What the fuck is wrong with you man?"

Scott turned to them both and spoke clearly, calmly and firmly.

"By the time we get down from this hill, a newsflash will have been broadcast on all state and private media. It will go something like this. *A helicopter carrying four dangerous fundamentalist prisoners was hi-jacked today as it was transferring them away from a death plot in Belmarsh Prison to the safer Muslim occupancy prison in Leeds. The craft was hi-jacked during its planned refuelling near Manchester and crashed shortly after on the West Lancashire Moors. It is not yet known what caused the crash but it is believed that the hi-jackers were not qualified to fly such a sophisticated and complex machine... blah, blah, blah.* Come on Sean. You didn't really believe that Mellor was ever going to let them get away did you? We had hoped to get at least one of the kidnappers alive but there was always a risk of losing them when the shooting started."

"So why did the shooting start?" Sean was still not getting this.

"When the first guard got to the helicopter I tried to wound the second one and disable his rifle. We suspected that his partner would have been briefed to get the chopper in the air if anything like that happened, and it did... and he did."

"But their pilot was not at the controls," Sean pleaded, "ours was. You committed an innocent man, a fellow serviceman to certain death! I fucking get that you are a spook and not a screw but who gives you the power to sacrifice our team? Were Farah and I just lucky to make it?"

"Don't get emotional, Sean. You and Farah were always going to make it. That was a given. There was no way that Phil Thorley was ever getting off that helicopter, whether they escaped or not. Their man probably couldn't even fly the fucking thing and even if he could, they would have kept Phil hostage to prevent any attacks from ground or air."

"Well it didn't fucking prevent you did it? Our colleague has just been killed and you stand there like Bruce fucking Willis, telling me he took one for the team!

"It was part of the plan, Sean. Phil Thorley had booked himself into the Bristol Dignitas clinic for a scheduled termination, two months from today. He had pancreatic cancer with absolutely zero chance of survival and a pretty shitty three months to look forward to for him and his family. He told Mellor about it months ago. They go back a long way. Mellor gave him this last job and insured his life for a million pounds. He gave his family, in death, what he could never give them in life… security and a future. He died a happy and proud man."

Lakin took some time to allow this to sink in but could still not understand the rationale behind the events that had just unfolded. "So let me get this straight. Tom Mellor knowingly sacrificed a helicopter, a pilot and a million pounds, just to get my detective inspector back? I don't believe it."

"No, Sean, you're right, it's not quite that simple. To the general public, this is a prisoner escape gone wrong. They knew nothing of Farah's kidnap. To ISIS and IBIS, however, this is a strong message. We don't negotiate with terrorists, we kill them. We still don't know for sure whether the goons in the helicopter had anything to do with the London bombings but we sure as hell knew that their leadership desperately wanted them back. ISIS know that this was not a hi-jacking gone wrong. Their people will have been watching every move. They will know that we took them out. They will know that we no longer play by the rules. We sent them a message, Sean, and we got Farah back safely."

Throughout this exchange Farah had been listening intently and objectively. Her relief at being released had not undermined her professionalism and she had taken in every word of that last exchange. She stepped forward and spoke:

"I don't believe that this was in any way related to the bombings, other than a fortuitous opportunity to catch me off guard in a

Muslim controlled territory. There was nothing in my meeting with Chatha to suggest he knew anything about the London bombs and he proclaimed genuine anger that the attack would set back their cause and the establishment of a British Muslim state. He even went so far as suggesting a crazy conspiracy theory that our own intelligence services carried out the bombings to further incite hatred against UK Muslims. My captors kept up the same rhetoric, telling me that my colleagues were responsible for killing their friends and relatives in London that day."

Sean introduced Scott Douglas to Farah but all three knew that none were being especially truthful in respect of their identities or relationships. They all seemed to understand and expected others to accept that each had a life to conceal. Scott Douglas continued, feeling that the police officers deserved further insight and felt safe in the knowledge that neither would betray his trust.

"I am genuinely disappointed that we could not take either of Farah's captors alive but our action does herald a new phase of the war against ISIS and IBIS in the UK. If they want to wage war to achieve an independent British Islam state, we are going to start to show them what that state looks like. We have much to learn from Saddam Hussein, Gaddafi and Assad. There were no dissident groups openly perpetrating terrorist attacks against the state under their regimes. They ruled with a rod of iron and employed the only form of government that these people respect: fear; the fear of fear and fighting fire with fire. When Blair and Cameron foolishly interfered in those regimes, they opened a Pandora's Box that allowed savages to enter into an ordered world. Those savages are now over here, living and operating amongst us, and against us. Since 2015, thousands of UK Muslims have disappeared to join the ISIS Jihad and tens of thousands came the other way. Well some of them are about to disappear again. They will have interesting tales to tell."

Douglas then realised that he had spoken for longer than he had intended to and had said more than he should have.

He consciously relaxed his expression, unclenched his fists and allowed a smile to form on his face just a fraction of a second before it was a blown away by the high velocity bullet fired from the sniper gun just over four hundred yards away... Sean grabbed Scott's blood splattered weapon from the floor below him and dragged Farah into the tower and up the stone stairway to the Perspex dome above.

Perspex would offer no protection against the type of weapon that killed Scott Douglas, so Sean positioned himself and Farah at opposite sides of the dome where they could each manage a one hundred and eighty degree view of the surrounding moor without exposing too much of their heads. With only one narrow, spiral stairway to the top of the tower, they could easily shoot anyone stupid enough to rush them, but they would be equally exposed should they try to exit: a Lancastrian stand-off.

As Farah peeked above the four foot high stone wall and behind the twelve inch wide steel arch that supported the not quite clear plastic window, she saw a hooded figure crouching behind the body of the captor that she had become to know as Hardy, and Sean had known as Tariq. His arm waved, motioning forward two comrades on quad bikes. One, presumably, to retrieve the body of a fallen comrade, the other to carry away the sniper who had Sean and Farah penned into Darwen Tower.

Reminding himself of Scott Douglas' last words, he motioned Farah to stay where she was with the pistol he'd passed her and he slid quietly down the stone steps with the rifle. He calculated that the local police would be close now, having had a constant update on their position since they landed just over eleven minutes ago. Although Sean could see the town below, he had no idea of the accessibility to their position but instinctively felt that they had to be approaching the scene. If he could pin down at least one of the quad bikes until the police got here they might just get someone to interrogate after all. With both quad bikes passing two hundred yards in front of him, from left to right, he considered the risk of moving out of the cover of the tower's pillars to take a shot. If there were more of Tariq's buddies behind his position he would be a sitting duck.

He looked around and there were, indeed, a group of black clad bodies clambering through the brambles and over the top of the hill. The cavalry had arrived! Sean ducked back behind the pillar and peeked out to count their number. Three, four, six, another four and then the sight of a bright blue and yellow chequered all-terrain vehicle behind them prompted him to act. He darted back to the other side of the tower where the two quad bike riders were hauling the corpse onto the pillion seat while the sniper had his sights on the top of the tower. Sean was a pretty accomplished marksman but it had been some time since he had pointed a rifle in anger. This time though, he was not aiming at moving bodies but at two very bulky vehicles, revving noisily, awaiting their load.

He glanced back at the approaching police squad and realised that he was putting himself between them and the bad guys, but if he did not move quickly they would all get away. As a policeman, he instinctively removed his jacket and shirt before peering from behind the pillar to spray shots towards the quad bikes. He hoped that his shots would alert the advancing police towards the side of the tower not yet visible to them, and when they saw him, they might realise that he was not one of the Jihadists. In three short bursts, he fired off seventeen shots and heard most of them clatter against random pieces of steel, aluminium and plastic. If the machines were still viable, he thought, the Chinese had become much better engineers than the world had imagined. They weren't.

As the police approached, the semi-naked Sean tossed down his gun, threw his hands in the air and motioned them around the tower. The ensuing exchange was short. One man joined his fallen comrade in paradise, the other two were injured enough to prevent them from finishing themselves off but not quite badly enough to avoid the next few months in various transit centres answering rather difficult questions. They were about to disappear from the moor and the face of the earth. If they were heading for paradise, their journey was to be a long and painful one.

37

FRIDAY MARCH 15TH, 6:00PM

The Cabinet Office seemed a forlorn and foreboding cavern as the five senior ministers awaited the arrival of their leader. The Home Secretary, Clive Mountstevens, had hastily convened this meeting as soon as the news had emerged from Darwen Tower. He demanded the presence of the Defence Minister, Robert Brockington and the Foreign Secretary, Matthew Sadler. He requested that the Prime Minister chair the meeting and Graeme Mitchell agreed but suggested that his deputy and the chancellor should also be present. There was a degree of awkwardness and a noted absence of opinion in the room as each of the occupants seemed unwilling to state their position on the outcome.

Mitchell swept into the room and took his seat between Mountstevens and Faraday, immediately opposite Brockington and Sadler. The chancellor, John Gemmell, sat two chairs away from Sadler. The Home Secretary rose immediately before any unnecessary pleasantries were exchanged.

"Prime Minister, gentlemen, thank you for making yourselves available at such short notice but in the light of this afternoon's events, I felt it imperative that we deal with this matter and its potential implications, immediately."

The five men in the room were among a group of twelve who knew, officially, about the kidnapping of Farah Karim and the operation to retrieve her. Mountstevens lowered himself into his chair as he continued.

"You will all be aware that I have been uncomfortable for some considerable time about the presence of Tom Mellor around this table and, following the disastrous events that unfolded today, I feel justified in either demanding his resignation or dispensing with his services forthwith. It is entirely inappropriate to have an unelected, maverick mercenary dictating intelligence and military strategy, especially one who has ridden roughshod over all conventional procedures and presided over this monumental disaster at Darwen Tower. There is no place for such cowboys in government."

"Get off the fence, Clive," Neil Faraday quipped. "He's not here. You're safe to say what you like. He can't give you a smack!"

Rob Brockington rose, though he really did not need to do so. At six feet four, the retired rear admiral already towered above the group from a seated position. This was probably the reason that he had never served on submarines.

"I can understand your sentiment, Clive, but I believe that you are being both hasty and harsh. As you know, it is not uncommon for government departments to have independent advisors and I have found Mellor to be as reliable and valuable to my office as the senior civilian advisors to the Exchequer, Health Ministry and Energy are to theirs. He has, in my opinion, every right to hold his position and he should not be judged until all the facts from today are known."

"The facts are these," Mountstevens fumed. "He went behind our backs to the police commissioner, he enrolled his own team of intelligence agents and mercenaries. He used false credentials to procure a private helicopter and caused the deaths of at least four martyrs of Islam, two of our own and a helicopter bill approaching two million pounds. For what? The release of a policewoman.

Don't get me wrong, I am pleased that she's safe and well but not only do we not do deals with terrorists, we don't go blazing in like Sylvester Stallone reprising his role in *Rambo*! The man is a bloody liability and I fear riots and reprisals when the truth gets out."

Matt Sadler, at thirty one, was the youngest minister in the Cabinet and was appointed for his fluency in seven languages and diplomatic grooming by his father, a former ambassador to The United States and Israel. A tall, handsome man, he was hotly tipped to become a future leader and demonstrated his powers of diplomacy effortlessly.

"Clive, I respect your perspective and the potential implications within my ministry also, but I remain convinced that Mellor was acting in the best interests of the nation in securing the return of a brave police officer without surrendering a ransom or returning hostages. I accept that there will be those that doubt the hi-jacking and crash scenario, but there will be no reliable witnesses and any statements disputing this version of events will be derided as Islamic propaganda."

It was Faraday's turn to pitch in. "Personally, I would be very happy to declare that this was a planned operation to recover a kidnapped officer and to demonstrate that we will use whatever force necessary to meet the challenge of terrorism head on, both overseas and within these shores. Let the Muslims believe what they want. We have been a soft touch for too long."

The Prime Minster leaned forward and raised his hands to calm the heated exchanges that now began to reverberate around the room.

"Gentlemen, this is not the outcome we expected or desired, but I was not prepared to stand by and have the nation witness another beheading video. Let us remember that this chain of events leads back to the Cenotaph and the multiple killings in Belmarsh by the suspected bomber. Clive, I accept that your relationship with Tom Mellor is uncomfortable but he is with us, primarily, to advise Robert and Matthew in defence and foreign matters, where it seems that his input is valued. Robert, what do you have to say on the matter?"

"Well, Prime Minister, the defence department is certainly stretched. We are fighting a ground war in Syria, defending our territory in the Falklands and Gibraltar, our ships are constantly engaged in futile cat and mouse manoeuvres with the Russians and the recent uprising in Corfu has required the deployment of another thousand troops into the Greek islands."

Corfu had been ceded to the United Kingdom following the collapse of the Greek economy in 2018 when her government steadfastly defaulted on demands to repay a single penny of the three hundred billion euros of debt they had racked up with European Union countries. The Greeks had gambled that forcing them into bankruptcy would bring down the Union, but the EU summarily decided to seize the assets of the nation and apportion them to the indebted member states. The UK received Corfu, a popular destination for British tourists and now their expenditure on the island was being channelled back into British banks rather than down the rather large toilet that Athens had become. Most Greeks accepted that this solution provided their best chance of security and prosperity but there were pockets of resistance against what they saw as occupying nations. Across the mainland and other Greek Islands, security was enforced by the Federal European Military Union but the United Kingdom were not a party to this.

Greece and its islands had now become the most popular tourist destination in the world since the European Union had placed blanket sanctions on tourism to the African continent. A wave of tourist atrocities against people, property and planes in Tunisia, Egypt, Morocco and The Gambia had rendered these resorts unreachable to Westerners. The EU could not impose outright travel bans but introduced punitive tariffs and withdrew consular support and travel insurance for those destinations.

Three of the less developed Greek islands had also been allocated to the United Nations as settlement colonies for the genuine migrants and refugees fleeing the Middle East and Africa between 2016 and 2018. European and foreign aid budgets had been diverted to help develop the infrastructure of these settlements. Prior to this solution, European ports and capitals had been brought to a standstill by the swarms of political and economic migrants flooding from war-torn African and Middle Eastern regimes. They were given building and agricultural equipment, temporary shelter and food until the fruits of their labours began to blossom. Now, they too, were struggling to secure their borders as Greeks from the mainland strove to reclaim their birthright.

"I have found Tom Mellor's military experience, strategic thinking and global networking invaluable in helping me to keep the plates spinning on so many fronts. We both share the view that the five year freeze on increased defence spending has rendered our armed services understaffed and vulnerable. I formally request that the chancellor review this policy with immediate effect. Mellor is respected by the heads of our services and I would consider him to be a massive loss if he were forced to step down. I am sorry, Clive, I need him and admire him despite, perhaps, even, because of his cavalier approach."

The Home Secretary could hear his argument crumbling around him and saw no sense in entrenching himself in battle that he would not win. He was not a man to back down easily, however.

"All right," he huffed. "If you are happy for him to trample his muddy, and bloody boots all over the Foreign Office and Ministry of Defence, so be it, but I do not want him anywhere near the Home Office or police service. He reports to you Matthew so keep him under control and out of my way."

Mitchell was uncomfortable with the Home Secretary dictating in this way but with such a crisis developing around them, he was both patient and judicious enough to avoid unnecessary confrontation with who, for all his faults, was a wise and loyal servant.

"Clive, nobody is forcing Mellor upon you and I recognise your concerns regarding his relationship with the commissioner. Don't be too hard on your man at the Met and I will tell Mellor to keep away until we have the space to conduct a proper review on the scope and remit of the role of our Homeland Security Advisor. As Matthew and Robert have already pointed out, we have enough battles to fight out there without tearing into each other in here. We have the Scots, the Irish and the Muslims over here, ISIS in Syria, Iraq and Afghanistan. The Argies are threatening another pop at the Falklands and we have to decide whether to defend Corfu or sell it to the Russians. The Spanish are quietly sneaking up on Gibraltar and we cannot ignore the evolution of the European federal forces. Right now, Clive, I would suggest we need all the advice we can get unless we simply accept Robert's request for a massive increase in resource and the defence budget."

Gemmell did not say a word but his silence spoke volumes. The Home Secretary sensed that he had gained some leverage here and tested Mitchell's resolve. "I accept your decision, Prime Minister, but given the increasingly delicate pattern of events that are unfolding, I am concerned that there may be a lack of cohesion between domestic and international events and I must insist on a closer working relationship with Matthew and the Foreign Office with the right to be consulted directly on matters that impact on Home Affairs."

Mountstevens knew this to be a completely spurious demand as most foreign affairs would have a domino effect on domestic policy but this was, to him, an opportunity to hang onto the tailcoat of the new rising star and to bask in the reflected glory of his young colleague's future strategic decisions.

The Prime Minister switched his attention to Matthew Sadler who astutely recognised the meaning of the smile he was afforded. "Matthew?"

"Of course, Prime Minister. I am sure that there are a number of areas in which Clive's undoubted talent and experience would add enormous value to the Foreign Office." His inner voice continued to speak but the words remained behind his smile; *I will bring one of my old toothbrushes and set the old fart to work scrubbing the dried turd stains from the pans of the fucking foreign office toilets. He can get his hands dirty and help us to clean up foreign issues with domestic tissues!*

With the Home Secretary back in his box, Mitchell turned again to his Foreign Secretary. "While we are all together Matthew, it would seem to make sense to bring us up to speed on your meeting with Trade and Industry on the Saudi Air Force issue."

"Yes, of course, Prime Minister," Sadler opened his tablet, pressed a couple of keys and a screen emerged on the wall with images of aircraft, bar charts and pound signs.

"This is perhaps the most sensitive and complex issue that the Foreign Office, Defence Ministry and the Department of Trade and Industry have had to contend with over the past fifty years."

Neil Faraday chuckled to himself and grinned openly at the old man's exclusion from what was, quite clearly, a matter of significant national importance.

"The Saudi Defence Ministry are at the most advanced stage of negotiations with UK Aero Industries for the extension of their trade agreement to supply the Saudi Air Force with a further seventy Hen Harrier Fighters. The order is of huge strategic importance to the Saudis and even greater economic importance to the company and the UK economy."

"Nice business if you can get it!" Faraday quipped. "I bet that deal cost more than the customary bottle of Scotch in a private room at Spearmint Rhino." Nobody else laughed.

"As you know," Sadler continued, "relationships between Saudi Arabia and the United States have been deteriorating markedly since America has been forging closer links with Iran. The Saudis have reluctantly tolerated the Israeli relationship but the US recent trading treaty with Tehran is starting to unnerve the Crown Prince."

"I would have thought that it's the Israelis who should be pissed off with the Yanks, not the Saudis." Faraday was almost dismissive in his comment, making a show of removing a speck of dirt from under his fingernail with the paperclip that had formerly bound his ministerial paper on the matter.

"Iran has become an increasing threat to the Saudi system to the point of imminent confrontation." Sadler was now in his stride. "The Saudis have got wind of the potential tie-up between UK Aero Industries and Boeing and will not commit to any deal with a UK company if there is a possibility that they form a US joint venture."

"So tell UK Aero Industries to flatly deny it," Faraday offered. "Seal the deal, sign the contract, and stitch the Saudis up. Start production and commissioning so they are reliant upon our technology, then do the deal with the Yanks."

"Unfortunately," rebuked Sadler, "the Saudi business principles are every bit as cynical as yours. They are two steps ahead of you and are now insisting that they will only do the deal if UK Aerospace sell the Saudis twenty-five per cent of the business. They are prepared to offer a seven per cent premium on today's share price and agree to the procurement cost of the aircraft with no further contractual negotiation. If Aero Industries don't do the deal, they will switch their order to Aerospace Français. Needless to say, the UK business is thrilled by the prospect. They need a full order book and they need a new investor. It's a win, win, win."

This time, Clive Mountstevens beat Faraday to the sucker question. "So what's the issue? Deal done, everybody happy!"

"Actually, Clive, everybody is far from happy." It was now the Prime Minister's turn to pick up the thread from Sadler. "The United States are apoplectic at the prospect. They are accusing the United Kingdom of openly embracing not just a commercial alliance with the Saudis but a political and economic one. They contend that ISIS is funded and organised by Saudi Arabia and that this new deal would see the UK supplying aircraft and weaponry that will be used against NATO forces as the conflict escalates. The prospect of Saudi Arabia owning a stake in our biggest military manufacturer fills them with horror and they are threatening our status within NATO."

This was not a particularly difficult perspective to understand and even Faraday could see the conflict of interests. "So if we do the deal, we piss off Uncle Sam and if we don't do the deal, we piss off our biggest export market, wind up UK Aero Industries and put five thousand highly skilled workers on the dole."

Sadler now afforded himself a smile. "Well actually, it's not quite as straightforward as that. The US ambassador has advised that they fully understand that the contract is crucial to the UK economy. He has suggested that if we encourage UK Aero Industries NOT to do the deal with the Saudis, America will purchase all excess capacity to re-arm the Israeli Air force and subsidise Boeing to pay a nine per cent premium on the current share price for a thirty-five per cent stake in the business."

The Prime Minister had the final words on the matter.

"So this is not a win, win scenario… this is very much a win, lose scenario and we have the unenviable task of deciding who loses. The Americans, the Saudis, the French… or us."

38

As happy as Rosie Hunter was with the news that her boss and colleague were safe, she felt a little cheated that the operation had been concluded so swiftly thus restricting the opportunity to make a name for herself in Sean's absence. She admired Sean and, on occasions, her admiration had become dangerously close to something more but she would never, ever, allow personal feelings to interfere with her professional career and, most importantly, her stellar ambition.

She buzzed with excitement, therefore, when she received the call from the deputy director of MI7, suggesting that there might be signs of a breakthrough in the communications trace of the Istanbul, Paris, Riyadh and London network exchanges. When she arrived, Paul Cruse led her to his office and she surprised herself by failing to withdraw her shoulder from his right hand as he shepherded her through the door. She considered him to be a person of considerable interest on both professional and personal levels. Bizarrely, she found herself recalling the first meeting of Julia Roberts and Richard Gere in the film *Pretty Woman*, before she was revealed as a whore, of course. She was slightly deflated when she saw a young man with his bespectacled, curly-haired head peering closely into a trio of digital screens behind the deputy director's desk.

"Inspector Hunter: Alec Brunson, one of our senior analysts in the Transmitted Data Section."

TDS was the heartbeat of MI7. The most sophisticated electronic tracking systems on the planet, with the possible exception of NASA, were manned by the most brilliant analysts that Cambridge and Cranfield had ever produced. They were almost bred for the task and raised with their machines. Personality was a positive barrier to success, as became apparent by Brunson's failure to recognise that Rosie was even in the room.

Brunson fiddled while Cruse spoke. "At around one o' clock this afternoon, we experienced a systems alert that signified that the four network terminals we had been monitoring in the Colin Richardson investigation had all become live, active with Istanbul, Paris and Riyadh triangulated with each other. Istanbul spoke with Paris and London, Paris spoke with Riyadh, and Riyadh spoke with Istanbul. In previous exchanges, all we have been able to determine was the link between the three terminals. The communications devices themselves were completely inaccessible to any form of data extraction."

"So you knew they were talking but didn't know *who* was talking, or what they were saying," Rosie was just confirming that she could cut through the jargon.

Brunson did not lift his head but his monotone mutterings had Rosie straining her ears towards him.

"We still don't. This is not a simple case of phone tapping but we do seem to have penetrated a further two layers of security which were probably accessed by one of the parties inadvertently opening communication on a commercial frequency. This allowed us to trace the signal back to the other three."

"So what does this give us?" asked Rosie, anxiously. In her head, she almost had her hand on her warrant card.

Cruse sought to manage expectations. "This is a significant breakthrough, but it doesn't yet, give us names, numbers or transcripts. It does, however, give us network IP locations through which the calls were routed and these have provided the exact satellite locations from which the calls were made and received. The IP addresses may service a multiple number of phone or computer terminals but using the exact time of the communication exchanges, we should also be able to identify precisely which and whose devices were used."

"That's amazing!" cried Rosie. "Mr Brunson, you are a genius."

"Actually, I am not, Inspector Hunter. It seems that the Istanbul party is a bit of a fool. Or uncharacteristically careless."

"Thanks Alec." Cruse nodded. "You can leave us now. DI Hunter will be investigating the London connections and we already have a man in Istanbul. Can you focus on the Riyadh and Paris contacts as a matter of priority please?"

The deputy director was clearly not expecting a response as Brunson bundled up his kit and shuffled through the door without any form of departing courtesy. His head was already in Riyadh.

"So, Rosie, you don't mind me calling you Rosie, do you? We now have a very positive but very, very, sensitive line of enquiry to pursue."

Rosie did not mind him calling her Rosie but was rather disappointed when he did not invite her to reciprocate when she answered. "No, of course not, Deputy Director."

Paul Cruse continued. "The early triangulation trackers approximated the signal source to the Whitehall area of London. Brunson's team have now tracked the IP address of the server powering the computer and telephonic device back to the address of: 70 Whitehall, London, SW1A 2AS... The Cabinet Office."

The words, "Oh, shit," had tumbled from Rosie's mouth involuntarily so she offered no apology. "So where the fuck do we go from here?" This time she did apologise.

"Don't worry, Rosie. I gave a similar reaction but not quite as civil. In answer to your question, I go to the head of civil service information systems security, and I suggest that you go to your Superintendent Lakin and agree between yourselves which of you will accompany me when I get the clearance I need to knock on some cabinet doors."

Any sexual sensations that Rosie might have imagined with Cruse were now well and truly surpassed by the electricity that now charged through every nerve of her being as she shook his hand and shot out of the room.

39

Sean and Farah were enjoying a rather large, fine malt whisky in the sedate surroundings of the sitting room of the Chief Constable's residential suite at Lancashire Police Headquarters in Hutton, near Preston. This was not a celebratory drink nor the prelude to a romantic evening together, this was just a necessary relaxant to help them both distil and understand the events of the last eight hours. They were both mature enough, and brave enough to admit that they were probably in a state of shock. There had been the obligatory debriefing by the Chief Constable and they knew that there would be more to come, locally and back in London with the Commissioner and security services. Farah had been taken immediately to the Royal Preston Hospital to have her finger wound treated and received the expected news that there was no possibility of the original digit being replaced but it was highly likely that a replacement could be grown and grafted by stem cell technology. She was also advised that she would certainly be required to assist in the interrogation of the highly valuable assets collected on the top of Darwen Tower but they would be allowed to soften up a little first. Farah understood the terminology and found herself feeling surprisingly ambivalent about their ordeal.

Farah's first priority following her treatment and debriefings with the Lancashire Constabulary was to call Ava in Paris. Her daughter was blissfully unaware of the trauma and distress that Farah had been suffering, which, to Farah, was the ultimate blessing. She could never have forgiven herself if her daughter's big adventure had been blighted by her mother's stupidity in allowing herself to be kidnapped. From the absent expressions of love and the hint of attitude, it was clear that Ava was in the company of her classmates, and probably others. When they spoke, Farah knew that her daughter would have been far more emotive and expressive had she been alone... or maybe she was just growing up? No, the nonchalant, apathetic tones of an arrogant teen were alien to Ava, who was clearly too embarrassed to express just how much she loved and was missing the mother who had devoted her whole self to her daughter. Not surprisingly, Farah was worried about how much Ava would be worrying about her tone so they were both hugely relieved, thirty seconds after they had closed the call when the digital message pinged on to Farah's screen, accompanied by a suitably slushy background video of music and roses. "Sorry I couldn't say all the things I wanted to say Mama, but I love and miss you more than you will ever know. Can't wait to see you again next Tuesday. Big, big, big, hugs from your little girl!"

Farah left Sean in the sitting room as she went out to sob tears of relief, joy and sadness. Ava was not the only Karim that had difficulty expressing her emotions publicly.

The Chief Constable's residence was a three bedroomed lodge within the grounds of the headquarters at Hutton and was, as such, as safe a safe house as could be found in the area. The Chief Constable rarely used the place unless he was entertaining visitors of similar rank and status from other forces. Tonight, he just showed Sean and Farah their respective bedrooms, invited them to make themselves at home and to avail themselves of his wine rack and cocktail cabinet. He also advised them that one of the duty constables would be very happy to collect and deliver a delicious Indian takeaway, on the Chief Constable's account, from the award winning Bangla Fusion restaurant less than ten minutes away. Their order was to be delivered within the hour.

Sean, gently teased out of Farah the details that she had not disclosed to the debriefing team. These were not objective facts or observations that she sought to conceal, but feelings and emotions that she could share only with Sean. Sean felt such a sense of guilt for allowing her to travel to Blackburn alone at such a sensitive time but consoled himself that he would not have acted differently had it been Rosie Hunter or Brian Chambers making the trip.

For two hours, they had sat either together in the same room, or passed in corridors as police procedures took their course. Then just half an hour ago, they were alone. Sean locked the door while Farah closed the curtains and they just fell into each other's arms with such passion, force and intensity that neither was able to move. There was no kiss, no caress, no loving gaze, just a grip that promised they would never be parted again. The grasp subsided, the tension mellowed, the arms relaxed, the hands roamed, searched and reassured that they were indeed together again. Their faces slid from cheek to cheek before finally meeting full face in a kiss secured by Sean's shovelled hands around Farah's head and hips. Neither wanted to spoil the moment by finding a bedroom. They wrestled each other to the ground, grabbing and tearing any obstacle to the meeting of flesh upon flesh, muscle to velvet. They fumbled, they froze, they gripped, they shuddered, they thrashed together in a frenzy that neither had ever experienced and together, sighing and groaning, they collapsed away from each other and left hands conjoined.

Aware that the only pleasure that might come remotely close to the past twenty minutes was the special massala meal and a bottle of Merlot, they gathered themselves together and prepared a table for two. Intimate enough to share their feelings but distant enough to dispel the curiosity of the obliging constable who duly delivered their dishes.

They talked again about Farah's capture. Farah agonised about how she might have behaved differently to have avoided this huge embarrassment to the unit but Sean reassured her that even with the assistance of PC Pemberton, the local officer, the abduction was always going to happen and had been planned meticulously. She was feeling reassured, perhaps, on reflection, too much so as Sean's next statement hit her hard between the eyes.

"You know that I won't be able to take you home tomorrow don't you? We can travel to Euston together but I will have to go straight back into the Yard. I promise you that there will be a secure escort on the platform to meet you. You will then be on leave for a week while I work out with the commissioner, the details of your transfer out of the Special Investigations Unit."

"My what? My transfer!" Farah was genuinely incredulous. "You just admitted that this could happen to any of us. It wasn't my fault. I wasn't negligent. I didn't crack under interrogation. I stuck to procedures and played it exactly by the book. Sean, I can't believe that you would ditch me like this! I thought I meant something to you!"

"Farah," he took both her hands. "You mean more than something to me, you mean everything to me but I can't ask you to be my wife if we are working in the same unit together can I? Oh, by the way, will you marry me?"

40

Rosie Hunter was stepping out of the shower when her mobile device buzzed. She shouted her programmed voice command and the device switched to the audio output on her wall display unit. A different command would have given the caller an unexpected visual bonus as Rosie stepped into her robe and walked into the bedroom.

The digital display read 'Cruse' and her own internal face recognition system had already kicked in. She thought about switching to video but decided that might be a little too obvious a tactic.

"DI Hunter?"

"Yes, Deputy Director, this is Rosie."

"Thank goodness I've found you, Rosie. I hope this isn't too inconvenient?"

"No, not at all. I was just taking a shower and thinking about a quiet table for one at the Italian around the corner."

"Well you might have to eat a little later if that's all right. Have you spoken to anyone yet about the communications that we traced back to the Cabinet Office?"

"No, not yet. You told me that you were checking the calls out with security and in any case, my superintendent is incommunicado at the moment and I was loathe to call the commissioner until you gave me the green light."

"The light is red, I am afraid, so you have saved yourself from a sizeable dollop of egg splatting across your rather spectacular face."

Rosie did not know which surprised her most; the subject matter or the compliment. Cruse continued.

"It seems that the guy in Istanbul was not so stupid after all. I checked in with the head of security at Whitehall after you left and he just got back to me. It appears that although the four devices were indeed communicating with each other regularly, the Istanbul device is no longer in Istanbul, and Westminster have advised us that none of the IP addresses traced back to the London device is actually routed through their server or network provider. They seem to be bouncing the London signal around the globe but we have not yet verified or written off Riyadh or Paris."

"I see," said Rosie, totally deflated. She had resolved to press on with her investigations on Saturday morning, while Sean was still away and while security at Whitehall and Westminster would be light enough to allow her access to areas that might otherwise require advanced clearances. "I don't understand. Your Mr Brunson does not seem to be a man who can be fooled that easily. He seemed absolutely meticulous in tracking those networks and utterly convinced that he'd nailed them. Are we sure that the signals were spurious? Isn't it possible that someone in Whitehall or Westminster is covering up the location of the server?"

Now Rosie was really excited and was not at all ready to dismiss the possibility of a scandal or conspiracy leading straight back to the seat of government. This could be a career changing investigation.

"Two very good questions, Rosie. Alec Brunson is working on the first one and I rather hoped that we might meet to discuss the second."

"Well my boss should be back on Monday. I should probably advise him of the new direction that the investigation is taking and how to handle the Whitehall situation."

"I was thinking of maybe getting together before then and, for the sake of both our careers, I suggest that you say nothing to Superintendent Lakin until we have our facts straight. How about you scrap the Italian restaurant round the corner from you and join me at a rather splendid French one, just round the corner from me. The kitchen stays open until ten and it's a stone's throw from Green Park tube station. I'd send a car for you but I would rather observe professional discretion at this juncture."

Rosie was intrigued by the possible reasons for discretion and certainly compelled enough to suggest that she could be there within the hour.

"Meet me at nine-thirty outside the Piccadilly entrance," he said with mock intrigue. "I'll be the one in the raincoat holding a rose."

Rosie was juggling with a whole mess of emotions. Disappointment that the immediate line of enquiry had seemed to close down; intrigue that the enquiry was perhaps taking an even more opportunistic direction; professional pride that she was at the forefront of such a high profile case and, most pertinently, a very unprofessional sensation permeating her naked body that she had not felt during her ill-fated affair with a married merchant banker.

Rosie was as ambitious in her personal life as in her professional one. Perhaps more so. While she had the ambition, aspiration and ability to succeed Lakin at some point, she confided in herself that she would be prepared to sacrifice her sense of national duty for a life of luxury in the Cotswolds, Cote d'Azur and Chamonix. She was aware that she could not normally achieve this as the wife of the deputy director of a government agency but having researched this one rather carefully she had discovered that he was also the heir to a Dukedom and vast property estate spanning a good proportion of the home counties. More to the point, he was single and surprisingly easy on the eye.

Given the time constraints, Rosie dried her hair down around her slender neck, training it to fall effortlessly and reappear above her left shoulder. Her make-up was subtle, just enough to accentuate her high cheek bones and punctuate her piercing steel blue eyes. She dressed in a classic black one piece dress, practical enough for a tube journey but elegant enough for Le Caprice. Black two inch heels and a grey cashmere coat completed the look. She was satisfied as she stepped out and walked briskly, almost jauntily, to the Gloucester Road tube station, just two hundred yards from her apartment and three stops from Green Park.

She flashed the Oyster app on her phone and her entry to the station was recorded at nine-fifteen. She had timed it to perfection. Initially she had been slightly annoyed that Cruse had been allowed to curtail her normal two hour preparation time but she then prided herself on managing to look so good, so quickly and scheduled to arrive promptly but not over eagerly early.

The platform was quite busy. Friday evening around Gloucester Road heralded humanity at its best and worst. Well-heeled couples setting out or returning home, thirty-something professionals winding up their week with a well-earned celebration in one of the many wine and craft beer bars in the area and the inevitable smattering of Eastern European immigrants nursing cans of strong lager that probably offered more warmth than refreshment.

The illuminated board above indicated that the next train was approaching in one minute. Rosie was relieved to see this. Although she was an independent and confident traveller, her police experience had conditioned her to notice trouble and she had already caught the sneering exchange of glances between a pair of bearded, ragged looking migrants and three tall youths of African origin in grey and black hooded tracksuits.

As the lights from the train became visible along the dark tunnel and the mechanised voice warned passengers to stand behind the yellow line, the first punch was thrown by the tallest of the black men. The other two waded in and the two migrants were violently thrown backwards and sideways into a horrified Rosie who was bundled and bowled onto the tracks in front of the rapidly approaching train. Her beautiful head was completely crushed and fragments of bone, blood and flesh exploded from the tracks and splattered the tiled platform walls and advertising screens.

The fighters turned and ran from the platform. The three hoodies, pursued by the two migrants, ran up the escalators, over the gates and onto the road and down an alley where all five of them jumped in to the same waiting white van, beyond the range of any CCTV cameras.

Deputy Director Paul Cruse had been watching the events unfold on his tablet in a private booth in Henry's Bar across the road from Green Park tube station entrance. In the unlikely event of Rosie surviving the encounter, he would have crossed the road, greeted her warmly, and enjoyed a pleasant meal together before ensuring that her evening came to an unpleasant end on the way home. It was nothing personal; it was, he thought, rather regrettable but the previous day's discussions in Westminster and Whitehall left him little alternative.

He sipped his Sancerre as he switched applications from his elaborate CCTV tracker to the data tracker that Alec Brunson had forwarded earlier. Rosie Hunter's data devices, like everyone else's these days, left a digital trail – exhaust fumes, Alec called them – that quickly and easily recorded, analysed and detailed every text, email or voice message; outgoing and incoming, to any of her registered devices. Cruse scanned them and was satisfied that she had discussed their findings with nobody. Next, he turned to the film footage uploaded by Brunson, following her facial recognition profile from the seven thousand surveillance cameras that now covered central London. She had been nowhere near Westminster or Scotland Yard over the past twenty four hours. She had seemingly met nor spoke with anyone. "What a sad end to a tragically short life," Cruse was almost sincere in his sympathy.

41

Mehmet Osman, or Richard Collins as his sea pass signified, took the lime and soda from the waiter and placed the card into the pocket of his shorts, under the sun lounger in a secluded corner of deck sixteen. Christina was beside him sipping a coffee, and anyone looking their way, might have reasonably assumed from their easy manner that they were discussing last night's West End theatre production.

"Everything you requested is loaded," smiled Christina. "The materials came aboard in beer kegs, flour sacks and food boxes in the last three ports of call. Abdul Aziz has quarantined them in his quality control area. It is a perfectly normal procedure for such shipments to be stress tested for the voyage."

Osman smiled warmly at the 'wife' he had met less than a week ago but had come to respect and even regard with a degree of physical attraction, which was unusual for him. He was rarely distracted when working.

"Thank you, Christina. You have been of enormous assistance and have made this particular part of the job most pleasurable. I really could learn to enjoy this lifestyle. Perhaps you and I could do this again sometime, without the stress of two hundred kilos of volatile explosives below us. And to think, there are those who still insist that cruising is the safest form of travel and relaxation."

"How do you do it, Colin?" Christina did not know his real name and wouldn't have used it if she had. "I know that I am complicit in this but I am fighting for a cause that I am forced to support. You are a non-believer. Can you really live with yourself and face your God having killed so many innocent people, just for money?"

Osman was neither fazed nor offended by the question. He looked around to ensure that they were still alone and took another sip of his soda, smiling as he watched the even wake gently suffuse into the sea from the stern. He really was relaxing.

"Firstly, Christina, I am not the killer. I am merely an extension of the weapon. I am the sights and the trigger. Would you hold a guard dog responsible for injuring a burglar? Was the pilot who dropped the bomb on Nagasaki an evil man? Is a gun a tool of the devil? I am merely doing my job. As a soldier, I killed people on behalf of my government, for money. As a mercenary, I kill for other people, for more money. My paymasters make the decisions, I am simply their weapon of choice. If it were not me, there would be others."

He took another sip of his soda and lit a small cigar. He inhaled, sent a fine plume of smoke towards the ship's funnel and continued.

"And who is truly innocent in this world. Aren't we all stealing somebody else's oxygen? Are we not all breathing toxic carbon dioxide into the atmosphere, selfishly, to keep ourselves alive? Were the allied bombers over Syria killing innocent people or seeking to destroy military installations?"

"Isn't that different though?" Christina asked. "Isn't that war?"

"Exactly," replied Osman, casually. "In war, there are no innocents. There are two or more sets of soldiers believing that they are right because they have been told they are right, and there are two or more sets of civilians hoping that they are right. There are always casualties; without casualties, what would be the point of war? And what if there had been no war. How long would have those innocent people of yours have lived? How would they have lived? How would they have died? Croaking at their mother's tit for milk that had long dried up? Baking under a cruel, unrelenting sun with no clean water? Eating grass and pissing through their backsides? The world is always at war. Somebody always wants what somebody else has. Some humans will always be defined and deprived by the geography of their birth. What is so special about life anyway when we are all born to die? No, Christina, I have no trouble sleeping and I have no concern, no contempt, in fact no feeling at all, for those who use me as their weapon."

"Then I am pleased that my father, husband and brother were not men like you. They did not fight for money, they fought for the right to a homeland, a place to live," she hissed.

"In a land in which some other fathers, husbands and brothers lived before yours and lost to their loved ones. I do not belittle your loss, Christina. I have felt the agony of loss and it is perhaps that pain that has drained the humanity from me but if we are not prepared to share our world, we must be prepared to fight, die and kill for it."

"But not you," Christina spat. "You are not fighting for your world, you are killing for your wealth."

"Do I look like a wealthy man, Christina? Do I act like a wealthy man? Yes, I take money from wealthier men than me, but I also give it to poorer men than me. Do not judge me, Christina. The people you are helping me kill will not care that I make money while you make martyrs. We both make widows and orphans. If we did not do so, someone else would. It is our calling to do it better and cleaner. The people who pay us are the killers. We are just weapons and ammunition."

He blew more cigar smoke upwards and it disappeared even before it got near to the mighty plume from the ship's stack. He smiled at Christina as though this somehow proved a point.

"And the people paying you, us, to do this," asked Christina. "What are they seeking?"

"I do not doubt that they are convincing each other that they are fighting for freedom, for a better world, for unity, for the long term survival of the planet or for humanity, but the truth is Christina, they are paying us for power."

"Look around you, Colin. Look at these people baking naked in the sun, mocking those in my homeland who cower behind rubble to find the shade. Look at them guzzling their bright coloured drinks, polluting their minds, corrupting their souls. Watch them build mountains of food on their plates only to create the avalanches of waste when they have finished the dance of their silver forks and spoons. What do these fools know of life, of love and of loss?"

"But are they not innocent?" Osman questioned, quietly, quizzically. "Is their excess a mortal sin? Does their enjoyment of their vacuous vacation condemn them to perish? Which one would you like me to kill for you? The fattest? The richest? The most beautiful? The noisiest: the one enjoying life the most? For it is he, after all that has the most to lose."

"No, Colin, their time will come."

"And so, my dear Christina, let us enjoy our remaining time amongst them. Let us pretend that we, too, have lives to live and lovers to love. Who knows? We may even grow to love their lives as our own."

42

The call had come from Brian Chambers. Lakin had patched the link through to the wall screen so Farah could share the conversation but instantly regretted his ill-fated attempt at innocent inclusion as soon as Farah burst into tears and ran from the room. Even in the safety of Lancashire Police Headquarters she could not escape the fear of the life she lived, or was it guilt at the life that Rosie had just lost?

"An accident? A fucking accident on a tube platform? Come on, Brian, you know that stinks the fucking incident room out as much as I do."

Lakin wasn't sure he should have used that line and suspected that his grammar and formation gave it a meaning other than the one he had intended.

"Women like Rosie don't have accidents on tube stations. Fights don't just break then fade away after just one pissed up push. This was a set up. She was targeted. What do we have on CCTV?"

"The five men all ran off in the same direction, up the exit elevator. The remaining witnesses on the platform were too stunned to follow them. They recognised or remembered less than we have

266

here on screen." Chambers broke down. "I loved that woman, Sean. I fucking loved her. Not in that way. She would never fancy an old twat like me; but I loved her style, her mind, her ambition, her ability, her authority; and she lets herself get snuffed out by a bunch of bickering yobs on a piss stained tube platform. They are not getting away with this. I will fucking have them!"

That was Brian's problem. He loved everybody too much. He never found time to marry so the force was his family; his brothers, sisters, sons and daughters; he even found unlikely friendships in some of the many non-violent villains he had nabbed during his thirty-five years on the force. Unlike so many long-serving officers, he had never become sordid, sour or cynical. He was not one of those world-weary cops counting down the days to his engraved Citizen watch and days by the canal with a fishing rod. It was not unusual to see Brian expressing emotion but rarely had he allowed such a vitriolic outburst as this to betray his old school manner. He really did love Rosie.

The next call was from the commissioner. He took this on his handheld device and it seemed that Pollard too, had the red eyes of a man whose sensitivity rarely surfaced. Perhaps it was just lack of sleep or a retinal fault on the display. Although Nigel Pollard was not the warmest line manager Lakin had ever worked for, he was a man of compassion and always took the loss of an officer seriously, but never personally. Lakin repeated his suspicions, slightly more objectively and, to his surprise, Pollard readily agreed.

"It's too much of a coincidence and detective inspectors don't die on tube station platforms. I have studied the footage and there is too little interaction between the men for this to have been a spontaneous altercation. I concur that it was staged to look like an accident and to scare witnesses from interfering before, during or after the attack. It is either directly linked to the bombing investigation or one of her other current or recent enquiries. What else has DI Hunter been working on?"

Normally he would simply have called her Hunter, never Rosie; the use of her title was the measure of his respect and humanity.

"She was investigating the series of gang killings between the Afro-Caribbean community and the Eastern Europeans. The turf war is spilling over into Wandsworth and two Romanian enforcers were gunned down within a day of each other the weekend before the bomb. She was working her way through the usual suspects when we put it on hold for her trip up to Scotland."

"I suppose that such a gang could take her out in this way, but the ethnic mix doesn't look right." The commissioner seemed uncomfortable in his phrasing as he continued. "The three hoodies appeared to be black and the others were definitely heard to be speaking in pronounced Eastern European accents. This would be an unlikely collaboration. Where did the Scotland connection take us?"

Lakin bit his tongue and avoided answering 'Scotland.' Instead he went over the details of the report that he had filed to Pollard two days earlier. "She got the name, identity card, fingerprints and contact details of one of the prime suspects in the bombings, sir. She took the details directly to MI7 where she was working with the listeners to try to track down his location. She was also following anyone with whom the suspect had been in frequent contact with around the time of the explosions. We were due to meet on Monday morning to discuss their joint progress."

"Okay," nodded Pollard. "Leave that one to me. I am due to meet with the DD, Paul Cruse on Monday. I will brief you immediately afterwards."

"With respect, sir," retorted Lakin, with just enough of a hint of disrespect, "that's two days away and with the pace at which things have happened over the past five, I would request that either you, or I, bring that forward. I will be on a train from Preston at eleven and back into Euston before twelve and in the Yard by twelve-thirty. Could you perhaps arrange for me to meet with Cruse instead?"

Sean knew that the response was likely to be affirmative as Pollard rarely dared to disrupt his good lady's social diary over a weekend and such a meeting with Cruse might transpire to be more sensitively challenging than the boundaries of his comfort zone stretched.

"Of course, Sean. You are right. It would make sense from a continuity perspective if you spoke with him so I will tee it up for you straight away. Give my regards to Karim, by the way. I hope that finger business is not going to keep her away from the job for too long."

"I have a feeling that her finger might heal faster than her head, sir. She spent thirty-six hours believing that she was about to lose it."

"Yes, of course. Tell her to take a couple of days off with her family. I will ping you the details of your meeting with Cruse."

Sean switched off the device just before Farah emerged from the bathroom.

"The boss sends his best!"

43

Adam Albano was not sorry to leave Adnan Abadi behind in the mortuary. He had spent three years in London playing the Angry Young Man, the devout and studious scholar living the spartan existence of a foreign student. Adam Albano would be greater fun and much more interesting but he was in no doubt about the urgency of the task ahead of him. He had also been advised of the fate of Scott Douglas, with whom he had shared a close partnership over the past two years as they both infiltrated radical Jihadist movements; Scott in the prison community, Adnan in academia. Adnan's reports made it abundantly clear that the threat from university was a hundred times greater than that from behind bars. He would miss Scott. He admired him as an operator and was probably as close to becoming a friend as their mutual interests would allow.

The trip to Paris had been straight forward enough. Customs and security procedures on Eurostar were marginally less intrusive than at Charles de Gaulle airport so he travelled by train. Although no visas were required for European travel, all of Britain's former EU partners now insisted on rigorous passport inspections that entailed long queues before encountering officials specially selected for their inability to speak English. This was just one small part of the European strategy to punish Britain for leaving Europe and set a transparent example to any other nation contemplating doing so. Brussels, led by Germany, sheepishly followed by France and slavishly supported by the remaining twenty-five failed economies had set about engineering the economic ruin of its former ally from the day that article 50 had been triggered. It was openly believed in England that Germany was now planning to achieve economically, what they had twice failed to do militarily. As an American posing as a Maltese citizen Adam was spared much of the deliberate beurocratic delay and suffered only the normal levels of French incompetence.

He had been in Paris just a matter of hours but was already beginning to feel like an overworked drone under the piloted command of the uber geek of MI7, Alec Brunson. Brunson had given Adam precise sets of coordinates for the voice and data messages that had triangulated between France, Istanbul and Saudi Arabia. To their knowledge, this user had not been in contact with the UK server. Brunson had reluctantly, very reluctantly in fact, accepted the assertion from Whitehall that the London signals had, in fact, been rerouted from Edinburgh but could not agree with Whitehall how it had been possible to dupe him. Until fairly recently, it had been possible to intercept a call, text or email and track it back to a registered device or address but private and perfectly legal advances in personal security now rendered a higher degree of difficulty to the operation. The devices used in Paris had been tracked to three regular locations: the first was a business premises on the Rue de Libertine, the second, a rather exclusive and expensive restaurant in Montmartre, called Valjean, and the third was a residential apartment just a couple of hundred metres from the restaurant. All that Adam and the backup team at MI7 now needed to do was tie down one person with these three locations.

This was to have been a relatively straight forward job for an agent of Adam's capability and he told himself that Mellor had teed this cosy little Paris assignment up for him as a thank you for his painful experience breathing urine and stale cabbage fumes in Chateau Belmarsh. Alec Brunson had done all the desk work and Adam was little more than his drone, flown in and guided to provide the personal touch.

When Rosie had given MI7 Colin Richard's ID and handset details it had been a routine tracking task for Alec to isolate the devices with which it had communicated over the weeks leading up to, and days following the bombing. He could identify all the trace signals, digital exhaust fumes as he called them, from and to phones, computers and tablets. Predictably, all these devices incorporated sophisticated encryption protocols preventing the extraction of actual data but provided an accurate set of footprints for his network of contacts. Given the degree of caution that the target had utilised in his encryption software, Alec found it odd that Richards had been careless enough to allow geographical tracing but assumed that his current location, the only one that remained a mystery to Alec, somehow compromised the security screen. That, or for some inexplicable reason, the ring master was letting the audience take a closer look at the animals.

From the GPRS coding and satellite imagery that made the old Google Earth look like Betamax video technology, he could zoom straight to the doors of the identified properties. Adam had been sent to monitor and possibly penetrate three properties in Paris from which the most prominent and prolific exchanges emanated. The first was an exclusive and eye wateringly expensive apartment in the upmarket area of Montmarte, where nobility, artists and tourists brushed shoulders. The second was a small but even more exclusive restaurant less than three hundred metres away and the third, an office complex on the Rue de Libertine in the Business District. The offices were home to just five organisations, two of which occupied the penthouse floor and were inextricably linked. The first of the two was a boutique investment brokerage called Sapient, which appeared to specialise in the courtship, marriage and divorce of mid-sized entrepreneurial businesses seeking equity investment under the radar of the Bourse. The chair of the business was listed as Francoise Marie La Plume, the forty-eight year old daughter of Bernard, one of the country's most respected industrialists, still controlling a business empire the size of a large African country at the age of seventy-eight. The adjoining penthouse offices were the registered headquarters of the right wing Vive De Gaulle Party whose leader was the charismatic, some said mesmerising, Madame La Plume.

The apartment in Montmarte was also hers, where she lived alone and the reservations system of the nearby restaurant, Valjean, revealed that she was a regular and generous patron. Adam had his mark.

His assignment was to secure physical access to, or procure the memory from, any of those devices, which would allow Brunson to create a complete, unabridged version of any verbal or digital conversation conducted upon them.

As it was Saturday morning, he began work in the business district but a cursory stroll by the business premises was enough to persuade him that the security seemed impenetrable. Brunson's satellite surveillance had spotted layer upon layer of infra-red beams and just for safe measure, a pair of surly, burly security guards patrolled the perimeter with a sense of purpose that suggested that these were not of the variety that would work for minimum wage at the local shopping mall. Even as Adam walked by on the opposite side of the avenue he noticed one of the guards speaking into his lapel and his colleague promptly casting his gaze in Adam's direction.

Adam quickly reverted to plan B, asking Alec to hack into the reservation system of the restaurant, Valjean, to determine when Madame La Plume had her next planned visit. The response was prompt and positive. A table for two was permanently reserved in her name although this did not, of course, guarantee that she would use it every night. Alec had noted that certain evenings were highlighted, indicating that on those occasions, she was more likely to be present. Had Alec bothered to examine the ownership structure of the restaurant he might have discovered that not only was the lady a regular patron, she was also the majority shareholder. Adam made a couple of further requests of Alec before returning to his hotel for a spot of R and R... Rest and Research.

44

Neil Faraday was at home that Saturday morning. Once a week, either Saturday or Sunday, he took a break from being the pugnacious Deputy Prime Minister; the arrogant and bigoted leader of UKIP; flamboyant doyen of the Westminster drinks terrace, and exchanged these facades for the caring husband and loving father that his family had always known him to be. He sat beside Quentin on the double divan in the spare bedroom that had been hastily prepared for his beloved son's discharge from hospital earlier that morning. The young man clearly was unfit to return, alone, to his bachelor apartment in Shoreditch and his mother had absolutely insisted that he come back home to Kensington.

Neil looked down at his bruised and battered son. The boy's head was bandaged, the left side of his face swollen to a bulbous suet pudding and his right eye hidden behind a dark blue ball of throbbing flesh.

"I am so sorry, Quentin. I am so very, very sorry."

His son struggled to speak through two swollen lips and three replacement teeth that still did not seemed to have accepted him.

275

"You have nothing to be sorry about, Dad. Abadi was a lunatic. A violent, fundamentalist fanatic and an explosion waiting to happen. I just happened to be there when he detonated. It had nothing to do with you or your politics. His kind just need to lash out occasionally and they don't care who happens to be in the way."

"I would love to believe that you are right, son, but there are those who believe that many of the issues this country faces are down to me, one way or another. Perhaps they are right. I do things my way and my way is not always orthodox. Whatever I do, I do for the love of my country but I should have realised how much I may have been harming the ones I truly love."

"Look, Dad, you have always spoken freely and fought for the rights of free speech for everyone in this country. Of course you have provoked confrontation, but you know as well as I do, that we are all much more secure by having such views expressed openly, than having them simmering below the surface in the Finsbury Park Mosque. And who knows, after this week the country and the world just might wake up to the threat that you have been forecasting for years and do something about taking back control of England."

Faraday discreetly brushed the tear from the corner of his eye before composing his voice enough to mutter. "Let's hope so, son. For all our sakes I really hope so."

The bedroom door opened a little and Valerie Faraday cautiously edged her head round as though conscious that she might hear something that she would rather not. She announced her presence by nervously clearing her throat.

"Tom Mellor is downstairs, darling. He was hoping you could spare him fifteen minutes."

Faraday was genuinely surprised and instinctively replied that he would be down straight away. He rested his hand on his son's shoulder and simply said, "We must all live with the choices we make."

Faraday found Mellor sat in the conservatory with a mug of tea. "Tom. This is an unexpected surprise. You should have called, we would have prepared some lunch for you."

Mellor rose and shook his hand warmly. "I am trying to cut back on my cell call usage and respectfully suggest that you might do the same. In this climate, high office does not put you beyond the reach of eager ears on either side of the moral divide."

"I don't think I would have anything to fear from my mundane mutterings," laughed Faraday, not altogether convincingly.

"No, I'm sure you wouldn't, Neil, but the smart ones can not only hack you, they can clone your voice and have you making conversations from the other side of the world with people you have never heard of. It's a dirty world out there, Neil."

"Thanks for the advice, Tom, but I have a son upstairs who has just been reminding me of the importance of free speech."

"Yes of course. Delighted you've got him home. Others have not been so lucky this week and, between you and me, I am not sure that Graeme still fully understands the continued threats we face. You are his deputy, I am just an advisor but together I feel that we have to slap down the lily-livers in the Cabinet and start to shore up our position both at home and abroad. We can't let this week be for nothing. We can't let those poor people die for nothing and we can't let any more lose their lives to terrorists and enemies of democracy. If Graeme cannot, or will not find the courage to take the fight to *them*, we might need to be thinking about promoting a leader who will."

"I'm listening, Tom. But I thought that you and Graeme went back a long way."

"We do, Neil, but my arse and I go back a lot further back and I have no intention of having it blown off by the next bunch of chancers who see this country as low hanging fruit. I am more than a little concerned that Graeme is listening to the diplomatic arguments of the Foreign Office and defence departments and side-lining the dinosaurs like us and Mountstevens. No government can survive another disaster of the proportions we have witnessed this week. If we don't take decisive action now, the public will, quite rightly, demand a new regime that does."

"Listen, Tom. Graeme and I have our differences and you will never see us down the pub together, but he is the Prime Minister, I am his Deputy and it is therefore my duty to support him, not undermine him… On the other hand, if you are suggesting that he needs a little help to point him towards a more radical conclusion then sit down, I'll get us a beer and we can talk about it."

Faraday returned with two large bottles of Bombardier Ale. The irony was not lost on Mellor.

"Good health, Neil! I know that we have had our ideological differences but I can't be the only person around the Cabinet to believe that Graeme is becoming seduced by the liberals and beginning to see the world through a rose-tinted periscope. He is proposing further defence cuts at a time when we are fighting on three fronts in the Middle East, on the brink of Civil War with the Scots and Irish, facing a Jihadist insurgence from IBIS and sitting back while the European Union build an army of occupation to take the country, with or without our people, back into Europe."

Faraday nodded but was suspicious of Mellor's motives. Was he really plotting against his old friend or simply drawing the Deputy Prime Minister into a treasonous plot that might see Mellor himself installed as Mitchell's number two.

"We have debated these issues in Cabinet, Tom. Mitchell is convinced that our relationship with the USA is still special enough to protect us from any potential economic or military backlash from Europe and although IBIS, ISIS and ISIL continue to terrorise us internationally, he will not take action against the peaceful UK Muslim population. In fact, I believe that he is secretly in favour of giving IBIS their own state within our state."

"Then he is losing the plot even faster than I thought he was! America already views us, potentially, as the fifty-first state and IBIS won't be happy until the dome of St Paul's Cathedral is painted gold. Be in no doubt that the Scots, Irish and Welsh will side with the EU to achieve a complete capitulation and hand our sovereignty back to Brussels."

"Mitchell is still popular with the British public, Tom. I would be happy to rally my party together to challenge and oppose him but if we bring the coalition down right now, he is likely to take seats from UKIP and gain an even stronger hold on the country."

"Then the country needs to be made to realise that he is leading us blindfolded, with our hands tied behind our backs into obscurity. The country is being attacked on all fronts and Mitchell's only answer is to increase the Foreign Aid budget to bribe the third world to be nice to us. The public need to be reminded that the events of last week, indeed, months, are the result of a weak Prime Minister, too scared to confront our enemies at home and abroad. It's time for change, Neil, and I am backing you to bring this change about."

"You have the ear of the intelligence services and the armed forces, Tom. Can't you collectively bring pressure to bear, show the nation that we are losing the battle?"

"We might just have to do that, Neil, but I need to know that I can rely on your support in Parliament. Especially when things get nasty."

"As you know, Tom, I am at my very, very best when things get nasty!"

45

Farah flatly refused to take time off and requested that she be allowed to take the lead in investigating Rosie Hunter's suspicious death. Sean readily agreed as he knew that this would keep her focussed but away from the front line danger of the ongoing terrorism investigation. She agreed that she might take a few days with Ava when she returned from her school trip next Monday but right now, despite, or maybe due to, her aching hand she needed the adrenaline flow of a live investigation. Rosie was a close colleague but not a close friend. They shared professional competence but Farah found it difficult to comprehend Rosie's obsession with career progression and finding Mr Right – or more probably Lord Right. She did, however, deserve a thorough investigation and Farah would ferret out the ambiguities surrounding her dubious demise.

She began her investigations at Rosie's cubicle in Scotland Yard. She secured access to her colleague's personal computer which regularly networked and synchronised all her electronic devices and consolidated case notes chronologically. Farah was immediately drawn to meetings with Paul Cruse and Alec Brunson in pursuit of a breakthrough emanating from her recent visit to Scotland

and the suspected assassin's employer. Not surprisingly, Farah was curtly advised that Paul Cruse was unavailable at weekends and that any request to interview him would have to be approved by their respective superiors. Sean would not present a problem but the head of MI7 proved to be predictably elusive. Farah supposed that this was probably a prerequisite of the role.

A formal, but less robust degree of clearance was required to interview lower levels and less than two hours later she was sharing a coffee in a soundproof booth with Alec Brunson. Farah explained that she was investigating the circumstances of her colleague's death and Alec seemed immediately uncomfortable and defensive. He acknowledged having met with Rosie in the presence of his deputy director as though to indicate that this made him immune from any further questions.

Farah had noted from Rosie's early file notes that the digital exhaust trails seemed to lead to Saudi Arabia, Paris and London but that the London connection appeared to have been bounced from Scotland.

"Our suspect must be a highly skilled communications specialist to have fooled you like that," Farah suggested.

She noticed Alec's knuckles whiten as he covered his mouth and muttered.

"If he was that skilled, he wouldn't have left the trace in the first place. If he can conceal his own location, as he has, he could have easily masked the recipient's devices. He is either very sloppy or very lucky... maybe both."

"But smart enough to knock you off the scent by fooling you into thinking that the communications with Scotland were actually happening in London."

Brunson said nothing. Now both knuckles were covering his mouth as he stared at the floor.

Farah continued. "I understand that we now have assets on the ground in these locations. Was DI Hunter party to this information?"

"I wouldn't know," Brunson mumbled, without looking up. "I just extract and analyse the signals. The DD determines what actions we take." This wasn't strictly true but Brunson knew better than to declare his knowledge of the operation underway in Paris.

"Who would be most likely to follow up the Scotland lead?" asked Farah, innocently. "Now that they are an independent state, would it be MI5 or MI6?"

"I don't know and I really don't care!" spat Brunson. "They are not going to find anything there anyway. There is no way that I got that trace wrong. I have never got a trace wrong. If I miss them I miss them. If I get them, I get them right. The devices were in London."

"So why are we not following them up in London? What, or who turned attentions to Scotland?" Farah enquired, conscious that this line of questioning was heading away from Rosie and back to the bombing.

"I am an analyst, Miss Karim. I don't interpret that data, I don't issue instructions, and I don't make decisions. I analyse and I do as I am told. If the agency believed I had made a mistake, I wouldn't be here anymore and now I really don't think I have anything else to say."

Alec Brunson rose and shuffled out of the area briskly without saying goodbye or glancing back. Farah would never comprehend the anguish he had experienced as his professional competency had been called into question. Brunson would rather die than be wrong and was fearful that he was more likely to experience the former than the latter in this department.

Farah was led out of the department by the watching security guard. She needed to speak to Sean before he met with Deputy Director Cruse.

46

Montmartre was viewed by Parisians the way some New Yorkers view Greenwich Village and Londoners view Covent Garden. It had changed, but not for the better. It had become a theme park within a district steeped in beauty and tradition. The Bohemian set couldn't afford to live there and it was viewed by many as little more than a tourist attraction and a postcard parody of Paris.

Instinctively, Adam followed the crowds up the famous thoroughfare, narrowly avoiding having his portrait sketched every time the procession halted as he made his way towards the Basilica of Sacre-Coeur, the beautiful white church which sat on the crest of the hill. At the bottom was the Boulevard de Clichy, which was lined with bars, kebab shops, and more sex shops and peep-shows than one could possibly pretend not to have noticed and it was inevitable, therefore, that not everyone that made it to the top of the hill was a bona fide culture vulture.

As Adam was greeted at the entrance of restaurant Valjean by a charmingly dressed young lady in tailored black trousers, white blouse and pristinely starched white apron, he wondered for a moment whether a young Audrey Hepburn was a part of the theme park experience. She showed him to his table, diagonally opposite two rather large and coarse Americans whose voices and raucous laughter were attracting disapproving glances from customers and staff alike. Around two thirds of the eighteen tables were occupied and the remaining six all had reserved signs mounted on them.

One of the Americans glanced over to Adam, made some form of comment or gesture to his buddy and both proceeded to roar with laughter. They looked and behaved like sailors on shore leave though it was unlikely that even these idiots could stray so far from the nearest shore. Thick set, buzz cut hair bristled from the crown of their heads to where their necks should have been and disappeared beneath flowered Hawaiian shirts in red and pale green respectively.

Adam looked around and it seemed obvious that the object of his attention had not yet arrived. Alec Brunson had assured him that Madame La Plume was definitely on this evening's seating plan in her favoured table fifteen meters away and, he was sure she would feel far too close to Mutt and Jeff. As he perused the exorbitant, brown leather menu, he sensed a surge of excitement amongst the waiting staff as the door opened once more and an elegant blonde haired lady in a cream and blue, knee length dress and three inch beige heels swept into the restaurant and was led briskly, but courteously, to her table.

"Hey, buddy, check out the high-class hooker. She looks like an old Faye Dunnaway sucking a lemon!"

"Think you could find her something more interesting to suck? She could be Faye Done Our Way!"

Both men roared with laughter as one of them reached out and grabbed the lady's hand. "Hey honey, why don't you join us over here and help us read the menu? Maybe you can tell us which of these burgers is the one made out of horse?"

Madame La Plume withdrew her hand as if extracting it from a fire and shook off the imaginary germs that she had collected as she took the next five steps to her table and sat with her back to them, facing out of the window. Adam assumed that she would normally be facing inward, surveying her fellow diners and enjoying the looks she would inevitably attract from jaw-stricken men and jealous women. The nearest of the two rednecks was not yet prepared to take no for an answer and he sat himself opposite her with a half-full bottle of Burgundy while his pal chucked childishly.

"Aw, come on, cupcake! Tonight's your lucky night! You get a threesome and a free meal to boot!"

Before she could rise and walk away, Adam had reached the table and placed his arm firmly on the offending hulk's shoulder.

"I really think that you should leave the lady alone, settle your check and leave before you cause an incident that you will both live to regret."

Adam may have been expecting a blunt response but did not appear to have been expecting the left fist smash into his face as the intruder swung around and upwards onto his feet. Adam recovered his composure just enough to return a blow to the big man's gut but his partner's bottle to the back of Adam's neck put him down. The Americans, suddenly seeming to realise what had just happened, turned to each other with panicked expressions and charged out of the door, each thrusting a fistful of euros into the hands of the Maître d'. The remaining diners had all stopped eating and most were staring open mouthed at Adam who was staggering to his feet and guided towards an empty seat at Madame La Plume's table. Madame clicked her fingers towards the oldest and largest of the waiters.

"Jean Francois! La Salle a manger privee, s'il vous plait. Vitement!"

While the remaining waiters were fawning over the startled diners and pouring more wine as if to weigh them down into their seats, a heavily dazed Adam was led by the faithful retainer and Madame La Plume to the private dining room at the rear of the bar area. They sat him down and Jean Francois nodded and withdrew as the lady showed Adam her phone and spoke in almost flawless English.

"That was a stupid thing to do, Monsieur. I have just called my private physician and my private security chief. They will both be here within four minutes and that is precisely how much time we have to determine which of them will entertain you first. So we can start by you telling me why you would hatch such an elaborate, expensive and painful plot to attract my attention to you."

"Madame, I do not understand?" he protested, though he had always suspected that she would see through his little sham but was not particularly bothered so long as it had the desired outcome of an audience alone with this lady. He also felt slightly aggrieved that the two CIA operatives were perhaps a little too enthusiastic with their part in the charade.

"I apologise, Madame. I should have known that a lady as accomplished and astute as yourself might recognise my ruse for what it was, but at least I have achieved my objective of speaking with you in person."

"And you now have precisely two minutes to persuade me whether my physician heals your wounds or my security chief finishes what your two hapless gorillas started."

"Madame, the fact that I found you here should assure you that I have researched you thoroughly and I know how difficult it would prove to secure a meeting with you through conventional business channels. The truth is that I need your help, your expertise and your considerable networking capability to help me conclude a transaction that will earn you a very easy and very quick five million euros in the process."

The door opened and a powerful, grey suited man in his mid-forties marched in, followed by a middle-aged lady in a Chanel suit, carrying a medical case. Madame la Plume addressed them both.

"Yvonne, please attend to this gentlemen's immediate wounds and have him cleaned up. Gerard, when Yvonne has finished with him please bring him over to the apartment. Yvonne, I would like you to join them as we may well need your services again later."

47

The *Princess of the Waves* was cruising at a steady speed of eleven knots towards Sunday's port of call in Marseille. It was a formal night on board; an opportunity to dress up to the nines in tuxedos and ball gowns and to stand in line to have a photograph with a digitally superimposed image of the captain sitting at your dining table. Richard Collins and his lovely wife Christina chose the casual option, dining in the Sea Breeze Buffet on deck 12. This was a popular option for both passengers and crew. It offered an excellent choice of food; as much or as little as one liked and rapid service for those with bands to watch or shows to see. Officers were encouraged to mingle with guests so the couple were not surprised to be joined at their table by the olive skinned officer in a startlingly white uniform.

As provisions master, Abdul Aziz was, indeed, classed as an officer, signified by the gold band upon his cuffs and epaulettes. Each cruise line had their own ranking system and it was often joked that two stripes on Ocean Line signified that the bearer could either read or write but not both; one stripe meant they could do neither but knew somebody who could. Abdul could do both in four different languages, making him a valuable provisions master and an even more valuable Jihadist. He smiled at Christina as he placed his tray upon the table and casually asked whether the cruise was meeting their expectations. He then placed the couple at ease by informing them that everything was in place, contained in six beer kegs, personally loaded, checked and palletised by himself. Enough highly concentrated liquid explosive to obliterate the ship and create a tidal wave sixty feet high and the power to travel two hundred nautical miles.

The three of them sat at least six tables away from the nearest other guests, casually discussing the magnificence of modern munitions technology, safe in the knowledge that none of them should be around to witness the devastating effects of this particular pyrotechnic show. Aziz also surprised them by revealing how simple it had been to load these and other illicit items onto cruise ships on which he had served because security levels were significantly lower than the checks carried out on container ships and tankers. They speculated on whether the event they were planning might actually create a change in long term tide tables, affecting weather and even calendar movements. The only issue they did not discuss was the potential loss of life.

When they finished their meals they shook hands cordially. Aziz headed down to the theatre to witness a number of his colleagues making utter fools of themselves in the Crew Talent show while Richard and Christina sat out on the deck with strong coffee and cognac. The smoke trails from his cigar and her cigarette seemed to head towards the plume from the smoke stack as if that's what they wanted to be when they grew up. Richard placed his hand on Christina's and softly said, "I am going to miss you tomorrow."

"So why don't I come with you?" she asked

"Because we are very different people, brought together by very different circumstances and doing what we do for very different reasons."

"We are good together." She smiled.

"We are," he replied. "But I would never be able to trust you. I do what I do because I want to. Sometimes I do it for money, sometimes for mischief, sometimes for revenge and sometimes just because I want to see what I can make happen, what I can change. Whatever I do, I do all these things for me."

"And that makes you more honourable then me?" she looked at him incredulously.

"Oh no, never more honourable, but much more predictable. I have no cause. I have no mission and no master. You on the other hand are driven by your God. You will kill for him, you will die for him. Your duty to your God and your brothers overrides any other sense or emotion you may hold. I don't understand it and that makes you dangerous to me."

"You think I would harm you?"

"No, Christina, I know you would harm me. If Allah's will were passed down by the Mullah on your phone right now you would cut my throat without even questioning it. I could never understand that. I may have no morals but I do have a conscience. Come to bed. We have a busy day tomorrow."

They walked, hand in hand, along the promenade deck and into the huge atrium rising upwards from deck five to deck nine. The handrails were barely visible as a mass of black and white clothing stood applauding the captain below, whose skill and experience, according to a gushing cruise director, had steered them safely through troubled waters and would, all too soon, have them safely at their final destination. Christina and Richard just looked at each other, smiled and walked on.

Back in their stateroom, Christina sat on her single bed with her head in her hands while her partner donned his sleep suit in the bathroom. When he emerged, she turned to him and he viewed a facial expression that might as well have belonged to a different woman.

"You are wrong about me. I would not harm you. I am not a Jihadist. I hate my life and I hate those at home who have condemned me to it. Yes, I lost my family in the struggle for a homeland but this did not make me bitter and hateful; it made me sad and lonely. It also made me totally dependent and from that time I have had to do the bidding of my late husband's nephews. I am trapped; trapped in my country and in my culture. A woman alone has no place in my world. Without them, I would not survive but if I am forced to continue killing for them I am no longer sure that I want to."

This was a scenario that Osman had never considered. Having been paid handsomely for this contract by the Saudi and his French accomplice, it had been a relatively easy task to recruit the foot soldiers that he needed to execute the plan. His close friend at the United Nations gave him contact details within the ISIL leadership and they were ecstatic to be offered the opportunity to strike such a devastating blow to their European enemies. He charged ISIL a modest fee to cover his expenses, never revealing of course, that he had already been richly rewarded. He was given the services of Abdul Aziz, the provisions master, Christina and a young man from the village who had been easy to persuade that paradise would be much more preferable to the existence he might face if he did not offer up his support in the supreme, sublime sacrifice. The final member of the team, he now knew, was Christina's coercive cousin who bore just enough of a resemblance to Osman to pass the Filipino security staff when he was to take his place, boarding the ship after a day ashore in Marseilles.

Christina continued in her passionate tone and expressions that flared her nostrils, widened her eyes and stretched the smooth olive skin over her sharply angled cheek bones.

"Do you think I do this out of choice? Do you really believe I choose the Burka over the bikini? That I would rather wash clothes in a dirty river than bathe in a heated swimming pool? Why do you think that I marvel so much at the performances in the Princess Theatre? The only music I have heard before has come from outside the mosque that I am forbidden to enter."

Osman was genuinely taken aback by these revelation and severely ashamed of his behaviour towards her. "We all have choices, Christina. If you despise your cousins as much as you say do, then leave them."

"Firstly, my name is not Christina, it is Samira. Secondly, I am not their relative, I am their possession; they own me. If I try to leave them they will invent crimes against me that will see me stoned to death. You will do what you have to do tomorrow and I will do what I have to do, but tonight, let us both do what we need to do together."

48

Vastly relieved and hugely grateful that he had spent considerably more time in the company of Yvonne than Gerard, Adam felt rather more comfortable during the short walk from the restaurant to Madame la Plume's Montmarte residence just a couple of blocks away. His wounds were bruises rather than cuts. His attackers had been skilled but they had warned that there was no possibility of staging a convincing attack without inflicting harm upon their colleague. They would laugh when they learned that La Plume had seen through the ruse but she affirmed that Adam had deserved the beating for orchestrating the insults hurled her way. He walked between the medic and bodyguard as they turned the corner and stopped outside a small, but highly polished and ornate eggshell-coloured door. As with many Montmarte structures, the façade belies the opulence within and Adam was genuinely speechless as he entered the spacious hallway of the three storey townhouse. Everything before him was either Wedgwood blue, ivory or gold and he did not doubt that the ivory and gold were precisely that. Madame La Plume appeared and beckoned them towards the drawing room, similarly decorated, and poured herself and Adam a generous cognac.

"Thank you both. Please wait outside." She smiled warmly towards her other guests, suggesting that they were rather more than just the hired help. Her smile hardened as she turned to Adam and addressed him in a much less harmonious, though thoroughly respectful tone.

"My staff inform me that you are Adam Albano. I assume from your highly inappropriate and impudent manner that you are the Adam Albano that is Chief Executive Officer of the Maltese Dolmen Hotel Consortium."

"You are every bit as impressive and resourceful as my sources suggested. But then, I paid an awful lot of money to have them find someone like you."

"Someone *like* me? You disappoint me, Mr Albano, and I am still considering how best to exact retribution for that humiliating and vile stunt you perpetrated upon me at Valjean. You now add insult to my injury by suggesting that you were not specifically seeking an audience with me?"

"Madame La Plume. Firstly, please allow me to apologise for the very public and clumsy charade that my colleagues arranged earlier. Of course I admit that we staged the incident to allow me to speak with you and I calculated that you would either be grateful enough or furious enough at my intervention to afford me some time with you. I was reliably informed that a more conventional appointment might take months. Months that I do not have. And please, let me assure you, having given my people a brief and perused their shortlist, yours was absolutely the only name that was of interest to me; very considerable interest."

La Plume's body language suggested that she was thawing towards Adam. She still held him in her piercing gaze but her back had moulded into the blue velvet of the armchair, her elegant right leg had slowly crossed over the left and her right hand brought the crystal cognac goblet to her lips, which parted in a smile as she savoured a long draught of the ridiculously expensive liquid.

"A cursory glance at your website tells me that you are the Chief Executive Officer and principal shareholder of a very, very substantial and highly profitable hotel empire. You have over three hundred luxury hotels across the Southern Mediterranean and Arab States, the property value alone is measured in tens of billions and there is relatively little debt on your accounts. Why on earth would I be of interest to you?"

Much of the information on the corporate website was true. The business did exist, it was valued at billions, thirty-six billion in fact, and Adam Albano was listed as the Chief Executive and principal shareholder. The truth, however, was that those last two identities should have been listed as the President of the United States and the Central Intelligence Agency. The empire had been acquired, developed and resourced by the proceeds of every busted drug cartel, fraudulent finance scheme, mafia operation and money laundering corporation that the CIA had closed down in the past twenty five years. Dolmen Hotels had become their own enterprise: an ideal vehicle for shielding and laundering cash flow, a perfect network of safe houses for security operatives across the Arab world, and an invaluable source of intelligence as their employees surveyed every action of the highest of high rollers patronising these playboy palaces. Most of their named executives were CIA operatives though few had done little more than sleep occasionally in their luxurious rooms. An executive position with a global luxury hotel chain was perfect cover for an international traveller. Adam matched the posture of his host, and he too, melted into his chair and his cognac.

"The corporate website tells the customer and the corporate investor what we want them to know; every word, number and image of which is absolutely true. We are one of the finest and most successful hotel groups in the world and I will not retire until we are THE finest and most successful."

"And so where do I come in to the equation?" La Plume was now less interrogative and more intrigued. "Why am I so integral to your plans for world dominance? I know nothing of hotels other than how to terrorise receptionists, Maître d's and chambermaids."

"But, Madame, you know everything there is to know about brokering international mergers and acquisitions. Especially those that are best conducted beyond the gaze of the world stock markets. Your network of Arab financiers in particular, is reputed to be the most comprehensive and expansive in the world. I need a deal to be brokered, I need it to be brokered quietly and I believe that your Arab connections will have the financial capability and the ideological motivation to make this deal happen."

Madame La Plume rose and gently smoothed her elegantly coiffured blonde hair. The one thing that those would be thugs in the restaurant did get right was the resemblance to Faye Dunnaway but the great actress herself would have yearned to have attained the same level of stunning, dignified beauty and the similar age of forty-eight. She was flawless. She brought the decanter and topped up their goblets.

"I am intrigued to know what you think you know about me, Adam, and even more intrigued to know who told you."

"I may be able to help you with the first part but I am sure you will understand that the second part must remain strictly confidential, even though you will eventually have that person to thank for delivering to you the easiest five million euros of your highly impressive career. The money can be processed in such a way that will never be traced, particularly if you wish it to be used to further your political party ambitions."

"How astute of you, Adam. Our supposedly democratic government seems to frown upon republican parties of the right. We spurn the support from our natural allies and bow down to their masters over in Brussels and Berlin as our nation dissolves into little more than a puppet parliament of Europe. Britain prospers at our expense and we just…"

She realised that she was both straying from the point and displaying rather too much of her hand so she regained her composure both physically and mentally.

"Forgive me, I should not allow my political leanings to override my professional obligations. Do go on."

"On the contrary, Madame, in this instance, I consider the two to be intrinsically linked which is why I am absolutely certain that my proposal will be of interest to you."

"Well then, Adam, you had better proceed. I am sure that Yvonne and Gerard have better things to do with their evening."

"Then dismiss them, Madame. I am sure I will have no further need of the splendid Yvonne."

"But you may, Adam," La Plume's smile tuned downward faintly, "if I find myself in need of the equally splendid Gerard. Please tell me what you have in mind for me."

"The website, Madame, comprehensive though it is, gives investors the barest financial details, demanded of the regulators." He produced a data stick from his top pocket, held it out to La Plume then withdrew and replaced it as she reached to take it from him. "This contains the full financial breakdown of the business. P&L, balance sheet, cash flow, projections and, most importantly, a full and detailed allocation of the share ownership of the business. I am the major individual shareholder with forty-two per cent of the equity which is a combination of my own accrued shareholding and the thirty-five per cent inherited from my father. His brother, my uncle, also holds a thirty-five percent holding and the remaining twenty-three per cent sits in the hands of institutional and private shareholders. My uncle, sadly, has only weeks to live and his shares will pass to my cousin who does not share our passion for our heritage and our ethic for hard endeavour. I am aware that he proposes to sell two thirds of his shareholding to one of the larger US institutions to fund his profligate lifestyle and fund the theatrical ambitions of his American fiancée. The twenty-three per cent he proposes to sell, plus the sixteen per cent they already own, together with Paolo's retained twelve per cent, would effectively give them fifty one per cent of my company and wrestle control away from the family for the first time in history. I need you to help me to persuade some of your influential friends in the Arab world to preempt this position with the purchase of shares from parties that I know would be willing to sell, at the right price. I will commit to purchase the shares from them, later, at a twelve per cent premium and you will take a handsome commission for facilitating the transaction."

"These shareholders you speak of. You are sure they will sell?"

"Please Madame, see for yourself." He handed La Plume the data stick.

Madame La Plume strode quickly towards the statuesque white cabinet in the corner of the suite and pressed a small button which retracted the top to reveal a highly sophisticated home office. She held her palm to the screen and as it dawned into life, she inserted the card into the micro port on the side of her processing device. Seconds later, pages of financial data started to appear on the screen. A Nano second earlier, the entire contents of Madame La Plume's hard drive was downloading onto a device, eagerly watched and anticipated by a very self-satisfied Alec Brunson.

"Gerard will drive you home now, Adam. Give me your number and I will call you in the morning."

49

A generous selection of antipasti, Sean's favourite pepperoni pizza and a moderately priced bottle of Chianti had been procured on the way back from Farah's meeting with Alec Brunson and had been shared at Farah's place amidst candles and soft music. Sean was ecstatic, especially as the two had vowed to make the most of Ava's last couple of days away with her school, to practice what life together would look and feel like when they finally managed to bring their relationship into the open, as both now promised to each other, that they were ready to do.

Farah's abduction had finally made Sean realise that his feelings for her could no longer be suppressed and that he needed to remove her from the front line of policing, where Rosie Hunter's death had served to remind them both that the bad guys were still well ahead of the good guys. They would both attend the funeral next week, though Sean was unlikely to enter the church.

"Christianity has two major misconceptions," he frequently said. "The first is that we are all born equal and the second is that all human life has a purpose."

Farah was brave and loyal but smart enough to recognise now

299

that her career will always run a distant second to her feelings for Sean and Ava. They had vowed to declare their engagement to Ava upon her return on Tuesday and, on Wednesday, they would see the commissioner together to discuss Farah's career options.

As much as they had tried to keep their Saturday evening impurely unprofessional, their conversation inevitably strayed towards Farah's earlier meeting with Alec Brunson and Sean's impending meeting with Paul Cruse. Farah recalled Alec's fury at the suggestion that he had been duped into believing that signals recorded in Whitehall had actually been generated in Edinburgh but he steadfastly refused to discuss the matter further.

Sean was to meet Paul Cruse on Monday. Protocol dictated that the deputy director could be interviewed by no lower rank than superintendent and Sean was now investigating the bombing and the murder of one of his officers although no formal link had been drawn between the two incidents. Sean hoped, however, that the man responsible for the day-to-day running of one of the world's most sophisticated surveillance agencies, might be able to assist in both enquiries.

The highly charged, emotional and ultimately fatal hostage exchange had taken his attention away from the recurring scenes of anguish and misery suffered by the victims and relatives of those caught up in the Whitehall bombing. Every newsfeed and social medium carried tales of bravery, heartache and twists of fate that either led survivors to safety or the less fortunate to their graves. The commissioner had now told him that there were twice as many officers working on the investigation as there had been casualties and although they were still considering the deceased Adnan Abadi to be their prime suspect, he was unlikely to have been working alone. The Metropolitan Police were also allowed to voice openly, what the public feared silently; this could just be the start of another bloody campaign like those that brought Britain to its knees following the first ground offensive in Syria.

When the British Prime Minister and US President declared 'War on Terrorism' almost twenty five years earlier, nobody had expected that this would be a war brought to the streets of Britain. Sean knew that Farah could have easily been yet another casualty in that war and it was this thought that fuelled him as he had happily handed over for interrogation the terrorist survivors of the Darwen Moors. Publicly, of course, there had been no survivors. Molten, mangled lumps of human remains had been paraded before the press and nobody could count the number of heads or limbs. Sean was sure that, by now, those prisoners would have been praying to whichever God they purported to worship to release them from the highly skilled interrogators that were now keeping them alive and conscious, just enough to feel every blow, cut, flame and snip that followed every unsatisfactory answer.

Farah could see that Sean had drifted away to another place and time. Very skilfully, she applied a range of highly persuasive techniques of her own to bring him back to her. Sean offered very little resistance.

50

Those passengers with balcony cabins on the port side of the *Princess of the Waves* were the first to be awoken by the first resounding crash, boom and frenzied screaming. The ship had just drawn into her mooring in the port of Marseilles as one of the crew accidentally let go of one of the ropes that should have allowed him to lower the gang plank gently and silently from the exit hatch on deck two, down to the quayside below. The aluminium pathway had narrowly missed the port worker below who berated the crewman in every possible language he could muster and a vivid exchange ensued, curtailed only when a member of the security staff reminded them that the majority of paying passengers were still sleeping.

The first couple of hours in port were vitally important to the ship's logistics team. They tried to load as many supplies as they could before the passengers began to make their way down the gangplanks to the quayside, at which point the service hold areas had to be cordoned off and the fork lift trucks detoured away from the most direct route between warehouse and ship. The operations were executed with military efficiency. Waste materials were offloaded first; compressed cardboard packages neatly compacted into cubes before palletisation, then bottles and cans, all destined for the huge recycling plant at the end of the dock.

Next were the empty beer kegs. Six kegs on each pallet; one pallet stacked upon another and offloaded into the empties area. Abdul Aziz, the provisions master, rarely bothered to attend the offloading activities hadmade an exception this particular morning as a single layered pallet of full beer kegs was wheeled to the mouth of the loading hatch. The six kegs were tightly bound together by stretch wrapped polythene and attached to each of the four sides of the pallet were prominent posters displaying the words "Damaged Goods for Uplift and Credit." At precisely 7.45 a.m., as carefully planned, a white van emblazoned with the logo 'Brasseries Alexport, Specialist Wholesalers of Beers Wines and Spirits' arrived. Aziz met the driver and as his mate supervised the loading of the pallet into the back of the van, they exchanged jovial words, paperwork and an envelope containing a substantial wad of used Euros. Next into the van were four resealed cases of beer cans, the outer ones visibly dented, a wine case, a gas bottle and a selection of keg couplers. Less than seven minutes later, the van was heading out of the docks and towards a service area on the outskirts of town where the senior of the two would have breakfast with his young assistant and wait for the replacement driver to take the load to its next destination.

At 9 a.m. Richard and Christine Collins scanned their sea passes at the security point and disembarked the cruise ship with a succession of other eager tourists. Marseilles had undergone a massive transformation from the crime ridden city of sin of thirty years ago and billions of European Union investment had helped to transform the city into the second most affluent and desirable tourist location in France. It still played host to a sinister underworld of trafficked African migrants, drugs, prostitution and money laundering but an open understanding between the crime lords and amenable local government officials, ensured that both sides of the city co-existed in a virtual parallel universe. The two walked to the port car park, hand in hand, and took the first available taxi. They politely declined the driver's invitation to give them a full morning's guided city tour and he was as disappointed as he was amazed to be asked to drive them to a truck stop less than twenty minutes away. Upon arrival, Richard explained to the driver that he was here to meet a cousin who was working in the region to discuss the legacy of a relative's recent death. He gave the driver seventy-five Euros and promised him a further hundred and fifty if he returned in ninety minutes time.

Dressed conservatively, the couple did not look out of place crossing the car park and as they entered the café Christina spotted the cousin she despised so much, sitting with a younger man at a quiet corner table. They sat beside them; words of greeting were exchanged, but no names. Although Richard could see only the vaguest resemblance between himself and the man opposite, he knew that this would be close enough to deceive the cruise ship's South Asian security staff to whom all Westerners looked alike. He had also decided, however, that this minuscule risk was about to be completely eradicated. To Christina's total surprise, he announced that there was a change of plan.

"I fear that my client here in France might have inadvertently compromised my identity and it will not be safe for me to pass through the toll gates on the way to your destination. It will therefore be necessary for you, rather than me, to accompany this brave young man and help him to prepare for his mission."

"I don't understand," the cousin protested. "I am meant to be boarding the ship with Samira. It is too late to change our plans."

"No it isn't, and no you are not. Security on the ship is tighter than expected and with the mission so close to its critical phase, your leaders would thank neither of us for failing to expedite such a glorious event for the sake of a simple identity check. On the other hand, just think of the greater glory that will be bestowed upon you when I tell the leadership the full role that you played in making this happen."

The other man clearly understood that failure was not an option and that he, personally would be held responsible, especially if the contractor let it be known that he had refused to comply with his wishes.

"But I know nothing of explosives," he pleaded.

"Other than the ones that you strap around children's chests," Richard replied. "Don't worry, the technical work is done. The cargo will be completely safe during transit and I will show you exactly how to connect, prime, detonate and ignite the device. It is as easy to assemble as a ten piece jigsaw. A child could do it, in fact looking at your associate here, a child probably will do it."

Even if the younger man had understood the remark, it was unlikely that he would have expressed any exception to it for fear of offending either of the two men beside him. His attention seemed to be focussed on the one they called Samira. He would have welcomed some time alone with the woman but reflected that he would be able to have as many as he wanted when he arrived in paradise.

Richard rose and the others instinctively rose with him. "Let's go across to the van and I will show you how it works."

They left the table with a twenty Euro note which would adequately cover the bill and the tip. Any more would have been ostentatious and nobody wanted to draw attention to their presence and the possibility of being news headlines in three days' time. When they reached the van, Richard took a wrench from a tool box and hit three of the kegs hard on their tops and sides.

"Perfectly safe. You could be involved in a motorway pile-up and they would still not detonate. These kegs contain the most volatile and potent liquid explosives ever known to man but they are completely inert until connected to this gas cylinder and detonated. Together, these kegs have the destructive capability close to that which destroyed Nagasaki in 1945."

The other two men looked at each other. The younger was clearly thrilled, the elder less so, but it was he who spoke first, his quivering voice contrasting his brave words.

"So you must show us how to make the device active and we will begin our historic journey."

Richard opened the box containing the keg connectors.

"Each of these is numbered and simply snaps on to its equivalently labelled keg. The connector itself contains the detonator, the tube running from the detonator fits into the manifold, which, in turn, fits into the gas bottle. Fit the connectors to the kegs, couple the lines to the manifold and the device is assembled. You simply release the valve on the gas bottle to allow the gas to prime the liquid in the kegs and thirty seconds later, press the valve downwards to ignite the detonators. Nothing can go wrong... except for anybody who happens to be situated within half a mile of the device."

The two pupils looked at each other and the older one spoke to his younger associate in a language that all parties present clearly understood.

"You know that you will be on your own at that point? Do you completely understand what is expected of you? I will accompany you to the point of access but then you are on your own. The glory will be yours alone."

"And you will be worthy of it and the rewards it will bring you," Richard added.

The young man glowed as Richard asked him to excuse the rest of them for a few minutes while he contemplated his task and rehearsed the safe procedures. Richard took the older man by the arm and led him some fifty metres away.

"Christina, or Samira, as you know her, wishes to tender her resignation. The money that your organisation has paid to me will be her severance pay and she will now be totally self-sufficient. I don't know where she will go or whether you will ever see her again but it will be in your interests to wish her a long and happy life. If this lovely lady should die other than peacefully in her sleep at least sixty years from now, I shall deem you and your family responsible for the exertions that your demands have placed upon her. I will eradicate you and yours, just as swiftly and surely as that bomb will wipe out your foolish young apprentice. Do you understand me?"

The cousin stared, wide eyed at the man towering over him, gulped and nodded; once, then more vigorously.

"Good," smiled Richard as he walked back and took Christina's hand. "Say goodbye to your cousin. We have some sights to see and a ship to catch."

They remained in the car park long enough to watch the two men carefully pack the couplers and gas bottle away and drive onto the north bound side of the dual carriageway. Shortly after they left, the taxi reappeared. Christina looked up at Richard through tear stained eyes, pulled his head down towards hers and kissed a man passionately, with meaning, for the first time in her thirty-one years on the planet.

51

When his screen sprang into life in front of him at 21.02 on Saturday evening, Alec Brunson's eyes widened and the faintest of smiles formed in the corners of his mouth. Any other mortal might have leapt off their chair, hugged the cleaner and high fived the filing cabinet but this was not Alec's way. He absolutely understood the significance of the successful software that he had implanted into the memory card that was now copying and downloading every single bit of data from Madame La Plume's computer, together with trace lines to those devices with whom she had been communicating, but for Alec, this was just another day at the office; albeit a rather good one. As he watched the data scroll from screen to screen and tallied the thousands of files downloading onto his machine, he punched the button on his desktop speaker and instantly connected with his closest friend and colleague in MI7.

"Hi Alec, how's it going?"

"Rather well, Dicky. I'm having a massive dump on my machine here," Alec responded without any understanding of why there was riotous laughter on the video screen in front of him.

Richard Michael Greenfield, Rich to his mates, and Tricky Dicky Micky Meadows to those few who dared, was the complete opposite to Alec. While being a brilliant analyst, he was outgoing, humorous and personable; as though on a mission to prove that it was possible to be both brilliant *and* human. Rich had been recruited into the service directly from university where he had graduated in Latin Studies and Roman History. Quite how these courses had prepared him to be one of the most astute and instinctive analysts in MI7, nobody knew, though the director had promised himself to examine the lad someday, when neither were quite so busy. At six foot four, bald headed and with a trendy bushy beard, the thirty year old had risen through the ranks rapidly, gaining popularity and respect in equal proportions. Alec was the master of extracting data. Rich was the master of analysing and interpreting it. He had the uncanny knack of sifting through billions of bytes of data and isolating clusters of dialogue that presented patterns from which narrative was built. The ridiculously complex programs at his disposal helped him to search for significant threads but it was his own unique ability to sew these together into a meaningful tapestry that made him so invaluable.

"Congratulations, Al! I hope everything comes out all right for you. Look mate, I'm out tonight. Remember the rather pleasant looking lady from technology procurement? She's over at my place and we are about to undergo a review of my hardware. Can it wait until tomorrow?"

"Yes, of course it can. I will be here from seven."

And of course, he was. He always was and Rich joined him at eight. Alec briefed him on the background scenario. The four way dialogue between Istanbul, Paris, Saudi Arabia and London. He specifically emphasised London and told Rich of his concerns that the deputy director seemed to have undermined his expertise by valuing the judgement of the Whitehall spooks over his own. He spoke of Madame La Plume's business, social and political interests. He volunteered his concerns that while the four parties had highly secure encryptions on their communication devices, the lead communicator out of Istanbul seemed to have unwittingly created a temporary chink in the armour, allowing Alec to establish their locations. The massive breakthrough had been the insertion of the memory card into La Plume's computer but he was customarily modest and matter of fact in describing the work that had gone into creating this bug.

Rich listened intently, saying nothing, his mind already picking up the strands and weaving a context around the suspected link with the London bombings and what he ought to be searching for to bring the narrative to life. He knew that his boss, Paul Cruse, would be expecting answers when he returned to his desk on Monday morning, but instinctively, Rich felt that there might just be an even more important deadline to hit. He diverted the data feed to his own bank of computers and programmed six individual processing units to scan and search for key words clustered around the broad topics of terrorism, radical ideology , finance, political geography, symbolic landmarks and London. He then inserted filters to link the topics with the locations of Istanbul, Saudi Arabia, France and England. This would be enough to refine his initial screening from billions of bytes down to mere millions. The maestro whistled as he ceremoniously clicked the remote that set his computers dancing.

All around him the screens were scrolling, words and numbers flew from top to bottom, the odd ones occasionally being isolated, dragged out and dropped into a vast electronic bucket above the monitors. Pictures dashed in and out, the programme pinged every couple of seconds to celebrate another hit as Rich sat there like a conductor orchestrating the opening night of his latest symphony. The data counter suggested that the programme was likely to run for eleven hours to complete the initial screening but this did not prevent Rich from cracking on with his own instinctive assumptions based upon the recurring images, locations and names that flashed upon the stage in front of him. This, he felt, could be the performance of his life.

52

Graeme Mitchell usually tried to avoid working on Sundays though in truth, this was more Mrs Mitchell's decision than his own. Today, however, they both agreed that they must both join the rest of the nation in their outpouring of communal grief by attending the memorial service in Westminster Abbey for the victims of Monday's bombing. The Prime Minister had attended similar services for the other faiths affected by the atrocity over the last three days. For the Mitchells, this was not just a display of civic duty but a heartfelt desire to join in the collective despair. It was hardly the ideal preparation for the impromptu meeting called by Mellor and Faraday as he was often prone to think and act emotionally rather than objectively but this, Mrs Mitchell assured him, was not such a bad trait for a Prime Minister.

When they returned to Downing Street two hours later, Mellor and Faraday had been waiting together for over thirty minutes. The massive security cordon around Whitehall and Westminster had made access, even for those at the very highest levels of government, somewhat difficult. As he approached the meeting room, he was pleasantly surprised to hear the exchange of jovial banter between Mellor, Faraday and Clive Mountstevens. Less than a month ago, to allow these individuals to meet unsupervised, would have been akin to dropping three hungry ferrets into a small muslin sack. Matt Sadler and Robert Brockington entered behind Mitchell, much to the surprise of the two already seated parties. It was quite naïve of them to expect that the Prime Minister, a consummate politician, would have allowed himself to be compromised by holding a conversation on national security without the presence of his Foreign and Defence Secretaries. Although it was his deputy who had convened the meeting, Mitchell had no hesitation in seizing the initiative.

"Tom, Clive, we are almost a week on since the bombings and I have heard little from the police or intelligence communities to suggest that we are any closer to a resolution."

Tom was first to respond.

"I am sure that if Adnan Abadi had survived his short spell in prison, he might have shed more light on the investigation. There seems little doubt that he was actively involved, but the inability of the prison service to protect him has denied us the immediate opportunity to get to the nucleus."

Clive Mountstevens shot a wounded glance towards Mellor who displayed no shame in either exposing his superior or deceiving his Prime Minister. Rather than rise to the bait, Mountstevens deflected the criticism by announcing that MI7 were actively pursuing a number of leads that pointed towards Scotland, Saudi Arabia, Istanbul and France.

"Indeed, we currently have an agent on active deployment in Paris and with the splendid support of my MI7 team, they seem close to unravelling a network of communications that could lead us back to the source and, more importantly reveal the possibility of future threats to security." He slammed a file onto the table, on top of Mellor's tablet, as though to trump his ace.

Faraday rose to his feet.

"I, of course, have my own personal reasons for preferring

that we kept Abadi alive but I certainly echo Tom's concern that the inability of Clive's handpicked governor to keep him alive in Belmarsh, has almost certainly made us more vulnerable to future attacks. The bastards have tasted our blood again and they are not going to leave it there."

He turned his gaze towards the Foreign Secretary and Defence Secretary, sitting either side of their leader, as if they were symbolically protecting him from the expected onslaught.

"Between you three, you have antagonised just about every radical Islamic regime in the East and you have helped to create more criminals in the region than Ali Baba. Your predecessors removed the only type of leaders that could keep these savages in tow and you have systematically reduced our international diplomacy and military capability to that of a geography graduate on work experience, backed up by a combination of Dad's Army and a bunch of Boy Scouts. Our defence capability, at home and abroad, is such a joke that we are positively inviting the world to have a pop at us and it's about time that the general public were alerted to the dangers that you three are exposing us to."

Mitchell remained calm, outwardly, though under the table his knuckles were struggling to contain themselves within the thinly stretched layer of skin that bound them.

"Well, Neil, thank you for your characteristically loyal assessment and expression of support. Perhaps you could help us all by telling us exactly where and when you would like us to fire our nuclear weapons?"

"Don't be fucking ridiculous, Mitchell. You know what you need to do. We have been telling you for years but the truth gets lost in that airy fairy, ideological, liberal head of yours! We need to take on the radicals at home and abroad. We need to round up the terrorists over here and get them back to the Middle East and then send a proper armed response over there; bombers and ground troops to wipe out the Islamic State once and for all. I am giving you notice now that unless you announce an immediate rebuilding of the armed forces, the abolition of IBIS and a full scale attack on Islamic State, my party will withdraw from the coalition, we will go to the nation and give them a chance to elect a government with the balls to defend itself! The pathetic performance of the last week will have persuaded the public that you are no longer fit for purpose."

The room was stunned. Sadler and Brockington sat open mouthed. Clive Mountstevens turned his eyes to the ground and Tom Mellor fixed his gaze upon the Prime Minister who simply rose, walked to the door, turned to Faraday and said, softly but assuredly, "Do what you feel you have to do. I will announce your resignation from Cabinet when the house sits on Tuesday, unless you want to go sooner."

Faraday sneered triumphantly. "Tuesday will be fine, but I will make the fucking announcement myself!"

53

The beer delivery van was parked up at the AutoRoute service area just outside Lyon. Suleiman, the elder of the two travellers was on his mobile phone in the car park while Aslam, the young apprentice was calmly enjoying coffee and pastries in the restaurant. No expense was to be spared on Aslam as he prepared for his final days on earth. He was resigned to his fate and perfectly at ease with himself. Suleiman, on the other hand, was rather more stressed. By now, he should have been sitting aboard a cruise ship and out of harm's way. He stroked his stubbled chin, shorn of his obligatory beard for the first time in his adult life and waited for the connection. Osman had already alerted the ISIL leadership of the necessity for the change of plan and indicated to them that Suleiman had not seemed entirely comfortable with the new arrangement. He had warned them that this was the only way to ensure the success of the mission and that Suleiman must be made to realise that it was his duty to guide Aslam to glory. As Suleiman placed the device in his pocket, the message was ingrained in his memory, as were the consequences of non-compliance.

He was bitter, angry and humiliated by the actions of the stranger. He had been deprived of a cruise ship experience, exposed to a degree of danger that he had never anticipated and deprived of the services of his beautiful and malleable cousin. He had long term personal plans for Samira once her prescribed period of mourning had passed. Who was this arrogant intruder to turn his life upside down? When the mission was accomplished, he vowed that he would hunt the man down, kill him and recover his prized trophy. He would later admit to himself, of course, that this was pure bravado and first, however, they had a schedule to observe. Suleiman collected Aslam from the restaurant and after a brief toilet visit, they returned to the van and undertook another rehearsal, assembling and disarming the device. Only when the older man was absolutely certain that Aslam could be trusted, would he be able to leave him at their destination and head home to safety.

He reflected on the words of the stranger. It would indeed be Suleiman that had delivered the device. It would be he that had coached and mentored his assistant. It would be he that had assembled and delivered the device. It would be he that would have delivered the most significant blow against the infidel in the history of Jihad. It was he who would return home a hero. Perhaps then the brotherhood would help him to exact his revenge on the stranger.

54

That Sunday morning in Montmartre was a real-time tourist video; bright, vibrant, relaxed yet bustling as Parisians and tourists alike strolled the avenues, perused the works of local artisans and sipped coffee and pastis at the myriad al fresco bars that lined the cobbled streets. Adam Albano was sipping one such coffee at one such bar when his mobile buzzed on the table. He activated the call but before he could acknowledge the caller, the voice at the other end of the connection took complete control of the scenario.

"Adam!" her voice was eight tones brighter and six tones lighter than the previous evening.

"Madame La Plume, how lovely to hear from you."

"Please call me Francoise. If we are to be business partners, as I hope we shall be, we must try to temper professionalism with a degree of cordiality. I like to believe that business and friendship are not mutually exclusive commodities."

Adam flicked his device to 'face' mode and the two parties exchanged very cordial, almost flirtatious smiles.

"I have now had time to examine your company structure and to evaluate your proposal. I can fully understand why you would

317

be concerned that your cousin's investment, or rather, divestment plan might have disastrous consequences for the organisation and I feel confident that my friends in the Arab world would view this opportunity favourably."

"That is splendid news, Madame... Francoise. How quickly could we get together to discuss the transaction? I am perfectly happy to travel to the Middle East and it would be an added bonus if I were to enjoy the pleasure of your company. Perhaps you could establish a date and venue with your contact?"

At the same time Adam switched to 'face' mode he had also pressed his tracker key to record and transmit the conversation back to Alec in London. He would now be alerted to monitor Madame's conversations and establish a positive identity in Saudi. This could establish whether the potential investor was also the co-conspirator.

"Yes, of course, Adam, but let's take things one step at a time. If we were to meet for lunch in, say, one hour's time, we could agree on how, when and where we would like to engage the third party. You haven't already eaten have you?"

"Not since breakfast. Did you have anywhere in mind?"

"Can you remember how to get to my place? We can discuss the matter much more discreetly there and at a much more leisurely pace."

The smile seemed to shift from flirtatious to seductive but Adam was prepared to do whatever he had to do for the cause.

"Yes, of course, Francoise. I can be with you within the hour."

"Excellent. I shall have one of the chefs from Valjean come around to prepare lunch. You are not allergic to seafood are you? We have some of the most succulent oysters in the world and his lobster thermidore is orgasmic."

"Sounds like a perfect Sunday in Paris. I shall see you in half an hour."

One click later and the seductive expression of La Plume was replaced by the disapproving frown of Brunson.

"Isn't she a bit old for you?" he asked, without any humour or irony evident in his voice.

"Now, Alec. You be a good boy and monitor the exchanges with the Saudis but no listening in when I get round there. You know how those naughty thoughts play havoc with your acne."

Adam closed the call before Alec could complete his two word response, but there was little doubt that the second word would have been 'off'!

55

La Plume took five minutes to gather her thoughts before keying in the secure Saudi code. She lived a varied and dynamic life, juggling her political ambitions with her business obsession but even by her own standards, this was a particularly exciting scenario. She was about to contribute towards a truly world changing event, she had been offered a business opportunity that could wipe out the costs incurred in funding her political party and she could even afford herself the luxury of a flirtation with a handsome and powerful man who was half her age; whether he liked it or not.

It took less than five seconds for the connection to be activated.

"Good morning, Opal, it's Sapphire here, I need to speak with Emerald." It was a fairly unsophisticated and probably futile set of codenames but it seemed to make the Saudis feel more comfortable.

"His Highness is will be available in five minutes and I will arrange to have him call you."

"No, Opal. I will set up video conferencing facilities in ten minutes. There are documents that I need him to review and discuss. Computer connections are more secure than phones in any case. Please have His Highness available at your console." The connection was closed.

La Plume scoffed, scornfully at the reference to 'His Highness'. She knew perfectly well that Abdullah bin Abdurrahman, or Emerald, had no greater access to the Saudi royal family than she had but his political connections and obscene wealth were sufficient for her to indulge his delusions. Most illegitimate offspring of Saudi royal descent either died or disappeared before their first birthday, but Abdullah was a rare exception. His guile, his cunning and network of connections, coupled with the photographs, videos and the DNA evidence harvested by his long dead mother had ensured that he was able to thrive, indeed survive in his underworld but would be looking over his shoulder for the remainder of his life, fully understanding that there were those who would dearly like to detach his head from it.

Ten minutes later, La Plume dialled up the advanced Lync connection. Under normal circumstances, her assertion that computer communications were more secure than digital phones would have been absolutely correct but the programme that she had inadvertently installed from Adam's flash drive had now rendered her system totally vulnerable as would be any device with which she connected. The Lync programme allowed real time voice and video contact together with split screen technology allowing both parties to access and view file documents or internet links. The second the connection was established, every sound, every pixel and every word was being relayed back to the eager eyes and ears of Alec Brunson.

Abdullah's face shone out of La Plume's monitor. He was in his mid-thirties with darker than olive skin and jet black, shoulder length hair, parted in the middle with a floppy fringe which seemed to contradict his tightly clipped moustache and beard. By any standards, he was a handsome man but with discretion said to be wiser than valour, his hairstyle and facial hair helped to disguise his likeness to his high-profile lineage. La Plume often hoped that they would eventually have the opportunity to meet in a more relaxed and convivial context.

He was first to speak. "This is a pleasant surprise, Sapphire. I thought we had agreed to deny ourselves the pleasure of each other's company until the conclusion of our impending venture. There is nothing unpleasant for me to be concerned with is there?"

Even though both believed the channel to be absolutely secure, they had always preferred to speak in coded clichés.

"Everything is in order, Emerald. The wedding celebration is as scheduled and the bride and groom are travelling to the church with the cake. There is an unrelated matter that I wish to discuss with you, however."

"I am intrigued, Sapphire, please go on."

"I have been presented with a fascinating investment opportunity. The CEO and principal shareholder of a huge and highly successful hotel empire is in urgent need of funds to purchase a swathe of family shares to prevent them falling into foreign hands and creating the likelihood of a hostile takeover by American shareholders." She saw his jaw clench slightly by the reference to Americans whom he despised almost as much as he did the English.

"And what scale of investment is your party seeking?"

"I believe that a figure of seven hundred million dollars would secure the shareholding he requires. The CEO would then commit to purchase the shares back from you over a phased period at a minimum premium of five percent in the first year, rising by a minimum of five per cent above that purchase price for every year you hold them."

"And what if the share price goes beyond these premiums? I assume that I will be at liberty to sell freely at the market price?"

"That is so, Emerald, but not until the CEO has purchased sufficient shares back to ensure that he has the controlling interest. He must always be given first option on disposals. Of course, there is nothing to prevent you, discreetly of course, from securing more shares and either challenging his ownership or inflating your selling price even further. In the meantime, you have a rock solid investment in a blue chip global business and an opportunity in which to invest some of your more questionable equity away from the gaze of global financial observers. You can also take satisfaction from the knowledge that such a transaction would be a significant blow to English and American investors who are keen to seize control of the group."

"What more detail can you share at this stage?"

La Plume quartered the screen, positioned the corporate website in the top right hand corner, the audited accounts bottom right and the share structure bottom left. She then passed control of the screen to her co-conspirator.

"Clearly, Emerald, I am not expecting a snap decision but the transaction will need to be concluded within days if we are to prevent the CEO's black sheep of a cousin selling out to Western capitalism. I strongly suggest that you look closely at the numbers and we should arrange to meet sometime next week when we might also celebrate the consummation of the wedding we spoke of."

"This sounds like an excellent plan, Sapphire. I am sure we shall both hear when the earth moves for them!"

56

One glass partition and three cubicles away from Alec, Dicky Meadows, or Rich, as he much preferred to be called, was sifting through the hundreds of thousands of words, phrases and sentences that he had lifted from the download of the La Plume laptop. He had already seen enough to draw the conclusion that the number and nature of communications between Paris, Istanbul and Saudi Arabia were neither simply business nor leisure related. The word search had already isolated numerous references to politics, insurgence, anarchy, direct action, casualties, but nothing yet linking any of the participating parties specifically to the London bombings. Rich had worked on enough of these cases, however, to see a pattern emerging that suggested something sinister was lurking behind the narrative.

Now that Alec had been able to open up access to the device in Riyadh he sent the data hurtling towards Rich who, rather than being overwhelmed, just altered the speed, scope and tolerances of his phraseology programmes and let his machine isolate interesting conversations.

With the two devices now linked, it was much easier for the programme to isolate exchanges that fell within the search criteria.

The screen in front of him scrolled words at the rate of two thousand per second. Any word or phrase matching the search sensor was amplified and dragged into a keep net where the secondary screening level pieced together words, phrases, sentences and paragraphs in sequential, chronological order. At this point, Alec and Rich could only extract data from the devices in Paris and Riyadh but anything of significant interest sent from those devices to those identified as Istanbul and London would fall within scope. They were acutely aware that despite the billions of pounds expended in the most sophisticated data monitoring systems on the planet, commercial communications providers had spent equal amounts developing and selling blocking devices. Without the flash drive in La Plume's laptop, they would have nothing more than vague locations. With the flash drive programme loaded and the Paris-Riyadh connection established, the investigation was coming to life, before their eyes.

Most frequently used words loomed and lingered longest. Others of significance but appearing less seldom flashed and evaporated like wasp stings. Rich called Alec through to observe as the conversation clues unfolded and formed before them. He deserved to see this; it was his initiative, his technical genius and Adam's fieldwork that seemed to give them their first tangible lead into what had been happening over the past week and, more importantly, what was about to happen next.

"It seems like the old trout has taken the bait." Rich remarked with a thumbs up to Alec. "To be honest, it doesn't much matter whether the Arab bites. Now we have access to his computer we have pretty much what we need."

"I thought that the idea was to get them to invest half a billion into the CIA front company to tie their assets up?" Alec was not party to the full strategic plan. His principle role was to provide access to the data. It was down to Rich and his team to translate it into strategy.

"That would be a bonus, mate. It certainly seems from the direct conversations that I've lifted so far between the old bird and the Arab, they have certainly been using funds to undermine the political and economic stability of UK interests, though nothing yet to directly implicate them with terrorism."

"How does that work?" asked Alec. It seemed odd to Rich that someone as technically brilliant as Alec seemed to lack the creative capability to expand and extrapolate the data that he was unlocking. Left brain versus right brain, he thought. Right brain wins.

"They seem to share an ideological hatred of the United Kingdom for different, but related, reasons. Both agree that former British colonialism gave our tiny nation far too much influence on the world stage and the Saudis certainly believes that Britain and now England have been interfering far too much in the Middle East and aligning ourselves too closely with Saudi royalty. It is no secret that much of the ISIS funding comes from Saudi Arabia and there are growing factions within their regime who want to break down the cosy relationship."

"And the French bird? What's her beef?" Alec was quite nonchalant but nevertheless intrigued. "I was under the impression that the French despised Islamic State as much as we do. Didn't they declare all-out war on ISIS in 2015 following the Paris bombings? Why would she be helping them to inflict further attacks in Europe?"

"You might be aware that she is amongst the leadership of a high-profile, albeit fringe, right-wing activist party in France. From a political point of view, she and her party hold a deep rooted, historical resentment of the UK and this is exacerbated by our prosperity since leaving the European Union. Their followers still feel deep humiliation that Britain released them from German occupation in the Second World War when many of their political elite had already thrown their hats into the Vichy arena. From a personal economic perspective, a number of her business interests have been adversely affected by UK economic policy and this, in turn, limits her ability to support and further her political ambitions. I don't doubt that she is equally hostile towards Islamic

State and the Muslim population of France. It was a huge smack in the face for them to learn that the Paris bombers operated out of Belgium, but an Islamic attack on England would kill two birds with one stone; she would strike a blow at the very heart of our nation and economy while whipping up even greater international pressure on Islamic State. This woman is a real piece of work. She is totally ruthless and seems to be exploiting the current anti-English factions in Saudi Arabia.

"So they have a mutual dislike of the UK," remarked Alec innocently. Rich thought it inconceivable that someone so technically brilliant and highly regarded within MI7 could be so disinterested in the murky world of global politics within which he operated. On the other hand, he supposed, this simply allowed Alec to focus on his core responsibility without the distraction of trying to interpret the events he monitored.

"They certainly have that, my old mate, and more importantly, they both have very heavy financial interests in the French aerospace industry and it would be a very major coup for them if they were able to destabilise UK and Saudi relations while the negotiations are underway to replace the Saudi air force military capability over the next fifteen years."

Alec grasped the significance of this statement rather faster than Rich imagined he might. "So if terror campaigns against the UK were found to have been planned, promoted, executed or even funded by the Saudis, the shit would hit the fan!"

"Beautifully put, Alec, but as yet, I can find nothing in these direct exchanges to confirm that they have been complicit in any of the past week's crap. We have, however,, tapped into a highly suspicious conversation regarding an impending wedding and neither of these two arseholes strike me as the romantic types."

"And what about the London and Istanbul connections?" Alec asked.

"As you know, I can't lift the conversations between those parties but SNOOPER is isolating significant words and phrases that have passed between the four locations and devices. At the moment, it's just a list of the most frequently communicated words in alphabetical order but the software will get to work on that list within minutes."

Rich switched screen views and the list of words scrolled continuously in front of them. Occasionally, certain ones would be brought to the fore, enlarged and emboldened. "Those are the ones that arise most frequently and the ones that SNOOPER identifies as having contextual links."

ablaze, abomination, absolute, accident, accomplice, acid, actinide, activist, admonish, adversary, agent, aggression, aggrieved, aircraft, ambush, amok, ammunition, anarchy, anger, Anglophobes, annihilate, artillery, assault, atomic, banish, barbarian, battle, biological, blaze, bloody, bomb, brave, bravura, break, breach, British, burn, Calais, camouflage, carnage, catalyst, cauldron, Cenotaph, channel, charred, Christians, CIA, clandestine, condemn, conflict, conquer, damage, danger, dead, decimate, demolish, deploy, destroy, detonate, discipline, discharge, discord, dislodge, dissident, distress, dominate, dread, dynamite, dystopia, economy, eject, electronic, elite, embassy, empire, enemy, enlist, epilogue, escalate, escape, evict, execute, expedite, explode, extreme, fatal, fatalities, fight, fire, flatten, force, Folkestone, fundamentalist, fury, gamble, gas, geology, germ, geothermal, glory, glycerine, gore, graves, guards, guns, hack, hazard, helicopter, hurt, imam, immigrants, immortal, imposter, ignite, infidel, inflict, injure, insurgent, interrogate, invasion, irreversible, jihad, jihadist, justice, kegs, kidnap, kill, laser, lager, lunacy, malignant, mandate, manhunt, massacre, mecca, minister, mortuary, multilateral, nemesis, nuclear, obliterate, occupy, oppose, orders, overrun, overthrow, paradise, pariah, password, pathologist, penance, peril, phosphorus, political, politicians, port, post-mortem, prison, proton, psychopath, pummel, pulp, pyrotechnics, quake, queen, Quran, race, radiation, rail, railway, ravage, recriminations, refugees, reign, religion, remorse, requiem, ritual, sacrifice, savage, scheme, shard, sheikh, ship, slaughter, station, structure, subterranean, Taliban, tectonics, threat, tide, tomb, track, train, tunnel, Turkish, unassailable, ungovernable, unleash, unprecedented, violent, warriors, war.

"That's quite a game of Scrabble going on there isn't it, Rich?"

"Shit!" exclaimed the analyst. "I think it's time to bring the grown-ups in. Call the deputy director!"

Alec strode purposefully to his desk and pressed the green emblem on the display of his communication screen. The face of Paul Cruse appeared but the continued beep and lack of animation signified a lack of connection. After a period of sixty seconds the message "Contact Unavailable" flashed on screen and the display faded. Alec's upturned hands and shaking head told Rich that the boss was probably out fox hunting or hurling his Aston Martin around Bedford Autodrome; not for him were Sundays work days.

"Okay! Forget the DD." shouted Rich. "Call the Director himself!"

57

Sean Lakin subconsciously bowed his head as he walked through the capital. The stillness of the streets was eerie, disconcerting and although his rational mind disagreed, he felt guilt that as a senior police officer in the city he had been unable to prevent the tragedy or at least be sure that the perpetrators had been brought to justice. As he walked over Westminster Bridge on his way back to Whitehall, he was totally overcome by the wall of flowers that completely covered the sides of the bridge and were now sprawling over the pavement in a multi coloured deep but delicate carpet. A heartless cynic might have suggested that the bombing had been masterminded by Interflora to boost their ailing business.

However busy the bridge, however hurried the pedestrians crossing it, it seemed as though not a single petal had been harmed as the sanctity of the offerings were respected. The bells of Westminster had been sounding sombrely all day. One hundred and sixty-six chimes at ten second intervals, every three hours. One for each of the lives lost just under a week ago and the death toll still rising.

Sean's guilt was not just for the dead of the city. He hated himself for allowing Farah to be exposed to such unimaginable terror and for putting her life at further risk in the rescue. And now, he felt even greater guilt at the realisation that these events, the suffering of countless others, had finally brought their love to the surface. Amid this misery, he had never felt so happy, fulfilled and optimistic about the future. He was ashamed of himself.

He had spent another long and wonderful night with Farah, making the most of Ava's absence. They slept little, both understanding that their time together was too precious to pass over to dreams; none of which could ever match the ecstasy of these awakened hours. They made love once last night and once this morning. In between, they held each other, they looked at each other, and they stroked each other and lay awake in each other's arms defying the hours to defeat them.

At eleven he had torn himself away to pick up a change of clothes and his computing pack to prepare for his meeting with the deputy director of MI7. The prospect worried him. He was not sure whether he should be focussing upon the terrorism inquiry or the suspicious murder of his friend and colleague. He was sure that the two were somehow linked and perhaps tomorrow he might find out how.

He arrived back at Farah's and let himself in. Fortunately he had not shouted anything indiscreetly as he entered and Farah, still facing the video screen on the wall of her lounge, held out a hand to Sean which he understood immediately. Farah was speaking to Ava and it might be difficult to explain why Sean, beaming from ear to ear, would be able to walk straight into their home. He sat quietly on the stairs. He listened to their conversation; not because he was nosey but because he wanted to understand and immerse himself into the love that Farah and Ava displayed for each other and hoped that he could add to, rather than dilute the pool.

Farah somehow managed to convince Ava that her own week had been far less adventurous than her daughter's. Ava and her school friends had experienced the culture of Paris, the thrill of independent friendships, the adventure of the French countryside and the attention of too many boys of both nationalities but for all this, she declared, she had never imagined how much she would have missed her mother and could not wait to see her when their coach arrives back into Victoria on Monday evening. They were scheduled to arrive around six but the coach driver had advised them that they could be an hour or so either side of that depending on how slow security was on both sides of the Channel. Sean found himself wishing that he could be the one to pick her up, or at least be with Farah when she did so but they had discussed this; he would need to be patient.

Farah and Ava made virtual kisses and waved. The screen faded and Farah summoned Sean inside. They kissed for real. She stepped back and looked at Sean, straight into his eyes.

"She is going to love you. She really is."

"I hope so," Sean sighed. "I will do everything I can to encourage her but for starters I will just settle for her allowing me to share a bit of your love for each other."

She looked at his overnight bag and computer case. "You can be quite a romantic when you're not being a snotty superintendent, can't you? Go and sort yourself out while I prepare us some dinner."

Just as she spoke, Sean's video phone vibrated on the table. The Police Commissioner's face shone towards the ceiling and now it was Farah's turn to dodge the gaze as Sean engaged his boss. This was the first time in four years that they had spoken on a Sunday.

"Good afternoon, sir." Sean offered with a suitable blend of courtesy and surprise.

"Good afternoon, Sean. Sorry to have to bother you on a Sunday but I thought I'd better give you the news now to allow you to arrange your day tomorrow. I've just had the director of MI7 on the line and I'm afraid that your meeting with Deputy Director Paul Cruse won't be taking place."

"What? The director has vetoed it?"

"Oh no, Sean. On the contrary. The director was keen for the meeting to go ahead but Cruse has just been killed this afternoon in a car accident."

"No, no way. This isn't happening. Are you smelling the same big stinky rat that I'm smelling, sir?"

"Well I might not have your refined nose for these things, Sean, but I certainly find something suspicious in the death of one of our officers within days of meeting with the deputy director and then his own sudden demise a further two days later."

"Well, sir. In that case it does sound like you're smelling exactly the same smell as me. So where do I go from here, do I go up or down the chain?"

"I would suggest both. You worked with Tom Mellor last week. Did you two get along well enough for an off the record?"

"Well, on the grounds that you obviously haven't received a complaint about me, I would say yes. I think so."

"Okay then, sound him out but also have a sniff around the DD's direct team at MI7. Start with the chaps who were handing Rosie Hunter's Intel. I will get you the clearance you need."

"Will do, sir. Can you set that up for tomorrow?"

"Consider it done, but Sean, keep me in the loop. This is highly sensitive stuff. It probably goes beyond even my pay grade."

"I very much doubt that, sir. I read the *Telegraph*'s Rich List last month. I'm sure that I saw you up there."

"Report back to me tomorrow, Sean. Enjoy the rest of your weekend."

Sean recounted the conversation with Farah. He wasn't being indiscreet as Farah was officially assigned to the Rosie Hunter case and it was fair to assume that there might be a link between the two unexpected deaths.

"Alec Brunson." she assured. "Too thorough and too straight for subterfuge. He's a bright guy but approaching stratospheric on the autistic spectrum. He was clearly uncomfortable speaking with me and it will be interesting to see how he behaves when he hears about Cruse. It could send him one way or the other. Would you like me to introduce him to you?"

"Maybe. If possible I would like you to handle that end of the equation and I will try to get to my new best buddy, Tom Mellor. If I have friends in high places, I am sure that he has friends in even higher ones."

"Well just make sure you don't go climbing too high. I don't want you falling from any great height just I have got you down on the ground."

"I'm not quite on the ground yet, but if you turn the heat down on that pan, I will be happy to oblige."

58

"With all due respect, Miss, although the director has authorised me to speak with you, I don't know what I am at liberty to talk about. I am pretty sure that I can discuss my conversations with Miss Hunter and Mr Cruse but the actual content of the data they were discussing is a matter for national security rather than the police."

"Please, Alec, call me Farah or Inspector if you must, but not Miss. Perhaps I could have my boss get your boss down here, but is that really necessary? We are both grown-ups and we are on the same side. The director has authorised me to talk to you because we believe that the deaths of Rosie Hunter and Paul Cruse are linked to each other, AND to the investigation that you are conducting. It will save time, and possibly more lives, if you can be open with me. I am sure you will be aware of my own experience last week. I can assure you that I am just as fully immersed in the wider picture as you are."

She held up her bandaged hand and he nodded his acknowledgement and understanding.

"I will tell you what I know, but you will need to get your boss to talk to his boss to talk to my boss if you want to know what goes on out there" He pointed to the cubicle in which Rich Greenfield sat scouring a screen with one hand on his headphones and another on a pen.

Farah hit one button and relayed her request to Sean.

"Leave it with me," he said. "I will get back to you but just remind me what you have so far. I am seeing Tom Mellor in ten minutes."

Farah reminded Sean of Alec's insistence that there had been a direct line of contact between the communications device known to have belonged to the suspect Colin Richards and a device or devices in Whitehall. Deputy Director Cruse had been following this up and it was he who asserted that Whitehall was, in fact, a white elephant. The communication had been routed via Edinburgh. Brunson completely refuted this but was instructed, bluntly, to erase the records of the spurious device in Whitehall as this would only cause embarrassment to the department. His professional pride had obviously been bruised, his integrity battered but had his resolve been broken?

"Before I go, Farah, have another word with this Brunson guy. If he is as straight down the line, borderline autistic as you suggest, will he really have deleted details of the Whitehall device? Turn on the charm Farah. Melt him down."

Farah was a trained psychologist and just as Alec could receive the signals he was receiving, Farah could read the signals he was emitting. He showed little emotion at the death of his deputy director and the little emotion he did display, looked like relief. Farah went back to work on him. Massaging his ego, wondering openly and praising his gift, lauding the unique contribution he was making to national security and complimenting him on his unique ability to assess and judge the integrity of those around him. His head slipped slightly to one side, eyes widened and lips parted like a Labrador puppy. The iceman melted.

True to his word, he would not reveal the conversations that were unfolding in Rich Greenfield's domain but he strongly suggested that her boss get the director to bring him over as soon as possible as Rich was making significant headway in decoding and interpreting the narrative. For his own part, Alec volunteered that he considered Paul Cruse to be a doddery incompetent who lacked the courage to stand up for his team. Alec had not erased the Whitehall data. He had the satellite location of a computer processor and the access frequency of a mobile phone. Farah eagerly requested the numbers for both of these but predictably, with Alec, it was not quite that simple.

"My software doesn't just produce IP addresses or mobile phone numbers. Security technology is far too advanced to allow that or you wouldn't need people like me around. I have digital pulse patterns and call connection frequencies that are unique to those particular applications but can only be accessed from my system here. I can't lift or translate data from them but I can communicate with them. It's totally illegal of course."

"Of course it is, Alec. Right then, it looks like we have a busy morning ahead of us."

59

Like most coppers, Sean had an inbuilt aversion to politicians. Not quite the pathological hatred he had developed when he was in the military, but he always remained convinced that while he was serving his country, they were serving themselves. Tom Mellor was different, though. He was not one of them. He took no bullshit and the PM had brought him in specifically to rattle the cages of politicos and the self-serving civil servants, and not worry too much about the diplomatic niceties. Sean liked him. He liked him even more when Mellor had readily agreed to meet with him in Whitehall to discuss new developments in the case and any possible overlap in the suspicious deaths and the ongoing national security issue. This was, of course, still very much within the remit of the Special Investigations Unit. His meeting was scheduled for nine forty-five but he had arrived early in anticipation of the heightened security in and around Whitehall. He judged it well as it took twenty minutes for his identity and credentials to be checked before he was led to Cabinet Office ante-room 3. The security officer led him to the door, Sean knocked firmly and was invited to enter. The room was surprisingly small and stark. The oak panelling was badly in need of a coat of varnish and a thick layer of dust was gathering on the solemn portrait of Her Majesty, Queen Elizabeth, who seemed to look disapprovingly at the two individuals below her. Sean was surprised to see Tom Mellor sitting opposite Neil Faraday with one laptop, one phone and dozens of archived paper files between them. Sean was as unhappy to see Faraday as he was delighted to see Mellor. His aversion to politicians rose to nauseous contempt at the very mention of the Deputy Prime Minister's name.

"Won't keep you waiting long, Sean," Mellor beamed. "Just a few strategy protocols to agree with the DPM."

Faraday rose and stretched out his hand to Sean. "I understand that you led the investigation into my son's assault, Superintendent. Well done on the outcome. You saved the prison service millions!"

"It wasn't exactly the outcome we desired, sir, and I accept no credit for it. His death has left us with a lot of unanswered questions."

"Yes, of course it did. Excuse me for not seeing the bigger picture on that one but when it's one of your own, rationale and reason can fly out of the window. Was the bastard's death as gruesome as I hoped it would be?"

Just as Sean was about to answer, the phone rang. Both men looked at it and ignored it.

Sean created a laboured smile and replied. "I am sure you would have approved, sir. There weren't any pals of yours in the prison at that time by any chance, were there? You know, some of your more zealous and less diplomatic supporters? Perhaps that's another investigation for the future. Anyway, I hope your son is on the mend."

Mellor sensed the intense unease and broke the tension by addressing the security guard. "Simon. Would you please take Superintendent Lakin to the kitchen and make him a coffee." He smiled at Sean. "I will be with you in no more than ten minutes."

Sean's courteous reply was almost drowned by the second, and more persistent, ringing of the phone on the desk which, stubbornly, remained unanswered. Simon took Sean twenty yards down the corridor to a small, sparse but functional kitchen and left him to fend for himself. He made a cup of strong instant coffee to wash away the bitter taste of his exchange with Faraday. His admiration for Mellor rose even higher, knowing that he had to deal, probably daily, with a knob like Faraday without resorting to violence.

He was snapped out of his fantasy of doing to Faraday what Abadi had done to his son by his own phone vibrating in his pocket. He lifted it out and beamed as Farah's face looked out at him.

"How's it going?" he asked, efficiently but softly, in case he was audible on either end of the connection.

"Making good progress here, but you need to get the Commissioner to speak to the director of MI7 to get you access to the guys next door to me. I can't be sure of anything with these guys but they seem to be on the verge of a massive breakthrough."

Farah briefly explained the process of data extraction and analysis from the Paris and Riyadh systems. She didn't know the content but Alec assured her that Rich was on to something big. She also confirmed that the Whitehall connection was live again and that it was Edinburgh, not London that was the red herring. She told him that Alec had tried to connect with the phone device twice in the last five minutes but as yet, there had been no answer. She had told him to keep trying. Just as he was about to respond, Mellor strode into the kitchen.

"Sorry about that, Sean. Faraday has a meeting with the PM to discuss the announcement of his resignation and he asked me for an intelligence update."

Sean was startled but quickly recovered his composure.

"Thanks Farah. I have to go now but I'll call you later. Sorry about that, Mr Mellor. One of the team seems to be making some progress over at MI7. Faraday requested an intelligence update? I presume you advised him that he doesn't have any!"

"Now Sean, that's a bit harsh. True, but harsh though he does serve a purpose. That's excellent news from the listeners though. I am heading across there myself later this morning. Maybe you'd like to come with me?"

"That would be really helpful, but I believe that my commissioner needs to get clearance from the director for grunts like me to be involved."

"I'm sure we can clear that up before we leave. There are certain privileges that go with being National Security Advisor to the PM Anyway bring your coffee and come on through."

Sean followed Mellor down the corridor and back into the anteroom. Sean felt distinctly uncomfortable in the seat recently vacated by Faraday, more so because it was still warm. The files remained, though now stacked tidily in the centre of the table. The phone and the laptop were gone.

"I don't know where this is going, Mr Mellor, but the deaths of Rosie Hunter and Paul Cruse are just too suspicious not to be considered part of the wider investigation."

"I totally agree, Sean, and please, call me Tom. I work here but I'm not one of them."

"Thanks, Tom. My officer met with the deputy director on Friday to discuss details of evidence she had gathered against the possible bomber. She died in suspicious circumstances the same evening. Two days later, Paul Cruse himself, a skilled petrol head by all accounts, dies in a road accident. The forensics team and pathologist are pulling out all the stops to give us some insight but there's nothing abnormal emerging, as yet."

"It's more than suspicious, Sean. The odds on these deaths being coincidental must be greater than you inviting Faraday to be Godfather of your firstborn. You haven't got kids yet have you, Sean?"

"Never quite got round to it and not sure I'd want to bring any into this shitty world."

"Well, it's up to the likes of you and me to make it better then isn't it?"

Mellor sat back with his hands behind his head and continued. "Inspector Hunter had information regarding possible communications from the bomber's phone. She's invited to meet with Cruse and they exchange information. Apparently, they then arrange to meet later that evening, either professionally or socially… maybe a combination of the two, but she doesn't get there. Before you have the opportunity to question Cruse, he is killed in a questionable car wreck. You have every right to smell a rat, Sean, because I certainly do and I'd be very disappointed if you didn't."

"What do you know about Cruse, Tom?"

"Establishment background, public school, family dripping with meaningless titles, safe service record, never strayed from the straight grey line in his intelligence career. All the hallmarks of the fuckwit son shoehorned into the service by some arsehole wanting to suck up to nobility. Don't get me wrong. I have nothing at all concrete against him but in my role as advisor, I had the responsibility of meeting all the senior leaders of the intelligence units and he was, in my mind, the least impressive and the least likeable."

"But nothing to suggest anything more sinister than nepotism and incompetence?"

"No, Sean, not in my opinion. I'm going to make a suggestion now that you might not like. I don't want to belittle the death of your officer or indeed a senior member of the intelligence service but I think that we are both agreed that they are more than likely linked to the wider events of last week. I am more concerned about the implications for the future than the past and I think that we need to ensure that there is no further immediate threat to national security. It might be distractionary and unproductive if we spend too much time and energy on these two investigations."

Sean took a few seconds to reflect on those words and admitted to himself that he was perhaps too focussed on last week and this weekend than the possible implications for the next weeks or months. Farah's excitement at the possible new revelations from

MI7 dragged him back to the table and he addressed Mellor directly, quickly outlining her conversation regarding Rich Greenfield's data extraction analysis.

"Can you get me in there with you, Tom? It would be cleaner if the director ticked and passed it with the Commissioner but I suspect that you might be able to make that happen."

Mellor removed his phone from his pocket, switched it on and made two calls. Three minutes later a car was waiting to take them on the short journey to MI7 headquarters.

Charles Murphy, director of MI7, was waiting at the entrance to usher them through personally. He advised them that Commissioner Pollard had already arrived and that his team were ready and waiting. Murphy was, himself, a military veteran but his objective professionalism would not have permitted the former status of his guests to influence his decision to admit them. Now in his early fifties, tall, slim and sandy haired, his ready smile belied the steely character that lay behind it.

"Thank you, Charlie. I appreciate this and you can be assured that Pollard and his team have very good reasons to be here and, more importantly, all the credentials to help."

"I understand that, Tom, and looking at the data being extracted from the Paris and Riyadh connections, we are going to need all the help we can get and as fast as we can get it. Come on up."

There were the customary finger print and retinal recognition screens at each of the doors and Sean had no doubt that the bank of surveillance cameras would ensure that armed response units would be on the floor within seconds when required. They walked through an open plan area where Sean nodded at Farah who was still sitting with Alec. The director led them into a soundproofed, glass-walled office in which Rich Greenfield, with another smart young casually dressed man, and Nigel Pollard were sitting calmly around the table, all eyes focussed on the wall monitor. As the last three entered, screens descended and the wall monitor was illuminated. Introductions were effected efficiently. Peter Coyne

343

was a team leader from MI5 who was eagerly anticipating a busy few days ahead of him.

Director Murphy quickly outlined the processes and roles of Alec Brunson and Rich Greenfield then quickly handed over to his senior analyst who seemed to relish his captive audience. Rich tapped a few keys and motioned his hands to the monitor in a 'voila!' moment. He began by explaining the term recognition technology that isolated recurring words within carefully defined parameters. He quickly displayed the first screen and then the distilled version with the most frequently used and sensitive words dragged to the foreground.

ablaze, abomination, absolute, accident, accomplice, acid, actinide, activist, admonish, adversary, agent, aggression, aggrieved, aircraft, ambush, amok, ammunition, anarchy, anger, Anglophobes, annihilate, artillery, assault, atomic, banish, barbarian, battle, biological, blaze, bloody, bomb, brave, bravura, break, breach, British, burn, Calais, camouflage, carnage, catalyst, cauldron, Cenotaph, channel, charred, Christians, CIA, clandestine, condemn, conflict, conquer, damage, danger, dead, decimate, demolish, deploy, destroy, detonate, discipline, discharge, discord, dislodge, dissident, distress, dominate, dread, dynamite, dystopia, economy, eject, electronic, elite, embassy, empire, enemy, enlist, epilogue, escalate, escape, evict, execute, expedite, explode, extreme, fatal, fatalities, fight, fire, flatten, force, Folkestone, fundamentalist, fury, gamble, gas, geology, germ, geothermal, glory, glycerine, gore, graves, guards, guns, hack, hazard, helicopter, hurt, imam, immigrants, immortal, imposter, ignite, infidel, inflict, injure, insurgent, interrogate, invasion, irreversible, jihad, jihadist, justice, kegs, kidnap, kill, laser, lager, lunacy, malignant, mandate, manhunt, massacre, mecca, minister, mortuary, multilateral, nemesis, nuclear, obliterate, occupy, oppose, orders, overrun, overthrow, paradise, pariah, password, pathologist, penance, peril, phosphorus, political, politicians, port, post-mortem, prison, proton, psychopath, pummel, pulp, pyrotechnics, quake, queen, Quran, race, radiation, rail, railway, ravage, recriminations, refugees, reign, religion, remorse, requiem, ritual, sacrifice, savage, scheme, shard, sheikh, ship, slaughter, station, structure, subterranean, Taliban, tectonics, threat, tide, tomb, track, train, tunnel, Turkish, unassailable, ungovernable, unleash, unprecedented, violent, warriors, war.

Two clicks later and the screen now displayed:

annihilate, bomb, Calais, carnage, catalyst, Cenotaph, channel, demolish, detonate, economy, escape, explode, extreme, fatalities, Folkestone, fundamentalist, geothermal, guards, immigrants, jihadist, kegs, nuclear, obliterate, paradise, politicians, port, pyrotechnics, rail, railway, sacrifice, station, subterranean, tectonics, tide, tomb, track, train, tunnel, war.

Rich then proceeded to relay the text of those direct conversations between Sapphire and Emerald which clearly described their political and economic motivations for perpetrating acts of terror in the United Kingdom and at least one further devastating strike designed to cripple the UK politically, economically, geographically and morally. It did not take any of the group more than three seconds to assemble the pieces of the puzzle but they left it to Charlie Murphy to articulate their conclusion.

"The Channel Tunnel. We don't know when, and we don't know how but I'm pretty sure that we know what. It would also help if we knew where."

Tom Mellor was the first to respond. "We have to assume that it is imminent and need to get into action immediately but… not a word to anybody, and I mean anybody outside this room without my express clearance. I will go directly to the Prime Minister. Charlie, I assume you will mobilise the other intelligence agencies and get feet on the ground on both sides of the Channel."

60

As the room was dismissed, Sean asked the director if he could join his inspector at Alec Brunson's work station. To Sean's surprise and intense frustration, the director refused and insisted that Farah leave immediately. Adding insult to injury to Sean, he reminded him of his duty towards confidentiality. As they left the building Sean suggested to Farah that rather than going back to the Yard, they should grab a coffee together in the Wetherspoons around the corner. As he walked back from the counter with his black Americano and her skinny latte his temples were pounding and he struggled to disperse the lead weight lodged in the pit of his stomach. He knew that Ava, Farah's only daughter, was due to travel back from France tomorrow but wasn't sure whether it was to be over or under the Channel. Either way, above or below the seabed, a major explosion in the tunnel could have disastrous consequences. He could not tell Farah yet but knew that he had less than twenty-four hours to change his mind. For just a second, he found himself questioning whether his sense of duty should override his instinct to share the dilemma but concluded that this would serve no useful purpose.

He sat by her; not opposite, not quite alongside, but just distant enough to dispel any unwanted attention should a colleague drop into, what was, a popular coffee stop for those fearing for their stomach linings under assault from Scotland Yard machine coffee. She looked excited, almost animated by the progress in the investigation and was eager to hear what Rich Greenfield had uncovered. Sean was sensitive enough not to cut her out completely, but professional enough to honour his commitment to his superiors.

"There is evidence of a further plot against the UK but at this stage the target would just be speculation. The protagonists appear to be in Paris and Riyadh but it's highly unlikely that either of those arseholes will be getting their hands dirty. There's at least one more party actively involved and that party could either be the power behind all this or merely the hired help. It's vital that we pinpoint those final two phone connections."

"I had Alec try to activate the London connection three times this morning. No answer. The first couple of times we did get a ring tone but the third flat-lined."

"Have you tried again since?"

"It's not that easy, Sean. We don't actually have a cell phone number. It's just a frequency or some sort of digital sequence that Alec can access from his console. We haven't a clue who, if anybody, is on the other end of it other than the satellite signal is pointing at Whitehall."

"Could you call Alec again and ask him to keep trying and after each attempt, trace the satellite location? If the device is still active, its movements might give us a clue."

Alec had given Farah his direct line number but had warned her that every call to and from it was monitored and recorded. The line was to be used strictly for official business only. Farah remembered this as she started the conversation.

"Mr Brunson, this is Inspector Karim of the SIU. That line of enquiry we were pursuing this morning. Could you please try again

347

from time to time and keep a track on its location? It could be important to my inquiry."

"Of course, Inspector. I will get back to you as soon as I have something to report."

Their coffee was still too hot to drink when less than two minutes later, Farah's phone flashed and Alec's face appeared. She set the device to discreet mode and held it to her ear.

"Right, thanks Alec. Keep trying and keep tracking." She turned to Sean with a confused and disturbed expression. "The two calls this morning were both tracked to a cabinet ante-room in Whitehall and another failed call a minute ago was located at an address in Downing Street. What the hell is going on, Sean?"

61

Mellor had phoned ahead to alert the Prime Minister's private secretary that he was on his way and needed to see him as a matter of extreme urgency. Janet advised him that his meeting with the Deputy PM was currently overrunning but she would use this as an excuse to rescue Mitchell and keep him free until Mellor arrived. Sure enough the two crossed on the stairs. Neither had the opportunity to speak but they exchanged knowing glances. Janet showed him through carrying a pot of tea for two and six Jaffa Cakes. In the time it had taken for Graeme Mitchell to polish off four of them, Mellor had brought him up to speed with the morning's developments.

"The Channel Tunnel? Christ! Are we certain?" he pushed the two remaining biscuits to Mellor who, of course, had no chance to take them as he was too busy replying. Mitchell did not let them go to waste.

"No, Graeme, we can't be one hundred per cent certain. All we have to go on are coded transcripts of computer conversations between France and Riyadh, plus a series of random, but closely related and highly significant words, isolated and assembled by MI7's

349

most sophisticated software. It was this piece of kit and the same analyst that thwarted last year's Heathrow terminal 6 bombing."

"And your assessment, Tom?"

"Much too much to ignore. We have to take it seriously and act accordingly."

"But we can't act in isolation, Tom. Not only does this have national security implications it has massively serious international, political and economic ones. At the very least, we have to involve the French. And what about other European trading partners and tourists?"

Mellor looked closely at his old friend. He had mentored him through many crises but had never seen him so ashen and vulnerable as now.

"Don't you think that the French might already be involved? There is absolutely no love lost since we imposed tariffs on their wine and cheese. They are no longer exporting cars to us so maybe they don't think that the tunnel does much for them these days. However much Francoise La Plume might be considered an extreme right-wing fringe politician, don't underestimate her influence. It wasn't too long ago that we regarded Neil Faraday as a lunatic."

"And some of us still do, Tom, but that's for another day. I need to call a Cabinet meeting urgently."

"Do you really need to do that? Do you think we have time to do that? For all we know there might be a nuclear device clamped to the top of the tunnel just waiting for the next train through to set it off."

"And for all we also know, Tom, or rather don't know, this could be at best, pure speculation or at worst, a plot that's just incubating and might not hatch for years. It could even be the reddest herring that's ever graced the Channel."

"And you are prepared to take that chance?"

"I am not prepared to unilaterally shut down the most significant travel route in Europe, if not the world, without at least consulting my own Cabinet and the other commercial and political stakeholders. Eurostar is operated by the national railway companies of France and Belgium, SNCF and SNCB and by Eurostar Ltd. If there is an imminent threat we don't know whether it's to passenger, freight or just the infrastructure itself. I respect your views, Tom, I really do, but I can't go it alone on this one."

"I understand and I will do whatever I can to help."

Mitchell pressed the button on his desk and Janet's image appeared on the wall in front of him.

"Janet. I need you to summon an emergency Cabinet meeting for 1.30 today. Get as many as you can. Tell them it's a matter of the utmost importance and that a decision affecting the security of the nation will be taken at 2.30 whether they are in attendance or not... and clear my diary for the rest of the day."

"Yes, sir. You remember that you are due to meet with the new Labour party leader at 5.30. Am I to cancel him as well?"

"Yes, Janet. At least that's one good thing to come out of this."

"Would you like me to be present, Graeme?"

"Yes, Tom, I would. Of course you won't have a vote but I shall be relying heavily upon you to support my opinions and back them up with your own."

"And what are those opinions likely to be?"

"I don't know yet but I need you to trust me. This could be just the opportunity that Faraday needs to screw me over. Whatever the consequences."

"You can rely on me. I will be back at 1.30. In the meantime could I use the bunker? I have a number of calls to make on the secure lines to prepare us as fully as I can. With your permission, I think I should brief Mountstevens, Sadler and Brockington before they arrive. Officially, I do report to them."

"Yes of course, Janet will give you the code for the door."

Janet wrote down the five digit code and Mellor climbed the two flights of stairs to the bunker. It was an anachronism that the room was at the very top, rather than the bottom of the building but was located there to ensure the strongest possible digital communications signals as opposed to nuclear protection. That place was called the doomsday room. As suggested, he called the Home Secretary, Defence Secretary and Foreign Secretary. He kept to the same brief script, even tone and summary conclusion. He could not debate further online but would be at the Cabinet meeting to answer further questions. He was of course, throwing the responsibility back to them and they would already be irritated that he had got to the PM before they had. That, however, was for them to sort out. In the meantime, he had enough on his plate.

He sat quietly in the bunker and stared through the window, over the city. His gaze drew him to St Pancras, the UK terminal of Eurostar which, for all he knew, might be due to erupt with devastating consequences at any given moment. He removed his personal communication device from his pocket and looked at it for a good thirty seconds before activating the security code and hitting the most confidential of his coded contacts. He knew that the chances of a response were minimal but he was encouraged to at least hear a ring-tone. After almost a minute he was about to disconnect when he heard the familiar but fearsome voice at the other end.

"Mr Black. I thought I had warned you of the consequences of calling me again. You should know by now that I am a man of my word. I always deliver on my commitments."

"And is now one of your commitments to blow up the Channel Tunnel?"

"Well, Mr Black. Congratulations. You see, I am not the callous unfeeling monster that I am sometimes made out to be. I threw out some seed for your carrier pigeons to feed upon and they eventually brought the message home to you."

"I am sure you had your own reasons for doing that. Particularly as you would be safe in the knowledge that while contactable, you are untraceable, whereas I would always be at the mercy of your discretion. Discretion that, these days, seems to be sadly lacking. Have you thrown me to the wolves?"

"Not at all, Mr Black, but I just figure that while your MI7 colleagues are looking for you, they are not so busy looking for me."

"So it's true then. You are going to take responsibility for destroying the Channel Tunnel?"

"No more than the responsibility you took for destroying the Cenotaph, Mr Black."

"I ordered a symbolic monument to be destroyed. I did not order the massacre of hundreds of civilians!"

"Calm down, Mr. Black. If it is of any comfort to you, the more devastating explosions had already been commissioned by another party. I simply switched the order and venues around. I did their devastating one first and your own futile, symbolic one second. With or without you, it would have happened anyway. As I said, I always honour my commitments."

"So the Channel Tunnel? When, where and how? Are you really prepared to let hundreds, maybe thousands more die?"

"That is a question that you should be asking yourself, Mr Black. If you are so sure that the tunnel is to be bombed, all your Prime Minister needs to do is close it now and nobody will be hurt. Unless of course, my people are already in there. I suppose I should check, but it really has nothing to do with me anymore. In fact I am currently contemplating retirement…"

"Just give me a clue. Anything…"

"No, Mr Black. I will give you nothing more. As you say, my device is completely untraceable. Yours is not. If you ever, ever try to contact me again, I will send a copy of this conversation, together with your personalised voice profile, to your Ministry of Defence. Now I suggest you destroy your phone immediately. Goodbye, Mr Mellor."

Mellor placed his head in his hands and fought back the tears. Yes, it was some consolation to him that the Whitehall deaths and subsequent events were not directly of his making but he would never forgive his own stupidity and ill judgement. He had felt himself to be fully justified in trying to stir his Prime Minister into firmer action at home and abroad by exposing the country's vulnerability to those who would do it harm. The PM was not listening to his Cabinet. He was ignoring the military build-up in Europe. He was going soft on Islamic terror. As Security Advisor, Mellor felt that he had an obligation, a duty, to shake Mitchell from his pacifist apathy. Now he realised that his plan was all crumbling around him but consoled himself that the terror attacks would continue with or without him and his association with the assassin gave him an insight that the security services would never have uncovered.

He would have to find a way to right his wrongs and that way might just be sitting in Paris right now. The next contact in his list was simply entered as AA. Once it had been Adnan Abadi, now it was Adam Albano. He called his 'on loan' agent who answered promptly.

"If you can speak," he whispered, "don't answer me now but call me on the emergency number in five minutes."

Mellor opened his device, removed the data card and replaced it with one from the lining of his suit jacket. He completely stripped the intricate metal foils from the original card, rolled them into a little golden ball and flushed it, along with the scarred blank card, down the bunker's adjoining toilet. Five minutes later, he checked his watch. He still had another forty minutes before the Cabinet meeting commenced. On cue, his phone rang on its new number.

"What's happening at your end?" Adam asked.

"The data dump was a complete success. We have La Plume exchanging communications with her Saudi contact that suggests they bought the investment scam and are considering proceeding. We've also been able to lift more vital clues that suggest an imminent attack on the Channel Tunnel. Have you picked up anything about that?"

"Not a thing, Mr Mellor, but my focus has been on keeping her communicating with the Saudis. She is a very astute and careful woman."

"I am sure she is but I'm afraid it's time to up the ante and go for the less subtle approach. It will mean blowing your cover so you might want to try to get her on your own territory but it needs to happen quickly. It might already be too late."

"I'll see what I can do but you will need to get me a safe route out of here. I might not get past airport security and I am sure you will understand my reluctance to chance Eurostar."

62

The Cabinet meeting lasted exactly thirty-three minutes. Sixty per cent of appointed ministers were present and the outcome was unanimous. The Prime Minister and Foreign Secretary would engage immediately with their French counterparts. As if that conversation would not be difficult enough, they then, reluctantly agreed that it would be necessary to brief the President of the European Union.

The Industry Secretary and Home Secretary would then summon the UK heads of Eurostar and Eurotunnel to Downing Street.

When Matt Sadler called his opposite number in the French capital he was brusquely advised that Monsieur Verne would not be available for at least another hour. Relations between France and the United Kingdom had become increasingly cool since the UK's departure from the European community but diplomatic relations were still respected. Sadler quoted the internationally recognised code that was agreed between the two nations to denote a crisis of epic proportion and while the Foreign Secretary was still unavailable, it was agreed that the French President, Alain Baroux

356

and his Prime Minister, Michel Audran, would host a secure video virtual conference at precisely 2.20 p.m.

Clive Mountstevens and Michael Hoyle, the UKIP Industry Secretary, could now prepare for a difficult meeting with the Eurostar and Eurotunnel supremoes. Government vehicles were on their way to collect them as part of a well-rehearsed protocol leaving the executives in absolutely no doubt of the reason for the meeting. This would commence at 2.30 p.m. and the two meetings could be brought together at any time in an enlarged virtual conference room.

Diplomatic niceties were briefly observed before Graeme Mitchell delivered the lightning bolt that reliable intelligence sources have unearthed an imminent plot to explode a device inside the Channel Tunnel. They did not know when, in which tunnel, by whom or how but they were absolutely convinced of the validity and veracity of the threat. Baroux and Audran sat in stunned silence. There had been security incidents in the tunnel before; genuine accidents, fires, suicide attempts and countless incursions by illegal immigrants but terrorist threats had remained precisely that; threats. They had created fear and chaos but nothing worse. Why should the French Government now believe that this would be any different, especially given the sparse detail of heavily coded communications between two unknown parties? France had become extremely sensitive to terror related issues as numerous acts had been perpetrated on her soil by, it would appear, French residents and French Nationals.

The identity of Francoise La Plume had not yet been declared as Tom Mellor had advised that he might be able to extract a confession out of her and would prefer to have his people speak with her before the French Government become involved. If the worst did come to the worst, the blame might yet be lain at a door in Paris.

At 2.50, the two video conferences converged. The communications rooms on either side of the Channel were constructed in such a way that the three hundred and sixty degree screens and three dimensional hologram imagery presented the illusion that all eight parties were seated around the same table. Mitchell was clear that he wanted the tunnel closed immediately. Kenneth Bull of Eurostar was prepared to halt operations quoting technical difficulties for a twelve hour period but insisted that the supposed cause would have to be deflected onto the tunnel infrastructure rather than his rolling stock. Serge Roussell of Eurotunnel was horrified by this suggestion and proposed that if there were to be a temporary closure it must be attributed to the computerised border control systems within the UK zone at Calais. Success, it seemed, had many parents but disaster was a true bastard.

Since 2015, the UK Government had leased a one mile square area around the Eurostar terminal in a multimillion Euro, ten year rolling arrangement. A garrison of two hundred troops had permission to operate within the confines of the militarised zone and it was here that all UK border checks were completed and the tunnels were guarded. A further quarter mile strip separated the UK zone with the French border and this lay under the jurisdiction of the United Nations who supported the security initiatives and helped with the processing of individuals, mainly from the African continent, who have been denied asylum by either the French or the English. Security is robust but with over fifty trains passing through each of the tunnels every twenty-four hours, it would be impossible to guarantee absolute impenetrability without suffocating the system.

At 3.00 p.m. the French leaders and the heads of the rail networks concluded that there was insufficient evidence upon which to close down the operations and offered to review the situation on an hourly basis in the light of any further, more concrete intelligence. Matt Sadler, with the apparent support of his Prime Minister advised the meeting that if the UK Government felt justified in doing so, they would advise United Kingdom citizens of the perceived threat but would hold off for a further sixty minutes to formulate the wording and communication of the notification. The screens went black and the holograms vanished.

63

Francoise La Plume was excited by the prospect of meeting Adam's broker. He had called only thirty minutes earlier to tell her that Neville Hall had made an unscheduled visit and had a free half hour if she could get across to the Regency Suites quickly. He had given her the code to access the private elevator that would take her directly to the door of his penthouse suite; one of the perks of being CEO. As she approached the suite, the security camera recognised her profile and the double doors silently opened inwards. She strode through, smiling imperiously, but from the corner of each eye she detected shapes looming towards her from behind each of the doors. By the time she had recognised the two goons from the restaurant, one had secured a tie wrap roughly and tightly around her wrists, behind her back, while the other stuffed a balled-up handkerchief into her mouth and secured it with tape. Her heels left two fine trails in the deep pile ivory carpet as she was dragged through the sitting room and into the adjoining wet room where the shower was already running. She was quickly and inelegantly stripped to her pearl satin underwear. Where the sleeves failed to slip over her hands they were simply ripped apart.

Her screams could only echo inside her as she was thrust into the surging spray of ice cold water. Hundreds of thousands of never ending needles penetrated every inch of her porcelain skin. She was held there for a full minute and then dragged across the room to the huge oval bath. It was half-full of water and a further quarter supported floating ice cubes. She was lifted by her feet and shoulders, submerged through the iceberg and her head held under for a ten seconds that, to Francoise, must have seemed like ten minutes. She was totally disoriented and filled with absolute terror. Within one hundred and twenty seconds she had been propelled from the highest prospects of prosperity and privilege to the deepest chasm of stark, freezing, humiliating pain and despair. Adam strode slowly into the bathroom.

"We make no apologies for the temperature of the water, Madame. You will find that it is your very best interests that you are completely alert when I ask you the next five questions. I will give them to you all at once and prefer it if you would answer in the order in which they are presented."

The look of terror in her eyes was even more grotesque with the constant involuntary trembling induced partly by the cold but mostly by the naked fear that encased her whole being.

"I am going to make this simple for you, Francoise. We know that you are planning to explode a device in the Channel Tunnel. We know this as an indisputable fact. We have your transcripts and most importantly we have one of your accomplices. What we don't know, but what you are going to tell us are: When is it going to happen? In which of the two tunnels, North or South? What type of device is it? How will it be transported? Who will detonate it? For each of the five answers I do not receive, you will spend a further ten seconds under the water."

One of the CIA operatives ripped the adhesive tape from her face and dragged the handkerchief from her mouth.

Adam continued in a tone so menacing that even he did not know he was capable of producing it.

"You have ten seconds above the surface to start giving the answers."

"I don't know! I swear I don—"

She screamed but before she could complete her protestation Adam had signalled to the head man to dunk her. He counted evenly to ten. As her bedraggled hair smeared her mascara and lipstick across her face, she choked and coughed uncontrollably. Adam took his time and showed no emotion whatsoever.

"I will make it easier for you, then, and allow you to answer one at a time in any order. The questions, remember, are when, where, what, who and how. 'Don't know' is not an answer."

He nodded imperceptibly to his henchmen to ease up on her a little. He knew that even if she wanted to talk, the shock, the cold and her confusion would be confounding her communicative functions. Right at this moment she was probably incapable of thought, let alone speech. He allowed her ten seconds for reflection before looking directly into her eyes and whispering,

"Speak and you live. I may not even reveal your role in this. Stay silent and you die; slowly and horribly."

She motioned to sit up and she was dragged upright. She breathed heavily, panting, heaving and trying to produce words. Adam rotated his hands patiently but urged her to speak soon.

"It will be sometime this afternoon or evening," she gasped, she shivered, but she knew she had to continue. "I don't know what kind of bomb it is or who detonates it but it goes on from the Calais side in some form of vehicle. I swear, I absolutely swear that's all I know. Please, please, that's all I know! I had no part in this. I just handled the money!"

Adam did not believe for one second that this was the extent of her knowledge or involvement but he felt that he had no time to lose in relaying what she had told him back to Mellor. The attack was real and it was imminent.

Another nod and La Plume was hauled, shivering, quivering from the bathtub. He threw her a robe and sneered.

"Cover yourself up. You look like that sad, sole plucked turkey left hanging in the butchers after Thanksgiving. You disgust me!"

And that was when the sobbing started.

64

Aslam had completed the last six kilometres of the journey alone. As instructed, he had driven Suleiman to the Gare de Calais-Ville where he would take a TGV connection back to Marseille and join a cargo vessel destined for Syria. Before he left, both men climbed into the back of the van and carefully moved aside the genuine beer kegs to allow access to the six kegs of high explosive that lay amid and below them. Aslam demonstrated once again that he was capable of connecting the detonators to the keg couplers and priming the device. When Suleiman was completely satisfied, he bade his young colleague farewell in the hope and expectation that they would never meet again; at least within this universe.

Aslam continued his journey towards the French border crossing. Suleiman advised him to wait in a layby until he saw a sizeable convoy of articulated vehicles approaching and to filter in between them. He had only a short time to wait and little difficulty in tucking in between the third and fourth of a line of eight. As a devout Muslim, he felt more uncomfortable about the beer in the back of the van than the explosives but knew that it was God's will. He knew nothing of beer other than to tell any inquisitive guards that this was the new global lager sensation from the South of France; much sought after in those unique boutique restaurants in London where customers thought nothing of paying fifteen English pounds for a goblet of fizz.

The French border control personnel paid little attention to the traffic passing through their barriers. A cursory glance at the driver's passport and the obligatory look inside one vehicle every forty minutes seemed to fulfil their obligations to the international community. Since the former Britain exited the European state, France, Greece, Italy and Germany were actively encouraging their African and Eastern European migrants to make their way to England.

Beyond the French line, the convoy of vehicles was divided into four random lanes to pass within the United Nations controlled zone. The primary role of this force was to receive migrants rejected by the English Border Control Agency so it seemed sensible for them to catch illegals and return them to France before they reached the English line. By tucking himself in between articulated vehicles Aslam knew that he was more likely to be waved through without inspection. Illegals were more likely to be smuggled in container trucks than vans.

At the English border, the pace slowed considerably. Illuminated signs advised drivers how long they could expect to wait before loading and Aslam was relieved to see that he could expect to be on board within twenty minutes. At the first control gate, his vehicle was approached by a stout lady in a dark blue tunic. Her badge introduced her as Monica, Border Control Agency. Monica smiled politely as though this required less effort than a spoken greeting and held out her hand for Aslam's passport and driving licence. His carefully forged and aged documents heralded him as a twenty-six-year-old French national and a commercial vehicle driver by profession. Monica scanned the documents with her hand held terminal, nodded to the green light that lifted the barrier and stepped back as he smiled and drove through. Three minutes later, two English soldiers stepped into the road and waved him over into one of eight inspection laybys.

"Good Morning, sir. Do you speak English?"

"A little," Aslam's strained vocabulary and pronunciation helped to mask the terror that was now building inside him as a third soldier walked around the van. There was now one at each of the driver and passenger doors with the third, he presumed, now at the rear.

"Would you step out of the vehicle, sir? Routine inspection." The soldier's expression seemed to suggest that this was anything but routine and Aslam's hand trembled as he opened the door and shakily stepped down from the cab.

"Beer is it, sir? Open up then, let's have look."

Aslam walked around to the rear of the vehicle where all three soldiers were now assembled. One carried a clipboard, the other two carried short range MX 21 automatic rifles. Aslam released the coded padlock and opened the right hand rear door. The clipboard-free hand reached inside and released the latch on the left hand one. Inside, there were two layers of thirty litre kegs; four pallets on each layer, four kegs per pallet; thirty two kegs in total. The load was compactly secured but there was sufficient space in the long-wheelbase, high sided van to manoeuvre if required.

"Why such a small load, sir? I thought that beer came over in tankers or containers."

Aslam coughed nervously as he recalled his rehearsed explanation. "This is highly specialist, organic craft beer, brewed in the Lambic tradition and has only a short shelf life. Those who like it are prepared to pay more."

"Is it any good?" asked the first rifleman.

"I do not know, sir, I do not drink, I only drive, but your countrymen seem to like it in London."

"Any free samples then?"

"Yes, of course," Aslam stuttered but mustered a muted smile. "The keg in the middle on the bottom layer. Help yourself."

"Nah, I think we'll give that one a miss thanks. Bring us some cans next time. You can close her up now. Have a safe trip."

"Thank you, officers. And you have a safe day." Aslam was just about to climb into the cab, relieved but shaking inwardly when the first soldier shouted. Aslam froze.

"Hey! Get back here!"

Aslam was now contemplating whether to run or jump back into to van and crash through the barriers when he saw the smile on the squaddie's face.

"Don't forget to put the padlock back on. You don't want the illegals having a piss up on the way across!"

"Oh! Of course, sir. Thank you, sirs." He kept his arms close to his sides as he climbed in the cab, hoping that nobody would notice the saddlebags of cold sweat that had formed around his armpits. He drove off slowly and was waved into the outside lane behind a fifty-two seater coach. Ten minutes later, the coach, the van and a Mercedes ML SUV were securely parked within their transportation carriage. A row of teenage girls on the back row of the coach waved cheekily, provocatively, to Aslam. He smiled and waved back dismissively in the knowledge that there were many more virgins waiting for him at the end of this short journey.

65

Tom Mellor was sitting alone in a ten Downing Street office, two doors away from the Prime Minister's. His videophone buzzed into life on the desk in front of him and he knew that this would not be good news as soon as he saw Adam's pained expression.

"It's the shuttle as opposed to Eurostar. A destructive explosive device will be loaded sometime today in an unknown vehicle at the Calais end of the tunnel. La Plume admits to brokering a financial arrangement with a Saudi backer with links to the royal family who is bankrolling the operation. The plot itself was masterminded and offered to the Saudi by an unnamed assassin, probably the one we know as Colin Richards, but the logistics, the legwork and the execution is in the hands of ISIS. We now have concrete evidence that Saudi Arabia is sponsoring Islamic State."

Mellor was nodding to himself as he took all this in. It was pretty much as he had suspected and feared.

"And La Plume. You are certain that this is the full extent of her knowledge and involvement?"

"I can't be certain, Mr Mellor, but it seems that this would have happened with or without her. It just happens to suit her own political and career ambitions to have the UK at loggerheads with Europe, Saudi Arabia and the rest of the Muslim world. What do you want me to do with her? Do you need her to have an accident? She could very easily fall getting out of the bath."

"No. Not this time, there is no mileage in that. Just make it very clear to her that we have absolutely everything on record. If a single life is lost on that train, we have her as an accessory to mass murder. Her political career would be over and we would confiscate every single Euro of her assets. If, on the other hand, she decides to play nicely with MI5 and the CIA, nobody needs to know how she was involved in all this. In a nutshell. Make it clear that from now on, she is owned. We own her."

"I understand, but…"

"Not now. I need to brief the Prime Minister and make sure that we can stop this thing happening. How quickly could you get to Calais?"

Mellor didn't wait for the answer before he closed the connection and burst into the PM's private office. "Sorry Graeme, but you need to know this. It's on for definite. A bomb will be smuggled onto the shuttle in Calais sometime today. It's a totally reliable source but not one that we can declare to the French so you have to make them understand that and get the service closed down as soon as possible."

"Oh my God! Holy shit! Find Sadler and Brockington for me would you and get them in here." He pressed the intercom on his desk. "Janet, please restore the video conference with Alain Baroux and Michel Audran; urgently. Tom, could I suggest that you get over to MI7 and get the watchers and listeners to pick up absolutely anything and everything remotely communicated on this matter."

Mellor was out of the door almost before the PM had finished speaking.

As soon as Robert Brockington and Matthew Sadler were found, the video conference was resumed and the three of them sat opposite, virtually, the French Prime Minister and President. It was agreed that Sadler would speak first allowing the Prime Minister to escalate the conversation as they expected would be necessary.

"Sir, we now have absolutely irrefutable evidence that a terrorist attack will be perpetrated on the Eurotunnel from a passenger shuttle or freight service out of Calais. The CIA have authenticated this intelligence and we need to close down the service immediately. As we speak, my Trade and Industry Minister is advising both Eurostar and Eurotunnel that they must do so."

The French President remained calm. "May I be privileged to see or hear some of this irrefutable evidence you speak of?"

Mitchell intervened. "I am afraid not at this precise moment, Mr President. We have a very delicate arrangement with the CIA and cannot reveal evidence or its source without their express consent which, at this stage, we do not have. I can assure you, however that it is absolutely genuine and I, personally, will accept any financial or political repercussions should this intelligence prove to be inaccurate, which I guarantee that it will not."

"Very well, Prime Minister. You do what you need to do and we shall do what we need to do. May I suggest an announcement that scientists may have unearthed a geological flaw on the seabed and we have taken a cross channel decision with the operating companies, to postpone operations until the matter has been thoroughly investigated?"

"Very wise counsel, Mr President. How soon can you have a press statement and news alert ready for release?"

"What time do you have now?"

The question was superfluous as two virtual clocks shone on each side of the video image. It was now 15.10 in London and 16.10 in Paris. Mitchell took the initiative.

"Let's make a joint statement at 1700 Central European Time, 1600, GMT, but in the meantime, I am going to initiate a computer failure at our border control to prevent any vehicles accessing those trains."

"Good luck, Prime Minister."

"And to you, Mr President. I am sure that we both have citizens and interests at risk here."

66

Aslam stepped out of the cab, walked around to the back of the van where he removed the padlock and opened the doors. He looked into the black Mercedes parked behind him. The driver stared out at him. He looked familiar; he looked like the soldier with the clipboard, but he quickly told himself it couldn't be him. There would not have been time to get so close behind him. It did look like him though. "Why is he following me? Do I have to kill him first? No Aslam, you are being paranoid. It is not him."

He climbed into the back of the van just as the train began to pull slowly but smoothly away from its platform.. Although in theory, he now had thirty-five minutes to get the job done, the optimum time would be twenty-one minutes because at that time, if they were on schedule, the train would pass under the point at which the distance between the tunnel and the seabed was at its minimum; around forty metres.

Moving the kegs around in the back of the van might have been more difficult had he and Suleiman not rigged a light fitting or insisted on so many logistics rehearsals. It was almost like playing one of those handheld games that he had enjoyed as a child. A plastic grid

372

within which he could move fifteen plastic squares up and down, left and right to create the blank space in the middle. Within four minutes, he had isolated the six explosive kegs, fitted the keg couplers and connected them to the red gas bottle that he placed between them. He opened the valve on the bottle and heard gas hissing through the lines, through the keg connectors and into the kegs where the fusion with the highly volatile liquid explosive created a devastatingly lethal compound. The detonator was a coded key on his mobile phone that he kept in the cab to avoid the possibility of a misfire. All he now needed to do was insert six numbers and press send. He looked at his watch. They had been travelling for eleven minutes. He switched off the light, climbed carefully through the kegs to the back of the van and released the latch on the right hand door. As he opened it he stared directly into the face of the driver of the black Mercedes who was just a metre or so from the back of the van. Aslam had been right. It was not the soldier.

***

Ava was disappointed that the holiday was at an end but she genuinely wanted to see her mother. This is the first time that they had ever been apart for more than two days and although she joined her friends in their mock crocodile tears on leaving France, she could not wait for the train to arrive back in Folkestone. She kept up the pretence that she, too, had become an independent female adult on that trip but her face was a better liar than her heart. She was excited about the journey through the tunnel and pledged to stay awake, knowing they would all probably sleep on the onward coach journey to Victoria. There was no internet signal on the coach in the transit carriage so the girls would be forced to actually speak to each other. As conversations ignited, the volume rose into an excited and indistinguishable frenzy of speaking, laughing and shreaking. The poor diver could only pray that somehow, they might be silenced.

67

Mellor burst into the conference room at MI7 headquarters and was surprised to see Sean Lakin and Farah Karim seated opposite Director Charles Murphy. Mellor instantly realised that Sean had not been able to take his advice and set the suspected murder enquiries aside for the time being.

"Sorry to interrupt, but Charlie, I need to speak with you urgently, in private."

Sean rose and motioned Farah to do the same. They walked out of the conference room. Sean stood just a few feet away, while Farah quickly moved over to Alec Brunson's work station, spoke a few words and then looked towards Sean and nodded. She also checked her own phone: two missed calls from Ava and a text message. "Hi Mama. Looks like you might have to pick me up earlier than we planned. We are on schedule to catch the earlier shuttle. Love you Mama. Xxx" She put the phone away.

Alec tapped half a dozen keys and hit enter. Sean was close enough to the conference room to hear the voices from within but not the content of the conversation. He was certainly close enough to hear the shrill ringing of the phone and saw Tom Mellor remove it from his pocket and hit the red key. Sean nodded back to Farah who, in turn, nodded to Alec. The same six keys were tapped and Mellor's phone rang again, much to his concern and consternation. When Director Murphy left the room, Sean stepped back in and closed the door.

"You've just missed a couple of phone calls, Tom. Don't you want to call them back?"

"No, it's just my brother trying to organise a round of golf with me."

"Your brother lives in Turkey does he, Tom?"

"Err, no, what do you mean?"

"Those calls, Tom. They were signal interventions from a coded frequency that was harvested from a device known to belong to our suspected terrorist know as Colin Richards. It's the device that Rosie Hunter was chasing down during her meetings with Deputy Director Cruse. It's the device that Cruse told her was actually located in Edinburgh when he went across to Whitehall to follow up the lead, just hours before Inspector Hunter was killed. Who told him that, Tom? It wasn't the Whitehall IT guru. We asked him. Just who is it that you've been talking to on the other end of that phone?"

Mellor looked ashen but with the prospect of the Eurotunnel bomb at the front of his mind, he didn't have the mental capacity, or will, to create much of a cover story.

"In my role, Sean, we sometimes have to deal with some very unpleasant people and do some very unpleasant things."

"Did you have Rosie Hunter killed?"

"No," Mellor lied. "Paul Cruse took that upon himself. It was his mistake and I saw to it that it was the last one he would ever make. There was no mileage in dragging it through the courts. None of the evidence could ever have come to light under the Secrets Act so believe me, Sean, it's best to just leave it there."

"I need to know who you have been talking to at the other end of that connection. He is behind last week's bombings isn't he? Tell me, Tom. Why have you been speaking with him? What did you know? What do you know?"

"I know, Sean that he is a very dangerous individual but beyond that, I know little more. He is an international assassin, a cold, dispassionate gun for hire, irrespective of the cause. You don't call him, he calls you and he can be very good at making problems go away."

"And it seems to me that he can also be very good at creating them."

"As I said, Sean, for the good of the nation, we all have to do things that we would sometimes prefer not to and that includes you, Sean. For your own good, for the good of the unit and for the good of those around you, just accept that sometimes you just have to let some things go. Now if you will excuse me, I have an international crisis to try to avert."

Mellor pushed past Sean and strode off down the corridor towards the director's office. Sean was walking across to collect Farah from Alec's desk, desperately wondering how he could possibly relay his conversation with Mellor to her when the world seemed to stand still. Operatives froze at their work stations. One young man screamed, then another before the whole room fell silent. Charles Murphy came dashing out of his office and almost bowled Tom Mellor over.

"We've just had reports of a massive explosion in the Channel Tunnel!"

68

The Mercedes driver had approached Aslam and reached into his inside pocket. If Aslam had waited a moment, he might have seen the map of Southern England being produced and heard the Mercedes driver ask for advice on the quickest route in to London. Aslam saw nor heard either. He panicked and pushed the man out of the way, dashed back to the cab, grabbed his phone from the dashboard and keyed in six numbers. 739625. The numbers had no significance whatsoever other than it was they that would end his life and those of a further four hundred and twenty-seven passengers on this train. He closed his eyes, held the phone to his chest and hit the send button. Nothing happened. He allowed his eyes to open two seconds later, confused and concerned that he had let the leadership down. He need not have worried. He had served the Caliphate well. His family would be proud of him. He would have known nothing of this. The blinding flash of light snatched away his vision, his consciousness and his life. He felt nothing. He was nothing.

The compartment encasing the coach, the van and the Mercedes was instantly vaporised. Osman had calculated and

377

feared that if the container had been too far from the engine unit when the bomb detonated, that the front carriages might escape the blast and be dragged to safety by the power unit. That was never going to happen. The scale of the blast immediately lifted the whole train from its tracks while completely shattering and shredding the shell against the walls of the tunnel. Those that were still conscious would have first seen the blinding flash and felt the thundering fireball raging towards them. They may have heard the deafening blast but would have been spared the grating and grinding of metal against concrete or agonised screams and wailing of the dying. Those within a two-carriage distance of the blast container avoided the agony of burning, choking or being crushed to death. They were simply and mercifully obliterated immediately. The less fortunate would have probably died, agonisingly, within minutes but nobody would ever know. There were no survivors. Not a single one would ever relive the horror. Their surviving friends and relatives would, forever, relive it on their behalf; hoping they had died peacefully but realistically imagining the very worst.

The blast did not immediately breach the underside of the seabed but compression within the tunnel sent the tremor and fireball hurtling through the service passages that connected the North and South thoroughfares. Hellfire hurtled headlong into a Eurostar passenger service heading from St Pancras, London, with over eight hundred and sixty passengers on board. The bodies from both tunnels were never recovered. The cylindrical structures collapsed completely. The walls imploded with the earth, rock and sand burying their bodies and scattering their ashes.

The tunnel did not flood immediately. Because the device was detonated prematurely it exploded at one of the less vulnerable, strategic points of the structure. Seismologists and geologists would be studying the seabed for years to determine whether it might ever be safe enough to attempt to enter the tunnel again. They doubted it ever would.

The ISIS leadership had hoped and dreamed of a massive, biblical tsunami created by a ritual parting of the sea. Their vision of fishing boats and ferries being tossed from the tide to the shores of Southern England and Northern France in massive, unremitting waves of fury hadn't materialised. The scar on the face of the seabed, however, was a lasting threat and reminder that one day it might still do so.

The unthinkable had now occurred. For almost thirty years, the threat of a terrorist attack on the Tunnel had loomed large but remained unspoken. Its voice would now shatter nations.

69

The control room of MI7 was in complete chaos, verging on meltdown. Buzzers, bells and sirens sounded. Lights flashed, screens projected images so rapidly that the effect was stroboscopic. The staff in this department had been specially selected and trained to deal with the most critical of situations but this one had been missed from the manual. Operators and analysts ran between work stations screaming instructions and demanding connections. Sean Lakin, Tom Mellor and Charles Murphy just looked at each other in stunned silence, each, instinctively, pondering inwardly what they might have done differently to prevent this catastrophe. At that very moment, this was not the responsibility of ISIS, or Francoise La Plume, some Saudi royal flunky or a crazed Jihadist; it was their responsibility. They had failed their nation.

Farah Karim sat alone at a desk. She was holding a phone in front of her, slowly shaking her head from side to side and occasionally gulping to remind her body to breathe, when her mind had surrendered any conscious desire to do so.

Her phone flashed again, and a new SMS message envelope appeared with Ava's name across it. Farah instantly recalled stories

380

of text and voice messages sent as the twin towers came under attack but before they came down. Parents and spouses had locked those phones away to preserve the last words of their loved ones. Farah did not think she could bear such agony but knew she had to open it.

"Hi, Mama. Forget my last message. Bummer! Army closed the Tunnel because some crummy computer has crashed or something! I knew I should have sat with Becky. They left half an hour ahead of us. Lucky cow! Could be sat here in Calais for hours now!! Sorry to mess you around Mama. Luvnmissu! Xxxxxxx."

Farah sobbed. She sobbed as she had never sobbed before.

70

It was estimated that sixty-nine per cent of the population of England and Wales watched the broadcast with a further two million in Scotland and Ireland. Four hundred million viewers worldwide were tuned in live, irrespective of their time zones.

"The following statement is delivered to you by His Royal Highness, King William VI from his stateroom in Buckingham Palace, London."

"I am deeply saddened by the horrific events both of yesterday and of one week ago. As you know, my own family have lost loved ones in politically motivated incidents and we therefore have some understanding of the immense loss of innocent life in the zealous pursuit of futile causes.

"The primary responsibility of Government is to protect and preserve the peace, prosperity and security of its citizens; sadly, my government has concluded that it has been unable to deliver against this noble, but fundamental commitment. I have therefore, with sadness and reluctance, accepted the resignation of my Prime Minister, the Right Honourable Graeme Mitchell.

"An election will be held within the next three months and a new government will be formed in July. There should be no doubt that the new administration will have an absolute mandate to seek out and eradicate acts of terrorism that threaten the well-being of our citizens both at home and abroad. I have personally received numerous messages of support in doing so from leaders across the globe, and within Europe.

"In the interim period, my Deputy Prime Minister, the Right Honourable Neil Faraday will lead a temporary coalition government with emergency measures to radically increase resource and expenditure in the defence of our nation.

"My family and I are in no doubt of the difficult challenges that lie ahead of us, but I have absolute confidence in the spirit and will of our citizens to restore peace, prosperity and pride to this Disunited Kingdom.

"May your own God bless you all."

71

In 1964, British Prime Minister, Harold Wilson declared that "a week was a long time in politics" but the events of the preceeding months precipitated such unprecedented change in the UK landscape that March might officially be declared a political eternity. Graeme Mitchell's resignation created such a feeding frenzy that the press delightfully dubbed Westminster a Political Pirhana Pool.

With the general election less than four weeks away, the United Kingdom Independence Party sat squarely behind the Conservatives with Neil Faraday holding twenty-five per cent to Matthew Sadler's thirty-six. Labour, under a slightly less eccentric and more patriotic leadership team, had shown some signs of recovery, marginally edging third place with eighteen. The Liberals and Greens polled less than three percent of public support between them.

Naveen Chaudhry of the British Muslim Party remarkably reconciled his family and political differences with his nephew, Rahim Chatha, who, by publicly denouncing Islamic State and formally dropping any demands for Islamic territories under Sharia Law in England, had effectively dissolved IBIS and paved the way for political and ideological integration. Chaudhry was appointed leader of The Integrated Muslim Party of which his nephew became deputy. They campaigned on a ticket of equitable political representation and the provision of resources to promote cultural and economic unity polling six per-cent. They were widely believed to hold the balance of power within Britain and were likely to play an active role in a coalition government if the Tories managed to conjure up enough votes to hold on to first place.

David Watters and Brendan Doyle formally brought together the Unionist factions of Northern Ireland and Scotland. They campaigned with a proposal to allow the Scots to re-join the United Kingdom in conjunction with a right for Ulster Unionists to relocate and reside in Scotland with funding provided by the Republic of Ireland. Scotland would restore its cultural and political membership of Britain and the United Kingdom; Ireland would edge closer to becoming an independent, Republican Catholic island, albeit heavily subsidised and controlled by the European Union. The rights of Northern Ireland citizens choosing to remain in Ulster would, claimed the Republicans, be preserved but its EU masters now had a number of leaders experienced in the black art of ethnic cleansing.

Together, The Unionist Alliance and the Integrated Muslim Party were marginally larger than the Labour party and as both the Conservatives and UKIP swore never to form another coalition government together, it seemed that the next government would feature one of these two parties. In actuality, three days after the election, the Conservatives were able to form a coalition with the Unionist Alliance.

Two weeks later, on a cultural visit to Pakistan, Naveen Chaudhry died in a mysterious car accident and Rahim Chatha seamlessly succeeded him as leader. He quickly forged an alliance with the Labour Party to perpetuate the perception of the world's most Disunited Kingdom.

72

The Armed Forces Recruitment Initiative masterminded and led by the new Secretary of State for Defence, Sir Thomas Mellor, had, within three months, generated an additional sixteen thousand service personnel, eight thousands of whom were already on active service in Iraq, Syria, Afghanistan and Libya. A further two thousand were deployed in International Development collaborative initiatives in Kuwait, Oman and the Yemen as diplomatic talks with Saudi Arabia were reaching crisis point. Officially, they were advisors, but not the sort of advisors it would be advisable to mess with.

Economic and diplomatic sanctions had been introduced in April and a multibillion dollar deal to equip the Saudi Air Force had been stripped from UK Aero Industries and awarded to France. Surplus capacity in UK military aircraft production had been readily seized by the United States who were currently negotiating a joint venture to create the largest military engineering group on the planet. Both countries knew that with their uniquely aligned approach to foreign policy, there would never be any danger of redundant overproduction in their output. If that ever happened, their governments were perfectly capable of engineering conflicts to utilise, destroy and replenish their inventory in perpetuity.

Closer to home, David Watters and Brendan Doyle were delighted to host a joint press conference to announce the establishment of a new military training facility on the outskirts of Enniskilen in County Farmagh. They celebrated bringing a much welcome boost to the economy in the region by advising that the infrastructure would be developed by a workorce drawn primarily from Northern Ireland and Scotland. The Garrison would be home to the newly formed Royal Hibernian Regiment. There was no shortage of recruits from Scotland to both build and man the facility.

It was neither surprising nor disappointing to the Defence Secretary that the regiment's name was the subject of heated controversy a little further south. Contrary to common perception, the word Hibernian was not just the name of an Edinburgh football club but was the latin name given to a native or inhabitant of Ireland.

Irish Republicans were constantly conspiring with their EU masters to escalate the tension and accelerate the annexation of the northern counties. If the establishment of the garrison itself was a severe boot to the collective groin, its choice of name was the steel toe cap.

Since Brexit, the strained trade agreement between the UK and Europe had created immense tension around the border areas and while both parties strongly contended that no border actually existed, neither did a United Ireland. With the Channel Tunnel closed for the foreseeable future, ports in both the North and South of the country were gearing up for the the inevitable exponential upsurge in traffic.

The UK Government had reconciled itself, some years ago, to the fact that the Good Friday Agreement had been nothing more or less than a shameful surrender to the IRA in return for the eventual annexation of the North into a united Republican Ireland.

Brexit dealt a major blow to this strategy and Tom Mellor knew it was inevitable that political tension would once again escalate into armed conflict. This time, the UK would be ready and if the EU chose to make this the first test for their army then so be it. "Bring it on!" he boomed.

73

As he slid the ring on Farah's finger, Sean fought back both tears and anger as he brushed the smooth stump on her adjacent knuckle. They both knew that the perpetrators had paid a hefty price for inflicting this imperfection upon her, but it would remain a constant reminder of the evil and ugliness that would forever contrast her kindness and beauty.

Sean and Farah's wedding was a small and simple affair.

Brian Chambers was best man, Ava was the single bridesmaid and Commissioner Nigel Pollard gave the bride away. He did so in more ways than one. In three weeks' time, when the newlyweds were scheduled to return from their honeymoon in the Caribbean, Farah, on Pollard's recommendation, would transfer to her new duties as Head of the Analysis and Research Unit of MI7.

Sean was delighted by this development. As much as he had wanted her away from the front line of homeland security, for his own selfish reasons, he knew that she had far too much to offer to be completely sidelined from the continuing war on terror. He was still battling with his own personal demons in determining exactly where the war would be fought. Would the next battle be abroad or within this disunited kingdom? He wasn't even sure he knew who the enemy was any more.

Ava had happily suggested that she might join a school study trip to Rome leaving the newlyweds free to enjoy their honeymoon. Of course, she knew full well that this would guarantee her a twin room with her best friend just down the corridor from her mother and stepfather.

There was only one train line on St Kitts; the scenic Sugar Train and it remained steadfastly above ground.

74

Mehmet Osman had spent a relaxing three months with his beautiful and devoted Samira. Having resumed their cruise in Marseilles, they sailed on to Barcelona where they disembarked and rented a spacious apartment in a quiet suburb overlooking Montjuic Park. During that time, they had enjoyed two further cruises around the Greek islands and the Adriatic coast. Samira was good for him. She became the sense of purpose that he had lost all those years ago as he fought fiercely, yet fruitlessly, for futile causes. Cruising held a special fascination for them. Not only had it brought them together, Mehmet now considered this to be the safest way of seeing the world. They simmered together in the pool deck Jacuzzi. They held hands on the promenade deck and they laughed at the shows in the theatres. They shared cocktails in the bar and shared the bed in their stateroom. They watched the news together and shared distress at the continuing violence across the world, conducted by those fanatics and fantasists that would seek to destroy their new way of life. Mehmet felt no guilt nor saw no irony in this but had no particular desire nor motivation to continue as their weapon of choice.

There had been no 'crossing of the Rubicon' nor a 'road to Damascus' moment for him. He fully recognised who he was and what he had done. If he removed himself from that world now, he was humble and realistic enough to know that he was not indispensable. There were others lining up to take his place and earn his fortune. He reassured himself that they would never be as effective as him, but he did begin to wonder whether or not he should be worried for his own safety and that of his new reason for living.

Mehmet Osman was a dangerous man but the true fanatics that hired him and that might replace him, were even more dangerous for they lacked intelligence and minds of their own.

75

The Channel Tunnel remained closed and although the joint owners believed themselves to be in serious negotiations with both the English and French Governments, they were rapidly reaching the conclusion that neither country wished to see the route reopened. From the English perspective, Tom Mellor secretly rejoiced in the added security that the closure brought to his country's border. From the French perspective, closing off this route to the Promised Land would deter the continuing flow of African and Middle East migrants from trekking through France and have them head straight to Germany instead.

The immediate impact on cross-channel trade had been nothing short of chaotic. It brought to reality the myths and threats perpetuated by the Remain Campaigns in the run up to the Brexit vote and in their futile attempts to halt the process. The movement of goods was crippled. Articulated vehicles were stranded on both sides of the channel and supermarket shelves were quickly depleted. The government introduced emergency rationing of essential supplies and deployed the Royal Navy and Airforce to assist in the movement of goods to and from mainland Europe.

The major beneficiaries, of course, were the freight shipping lines and ferry operators. Although the French controlled CMA group and Germany's Hapag Lloyd showed little appetite to increase their trips to the British Isles, Maersk Group of Denmark and MSC, the Italian founded shipping giant based in Switzerland, were far more receptive to the opportunity presented to them. Both stepped up their frequency of operations across the Channel and the North Sea. Joint venture and merger talks were quickly convened with P&O, the major UK ferry operator.

Despite the gradual easing of transportation issues, the mindset of the nation continued to change and gravitated towards the greater support for home grown produce. This provided a further boost for the economy but increased the strain on the employment market and resources to accommodate the welcome influx of the migrant workforce from Europe and beyond.

"Be warned," Neil Farady goaded Sir Tom Mellor. "Not all of those fit and angry young men arriving at our ports are here to work in the fields and factories to feed their absent families!"

Mellor smiled and nodded but knew that the threat was a serious one.

The European Union now comprised just twenty-two states. Turkey had become a full member, but this prompted the withdrawal of a further six. France teetered on the brink of withdrawal but her fear of German reprisals kept her in line and in the Union. The EU Army grew in size but also grew in incompetence and inefficiency. None of the world's foremost arms producers wanted to or were allowed to trade with the Single Market Superstate and its own technology was insufficient to produce anything that might match the might of the real world super powers.

Economically, they recognised that more European than British jobs were threatened by their isolationist trade policies and negotiations were convened to agree a set of wider tariff-free trade agreements.

Certain political factions, both abroad and at home, could only observe in horror.

76

Sir Tom Mellor was conducting a routine and informal debrief with Adam, his most accomplished and most prized asset. They sat sipping coffee on a rooftop terrace near St Paul's from where they had a full view of the renovation work underway around Whitehall. From the secure electronic tablet before them, they were absorbing some rather intriguing insight into the Machiavellian machinations of a revised French foreign policy, provided by his remarkably valuable new source, one Madame la Plume.

Their concentration and conversation was interrupted when Mellor's most secure phone pulsed quietly and unexpectedly in his pocket. He lifted the device and, immediately recognising the code on the call screen, he left Adam, stepped away from the table and walked across to the viewing platform. Although Mellor was fighting to force the coffee to stay within his stomach, he summoned his immense inner strength to sound confident as he spoke.

"I really thought that we were done. You served your purpose, and do you know what? The hundreds of lives lost under the Channel may have saved us thousands by stepping up our war against Islamic State. You have no further hold over me. My position here is perfectly secure. I have complete control over defence and intelligence. You can no longer blackmail me or hurt me."

"Ah, Mr Black," replied the voice, ignoring the vitriole and resisting the temptation to correct both assumptions. "It's so good to speak to you again and I wish you only well. The truth is, my old friend, I think I may be getting slightly bored with domestic life and I am, perhaps belatedly, finding fascination in the emerging new world order. I am considering a little project in the Middle East which I believe might just be of interest to you. As a trusted and loyal client, I would be happy to make you a very special offer…"

.